PRISON OF HOPE

By Steve McHugh

Crimes Against Magic

Born of Hatred

With Silent Screams

Infamous Reign (A Hellequin Chronicles novella)

PRISON OF HOPE

Steve McHugh

47N☉RTH

Published by 47North, Seattle

www.apub.com

Amazon, the Amazon logo, and 47North are trademarks of Amazon.com, Inc., or its affiliates.

ISBN-13: 978-1477828595
ISBN-10: 1477828591

Cover design by Eamon O'Donoghue

Library of Congress Control Number: 2014955279

Printed in the United States of America

For Harley, our very own little Quinzel.

LIST OF CHARACTERS

Flashback

Nathan (Nate) Garrett: Sorcerer. Once worked for Merlin as the shadowy figure Hellequin.

Lucie Moser: Half enchanter. Employee of Hades.

Kurt Holzman: Werebear. Employee of Hades. Married to Petra.

Petra Holzman: Werewolf. Employee of Hades. Married to Kurt.

Selene: Dragon-kin. Daughter of the Titan, Hyperion. Sister to Eos and Helios. Married to Deimos.

Pandora: Created by several gods of the Greek pantheon. Able to enthrall those she touches.

Hope: Immortal host for Pandora. Was a human girl.

Magali Martin: Human. Ally of Pandora.

Helios: Dragon-kin. Brother to Selene and Eos. Son of Hyperion.

Current Timeline

Nathan (Nate) Garrett: Sixteen-hundred-year-old sorcerer. Once worked for Merlin as the shadowy figure, Hellequin.

Thomas (Tommy) Carpenter: Six-hundred-year-old werewolf. Owner of a security company. Nate's best friend. Partner to Olivia. Father of Kasey.

Kasey (Kase) Carpenter: Fourteen-year-old daughter of Tommy and Olivia.

Hades's Family, Friends, and Employees

Hades: Necromancer of incredible power. Husband to Persephone and adopted father to Sky.

Persephone: Earth Elemental. Wife to Hades and adopted mother to Sky.

Sky (Mapiya): Half Native American. Birth parents murdered when she was a child. Adopted by Hades and Persephone. Necromancer.

Cerberus: Werewolf. Controls the Tartarus compound when Hades isn't there.

Kurt Holzman: Werebear. Ex-employee of Hades. Owns restaurant in Mittenwald.

Petra Holzman: Werewolf. Ex-employee of Hades. Owns restaurant in Mittenwald.

Wayne Branch: Guard at the Tartarus compound.

Avalon Members

Sir Kay: Director of SOA (Shield of Avalon). Brother to King Arthur.

Lucie Moser: Half-enchanter. Ex-employee of Hades. Current Assistant Director of the SOA (Shield of Avalon).

Olivia Green: Director of southern England branch of LOA (Law of Avalon). Water Elemental. Partner to Tommy. Mother of Kasey.

Witches

Mara Range: Coven member. Mother to Chloe.

Chloe Range: Fourteen-year-old daughter to Mara Range. Friends with Kasey.

Emily Rowe: Coven member.

Tartarus Inhabitants

Carion: Ferryman for Tartarus. Member of the Titans.

Atlas: Siphon. Member of the Titans.

Cronus: Sorcerer. Husband to Rhea, father of Zeus. Member of the Titans.

Rhea: Sorcerer. Wife to Cronus, mother of Zeus. Member of the Titans.

Lorin: Griffin. One of the guards of Tartarus.

Brutus, Friends, and Employees

Brutus: Sorcerer. King of London.

Diana: Half werebear. Roman goddess of the moon, the hunt, and birthing. Brutus's lieutenant.

Licinius: Sorcerer. Brutus's lieutenant.

Justin Toon: Head of security for Brutus.

Hera, Family, and Allies

Hera: Sorcerer. Head of one of the most powerful groups within Avalon.

Ares: Negative empath. Son of Hera. Husband to Aphrodite.

Deimos: Negative empath. Son of Ares.

Demeter: Earth Elemental. Mother of Persephone.

Aphrodite: Succubus. Wife to Ares.

Eos: Dusk walker. Sister to Selene and Helios. Daughter of Hyperion.

Selene: Dragon-kin. Sister to Eos and Helios. Daughter of Hyperion.

Hyperion: Dragon-kin. Father to Eos, Selene, and Helios.

Miscellaneous Characters

Donna Preston: Thirteen-year-old friend of Chloe and Kasey.
Robert Ellis: Australian. Vanguard member.
Sarah Hamilton: Witch.

PROLOGUE

Berlin, Germany. 1936.

The two Nazi soldiers stood outside the imposing four-story building, watching those on foot pass them by. The heat from the midday sun must have been hell on them; their shiny, smart uniforms weren't something I'd want to be wearing when I was standing out in the baking sunshine for a large portion of the day.

I placed the newspaper, an obnoxious piece of journalism that painted the Nazis as some sort of savior, beside me on the park bench and watched the two men nod to a pretty woman who walked past. The men were young, blond, and everything those in charge would want to show as their *master race*, whatever the fuck that was meant to be.

Nearly eighteen years previously, Germany had lost the Great War and was then humiliated by the British, French, Americans, and anyone else who happened to want a piece of their pie. The German people were angry and hurt by what happened, and that allowed someone like Hitler and his merry band of thugs and killers to come into power. It only took a few years for the Nazi flags to fly proudly on every street and for those deemed lesser, in their narrow vision, to be removed from sight.

For those people the regime had targeted, the Olympics had brought a brief respite, publically at least, but I knew it wouldn't last. The rumors of people forced to relocate to camps if they were the *wrong kind* of people, were rife. The rest of Europe, if not the world, had its head firmly buried in the sand, hoping against hope that the frankly obvious war that was looming wouldn't start anytime soon.

With the Olympics only a few weeks away, and the world watching, the Nazis had done the equivalent of putting their hands in the air to show they weren't carrying any weapons, while pushing a stack of guns under the table with their feet.

The majority of Germans were good people, but the minority held the power, and they were going to use it to do whatever they liked, no matter how many lives they destroyed in the process. And what they held in the building before me was going to make that destruction a thousand times greater than anything people could imagine.

As the civilians on the streets thinned out, the sun began to creep toward the west, painting the sky orange and purple. I picked up my fedora from next to the newspaper and after putting it on, walked across the road. There were few cars about, although no matter what country I'd traveled to, more and more seemed to be appearing with every passing year.

"*Guten Tag,*" I said to the two soldiers.

They stared at me, but there was no hostile intent in their body language; they appeared calm and relaxed. "How can we help you?" one of them asked.

I glanced past them into the empty reception area of the building. "I'd like to speak to Captain Dehmel."

The men glanced at each other.

"This is the Gestapo HQ for Department F, yes? He's expecting me."

One of the men removed a key from his pocket and unlocked the door, holding it open for me to step inside. Both men followed me into the expansive, but empty, foyer; the one closest to me pulled his revolver and aimed it at my head.

"You will come with us until Captain Dehmel can confirm your appointment."

I glanced over at his partner, who had also drawn his revolver. Both men were confident and experienced, and I had no doubt that they'd pull the trigger without hesitation if I gave them a reason.

I took a few steps and then stopped. "What floor is Dehmel on?"

"No questions," the first Nazi snapped, shoving me forward.

"Are you not listening to us?" the second Nazi demanded when I stopped walking. "We said move or we will shoot."

He shoved me again, but I rolled to the side and spun around, pushing his arm aside as he pulled the trigger, so he ended up removing a portion of his partner's head. The dead Nazi crumpled to the floor, while the sound of the gunshot echoed around the room.

A split second of hesitation on the part of the second Nazi, presumably brought on from the killing of his comrade, was all I needed, and within moments I'd removed his revolver and hit him in the jaw hard enough to knock him to the floor.

"Where's Captain Dehmel?" I asked.

"Go to hell," he snapped, so I shot him in the leg. Any pretense of getting to the captain quietly had evaporated the second the first explosion of sound had flown around the floor.

"Don't make me ask you again," I ordered as he writhed on the floor.

"Fourth floor," he said immediately through gritted teeth.

"How do I get there?" I aimed the gun at his good leg.

"There's a key to get onto the left stairwell. It's where all the experiments are run." With some awkwardness and pain, he fished the sizeable iron key from his belt and passed it over.

"Danke," I said.

"Are you going to kill me?"

"You never should have taken her," I said and shot him once in the head, dropping the gun onto his body.

I picked up my hat, which had fallen to the floor as I'd disarmed the second Nazi, and ran to the left side stairs. I used the key to unlock a silver gate that sat in front of the door and then continued my run toward the top of the building.

As I opened the door to the fourth floor, the silence hit me. There was no one in the hallway directly outside of the stairwell, and a few seconds of checking the nearest rooms showed there was no one anywhere. I was about to curse my luck and wonder if the Nazi had given me the wrong directions, when I heard the unmistakable sound of a scream, followed by a gunshot.

I made my way toward the noise, passing by laboratories with doors torn off and blood splattered inside. One room had a blackboard with smudged white chalk on it. What had been intelligible was now covered in blood splatter. Paper littered the floor, and a man sat hunched over in the corner, a puddle of blood underneath him. I took a step into the room as more screams sounded from the far end of the floor, and I quickly changed my mind.

The entrance, an airlock door, had been scorched and twisted, and was covered in even more blood. A young man lay beside it, a revolver in his hand. As I got closer, I saw the bullet hole in his head. A second man lay farther inside the airlock, his charred remains jamming the opposite door open.

There was a crash from the room beyond, and I darted inside, confronted with a dozen bodies, most of which appeared to have been bludgeoned or stabbed to death.

"Hello, Nathan," a woman said to me as I stepped over the body of a man in a now-red lab coat. "It's nice to see you again."

She was quite beautiful, her olive skin and long dark hair a product of her birth millennia ago. Her deep red eyes were from something much less human. She was naked. To many, she appeared to be a perfect woman; to others, she was the devil incarnate.

"Pandora," I said with a slight bow of my head, "it's good to finally have found you." Scorch marks licked the remains of the shattered window, and a man in a German officer uniform cowered in one corner, his eyes darting between Pandora and me.

"Dehmel?" I asked him.

He twitched slightly and then stood, waving a scalpel in my direction.

"What'd you do to him?" I asked Pandora. "And where did those burns come from?" Several small fires had been started on the far side of the room, destroying books and documents that had been piled up.

Pandora glanced over at the window and then down at a badly burnt soldier. "We had a friend help us. These men should not have overstepped their boundaries while we were in their company."

"I assume you allowed yourself to be taken. You could have left at any time, so why didn't you?"

"We wanted to see if they could help us with our needs. Obviously, their helpfulness has ended." Pandora always spoke about herself in the plural—some people call it "the royal we." I guessed that was what happened when you stuck a human and a monster in the same body. It took some getting used to.

She took a few steps toward Dehmel and whispered something to him. He immediately slit his own throat, dropping to the floor beside Pandora, who was busy putting on a pair of trousers and some boots that had been placed neatly on a nearby table.

"If you've got plans to run, Pandora, don't. It only makes things worse."

"Oh, my dear Nathan, things are going to get much, much worse." After she finished getting dressed and lacing up some army boots, she ran at the window, then jumped through without pausing.

By the time I'd reached the window, Pandora was speeding away on the back of a motorbike, her helper in control of the machine. I sighed and looked around the room. I walked over to the fires and found several singed documents that hadn't yet been consumed by the flames, but nothing was intact. More information about North Africa, and something about human test subjects. I put the documents in my pocket and searched for any survivors, but there was no one left alive to help me find Pandora's destination. And help was the one thing I really needed. Because if I didn't find Pandora soon, the Nazis would no longer be the worst thing that could happen to Europe.

CHAPTER 1

France. Now.

My mistake came in the form of saying "yes"—a simple, but powerful word that along with its brother, "no," can do a lot of good or a lot of damage. Once that first word had left my lips, I was duty bound to follow through. I could have come up with an excuse to get out of it—hell, I could have shot myself and said someone was trying to kill me. Should have, would have, could have. Instead, I convinced myself it wouldn't be bad, that it might even be fun. I was wrong. It was hell in a carriage.

I'd agreed, for some foolish reason, which I liked to believe had to do with drugged food and drink, to accompany Thomas Carpenter and his daughter Kasey on a school trip to Germany. Traveling along with my closest friend and his teenage daughter were over a hundred of her school friends, several parents and guardians, and their teachers. All spread out over a four-carriage train.

Avalon—the hidden true power of our world—arranged the trip, like it did for all Avalon-funded schools. But teenagers are moody and temper prone at the best of times. Throw in the beginnings of their powers, be those magical or otherwise, and you had the makings of a tense atmosphere.

Many of the kids with parents in attendance pretended that their parents didn't exist, while most of the parents silently watched their offspring with the attentiveness of an eagle searching for its next victim. Occasionally, one of the teenagers would say something inappropriate and receive a chastised glance or a discreet cough aimed in their direction, which in turn made the teen sigh or roll their eyes. It was like the Cold War all over again. I was half-expecting someone to turn up and start building a really big wall between the two sides.

Even Kasey, normally one of those rare teenagers who didn't mind sitting with her parents, was some distance down the ornate train carriage, surrounded by an unknown number of other teenage girls.

Fortunately for my sanity, I'd decided to take an eBook reader with me. Unfortunately, Tommy didn't have anything to do, so I'd managed about three pages in the hour and a half since we'd left London.

I glanced through the touch-activated tinted window beside me, as the scenery flew past. The train's interior reminded me of the Orient Express: everything was of the finest quality, and no expense had been spared. Despite the antique feel to many of the fixtures and fittings, there was nothing antique about the technology contained within. The exterior was no different; the train looked like one of Japan's bullet trains and was capable of speeds that easily matched them. Hades's engineers had worked wonders with the train, which was now in regular use, ferrying school trips from whatever country they came from to the compound in Germany.

"So, what's the book you're reading?" Tommy finally asked after holding his tongue for far too many miles.

I glanced up across the small table that separated his seat from mine, picked up the reader, and placed it in front of him. He touched the screen and tapped it a few more times as he read a few pages. "This is a grimoire."

"Yes, it is."

"It's in eBook form. Aren't they meant to be old and dusty?"

"Hades had his people change them to electronic form for ease of access. It used to take weeks to find what you were looking for; now it takes minutes."

"Why would a sorcerer even need a grimoire?"

It was a valid question. A sorcerer's magic is part of us. We think what we want to do, and if we're powerful enough, we do it. Only witches, or something else without an innate magic, use grimoires on anything close to a regular basis, by permanently tattooing their bodies with runes, and even then that's only if they really want to blow themselves up. Grimoires aren't really books on spells. They're books of ideas that you can use with the magic at your disposal—and in some cases, knowledge on how to access that magic.

A lot of grimoires show rune work and how someone with zero innate magical abilities can apply certain runes to their body to allow them access to some exceptionally powerful magic. It's why they're so dangerous; they can teach people who have no innate ability how to access magic, but not necessarily how to wield it safely.

"Yes, well, I'm trying to figure out how to do something and I thought maybe this would help."

Tommy tapped a few more screens and his eyes widened. "Do you know who this book belongs to?"

"Yes," I whispered.

"It's fucking Zeus's," he whispered in return.

"I just said I knew that."

"The last time someone took one of his grimoires, it started the Titan Wars. Prometheus chained to a rock, the creation of Pandora? You know all the really *fucking bad* stuff that happened."

"Right. First of all, you're beginning to get high-pitched and sound like a girl," I pointed out. "Second, Hades *gave* it to me. Zeus disappeared hundreds of years ago; I don't think he's going to miss it."

"What's the problem?" he asked in an abnormally deep voice, which made me smile.

"Look, you know how I can only use air and fire magic from the four elements that make up the first set of magic?"

Tommy rolled his eyes. "Yes, it's come up once or twice in the previous six hundred years we've been friends."

"Sarcasm's the lowest form of wit."

"That's puns. Get on with it."

I opened my mouth to argue and wisely closed it when I noticed the smile creep onto Tommy's face. Bloody wind-up merchant. "Right. Well, once you've learned those two types, and before you can move on to the Omega magic stage, you can learn how to merge your elements. So, fire and earth can create magma—that sort of thing."

Omega magic is only available to the millennia-old sorcerers and consists of mind, matter, shadow, and light magic. For the time being, they were beyond what I was capable of, but being able to merge my two elements was a distinct possibility, and something I was very keen to master.

"So, what about fire and air? What do they make?" Tommy asked, all sense of teasing now gone.

"Lightning."

Tommy blew out a long breath. "Well, I understand why you're reading Zeus's personal grimoire. You can learn how to wield lightning?"

I shrugged. "Not sure. Not all sorcerers can merge their elements."

Unfortunately, when Zeus wrote his grimoires, he believed only he would ever use them, and as he was already a powerful sorcerer, he had no need to explain control or patience. Besides, back in the day, Zeus didn't have a lot of either of those to go around. So, actually mastering something that Zeus didn't feel the need to explain in detail involved a lot of trial and error, but mostly a lot of throwing around dangerous levels of magic.

"Is the book helping?" Tommy asked, passing my e-reader over to me.

I put the device in my bag, which I made sure was shut tight. "I think so; it's just a matter of practice. When I absorb a soul, I can access it easier. I blew up a toaster at home."

For most of my entire sixteen hundred years of life, I'd had six dark, constantly changing marks on my chest. A few years ago, someone I'd considered a friend had sacrificed her life to save my own. It had the side effect of beginning the removal of the marks. An increase in my power and manifestation of necromancy were the first steps on my path to discovering what the marks were hiding. Four marks still remained, waiting until some arbitrary point when they'd vanish too. In the meantime, I practiced my necromancy, which comes in a lot of different varieties; mine allows me to absorb the spirits of those who have died fighting.

"Why would you blow up a toaster?" Tommy asked.

"Well I didn't mean to. I just sort of lost control. Earlier in the day, someone came and asked me to go with him and his teenage daughter to Germany. Shockingly enough, he mentioned nothing about the entire bloody school year accompanying them."

Tommy's face was a picture of innocence. "Don't know what you're talking about. I remember very clearly whispering about the school trip part. Besides, we're going to see Hades—it's not like that's the worst trip ever. I thought having you around might make the whole trip more bearable. Olivia had to stay in England, and dating an LOA director doesn't really make the other parents want to be too friendly with me."

Olivia was Kasey's mum and head of the southern-England branch of the LOA, or Law of Avalon, which is best described as Avalon's police force. They're a sort of mix of the FBI and Interpol. They're not always the most popular people, even to other Avalon members, and despite Kasey's school being Avalon funded, a lot of the parents would have loyalties to people who might have very different interests to Avalon's power and influence in the world.

Tommy had found making friends with some of the other parents to be hard work. Avalon politics is full of long memories and longer feuds, and Tommy's association with some powerful members of Avalon made people wary of him.

"It's nice to see you both for more than a few minutes at a time," I admitted. I'd been away from England on and off for just over two years, ever since my necromancy reared its head. I'd missed spending time with Tommy, Olivia, and Kasey.

"Will Sky be there?" Tommy asked.

"Probably—she does like to enjoy my misery."

Sky was one of several people whom Hades and Persephone had adopted over the years. She had been born in America a few hundred years ago to a female European missionary and male Native American chief, the latter of whom worked for Hades. When she was very young, rivals within the tribe had murdered her parents, who were both necromancers; their power had been inherited by Sky. After that, Hades and Persephone had taken her into their home. Hades had also erased those responsible from the face of the earth. It isn't wise to piss him off.

"You know, I never understood something about grimoires," Tommy said, taking the conversation back a few minutes.

"And that would be?" I asked after a few moments of waiting for my friend to continue.

"What was the point of putting in all the runes about how to access magic? The original grimoires were written by sorcerers, so surely they shouldn't have needed the knowledge."

"I don't really know the full answer, but basically a lot of sorcerers reach a point when they've mastered so much magic that they try to look into new ways of increasing their strength. Runes are a popular choice. And then, once Zeus's grimoires were given to the humans, they started practicing and making their own versions of the books."

"Hence, witches," Kasey said as she stepped out from beside me.

I turned to the young teen. "You need to start wearing a bell."

"Sorry, Nate," she said with a sly grin. Kasey was every inch her father's daughter in personality, although in looks, thankfully, she took after her mother, with long red hair, green eyes, and an elegant face. No teenage girl wants to be short and stocky with a permanent five o'clock shadow.

A few years ago, a then twelve-year-old Kasey had put herself between me and something so evil that I was certain I couldn't have beaten it. She'd stopped me from getting hurt more than I'd already been, possibly saving my life in the process. Considering the attention he'd get from both Tommy and me, I almost pitied the first boy she'd bring home. Almost.

Kasey sat opposite me, and I noticed that one of the parents farther down the carriage was giving me an evil glare. She'd been doing it on and off since I'd arrived at the train station, although I had no idea what I'd actually done to earn her wrath.

"Her name is Mara Range," said a young woman sitting on the opposite side of the aisle to Tommy, Kasey, and me. She had dark hair that was almost black, tied back in a ponytail. She wore a simple light-blue T-shirt, the same color as her eyes, with a picture of Led Zeppelin on the front. It hugged her figure, showing off both her athletic body and the tattoo that stopped just above the crease of her elbow. I couldn't make out what it was, but the reds and purples certainly made it appear colorful.

"Sorry—I saw you glance over at her. I'm Emily Rowe," she said quickly and shook my hand and then Kasey's and Tommy's. "I'm one of the lucky people chosen to help with the rabble. No offense." She aimed her last words at Kasey.

"None taken," Kasey said. "Your nails are awesome."

Emily wiggled her fingers, and indeed the little skull and crossbones on each nail must have taken some time and effort to achieve.

I had slightly more important things to consider, though. "And why does this Mara woman suddenly have an issue with me?" I asked.

"She's a witch," Emily said. "A lot of the coven members are on this trip. Unfortunately, because most of the higher ranked members stayed home, Mara is in charge of the coven."

I sighed. "Great. Nice to know there's going to be a frosty reception for the next few days."

"Why?" Kasey asked. "I don't understand what you've done. You've never even met these people."

"A lot of witches don't like sorcerers," I said.

"Why?"

I opened my mouth to explain and then stopped; I wasn't really sure how much to tell her. On the other hand, if I avoided the question, she'd never stop asking. "What do you know about witches?"

"They can use magic, but don't have an innate talent for it," she said as if she were reading from a book.

"Something like that, yes," I said. "Basically, witches are, for all intents and purposes, human. They could easily live a normal human life with no magic at all. But a long time ago, some humans were taught how to use runes to access magic. Unfortunately, where I have the innate ability to use it from birth, they have to make themselves access it. And whenever witches use magic, instead of extending their life, it actually takes time away from it. The more powerful the magic, the more life is taken."

"So they can't extend it at all?" Kasey asked, slightly shocked.

"There is very dark blood magic that allows witches to extend their life by hurting and killing people. Some witches aligned themselves with certain powerful people in Avalon who convinced them that sorcerers were keeping the magic from them. That was a few thousand years ago, and over time witches have maintained a very bad view of sorcerers. They think we're trying to keep them down and not allow them to reach their potential—that we show off just to rub their noses in it."

"They're jealous?"

I nodded. "That's the sum of it. After such a long time of being told it, many witches believe the lie."

"And what do sorcerers think of witches?" Kasey asked.

"We don't," I said with a shrug. "They're not powerful enough to concern us for the most part, and those that are will kill themselves well before they become noticed by Avalon. Occasionally, one of them does some dark stuff—killing a sorcerer for blood was an old trick of theirs—but for the most part, witches are seen as people to ignore. Because they're aligned with Demeter and Hera, they have enough members that they can affect a vote in Avalon, but that doesn't happen often."

"Why align with Demeter?" Kasey asked, clearly in her element of being able to ask every question her quick mind could think of.

"Demeter, Hera, and a few others were the ones who convinced witches that sorcerers were out to get them. They arranged for the witches to support them in Avalon matters in return for information on how to obtain true power. Information I don't think they've ever actually followed through with."

"So, do all witches think this?"

I shook my head. "No, just the stupid ones. I've met some very smart and pleasant witches. And I've met some evil ones too. A witch in a quest for power has the worst of human nature wrapped up in the ability to hurt a lot of people."

"A lot of witches are very nice people," Emily said, making an attempt to show that not every witch was a power-hungry nutcase. "Some of them only use magic to help others and try to spread a message of peace."

"Unfortunately, those who are in league with Demeter undo a lot of that good work. The witches think they have power and a say in what happens, when actually they're just being used to further the aims of those who would throw them to the wind the second they needed to."

"Yes, but like I said," Emily stated, "not all witches are like that. Some actually use their brains and don't want to follow like sheep."

"I'd like to meet more of them," I said, and then a horrible thought occurred to me. "You're a witch, aren't you?"

Emily nodded, and Tommy laughed out loud, gaining a few glances in our direction from other adults.

"Are you a member of the coven?" I asked, ignoring my friend.

Emily nodded again. "Have been for a few years now. You don't seem all that embarrassed. I could have been offended."

"But you're not, so you either agree with me, or you don't care. I'm going with the former."

"I agree with you. Too many witches crave power and are easily swayed to a life of serving those who don't really care about us. A portion of the coven would slit their own throats if Demeter told them to. Fortunately, they're in the minority. The coven leaders normally manage to shut them down before they start ranting."

"And Mara belongs to that smaller group, I assume," I said.

"Yes, she's probably in charge of it, although I have no proof of that. She's certainly not shy about her feelings toward sorcerers."

"Thanks for the warning."

"My pleasure. They're mostly all talk, though." Although she smiled as she spoke, it was the word "mostly" that stuck in my mind.

CHAPTER 2

Why couldn't we just fly here?" Kasey asked as we all exited the train in the town of Mittenwald, after a journey of over twelve hours.

"Because some of the children are unable to fly," Emily said. "Not every species on earth likes to be tens of thousands of feet up in the air."

Tommy chuckled. "Yeah, ask Nate."

Emily looked at me, a question ready on her lips.

"Don't like flying," I admitted. "Not unless alcohol is involved. Trains I'm okay with."

All along the private platform, more and more people piled off. The noise from so many people talking grew every few seconds until it was just an indistinguishable din. I had the sudden urge to get back on the train.

Several of the teachers motioned for everyone to follow them, and soon we were all setting off once more. It was like some weird version of the Pied Piper, with a clipboard and whistle, leading the children and adults out through the small train station and into a huge car park, where three massive buses were parked. Each bus was a long single-decker, all of them painted yellow and blue.

Kasey had met up with some of her friends and had merged into the throng of school children, leaving Tommy, Emily, and me to sit back and wait to see what happened.

"Have you been here before?" Emily asked me while I watched the teacher in charge try to actually *take* charge.

"Lots," I said. "Those buses are what they use to ferry all the kids up to the main complex."

"Are they safe?"

"Run-flat tires, bulletproof windows, and reinforced shells," Tommy said. "I've seen these things take a point-blank shotgun slug to the engine and keep going. Nothing short of a missile strike is going to stop it."

"Are you worried we'll get attacked?" I asked.

Emily shook her head. "No, I just worry about driving in places I've never been before."

"The hotel for everyone is ten minutes outside of town, next to Lake Ferchensee. It's another twenty minutes to one of the single most secured places on the planet. It's why the kids come here from *every* Avalon school all over the world. Hades and his people do this every month. Besides, that's why the parents and guardians are here."

"The guardians are mostly witches, who by your own words aren't something most worry about."

"*Most* sorcerers," I corrected. "And I've met a few witches I wouldn't want to cross. What is she doing?" I asked as the woman who had been glaring at me, Mara Range, was ushering selected people onto a fourth bus that I hadn't thought was part of the trip. It was more of a mini-bus, although it had clearly been modified for more rugged travel. It was all happening much to the obvious irritation of one of the teachers.

"She wants all the witches and their children to travel separate from the rest," Emily said.

"Why?"

"Because she's a fucking idiot," Emily snapped and walked off toward what was hastily turning into a row between Mara and the head teacher, a large woman who was possibly part troll.

"She's going to get her head torn off," Tommy said as he rejoined me after going off to help Kasey put their bags on the buses. Kasey and five more young teenage girls were alongside him, although I didn't recognize any of the newcomers.

"She's nuts if she thinks segregating the witches is a good idea," I said, and one of the girls with Kasey said good-bye and stomped off unenthusiastically toward the ruckus.

"Mara is Chloe's mum," Kasey informed me. "They don't get on."

"Poor kid," I said, mostly to myself, although I heard a giggle from one of the girls standing with Kasey. "What about her dad?"

Kasey shrugged. "She was close to him, but he left her mum a year or so ago. Mara started to go a little . . ."

"Crazy," Tommy finished for her. "You should see her at parent meetings; she's like a tiny, slightly less mustached Stalin."

"She still wears her wedding ring, though," Kasey added. "Although if anyone brings up Chloe's dad to her, she goes mad."

Emily eventually reached the arguing women, and whatever she said appeared to work, as the teacher threw her arms in the air and Mara smiled triumphantly. She ushered the children and adults onto the bus, including Emily, who stopped to say something that made Mara bristle. Mara's daughter, Chloe, was last on the bus, which caused Mara to stop her from getting on and say something that clearly upset the young girl.

"I don't like her," Kasey said.

"She's horrible to Chloe," agreed one of her friends, a short ginger girl, whose face was covered in tiny freckles.

"I can't say that I'm a big fan," I said as the bus's engine roared to life and slowly moved out of the lot.

"Nice of them to wait for everyone else," Tommy grumbled. "I guess this is setting the standard for her behavior for the next few days."

"I think it's more than just her," I said, as the clearly irate headmistress ushered everyone else onto the remaining buses. "If what Emily said was true, there are several witches here who think the same as Mara. It could make for a very long stay."

"We'll just avoid them," Tommy said as we climbed onto a bus and found seats near the rear. We were soon joined by Kasey and her friends, who kept glancing over at Tommy and me, probably sensing that there were more interesting things to come if they stayed nearby. I really hoped they were wrong.

The hotel near Lake Ferchensee was a sizeable ten-story building that held enough rooms for nearly five hundred people. In the various meeting, conference, and dining rooms that it contained, you could easily have walked its halls for several days without seeing everything it had to offer.

It took well over two hours to get all of the children, their minders, and teachers booked in, and even after another hour the massive foyer was still full of people asking for information or telling the staff that their room key didn't work.

I took my bags up to the ninth floor, dodging various teenagers who were without constant adult supervision and had decided that the hotel was now their playground to run around in at will.

Tommy, Kasey, and her friends had already gone up to their rooms on the eighth floor. The school had wisely put into place a policy that ensured a certain percentage of adults on every floor. Tommy's room was next to Kasey's, so I imagined he was facing down nights of staying up to ensure she'd gone to bed at the appropriate time and checking for boys every five minutes— even though Kasey wasn't really the type to either stay up all night or party with boys.

I dropped my suitcase on my comfy-looking bed and slumped down on a leather armchair next to the large window, which gave me an exquisite view of the lake and woodland surrounding it. Germany has always been a beautiful country, especially in the autumn and winter months, and the southern part of the country was one of those places that was just a little too special to stay away from for long.

It helped that Hades and his family often spent a lot of time in the area; I always had a place to stay. Even when the country was scarred by war and evil, Hades and his compound had remained untouched. Hades helped where he could to ensure that those who needed to vanish from the ever-present gaze of the authorities at the time did so without fuss, but he was reluctant to get too involved. The war was a human problem, and if Hades had fully involved himself, there was no telling how much it might have escalated. Hitler and the Nazis had support of the nonhuman variety too. People will always want more power, no matter how much they wield, and some will align themselves with madness to gain it.

I remember wondering at the time, if Avalon and its allies *had* involved themselves, whether the war would have even taken place, but the answer was probably still yes. The only difference is that it would have been much, much worse.

I cast my melancholy aside and took the kettle that was on a nearby table to the modestly sized bathroom, to fill it up in the sink before returning it to the table and switching it on. I liked to have a cup of tea after a long journey; it was nice to just take a few minutes to sit and relax while taking in new surroundings. I knew a few people who did something similar with alcohol, but I doubted any school trip would be too impressed with one of the guardians producing a bottle of scotch and settling in for a few hours, so tea it was.

I prefer white tea, which isn't tea with milk in it, but will gladly drink green or black. Never instant, though, which is pretty much like drinking muddy water. I grabbed a small sachet of brown sugar and tipped it into the mug before dropping in the green tea bag and pouring the water in. I'd just settled down to enjoy the drink when my mobile rang, the sounds of "Behold a Pale Horse," by Martin O'Donnell and Michael Salvatori, filling the room.

I sighed and picked up the phone and discovered that it was Tommy calling. I placed the tea on the table before continuing. "This had better be good," I said.

"You should come down to reception. Quickly."

I was about to ask what had happened, but Tommy had ended the call, so with another sigh I stood and left the room, grabbing my jacket on the way.

I took the lift down to the ground floor, where the sounds of shouting reached me before the doors fully opened to reveal an irate Mara Range screaming at the hotel manager.

I found Tommy nearby, standing next to several more adults from the trip, all of whom appeared to be watching with a mixture of interest and humor. "What the hell?" I whispered, unsure what the acceptable volume of speech was while watching a witch shout at the hotel manager.

"She's pissed off," Tommy explained.

I stared at him for a second. "No shit, really? I did wonder what the yelling was for. Any idea why?"

"She's mad at you."

That made me pause while my brain processed the new information. "Umm . . . what?" I eventually managed.

Before Tommy could reply, Mara turned toward me and raised a bony finger in my direction. "I refuse to share a floor with filth like him," she snapped.

I glanced with mock surprise all around me before looking back at Mara, as those to either side of me made a point of quickly stepping aside. I was unsure whether Tommy didn't move out of loyalty to me or a desire to be closer to the action. "What did I do?"

"Sorcerer!" she almost shrieked. "We were told that the witches had the ninth floor, and that *only* witches would be allowed there. Instead, you place one of *his* kind there too."

"I'm very sorry for your upset," the manager tried to explain— something I imagined he'd been trying to do calmly for some time. "But whoever booked Mr. Garrett was clearly unaware of this arrangement," the manager—a tall, thin man with a some- what haggard expression—said.

"Then remove him from floor nine this instant."

"As I've explained several times," he told her, this time with slightly more force, "we will not make anyone move rooms just because another guest tells us to."

"Would you be happy sharing a floor with a member of the Nazi Party?" she demanded to know.

The manager's face hardened, and I got the impression that Mara may have just launched herself over whatever line of good taste existed when one was accusing someone of being a psychopath. "Madam Range, I think there's a difference here between someone having to share a floor with those who actively hate others, and you having to share a floor with Mr. Garrett, who, to the best of my knowledge, has done nothing untoward to either you or your witches."

"I don't hate witches," I very happily told everyone. "If it helps, I'm not a member of the Nazi Party either. Just sayin', in case this conversation goes in that direction."

There were stifled laughs from those behind me.

"See?" the manager told Mara. "He wishes you no harm."

"We'll see how that goes when he's murdering us in our sleep," she said.

"I promise to clean up after I'm done," I said.

The manager gave me a "Was that really necessary?" look while someone behind me made no effort to conceal his or her snigger. Apparently my time of helping was over.

Mara Range stomped toward me and placed a finger on my chest. "I'll be watching your attitude toward my witches on this trip. If you step out of line, you will regret it."

I looked down at the digit and wondered for a second if I should remove it for her. I decided that would make matters much, much worse and ignored it. "So, I guess asking you out for a drink isn't going to work?"

"You're not taking me seriously," she snapped.

"That's because you're a fucking idiot," I whispered to her and then smiled while her face contorted with rage and she stormed off toward the lifts.

Everyone watched while she pressed the button and waited. After about ten seconds, I could sense that people wanted to laugh, but didn't dare. Another five seconds made it unbearable. Finally the lift arrived, and she stepped inside, causing everyone in the foyer to burst into laughter at once.

"Well, that was interesting," I commented.

"If I were you, I'd keep an eye on her," the manager suggested before walking off.

"Wow, she certainly doesn't like you," Tommy said after he'd finally finished laughing. "Now you can piss women off before you've even met them. That's quite a talent."

"Thanks, Tommy. That was, as always, incredibly helpful."

"Ah, don't be shitty; she's clearly got her knickers in a fucking twist over something. Nothing you can do about it."

I knew he was right. Whatever Mara's issue with me, there was very little I could do to make it go away. But that didn't mean I enjoyed being accused of something I hadn't done.

"Nate," Emily called out from the lift as the doors reopened. She ran over to me, an apologetic expression adorning her face. "I'm so sorry about Mara; sometimes she gets a little . . ."

"Psycho," Tommy helpfully added.

Emily glanced over at my friend and shrugged. "I was going to go with 'intense,' but your word works well enough."

"It's fine, I'm just going to go for a walk," I explained to them both. "There's a good place in town; maybe I'll grab something to eat there. It would be nice if when I got back to my hotel room, Mara hadn't wired it to explode upon opening."

"I'll talk to her," Emily promised.

"You need any company?" Thomas asked.

I shook my head. "I could use the walk. It would probably be best for me to avoid any contact with Mara or her coven, for the evening. I'm not certain I could hold my temper for a second time."

CHAPTER 3

The manager offered to have a bottle of Scotch sent to my room by way of an apology. I accepted on the condition that it be a decent bottle, but still told him that I was leaving for the evening.

About ten minutes of walking into Mittenwald was just long enough for me to enjoy the peace and quiet that came with taking a detour through the nearby forest. There are not a lot of predators to worry about in Germany—the days of bears and wolves stalking the land are long since gone, and although I'd heard that some wolves had started to be repopulated in the northern parts of the country, I wasn't really worried about coming across anything that might give me concern. In fact, the most dangerous thing I saw on my walk was a squirrel, and I think I could probably take one in a fight.

Despite the cold and the occasional flurry of snow, the real winter weather was probably a few weeks away. It was a shame because, as I exited the forest about a hundred meters away from the town, which was lit up in the night, I remembered how stunning the place was after a snowfall. Plenty of people travel a long distance to stay at one of the Bavarian towns during winter, and owing to the town's beauty, with good reason. It was still a busy time of year, and a group consisting of several men and women said hello to me as they walked past, the winter cheer easy to smell on them, which made me smile as I returned their greeting.

The bar I was looking for was about a ten-minute walk from where I'd entered the town, and by the time I'd reached it, I was glad that I'd decided to go out for the evening. Tommy would more than likely have his hands full with shenanigans brought on by imaginary slights, and I didn't trust Mara not to do something incredibly stupid at my expense. I didn't want to give her witches even more reason to hate me by breaking their leader into tiny chunks and scattering them over the hotel.

The bar that was my destination was called *Der Bär und Wolf*—The Bear and Wolf; the sign outside had a black bear standing on his hind legs beside a gray wolf. They appeared to be walking alongside one another, partners in wherever they were going. There was a large car park out front, which was nearly full to capacity with cars of various makes and ages.

I passed a couple of young men who were standing at the rear of their truck, whispering between themselves. They stopped as I passed by and nodded a greeting, which I returned without slowing down.

The noise from inside the bar began to wash over me as a few patrons exited the establishment, the open door allowing the sound, for the briefest of moments, to escape into the night.

I reached the door of the bar and opened it, stepping inside, where I took in the surroundings. I'd been to The Bear and Wolf several times since its conception several decades earlier. It was divided into two parts. The first held several small tables next to a sizeable bar. There were maybe twenty people standing beside the bar while a jukebox in the corner played the Foo Fighters's "Everlong."

Next to the door was a small plinth, on which sat an open book. A young woman with short-cropped hair stood behind it and smiled as I asked for a table for one. She grabbed a menu and beckoned me to follow her.

The second part of the bar was in the rear of the building, which I followed the waitress into. It was comprised of dark-red leather booths and wooden tables. Music played through speakers placed high on the wall, although it was piped in from the jukebox at the front of the bar. Oddly enough, none of the riotous noise from those at the front of the bar made it through to the rear. The acoustics were really something, although I think this had more to do with the rune work the owners had hidden on the bare stone wall between the two sides. It probably cost a fortune to have those runes created that would absorb sound the way they did in the bar, but judging from how busy it was up front, the owners probably found it worth the extra cost.

The waitress seated me in a booth about halfway down the restaurant. I ordered the house beer, and she left me alone to decide on what to eat.

Someone, probably Tommy, once told me that if you go out to eat, you should always order steak or lobster. Presumably because he's a greedy bastard. Lobster wasn't on the menu, but there were plenty of steak dishes. However, as I fancied a change, I went with slices of suckling pig and chips, with a side order of some bread. Bread and chips. You can take the man out of England, but not England out of the man.

I placed the order, along with a second ice-cold beer, and it came a few minutes later, carried by a petite lady who wasn't my original waitress. She appeared to be a good decade older than the previous woman, and her strawberry blond hair was in a braid down her back.

She placed the food and drink in front of me with a smile. "And you weren't going to come say hello?"

I got up from my seat and was launched upon, her hug taking my breath away as she lifted me from the ground with ease. "Hi, Petra," I managed to wheeze as she placed me back on my feet.

"Nate, it's wonderful to see you again. Kurt has gone out for the evening, but he'll be so glad that you're here." Petra Holzman's German accent was much less pronounced than her husband, Kurt's, a product of her spending so many years working abroad for Hades, helping with security for his various businesses.

We both sat at the booth, and I took a bite of the wonderful food, which tasted even better than it smelled. "Is Kurt still doing the cooking?"

Petra nodded. "He wouldn't give it up for anything in the world, although we have another half-dozen chefs who work alongside him. This place gets too busy for it to be just him anymore."

I glanced around at the dozens of other patrons, mostly in twos or groups, eating food that looked delicious and having a good time.

"It's been far too long," Petra said. "We heard you'd come back from the dead after being away for a decade."

"Ah, yeah—Mordred and his plans," I said with a forced smile.

"Kurt once told me that Mordred used to be a good man. It's a shame how he ended up."

"That was a very long time ago," I almost whispered. "And he's never going to hurt anyone else ever again." Mordred had removed my memories while trying to kill me, but I'd managed to escape. I'd spent the next decade living a life that wasn't mine. On the plus side, once I'd recovered my past, I'd taken a great delight in being able to put Mordred in the ground permanently.

Petra watched me for a second, and then a smile spread over her lips. "So, why are you here?"

I explained about the school visit and how there had been a few issues with one of the witches at the hotel.

"Witches," she said with a slight snarl. "I never understood them. Humans playing at being sorcerers, and angry because it doesn't work out how they want."

It wasn't the first time I'd heard witches described in that way. Even those who used to be human often saw them as humans with delusions of grandeur. "Well, apparently, this particular witch holds quite the grudge. Besides, not all of them are bad, Petra."

Petra snorted in disdain. "When I worked for Hades, I had the pleasure of dealing with Demeter and her damn witches on a regular basis. Their insanity gave me a bad impression of the whole lot of them."

"Demeter has that effect on people," I said and finished off my food while Petra laughed.

"So, since you've been back . . ."—Petra rubbed her hands over one another—"have you . . . you know, . . . have you seen *her*?"

"Her?" I asked.

"Don't be an ass; you know exactly whom I mean."

"No, I haven't seen Selene."

"I heard that when everyone thought you were dead, she was inconsolable."

"Bet that pleased her husband," I said with slightly more anger in my voice than I'd intended. "You know—the man she left me for."

"She still loves—"

I raised a hand to stop her there. Selene and I had been together for nearly thirty years, until the late 1920s, when she'd left me for another man. Despite many people at the time—Petra included—trying to explain to me that it wasn't as black and white as I made it out to be, I didn't care. Didn't care then, and still don't. She left me; end of story.

"Whenever Selene's husband or another of Hera's cronies visits Tartarus, she always comes here. She's always alone, and she always asks about you. *Always*, Nathan."

I shrugged. "She's made her bed; she can fuck her husband in it."

Petra's eyes narrowed. "If I thought you meant that, I'd slap you so damn hard."

"Whatever was once between Selene and me is dead and buried. It's best that people leave it that way. She married someone else." Petra opened her mouth, and I kept talking to stop her from interrupting. "I don't care what the reasons were; I don't care if she still harbors some unrequited love for me. If love were that goddamn important to her, she'd have stayed with me in the first place. So fuck Selene, fuck her husband, and fuck the idea of me seeking some kind of solace in the hope that she and I will get back together."

Petra slapped me.

It wasn't hard—more of a tap than anything. A true slap from a werewolf would have knocked me aside by a few feet, but it was loud enough that several of the other patrons stopped eating or talking, to glance my way.

Petra stood up, fire in her eyes. "You can be a cold, arrogant man, Nathan Garrett. Maybe you're not the only one who was a victim of what happened between you."

I glanced up at my old friend. "She's not a victim; she walked out on me and married someone else. All because her dad asked her to." My words were barely above a whisper. "I showed her how much she meant to me every single day. At least I did before she decided to run off with the jumped-up little prick who she currently calls her husband."

Petra's argument faltered with a sigh. "It's not that simple. She had no choice. Hyperion needed her help."

I sat back in the booth and took a deep breath. "Everyone has a choice. She just made a bad one. And I'm not sure why Hyperion needing her help equates to her marrying someone else. If you know more, Petra, maybe you should tell me."

Petra shook her head and walked off, and I went back to finishing my chips and bread. We'd had the same conversation since Selene and I had ended our relationship, and usually it wound up with either Kurt interjecting himself to calm things down or with Petra punching me. Clearly, after almost a century of being apart, it was finally starting to sink in with Petra that Selene and I would never be together again.

I wondered why Petra had such a hard time of letting it go. I'd heard the stories about how Selene's husband whored around and that the two of them barely spent any time in one another's company. And I knew that Petra and Selene had always been close, but I didn't care. She was miserable with a man I knew she didn't love, but she had married him anyway. I'd heard the excuses about not having a choice, and that Selene had to marry him for this reason or that, but none of them ever changed my mind.

I polished off the food and drink, taking my time as people came and went around me. Several beers later, and after adding a lovely warm chocolate brownie with a chocolate fudge sauce and fresh cream to my bill, Petra still hadn't come back to yell at me some more. I was almost finished with the brownie when a pretty, young woman sat down opposite me.

"Hello, sorcerer," she said. She had a South London accent, although it wasn't very pronounced.

"And you are?" I asked, looking up from my brownie and licking the remains from my spoon.

"Sarah Hamilton." Sarah was, from what I saw in a glance before she sat down, a few inches taller than me. She was thin, with pronounced cheekbones, long elegant fingers, and perfectly manicured nails, painted blue. She wore no jewelry on her hands or wrists, but two diamond studs sat in each ear. Her long, light-brown hair was swept back in a ponytail, which had fallen over one shoulder. She wore a black jacket, under which was a scruffy, light-blue, zipped hoodie that was at odds with the nails and earrings, as if she were trying to blend in with the casual appearance of everyone else I'd seen in town, but couldn't be without at least a few of her finer things.

"And how can I help you, Sarah?" I asked.

"Telling me your name would be nice."

"Nate," I said. There was no point in lying. Despite various sources throughout history saying otherwise, no one can do magic on you just because they know your name. If they could, a big portion of the world's inhabitants would be up to their neck in curses.

Sarah smiled. "Excellent. Well, Nate, I'm here to offer you a chance to leave this town before your presence means I have to deal with you on a much harsher basis."

I quickly glanced around the restaurant, not wanting to take my attention away from Sarah too much, but there was no one around I'd have considered a threat.

"Nothing will happen in this restaurant," she said.

I reset my gaze on Sarah. "Does this have anything to do with Mara and those witches? Are you another one of the coven?"

Sarah shook her head. "I am a witch—that much is true—but not part of Mara's coven. Mara is, quite frankly, an idiot."

Sarah produced a palm-sized, round rock from her pocket, placing it between us. It was smooth all over, and it looked a little like someone had drawn a compass on it, but instead of the usual "N," "S," etc., there were small runes. Three of the runes were black, while the one pointing toward me was white.

"Do you know what this is?" she asked.

I nodded. "I haven't seen one for a while." The small item was a witch finder and was used to track people who can wield magic. There weren't many witches who still made them; there was a time when people used them to actively track and kill witches, and no one wanted that period of history back. However, a simple change of the runes meant that it could be used to track a sorcerer instead, although it was a change that was rarely used. Very few people want to actively track a sorcerer.

"I was told to find a sorcerer by the name of Nate and offer him a way out. You are a sorcerer. Don't bother to deny it. You're the only one in town, from what I can tell."

"You made this yourself, I assume. That's a good chunk of magic."

As with most witch magic, her own energy would have been used to power the device. As if on cue, Sarah raised her sleeves, showing me the three runes tattooed on each wrist.

"That's quite a bit of power you've given yourself," I said. "You're playing a dangerous game. I wonder how much of your life you ebbed away just making that." I pushed the witch finder back toward Sarah.

"The amount of power I can access is hardly your concern."

I shrugged. I wasn't about to dissuade Sarah from the course of action she clearly wanted to take.

"So, why do you want me to leave this town?"

"Also not your concern," she said dismissively. "All you need to know is that you have twelve hours to pack and leave. Don't come back."

I rubbed the back of my neck and sighed. "The problem is that I'm not really one to be run out of town without knowing who's doing the running and why."

"If you stay, you'll find out. I was told to offer you one chance. It's been offered. If you ignore it, then what happens is of your own making."

I leaned back against the leather seat and crossed my arms. "And what will happen?"

Sarah stood up from the table and placed fifty euros on it. "The meal is on me. As for your question, I'm afraid you won't get the chance to learn that. Just know, if you stay, your death will be for a good cause. I hope that helps."

"Not really." I pushed the plate aside. Any appetite I'd had when Sarah first sat down had evaporated like the heat from the brownie.

"I think the person who sent me here would rather you didn't die, Nate. I have no interest in your ability to breathe one way or another."

I looked at her for a heartbeat. "You should know something too. If you come after me, or anyone I care about, I'm going to tear you and whoever you have with you into tiny, wet chunks of smeared meat. I'll end you and your friends, and then I'll go after whoever it is you're working for, and I'll end them too. You have no idea who I am, Sarah. But if you push me, you're going to find out."

She leaned near me and placed a hand on my shoulder. "I'll look forward to it," she whispered with a smile before turning to walk away.

"You shouldn't," I told her. "It won't be something you'll enjoy."

CHAPTER 4

I sat in the restaurant for another twenty minutes, allowing the information Sarah had imparted to ferment in my mind. I had no idea what her plans were or why she would have given me a warning to stay away, but clearly someone expected me to interrupt those plans if I remained. I liked interrupting plans of people who threatened me. I was good at it.

Petra reappeared as the customers in the restaurant began to thin out. "You plan on ordering something else?"

I glanced up at her. "You still mad at me?"

Petra's shoulders sagged, and she shook her head before taking a seat opposite. "I'm sorry for slapping you."

"Don't worry about it; at least you didn't punch me."

A smile crept onto her lips, but vanished just as quickly a moment later. "What's wrong?"

I reiterated my chat with Sarah Hamilton.

"So, what's your plan?" she asked after several moments of silence, once I'd finished talking.

"I'm going to stay around and see what happens. I'm off to see Hades tomorrow with the school, and unless she happens to have an army, I doubt very much that his compound is any sort of target."

"But it is possible."

I nodded. "Well, then it's a good thing I'm going. Although anyone attacking Hades or his family will clearly have some sort of death wish."

My original waitress came over and nodded slightly to me before whispering something to Petra.

"You're sure?" Petra asked, and the waitress nodded.

"What's going on?" I inquired.

"Apparently your witch friend is outside in the car park, along with several men."

"Well she's either engaged in a very alternative lifestyle, or maybe she didn't believe I was taking her threat seriously."

"I'd go with the second one. Which only leaves the question of did you take her seriously?"

"I always take threats seriously. *But* I've been threatened by more dangerous people than a witch with delusions of grandeur."

"So, what's your plan?"

"I'm going to go see what she wants."

The waitress walked away after picking up the fifty euros, taking the empty plates with her.

"My waitress told me the name of one of the men waiting out there." Petra said when we were alone. "Name's Robert Ellis."

"He from around here?"

Petra shook her head. "He's Australian, I think. He arrived a few months ago just before Christmas. Just after a krampus that people had spotted in the area."

That got my attention. "A *krampus*? You're sure?"

Petra nodded. "I saw it walking down the road, swinging its chains around. Those fucking horrific bell things were making noise. You can't really mistake a krampus for anything else."

In mythology, a krampus was a sort of anti-Santa. It would spirit away the naughty boys and girls to its lair. What it did with them is open to interpretation; some say it drowned the children and ate them, while some suggested it just kept them until they behaved and then brought them back. In most instances the truth is quite far removed from reality, but in the case of the krampus, truth and reality weren't all that dissimilar.

Krampus don't care one way or the other about the behavior of the children they steal. They take children back to their lairs and feast on their souls, tossing the corpse of the child into a nearby stream or river when they finish. Unlike animals that need to hibernate during the winter, krampus only feed during the coldest months of the year, before vanishing once spring arrives. Before the tenth century, there were hundreds of the bastards running around, although nearly all of them were killed after it was made illegal to create them.

Like most of the truly horrific creations in the world, krampus were made using dark blood magic. At one point, they'd been human, although once the magic had finished with them, any glimmer of humanity had been extinguished. They were considered a *crime against magic*, and their creation was punishable by death. Apparently, someone was unconcerned about the possibility of such things, if he or she had taken the time and effort to make a krampus and unleash it on the town of Mittenwald.

"How many did it take?" I asked, not really sure I wanted the answer.

"None," Petra said.

The shocked expression on my face said more than any words could have.

"I know," she continued. "We saw it, or heard it, for two nights, but no one was taken. Most of the permanent residents in town, human or otherwise, are aware of the world they really live in, so after that first night they took precautions."

"So how did this Robert guy come to hunt the krampus?"

"After the second night, we had a town meeting. They wanted to get Hades to come help before something bad happened."

"And?"

"Robert arrived at the meeting and went full-Brody on us all."

"What?"

" 'I'll catch him for three and kill him for ten,' " she said in a gruff voice. "You know, Brody from *Jaws*."

"I'm aware of the film, yes," I informed her. "He told you he'd find and kill the krampus for money?"

"Basically, except Robert didn't want payment as such. He said all he wanted was free accommodation and food while he stayed in town."

"Is he human?"

Petra nodded. "He didn't show any signs of being anything else. He had a rifle with him. Kurt told me it was a military one."

"You know what type?"

Petra shook her head. "I've never been concerned with human weapons. Not unless they're pointed at me, anyway."

"I don't understand why, in a town full of people who aren't human, you let one track something as dangerous as a krampus. Killing one is hard enough work for anything, but a human should have been torn to pieces the second he got close."

"Robert arrived at that town meeting, where we were about to put forward a motion to get Hades's help, and explained that inviting Hades to come assist us might set a precedent that meant we'd be running to him every time we had something big to deal with. He said that we should at least try to kill the krampus ourselves. He was so damn confident that everyone there agreed with him. It was the strangest thing. Thinking about it, we should have laughed him out the building. I know that no *were* wants to go tracking a krampus—not with those damn silver chains it has—but sending a human out there was insane."

"So what happened?"

"Robert took some people who'd arrived with him. They tracked it up to the mountains, and according to them, Robert shot it and it fell down a ravine."

"Any proof?" I asked, not really believing that a krampus would die so easily.

"A bell. The bullet shot one of them right off the monster. It has a bullet hole in it. I've seen it myself."

We sat quietly for a few minutes as the information I'd just been given swirled around in my head.

"What are you thinking?" Petra finally asked.

"That something very weird is happening in this town. Sarah said there are no sorcerers in town. Is that true?"

Petra nodded. "We occasionally get the odd one or two passing through, but none live in town. Why?"

"Krampus are normally a witch's creation, and having a witch turn up to threaten me while she hangs around with the man who's supposed to have killed a krampus doesn't sit well."

"If they're setting us up for a con, it's an incredibly long-drawn-out one. I've never seen that woman before, and Robert's entire bill is setting the town back a few grand at most. They put him in a house near the north end of town. He buys groceries once a week, and that's the extent of his monetary gain."

"He's here for a reason. Otherwise, why not leave once the krampus was killed?"

Petra shrugged. "You know, I've never thought about it."

"Like I said, weird." I stood up and put another fifty euros on the table. I wasn't about to have someone who threatened me pay for my meal.

"You need help out there?"

I shook my head. "It's just going to be a nice little chat between adults."

"And if they want to do more than chat? You can't turn my car park into a war zone; there are families, kids in town."

"A war implies that both sides will get a chance to fight. If it all goes to shit, I assure you, the only things they're going to be doing is whimpering and bleeding."

I stepped out into the cold night and breathed out, my breath condensing as I stood under a light attached to the front of the restaurant. Sarah and five other men—one of which I assumed was Robert—were standing together at the far side of the car park, next to two large four-wheel drive behemoths of one kind or another.

The streetlight above Sarah and her friends' heads didn't work well; the only light that reached them was the overspill from those outside of the car park. A small amber tip occasionally lit up as a cigarette was pressed to one of the men's lips; a second later a cloud of smoke was exhaled.

I strolled over to them, and they disbanded slightly, spreading out around me. "I assume you want to continue our little chat?" I asked.

Sarah smiled. "You weren't taking me seriously. I wanted a chance to impart just how much you need to leave this town." She placed a hand on the man beside her.

"And your man Robert and his friends are going to do that?" I glanced at one of the men nearby, the one still smoking a cigarette. "Is *he* going to be able to do anything before he coughs up a lung?"

"It's regrettable that it's come to this," Sarah said, ignoring my taunt.

I laughed. "See, this is why I can't take you seriously. You're standing there, all menacing, while your friends circle me, and you're expecting me to be scared. Unless one of them is a troll in the best disguise ever or something, it's going to be a short fight."

"This will make it longer," she snapped and showed me her bloody hands before slamming them onto the cold pavement.

Waves of power rushed over me as runes of bright red lit up over the tarmac beneath my feet. I've had my magic removed before, through runes and sorcerer's bands, but what Sarah had done felt like all of my power and energy evaporated into my surroundings. I dropped to one knee as I lost my breath and felt the world spin around me.

"You really are an arrogant little sorcerer," Sarah said with contempt. She turned to Robert. "He can still take more punishment than a human, but don't kill him. Just get him in the truck and take him away from here."

I tried to create a ball of flame in my palm, but it was barely a few millimeters in size and disappeared as quickly as it arrived.

Sarah was right: I'd been arrogant. I hadn't expected her to use so much power.

Sarah staggered back slightly, placing a hand on the bonnet of the truck as the five men encircled closer around me.

Despite the lack of magic, and the tiredness I felt, I shook my head clear of any cobwebs and got back to my feet, albeit slowly. I stretched my back and arms as I readied myself for a fight. I could have tried to make a run for it until my magic returned, but there was no way of telling how much area Sarah had managed to put her spell onto.

"You sorcerers are always so preoccupied with your magic," Sarah said with a snarl. "I wonder how well you're going to do without it."

"Okay then, ladies, who wants to get the shit kicked out of them first?" I asked.

The first person to move was the smoker, a huge barrel-chested man, who had removed his jacket, revealing dark tattoos over huge muscular arms. He flicked the cigarette toward me in an attempt to make me lose my concentration, and then darted forward. I stepped back directly into a blow to my kidney from someone behind me. It was hard enough to make me pause as pain rocked through my back, giving the smoker enough time to slam into me, lifting me from my feet. He kept running for a few steps before dumping me onto the nearest car's bonnet. The air rushed out of me in one go, and he ensured it wasn't going to get back in by punching me in the solar plexus and then pushing me off the bonnet and onto the cold ground, where I smacked my elbow as I landed roughly.

I rolled away, between the two parked cars, and got back to my feet, only to be kicked in the head by Robert, who vaulted over the boot of the nearest car, sending me sprawling back to the tarmac.

A hand reached down and grasped the back of my jacket, dragging me out from between the cars and throwing me back to the ground, where someone else kicked me in the ribs hard enough for me to lift up slightly. A second kick spun me onto my back. I was getting my ass kicked by humans. *Humans*, for fuck's sake! If they beat me, I'd never live it down. The once mighty Nathan Garrett, beaten by a bunch of people who didn't even know what magic really was, let alone know how to use it. Tommy would never shut up about it.

"This is pathetic," Robert said from somewhere behind me. "Sarah said that sorcerers can't fight for shit without their magic, but damn, boy, I figured you'd be able to put up a bit of a struggle."

I rolled onto my front and got back to my knees without anyone trying to fight me. I was hoping that in their own small victory, they'd gained a measure of confidence that I wasn't someone to be concerned about. One of my attackers, the larger smoker, grabbed my jacket again and pulled me upright, shoving me back against the nearest car and punching me in the stomach.

"This is fun," the man said.

"You smell awful," I informed him.

The man grabbed me by my hair and pulled my head back with enough force that I thought he was going to tear my hair out. "Not as big as you thought you were, are you?"

"One thing," I said softly. "You need to know one thing."

"And what's that?" he asked, his tone mocking, as the stench of his breath filled my nostrils.

I drove my cupped palms onto his head, one over each ear, with enormous force, possibly bursting an eardrum. Smoker released me and yelled out in pain. I whipped my head forward with speed and ferocity, driving my forehead into his nose with everything I had. The bridge of his nose crunched under the blow, and he staggered back as blood streamed down his face. I stepped forward, smashing my forearm into his face and then pushing him roughly onto the ground.

I took a deep breath and then breathed out as one of the four remaining men rushed toward me. I deflected his punch, slamming my palm into his throat. He dropped to his knees like he'd been shot, gasping for breath. I grabbed his long dark hair and drove his face into the headlight of the nearest car. I sensed movement behind me and spun round, catching the third man in the jaw with a kick, and then whipped the same leg down onto the choking man, using my knee to bury his face into the remains of the headlight. His face was now a mass of tiny shards of safety glass and plastic.

If you're going to fight a group, you go in hard and fast. The same can be true for any fight, to be honest, but when you're outnumbered, you want to drop those against you to a manageable level as quickly as possible. Of course, a big rule is also not to get taken off your feet, but I'd managed to fail that in the first ten seconds.

After my initial weariness from Sarah's spell, my energy had started to increase, and apart from the lack of magic, I felt okay. I was pretty sure the three injured men on the tarmac around me couldn't say the same.

"Are we done here?" I asked no one in particular.

Their answer was immediate: the fourth man rushed forward and jabbed at my face, which I blocked, but he'd forced me to step back, directly into the path of another of Robert's dangerous kicks. I moved to block the blow, but Robert saw it coming, and instead of catching me in the side of the head, he shifted his stance mid-kick and hit me in the chest.

The power behind the kick was immense, and I was forced to take several steps back as my chest screamed in pain. Robert grinned and started bouncing from foot to foot, shifting his stance with every few bounces so I couldn't tell which leg he was going to kick with.

His friend decided my plan for me. He moved forward while my attention was on Robert and threw a vicious hook to my jaw. He knew that I would either dodge back, right into a waiting Robert's path, or I'd block the blow, which would open me up to a second punch, this time to the gut. I stepped back, gaining Robert's attention, his foot leaving the tarmac. I darted forward and grabbed the fourth man's arm, immediately turning and dragging him off balance, forcing him to stagger into Robert's line of fire. Robert's leg was already moving faster than it had before—the trick of changing stances mid-kick was impossible—and his foot quickly found a home on the side of the fourth attacker's head.

The man's eyes rolled back up into his head, and he flopped forward toward me. I caught him and shoved him toward Robert, who darted aside and let his friend crash to the ground.

I didn't wait around to give Robert a chance to recover, and rushed him, throwing an uppercut to his jaw, which he avoided, stepping right into the path of a punch to his gut. He stepped away, but not fast enough to avoid a swift kick to the side of his knee, which caused him to shout out in pain as he dropped to his one good leg.

Robert threw a punch, which I pushed aside and I clasped my hands around the back of his neck, bringing my knee up as I pulled his face down. He managed to block the first two knee strikes, so I released my hands and kicked out, catching him on the chest and sending him sprawling to the ground.

I walked over to him, and he kicked out with both legs, but I managed to grab one ankle, and a quick kick to the side of his knee dislocated the joint. He yelled in pain as I applied more pressure to the injured limb.

"Now, what are you doing here?" I asked, managing to remain calm, despite his howls of protest.

"P-paid—paid to," he eventually managed.

I released the pressure a little. "By whom?"

Robert shook his head, and I was about to say something when someone smashed into the side of me, taking me from my feet and driving me to the side. I twisted in his grip, to discover that Smoker had found his feet and wanted some payback.

I slammed my palm into his broken nose. He immediately released me and yelled in pain.

I drove my forearm into his face once more. This time there was no lack of energy on my part, and his head snapped to one side as if hit by a truck. He spun once and then fell to the ground, probably with a broken jaw in addition to his nose.

"Right," I said with a slight cough. Smoker had managed to hurt my already bruised ribs. "Where were we, Robert?" I took a step toward him as Sarah appeared at the end of the car park.

"You are done here," she raged.

"Girl, if you test me, you won't find me in the mood to play nicely."

She brandished a dagger in one hand, which she drew across the palm of the other before dropping it to the ground. A second later, she pressed her palms together and closed her eyes as I began to run toward her, determined to stop whatever she was about to cast. Unfortunately, I was too slow, and as she exhaled, she pushed her hands out, palms toward me, and snapped one word: *"Effete."*

The effect was instantaneous. I crashed to my knees as if the weight of the world were suddenly pressing down on me. I couldn't move, could barely breathe as my body just stopped working. Every ounce of energy I had left me in a moment, and a second later I was lying on the cold car park trying to make my brain work enough so that I could figure out what was happening to me. Unfortunately, my brain had gone the same way as the rest of my body, and a deep fog had settled in my head, clouding any rational thoughts and ideas.

I watched in silent horror as Sarah picked up the dagger and stalked toward me, a set purpose on her face. She crouched beside me. "I tried to help you, but you just couldn't stop, could you?"

I glanced up at her and saw blood trickle from her nose. She'd used a lot of magic, and her body was violently protesting.

She noticed my gaze and wiped the back of her hand across her mouth and nose, noticing the blood for the first time. She stood, full of urgency and panic. "You can die here," she said to me and then went to each of her five friends, placing a hand on their bodies and healing them slightly before helping her dazed and aching comrades into one of the trucks and speeding out of the car park.

I shook my head and tried to clear the mental cobwebs that Sarah's magic had placed there. *Effete*—the word was familiar. I knew what it meant, I knew what had happened, but I couldn't make my brain wake up enough to actually form the words.

I moved slowly toward the restaurant, forcing myself forward an inch at a time. I wasn't going to die without a fight, I was damn sure of that. As I slowly dragged myself along the tarmac, my head began to clear; I must have been reaching the edge of the magic that Sarah had used.

The word *effete* burned into my consciousness. Sarah had used a blood magic curse on me. I pushed myself up to my knees and crawled forward until I saw rune marks that had been drawn on the ground in what appeared to be black chalk, making them almost invisible unless you were right on top of them.

My brain cleared further. *You were marked*, it told me. The knowledge slammed into the front of my thoughts; curses don't work unless you're marked first. The memory of Sarah placing her hand on the back of my shoulder tore into me, and I immediately ripped at my jacket, throwing it aside and then doing the same with my hoodie.

Only a fraction of my magic had actually been drained from me, but it rushed back into me like a freight train. If I hadn't already been on my knees, I would have been knocked over, as the power crashed over me in one huge wave. Tarmac cracked and broke around me, and my white and orange glyphs burned brightly over my arms and chest, despite the fact that I wasn't consciously using any magic at all.

It forced me onto all fours, my magic breaking the tarmac under my hands, destroying part of the runes, and releasing the contained energy.

My mind cleared in a heartbeat, bringing with it terrible news. If I'd stayed inside the affected area, I would have been weak for a few hours, maybe a day, but then my strength would have returned. The power collected by the runes would have returned to me until I'd regained my strength.

Breaking the runes had changed that. On the plus side, it meant getting my missing energy back much more quickly; on the minus side, it turned the car park into a damn bomb.

The remaining magic exploded outward like a nuclear shockwave. Windscreens and headlights shattered, tires blew from the pressure, and the lights and windows at the front of the restaurant rained down glass over the ground. The blast picked me up like I was made of paper and threw me aside. I felt a crunch as I collided, back first, with something hard. Pain rocked through me, and then, just as quickly as the magical energy had rushed outward, it stopped and all rushed back into me as if it were attached on an elastic band.

The final thing I remembered before passing out was that I cried out in pain.

CHAPTER 5

Berlin, Germany. 1936.

For the better part of a week, I scoured the city of Berlin, looking for any signs of Pandora or information on where she might have fled. Usually, a trail of dead bodies—like a trail of breadcrumbs—provided a pretty good indication of where she was, but on this occasion it led to nothing. She had simply escaped on the back of a motorbike, an image that seemed more romantic than the reality of all the murdered Nazis she'd left behind in the Gestapo building.

I decided the only course of action was to wait around until Pandora did something spectacular. She always did, but sometimes she liked to relax for a while first. In all likelihood, she was sitting in a hotel room somewhere in Berlin, drinking champagne and eating expensive food while plotting whatever scheme she wanted to carry out.

I spent a few days reading and watching the other occupants go about their business in a hotel lobby. I'd picked the place especially because of the number of foreigners who were staying there, hoping to overhear one of them slip up and discuss something inadvertently. Occasionally, Nazi officers would enter the hotel and wander around, asking people for their papers or generally being a pain. There was no overt threat, but it was clear from their tone and body language that they were begging for someone to aggravate them. They were just thugs—thugs with power, certainly, but the only difference between most Nazis and the common thugs you'd meet if you walked down the wrong street at night, was that the Nazis had shinier boots.

So, I found myself sitting in a comfortable green leather armchair in the lobby. I placed a German newspaper on a nearby table. I'd hoped it would give me a clue to something that might have sounded like business Pandora was involved in, but it was so pro Nazi, it should have come with its own flag.

Instead of reading what passed for journalism, I picked up a book from a local store and set about reacquainting myself with Lovecraft's dark tales. I'd known a few people in my life that I could easily have described as Cthulhu-esque, and I wondered for a moment whether Lovecraft had actually met any of them or if these tales were really just a product of his imagination. I wasn't sure which one of those two options concerned me more.

I was midway through a particularly good story, when someone sat in the chair opposite me. "Hello, Nathan." She spoke in what was almost a Southern drawl.

I lowered the book and glanced over at Pandora, who smiled. "Interesting accent," I said and carefully placed the book on the table beside me, as if moving quickly might spook her, and she'd run off.

"We're trying it out," she explained and raised a glass of champagne to her lips, taking a sip. "You weren't looking for an American, and we've spent so long in Tartarus that our once Greek accent has been sort of lost in the annals of time. Much like our ability to care about the human race or their petty conflicts."

"Have you fanned the flames of another war?" I asked. Pandora hadn't *started* the Napoleonic Wars the last time she'd escaped, but she sure as hell had managed to keep that particular fire well and truly stoked.

She shrugged. "You like it?" she asked, motioning to her hair. Her once long, dark hair had been cut much shorter.

"You didn't answer my question."

"No, Nathan, we haven't involved ourselves in any wars. These humans don't need our help to kill one another."

"Hasn't stopped you before."

She shrugged. "Yes, well, this time we're only killing people who deserve it. Indiscriminate violence is only fun for the first few millennia. After that, we had to find a new hobby."

"You feel like telling me where you've been? Petra and Kurt are searching Dresden for you at the moment."

She shook her head. "Doesn't matter. All that matters is that we're here right now, throwing ourselves on your sword. Metaphorically." She looked me up and down before taking my fedora from the table beside me and placing it on her head. "Nice suit. Makes you look like a gangster."

"That's what I was going for," I said sarcastically.

"We're going to keep the hat."

A young man walked past and winked at Pandora, who smiled in return. Pandora reached out and touched the back of the man's hand, and he stopped walking immediately and sat on the arm of the chair, offering Pandora a cigarette. She took it and licked her lips seductively as she placed it in her mouth, rolling her tongue over the tip as he struck a match and offered to light the cigarette.

"Pandora," I said, my voice stern.

The man glanced over at me and appeared to notice me for the first time. Even if Pandora hadn't been able to bewitch and enslave people, her beauty would have still stopped those who passed her by. Thankfully, due to an encounter long ago, I was immune to both Pandora's charms and her powers; it was why I always got sent to track her down after she escaped.

"The lady and I are talking," he said, his accent placing him from England, probably around the Manchester area. He had a thin moustache and slicked back hair. His smart suit probably cost a pretty penny, and he wore it with confidence. All in all, he looked every inch the respectable banker or lawyer, but there was something behind his green eyes. Something I didn't like.

"Actually, you haven't said anything to her," I mentioned.

He appeared to be confused for a moment, as if only just realizing that what I'd said was true. "Well, be that as it may, you can leave now."

"Pandora, knock it off," I snapped.

She glanced toward me and removed the cigarette from her lips, blowing the noxious smoke above her. "You don't want to fight for us, Nathan?"

I stood and sighed; I really didn't want to have trouble inside the hotel. And I knew that Pandora was thoroughly enjoying herself, but she'd hopefully get bored if I walked away. She always did like an audience. "Don't go anywhere."

I left the couple to talk and asked the smartly dressed, pretty, young receptionist at the hotel front desk for a phone to use for a private conversation. She retrieved one from under the desk and then walked away in order to at least appear as if she weren't going to listen in.

I connected myself with an operator and got her to put me through to a number in Mittenwald. To the rest of the world, it was a simple hotel, but I knew that it was the only way anyone could get through to Hades, who refused to have a direct number while he was at Tartarus. He said it was safer that way; I just thought he didn't like the idea of having a telephone that anyone could use to contact him.

It took a few minutes, but eventually I tracked him down. "*Ja, Nathan?*" he asked.

"I have Pandora," I reported, and waited for a few seconds for the information to sink in.

"That's excellent news. Was she . . . awkward to capture?"

I told him about the time I'd spent searching for Pandora, ending my account with the time a few minutes earlier, when she'd just walked into the hotel.

"Well now, that is unusual. Where are you at the moment?"

I gave him the address of the hotel and could hear the scribbling of pen on paper at his end.

"There's a private airfield about sixty miles outside of the city." He gave me more accurate directions, which I wrote down after the receptionist passed me a sheet of paper and pen. "Be there in six hours."

"Will do," I said, and nodded thanks to the receptionist as she retrieved her pen. "Something isn't right here."

"Something is never right with that woman," Hades said with a slight chuckle.

"More so than usual. I've never known her to just hand herself in without the preceding fire and brimstone she's always managed to create."

Hades paused for a second. "You think she's planning something?"

"Always. But this time, I think whatever she's got planned is already set in motion. Otherwise, why appear out of nowhere?"

"Okay, I'll think on it and talk to you when I get to the airfield." Hades hung up, and I passed the phone back to the young lady, who nodded her thanks before walking away to deal with a new couple who had arrived.

I heard Pandora before I saw her; or rather, I heard the commotion she'd clearly created. Two men, one of whom had given Pandora the cigarette, and a second dressed in an SS uniform, were arguing over who was going to talk to the woman seated between them. No one wanted to get involved in a row that a member of the Schutzstaffel was engaged in, but everyone appeared to be very confused as to why the officer wasn't just dragging the other man outside.

"I saw her first," the British man bellowed.

"She is mine to treat like a lady as she deserves," the German officer shouted back in English, following it up by shoving the other man in the shoulder slightly.

"You sir, are a cad and a bounder," the British man said and shoved the German back, with a little more force.

Everyone in the lobby took a deep breath. No SS officer was going to let someone shove him without meting out some serious punishment. I walked toward the two men, but didn't reach them in time to stop the German from removing one of his brown gloves and slapping the British man across the face with it. The crack of leather against skin brought winces from those nearby.

I stopped walking and glanced at Pandora, who had an expression of glee on her face. "It's like theater," she said with a slight giddy laugh; the Southern drawl was replaced with her normal tone, a neutral accent that contained traces of her Greek heritage.

"Stop them," I urged. "Before this goes any further."

Pandora tore her gaze away from the two men, who were now slapping each other across the face with reckless abandon, and glanced at me. "We aim to have some amusement before being taken back to Tartarus. Besides, if we weren't here, then this SS gentleman would have taken the other man outside and had him executed."

"If you weren't here, they never would have started doing this. *You're* making them fight like this. You made him say 'cad and bounder,' Pandora."

"We can't help it if men want to fight over us."

"Yes," I said softly, "you can."

Pandora's expression hardened, and she pointed to the German officer. "Nathan, this man here is a member of the SS. He has murdered and tortured people, and he likes it. A few weeks ago, while he was drunk, he beat an elderly Jewish man to death. He still had blood on his boots the next morning when he went to see his commanding officer. He believes totally in Hitler's propaganda."

Both men continued to slap each other, ignoring everything else around them. The British man had found a glove of his own, but the event was now escalating, as their faces became pink and painful. People in the lobby were clearly uncomfortable at what was happening, although no one moved to intervene or call for the police.

"This man," Pandora continued, her voice full of anger and disgust, "has raped four women just on his journey from England to here over the past few weeks. Two in Germany. He beat the second woman so badly she's currently in a hospital under sedation. He went to visit her and whispered things in her ears that would make your skin crawl. He believes himself to be above the law. He wanted to rape us, Nathan, do you know that? This piece of shit wanted to take us in the alley behind this hotel and hurt us, to make me scream."

I was sure she'd said "me" and not "us," but I couldn't be certain. "Are you making everyone in this place watch them?" I asked.

"We're ensuring no one calls the authorities, that's all."

"Are you going to check all of these people for evil deeds and punish them too?"

Pandora closed her eyes. "Jealousy, anger, rage, hatred, bitterness. All normal emotions, but no one here has killed for fun or hurt people for pleasure. They do not deserve our wrath."

"Did you know that these two would both be here?" I asked as the sounds of slapping had slowed down, and the men's faces were both raw and had been cut open several times.

Pandora ignored my question. "We can feel it, Nathan. We can feel the wants and desires, the anger and rage of every person we walk past. It's like a chorus of malevolence. And in the middle of all that is always that glimmer of hope and love. But these two, these two diseased pieces of shit, deserve to be punished for their actions."

Pandora couldn't lie to me; it was one of the benefits of the bond we shared. From my point of view, anyway. "Make them go outside," I whispered. "To the alley behind the hotel."

Pandora glanced up at me, her eyes ice cold and full of rage. "Someone here might remember us."

"Just leave with me; we'll go to the alley with them. Then you can release them."

"Will you stop me?"

I paused for a second. I was certain that Pandora hadn't said "we," or "us"—that she'd used the singular, not the plural.

"So, are you going to stop us?" Pandora asked.

I looked at the two men who had unwittingly set themselves into the gaze of someone as dangerous as Pandora. They were the flies to her hunting spider. And once she'd caught them and learned their true natures, they'd never stood a chance. "No, they're yours to use as you see fit. But after, you come with me, no arguments."

She nodded once, curtly. "Deal."

She stood and walked off toward the hotel's front doors, the two men trailing behind her silently. I glanced around as everyone went back to whatever they'd been doing before Pandora started affecting them; no one appeared to even know that anything had happened.

I caught up to Pandora and her followers as she walked down the steps outside the hotel and began strolling along the street outside. As it was mid-morning, it was fairly busy, and a few people gave noticeable glances to the two men who looked as if they'd been in a fight, although I doubted anyone would have come close to guessing what had actually transpired.

We all turned into a nearby alley and continued down the snaking path until we were behind the hotel. The alley was empty, and from the place where Pandora and the men stopped, it was impossible to be spotted by anyone, unless someone was looking out one of the windows of the hotel that towered above us.

The sun shone down, lighting up the alley and glinting off the pieces of glass and paper that littered one side.

"So, do you have a plan?" I asked Pandora.

Pandora turned to the two men, who swayed slightly as if drunk, and removed a pen and notepad from her pocket. "Both of you will write your confession of your crimes."

She didn't need to speak to anyone she'd enthralled in order to get that person to do anything, but I think she liked to verbalize her orders. Either as an idiosyncratic action that made her connect more to her human side, or maybe she just liked the sound of her own voice. I preferred to believe it was the former.

Pandora passed the notepad and pen to the SS officer, who set about furiously scribing the confession to his crimes. It took him nearly five minutes, and several pages, to get it all out, but when he was done, he passed the notepad and pen to the British man.

"Excellent," Pandora said, and the man beamed.

She tapped him on the shoulder, and he glanced around as if searching for something. Eventually, he found what he was looking for and walked off a few steps, stopping and picking up a three-foot piece of metal that at one point had probably been part of some railings. The metal was dark blue in color with a spike on one end that would have deterred people from climbing over whatever it had originally come from. He brought it back to Pandora, who smiled at him.

The officer beamed again, as if he were a puppy who'd been told he was a good boy, while the British man started his own confession in earnest silence. The officer placed one end of the pole into a drain nearby, ensuring that it was wedged tightly. Once forced into position, the spike was maybe two feet out of the drain. The officer knelt down in front of the spike and glanced over at Pandora, who nodded once. Then he drove his head forward as fast as possible, his eye making contact with the spike first, accompanied by a sickening sound. His own momentum and gravity ensured that the spike followed through the rest of his skull, coming out the back of his head with a crunch. The officer twitched for a few seconds and then went still, his body slowly collapsing to the dirty ground as he slid farther down the railing.

The British man finished his confession and looked down at the man he'd been fighting only a short time ago, but he didn't appear to notice or care. Pandora passed me the notepad, and I flicked through both men's writings. The officer had murdered or tortured well over a dozen people, and many, many more had been attacked. But the crimes of the British man were also contemptible, and he embodied the definition of a lifelong criminal. He'd raped and beaten many women in his lifetime, including girlfriends and wife. He wrote about the things he wanted to do to the woman he'd recently attacked, and how he was going to wait for her to leave the hospital before he visited her again. When I was done reading, I wanted to impale his head over that of the officer. Hell, I wanted to tear the fucking thing free of his neck and throw it down the alley. He was an evil little man who enjoyed the pain of others. Any concern over what Pandora wanted to do to him evaporated. Whatever she did wouldn't be enough.

"Are you okay?" Pandora asked me as I raised my gaze to the man, who was still ignorant to his plight.

I nodded and placed the notebook in my pocket. "Whatever you're going to do, get it done. We need to leave before anyone comes looking for his SS friend."

Pandora turned back to the remaining follower and whispered something in his ear. He nodded with total enthusiasm, and I turned to walk away.

"You don't want to watch this?" Pandora asked. "You're not squeamish all of a sudden, are you?"

"I'm fine with whatever you've got planned, but I've killed and hurt enough people over the years that I don't need to watch someone else do it. He'll be dead either way."

Pandora turned back to the man. "We'll be with you shortly then."

I stood around the corner from the alley, maybe fifty feet away from whatever Pandora was inflicting on her victim, but not once did I hear any cries for help or screams of pain.

I checked my watch and found that two minutes had passed. I glanced around the corner to see a prone man lying on the ground on his side facing me, Pandora liberally stomping on his skull, which, even from the distance between us, I could tell was now grossly misshapen. I walked toward them and saw so much blood on his face that it appeared to be a mask. It wasn't until I got a few steps closer that I realized that large portions of the skin on his face had been removed. Blood pooled out of his ears, combining with the blood that streamed from his face as if it had been torn apart.

"Pandora," I whispered as she gave one last crunching stomp on his temple. Her black boots were shiny and slick with his blood; a piece of skin dangled from the heel.

The man remained silent, a smile still on what remained of his lips.

"I'm almost done," she said.

"End it," I demanded.

Her head snapped up toward me, her red eyes burning with rage. "You don't get to tell *me* when to fucking stop."

"End it, or I will," I said, ensuring my voice was calm and level.

Her gaze remained locked on the man she was killing for just a moment longer before she glanced up at me, and her eyes softened. "As you wish." She stared at her victim, and a second later he was no longer enslaved to her. The pain that wracked his body very quickly overrode his expression of confusion, and he screamed out, gaining a swift kick to the mouth for his trouble. Pandora removed a compact from her pocket and showed the man his new face. Just to drive the point home, she dropped something on his chest: his actual face.

"We want you to know that all of this is because of what you are," she told him as he whimpered and tried to cry out, but Pandora stuffed the tip of her boot into his open mouth. "This is quicker than you deserve," she told him and removed a knife from her pocket. She took the boot from his mouth and then slit his throat with one quick movement. She stepped away as he bled to death on the filthy ground of the alley. He clawed at his wound, desperate to stop the bleeding, but it was no use, and he was soon dead.

When he'd taken his last breath, Pandora wiped her boots on the trousers of the SS officer and tossed the knife onto the ground. "Now, I'm done," she told me as she walked past me and around the corner to the end of the alley.

CHAPTER 6

Berlin, Germany. 1936.

Pandora had stolen the keys for a black Bugatti Type 50, which had light-blue stripes along each side. It was an ostentatious, but comfortable, car, and at least it meant that Pandora might behave herself for the journey if we drove in a car of her choosing.

Pandora said nothing from the moment she'd given me the keys, and remained quiet for the entire journey. It wasn't until we were only a few miles away that she finally found her voice. "Hello, Nathan." Her voice was still Pandora's, but it was quieter, less assured of itself.

"Hope," I said with a forced smile, "how are you?"

When Pandora was created all those millennia ago, it was by taking a normal human woman by the name of Hope and forcing her to bond with what is best described as a demon; a non-corporeal entity from another realm. It made her immortal, powerful, and dangerous. But it also left the demon in charge. She took the name Pandora. At some point, those responsible for Pandora's creation realized that Hope's consciousness was still inside. Over time, Pandora and Hope had come to some kind of mutual agreement, allowing each of them to be in charge as needed. Hope retained Pandora's anger at those who had forced her into the situation she'd found herself in, but Hope hated the use of violence. She once told me that she'd seen enough of it through her long life and didn't want to add to the tally of misery that Pandora had managed to accrue. She had a fair point.

"She's unhappy that you stopped us from hurting that man. She didn't think you were so weak. Pandora's words, not mine."

"I have no problems with killing or hurting people, but she did that for fun. I would have just killed him and been done with it. The theatrics were unnecessary; he had no information we needed and was bewitched anyway, so he only felt something at the very end. It was a pointless exercise of power to punish someone she wanted to hurt."

"She's angry. Although it's not entirely aimed at you."

"Well, wherever you're going, she'll have time to come to terms with whatever caused that anger."

"I'm not going back to Tartarus?" Hope asked.

I shook my head and slowed up as we reached a Nazi checkpoint. Hope remained silent as I wound down my window and passed my forged papers to the officer who asked for them. He spoke to me about my journey, and I informed him that I was taking my girlfriend for a drive in the country. He looked Hope over and smiled, wishing me a good day before allowing me to pass.

"Why aren't I going back to Tartarus?" Hope asked after we'd put more distance between the checkpoint and us.

"The second you escaped—"

"Pandora escaped," Hope corrected.

"Sorry—the second Pandora escaped, she caused a lot of people to petition Hades to have you moved. Avalon agreed with

Hera and a bunch of her cronies that you needed to be housed in a secure environment away from any influences."

"I liked Tartarus. Everyone was nice to me." She remained quiet for a few seconds. "I'm not going to be placed with Hera or any of her group, am I?"

"No, Hades wouldn't let that happen, no matter what pressure anyone might put on him." It wasn't a huge secret that Hera wanted to have control of Pandora. Apart from her talent of bewitching people, she was also immortal and pretty much impervious to harm, although she did feel pain. Hera would have very much liked to study her and see what she could learn.

"Hera has always wanted to use me again," she said, as if knowing my own thoughts. "She never showed any concern at what she and those closest to her created. Even Zeus begged me for forgiveness."

I opened my mouth in shock. I'd never heard of Zeus begging for anything, although I knew that Pandora's creation and what she had been used for had caused him many sleepless nights. Hades had mentioned before that it was the only one of a few occasions when he ever saw his brother Zeus have doubts over something he'd done.

Pandora was created as a weapon, the ancient Greek equivalent of a nuclear bomb. She could enthrall anyone she came into physical contact with, having the person do whatever she wished. During the Titan Wars, when the Olympians and Titans fought for supremacy millennia ago, the Titans destroyed an Olympian stronghold, killing tens of thousands of humans in the process.

In response, Pandora was created and sent to the Titan cities of Sodom and Gomorrah. She walked through the cities, ensuring that brother killed brother and wife killed husband.

She turned tens of thousands of people against one another and forced the Titans to burn the place to the ground so that no one could escape and infect anyone else. It was before the true nature of Pandora's power was discovered, when people thought that anyone enthralled could enthrall others. A combination of lies, half-truths, and deadly action turned two cities into scorch marks on the earth.

Some of the Olympians saw what had happened and were ashamed of what they'd created, ashamed of the awful destruction they'd wrought. Hera was not one of them.

"Hera wants power," I said. "She always has. And since Zeus vanished, that craving has increased. The group she's created with her companions has a lot of influence over Avalon, but not enough to get Hades to hand you over to them. There are too many powerful people who don't want to see any more power in her grubby little hands. You'll be taken somewhere neutral."

Hope nodded in understanding.

"Did you forgive Zeus?" I asked.

"Understanding why he and the rest of the Olympians created us and forgiving them for it are two very different things. His apology went some way toward me holding no anger against him. Although, given a chance, Pandora would like to punish him. Only Hera, Ares, Demeter, Aphrodite, Dionysus, and Hephaestus remained unapologetic. My anger is reserved for them more than those who showed remorse at what they'd done."

Of all the gods who had been involved in the wars that had been fought at the time, only Hades, Athena, and Hermes had refused to be involved in Pandora's creation. These three, Zeus, and Avalon had tried to keep Pandora as far away from trouble as possible once the war was over. Usually, only a few centuries would pass before she escaped again and caused havoc in the world, but once we actually managed to find her, she'd always been captured with a minimum of fuss. For the past thousand years, I had always carried out that particular task.

We reached the airfield a short time later, and I nodded to one of Hades's guards, who, along with his comrade, opened the fifteen-foot gate and let us in. I drove across the empty airstrip and parked the car beside the only hangar within the enclosed space.

Hades left the hangar before I could get out of the car; he opened Hope's door, and she beamed at him as she stepped out.

"Hades," Hope said with a genuine smile.

"Is that Hope? I'd . . . well, *hoped* that it would be you and not your alter ego. I was unsure how happy she would be at being captured after such a short period of time. She's normally free for much longer." Hades walked over to Hope and passed her two small bracelets, which Hope fastened on each wrist without complaint. They were designed to ensure that Pandora didn't try to take control of her while she was in custody. They dampened Pandora's abilities until she could be placed securely above whatever transport Hades was using; this vehicle would have the runework inside to ensure Pandora had no access to her power.

"She's okay with it," Hope said and looked over at me. "She expected Nathan to recapture us at some point."

"Is there anything you can tell us about what she's been doing?" Hades asked.

It was a question I'd wondered myself, although I knew that Pandora wouldn't have said anything unless it benefited her, and I didn't really want Hope to have to explain it to me and then Hades, so I hadn't bothered to ask.

"It's something to do with Berlin," Hope said, clearly unhappy that she didn't know more.

Although Pandora and Hope shared a body, and their emotions could be felt by one another, both of them could choose to hide things from the other. Pandora had learned long ago to hide her more violent tendencies from Hope, as they had begun to break Hope's human psyche. Pandora couldn't hide everything; things bled through whether she wanted them to or not, but she would endeavor to hide anything that would either cause Hope mental anguish or make her a liability if questioned.

"Do you know anything else?" a woman asked as she stepped around the side of the hangar.

She was one of the most staggeringly beautiful women I'd ever laid eyes on. The top half of her hair was so dark that it appeared no light could escape its snare, while the bottom half, which cascaded over her shoulders, was brilliant silver. I knew that the time of day affected how much of her hair was one color or the other; the later in the day, the more of it was dark.

Her lips were full and inviting, and her gaze filled you with the notion that she was both easy to talk to and fun to be around. A wicked temper hid behind the friendly exterior; it was something that anyone who crossed her was quick to feel. Her eyes were the most brilliant shade of green I'd ever encountered.

She was about five-four, although her high-heeled boots added another three or four inches to that, and she wore a dark trouser suit that would never have looked as good on anyone else on earth. Memories of her body, moving against me, tight and athletic, snapped to the front of my mind. I almost had to shake my head to remove the unwanted thoughts.

"Selene," I said, keeping my tone calm, my thoughts neutral. My anger in check.

She glanced my way and nodded once.

Hades tried very hard not to look at me.

I tried very hard not to jump back in the car and drive away as fast as possible.

"I'll take Hope for a chat," Selene said, motioning for Hope to follow her.

I waited until they were both back in the hangar before looking at Hades. "Selene?" I asked, my tone incredulous. "Who's unbearably stupid idea was this?"

"Apparently, Hera managed to swing the idea of putting someone with you to figure out whatever Pandora is up to. Hera suggested that she come see what's happening."

"And she *agreed*?"

"When I say 'suggested,' I mean she told her either she would come, or her husband's brother would. Who would you prefer—Selene or the complete absence of personality that is Phobos?"

I sighed and placed my head against the Bugatti's cool roof. "Great."

"I know this can't be easy for you," Hades said as he walked over to me and leaned on the car.

"At least I know Selene is competent and won't try to undermine me at every available opportunity. Besides, at least Hera didn't send Selene's husband, Deimos, instead, although it's nice of Hera to try to use her grandson's wife as a weapon against me."

"You got that notion too," Hades said with a sigh. "From what I hear, Deimos really hates you too. This probably won't help."

Deimos was, like his father Ares and siblings, an empath. Empaths came in two types, negative and positive. Although the positive empaths dealt with love, harmony, peace, and the like, the negative ones dealt in pain and anger and hate. Deimos, like all negative empaths, fed off people's pain, making him physically stronger. But all empaths have one emotion that they are in sync with. In Deimos's case it was terror. He could make you relive all of your memories where fear was prevalent. Empaths could even change your memories to increase the level of emotion they wanted from their victim. The more afraid the victim was, the more emotional the person became, and the stronger the empath would grow.

I nodded. "I don't know if it's because Selene was with me first, or because he thinks I'm a threat to their happy union, but he really does seem to have a bit of an issue with me." A thought popped into my head. "Oh—it's a little thing, but Pandora referred to herself as 'me,' not her normal 'we.' She did it a few times too."

"You positive?" Hades asked, concerned.

"Yeah. You think maybe Pandora is exerting more control over Hope? She went to the Gestapo for a reason; there were lots of notes in their offices about North Africa and human test subjects. You think maybe she was helping them find the old realm gate the Olympians used to bring out the demon that they put inside Hope?"

"That realm gate is one of the most secure places on earth. It's protected not only by Avalon but also by people I trust. But it's worth letting them know your findings. Although why Pandora would want another person to go through what she did is beyond me."

"Maybe that's why she killed them."

"Something feels rotten about this," he said and placed a hand on my shoulder before walking off into the hangar, leaving me alone as the midday sun beat down on the airfield. I removed my jacket and dropped it through the open window of the Bugatti before rolling up the sleeves of my shirt.

"Is this going to be a problem?" Selene asked as she walked around the car. She smelled good; I picked out vanilla in whatever perfume she had put on. It was a scent I'd noticed on the sheets and pillows after she'd left the bed . . . I took a deep breath.

"Your husband is a colossal asshole," I said. "And Hera an even bigger one for sending you here."

"Noted," she said sharply. "I'm not here to discuss my love life; I'm here to try to figure out what Pandora spent her time doing in Berlin. I was ready to join you before she gave herself up—an act, if you remember, she's never done before."

"She doesn't give up unless she's caught. But this time, she came and found you to wave the white flag. What was she doing between the time she was evading you at the Gestapo HQ and this morning?"

I didn't like the way she said *evading* me, but maybe I was just being overly sensitive, so I kept my opinion to myself.

"That wasn't a dig," she said, after reading the thoughts that were obviously written over my face.

Damn it—she knew me too well.

"I'm not here to cause problems, Nate," she said softly. "I offered to come because we both know that if Phobos turned up, he'd spend half the time trying to undermine or kill you. I'm not going to play stupid games. We need to find out what Pandora did before people get hurt."

"Nate," Hades called out from inside the hangar.

Selene and I put our conversation on hold and made our way round to the front of the hangar, where we found Hades gesturing toward Pandora. There was a man lying prone on the ground as Pandora held his arm, locking it behind his back. From the pain on his face, it was obvious that he was clearly uncomfortable with the situation.

"Pandora," I said, "I didn't expect to see you back so soon." The change from Pandora to Hope and vice versa took a lot out of them; usually it was at least several hours before they could swap back again. That, combined with Pandora's sudden use of the word 'me' was something I found very interesting. And even more concerning.

"We thought that Hope wasn't best placed to answer your questions, but we're wearing these ridiculous bracelets. We do not like that."

"Let go of him," I said, before finishing with a smile and adding "please."

Pandora released the man, who started furiously rubbing his injured arm.

"No shackles," Pandora snapped.

I picked up the handcuffs and threw them to Hades, who caught them absentmindedly and dropped them to the floor beside him. "I did try to tell him that they weren't needed," Hades said. "Apparently the staff Avalon sent with Selene think they know better."

I thought I heard sniggering from inside the aircraft nearby, and I was certain that Hades's men had decided to watch the fun and see what happened once someone tried to restrain Pandora.

The plane was a Douglas DC-3, a twin-propeller machine that I'd heard was going to help change the face of aviation. They'd only gone into general production a few months earlier, but I'd seen a similar aircraft being developed by Avalon nearly a decade before. Avalon technology tended to be ahead of anything humans might have access to, but eventually it filtered down.

"Is that your plane, Hades?" I asked.

Hades nodded. "Had it a few years, although it's about four generations above whatever the humans are currently using."

"If you two are done," Selene snapped, and she strolled past us. "Pandora, we need to know where you were in Germany."

Pandora laughed. "And you think we're going to just tell you? You're out of your damn mind."

"You will tell us what we need to know."

"The only thing we're going to tell you is how much you can go fuck yourself. If you'd like, we could take control of you and make you do it to yourself? You might get rid of some of the tension you've got there."

Selene's hands balled into fists.

"Pandora," I said, taking control of the rapidly escalating situation, "you remember I informed Hope that you weren't going back to Tartarus."

Pandora and Selene exchanged one last glance of anger. "Yes, we remember."

Hades took over the conversation, saying, "You have two options. The first one is that you're going to be taken to America. Nevada, to be exact. Once there, you're going to be lowered into a cell in an underground complex in the middle of the desert. You will have no contact with anyone ever again. Nate will not be permitted to go."

"What? They can't do that." Fear crept into her voice. The fear of being essentially alone.

"Hera has already petitioned the Avalon council. They agreed that if you don't cooperate with us, you won't see another living being for a thousand years. Originally, she asked if she could have you experimented on, but that was going too far, even for them."

"We would rather die than go there," she almost shouted, all fight evaporating in an instant. The idea of no contact with anyone terrified her. Hera had carried out a similar punishment soon after her creation. For a year, Pandora had been alone in a dark pit, where the only people she saw were deaf mutes who brought her food. It didn't take her long to break.

"However, if you agree to help us, you'll be taken to the second option, a facility in London that will allow you contact with other people," Hades told her. "Very specific people will be chosen to visit with you. They will be people you cannot enchant, but you will be able to have contact, to read and write as you wish. But only if you cooperate."

Pandora glanced around at everyone in the hanger before talking. "You won't be able to stop it."

"Then there's nothing stopping you from telling us," Hades said.

Pandora appeared thoughtful for a second and then shrugged. "We were staying in the house of a man by the name of Jean Martin and his wife, Magali. Jean was the man on the motorbike you saw. They're French nationals living in Dresden, working as part of an underground movement opposing the Nazis. We went to them for help, and a plan was devised. We would go to the Gestapo and tell them who we are and that we would help them win the coming war. In exchange, we wanted details of the security in Berlin for the upcoming Olympic games."

"Why?"

"Hera and her people are going to be there. We thought it the perfect opportunity to get to them. Once the Gestapo passed us the information we required, we killed them. Then you found us."

"Why were you naked then?" I asked.

"They gave us the information we requested and then drugged us to try to experiment on us. We could have broken free, but honestly we just wanted to see what would happen. They have some very nasty stuff waiting in their labs. It's a good thing it didn't harm us in any real way."

"Why were they looking in North Africa?"

"You saw that?" Pandora asked. "Yes, they wanted the realm gate where we were created. They wanted to put another poor girl into that realm and have her bonded with a demon. Just like we were. We did not wish for that to happen. Once they decided to go down that path, the humans were no longer of any use to us. We killed them and destroyed their findings."

A thought crossed my mind. "Did you send the German soldiers to scour the hotel, looking for me?"

Pandora smiled. "No, just the soldier who died in the alley. We needed to find you, but actually we were looking for two people."

"Did one of them happen to be the other man who died in that alley, by chance?"

Pandora glanced at me and nodded slightly. "Most impressive, Nathan. The rapist's last victim was someone who worked with Magali and Jean. It was coincidence that you were both in the same hotel. His punishment was a little revenge to repay those who had helped us. The SS officer had been under our control since we went to the Gestapo in the first place. He had allies in that dreadful group; it made infiltration easier."

"What's your plan?" Hades asked.

"We don't know," she said. "It's not our plan anymore."

"What does that mean?" I asked.

"We've given the task over to someone else. He has orders to do whatever he wishes to ensure it's completed. We have no say in what he does, but we're guessing it'll be spectacular."

"Pandora, we need more than that." Hades said. "Telling us that some random man in Germany is going to do something isn't exactly cooperation."

"He's going to kill Hera and her friends at the opening of the Olympic Games in Berlin. Is that specific enough for you? Anyone in his way is an enemy and will die."

She walked over to me. "Nate," Pandora said softly. "We're begging you. Leave this place. Leave Germany and get as far away as you can."

"I can't let innocent people die, Pandora. And they will if he attacks Hera in some way. She cares a lot less about the civilian population than most Nazis."

"Can you tell us more about this mystery man?" Selene asked.

"Yes. He's about six feet tall, with a constant deep tan and the yellow eyes of a reptile. He's not human, obviously, and is probably a match for anyone in this hangar, Hades excluded."

Hades and I shared a glance.

"We know what you're thinking: Send Hades into Berlin. Well, the problem with that is, we knew Hades would come himself to pick me up. Can't let someone as powerful as me just hang around with a bunch of security. So we left my friend with another order. If he sees Hades at any point during his time in Berlin, he's to consider the mission a failure and attack wherever he happens to be at that time. Thousands could die."

"You sick bitch," Selene snapped.

"Yes, well considering who you lie with every night, we could say the same about you."

Selene's cheeks burned red, but she kept quiet.

"And what about me?" I asked.

She stroked the side of my face. "My dear Nate. We care about you very deeply, but you can't beat this man. Not on your best day. If you stay and confront him, you will die. Although you'd have to find him first, which could prove difficult."

"What's his name?" I asked.

Pandora held eye contact for a few seconds and then sighed. "If you're so willing to die. His name is Helios." She turned to Selene, whose eyes were wide and full of fear. "Ah, we thought you'd recognize your brother."

CHAPTER 7

Mittenwald, Germany. Now.

I woke up in a comfortable bed that wasn't my own. It wasn't even one from the hotel. I looked around the spacious bedroom and tried to sit up, but my body ached as if it were the day after I'd done the first workout of my life, and the thick quilt, in its blue and white duvet, was cozy and inviting. I decided not to bother getting out of bed, and adjusted my pillows so that I could lie down while remaining slightly propped up.

A TV sat on a chest of drawers in front of me, but the remote was several feet away on top of a bedside table, and quite frankly I wasn't certain I could make the trip and return to the bed before the muscles in my back decided to make me yell like a little baby. I settled for looking at the expansive collection of artwork, mostly landscapes of the surrounding region, which adorned the walls.

There were three doors in the room. One was fully open, and I saw rows of clothes in the darkness beyond; a walk-in closet. The second door was closed, but as the third was clearly the exit from the bedroom to the house beyond, I figured door two was a bathroom.

Two raised voices could be heard from outside of door number three, one male and one female.

"It goes five, six, four," said the male voice, which was easily identifiable as Tommy's. Any concern about where I was evaporated. If Tommy was around, then he would have made sure I was somewhere safe.

"No, you ignorant werewolf," said the female voice, the German accent giving it away as Petra's. "It goes five, four, and six. No one puts six over four—that's insane."

"I guess you're feeling better," a second man said as he stepped through the open door, a cup and plate in his hands.

"Thanks, Kurt," I said, my voice a little raspy. I coughed and cleared my throat. "This is your house, I assume?"

He nodded and placed the cup and plate, some tea and toast, on the table beside me. "How are you feeling? Other than *better*, I mean?" Kurt was well over six feet tall and weighed close to three hundred pounds of pure muscle. His long light-brown hair was tied back, and his bushy beard had flecks of gray in it. His arms were covered in dark tattoos of swirling marks and pagan symbols. He'd had them done when he was human, which was roughly when the Roman Empire first invaded what is now Germany.

Kurt was one of the most respected members of the werebear community, and probably the only one of his kind in the south of Germany. I'd seen him fight twice, both times very long ago, and both times I was very grateful that he was on my side.

"I ache everywhere," I admitted.

"We found you embedded in the car of a staff member. She wasn't best pleased to find you there. You also did extensive damage to every other car in the lot as well as the windows on the restaurant. I'm not really sure how you managed it." His voice was calm and measured. Werebears, for the most part, are incredibly calm and let very little bother them. Due to the fact that the beast of a werebear is very close to the surface—much closer than the beast of a werewolf or werelion—they're forced to watch their emotions carefully to ensure that the beast doesn't override the person.

"I'll pay for the damage," I promised and then explained what had happened.

I'd just finished when Tommy entered the room. "Excellent—you're awake. Can you please tell this *philistine*"—he pointed to Petra who was standing beside him—"that episode six is better than episode four?"

Kurt raised an eyebrow in confusion.

"*Star Wars,*" I explained. "They're arguing over whether film six or four is better."

"What about five?" he asked.

"Everyone knows five is the best one," Petra said in the same tone you'd tell a small child that fire is hot. "So, what is it? Six or four?"

"I have no idea," I said.

Tommy stared at me for a few seconds. "Liar. Which one?"

"Tommy, Ewoks suck. They've always sucked and they always will suck. Four has Peter Cushing in it. If in doubt, always go with a film that has Peter Cushing in it."

Petra appeared to be very smug in her victory.

Tommy looked mortified. "But six has Jedi Luke and that awesome bit with the Emperor at the end."

"And Ewoks," I said. "Who, I'm pretty sure I pointed out, suck."

"And to think I was going to get you your own lightsaber," Tommy said in mock outrage.

Petra's face lit up like a child's on Christmas morning. "You have your own lightsaber?"

Tommy nodded. "Two of them."

"Why?" Kurt asked. "Why do you need a lightsaber? What can you possibly use it for?"

"I think the question is," Tommy said, "why *wouldn't* I need a lightsaber? And as for what I can use it for, I use it to look awesome. Really, really awesome."

"You just don't understand, my dear," Petra told Kurt.

Kurt didn't appear to want or need to understand anytime soon.

"So, you got beat up by some humans and a witch," Tommy said, barely containing his laughter. "Do you have CCTV?" he asked Petra, who chuckled.

"Are you both done?" I asked.

They nodded in unison.

"This witch used a huge amount of magic on me," I informed them both. "To use runes to drain my magic is one thing, but an *effete* curse is a whole other league of power. That's a decade of her life, right there."

"I don't understand why anyone would ever use a blood magic curse," Tommy said. "It's not like it's fun for the person casting it either."

"What do you mean?" Petra asked.

"There are several different blood magic curses you can cast on another person, and a few you can cast on yourself," I explained. "All of the curses do various things to the person they're cast upon, but the caster has to take some of the curse back onto him- or herself. So, in this case, Sarah cast the *effete* spell, making me exhausted and utterly useless, but a small portion of that will bounce back onto her. How long was I out?"

"Six hours," Kurt said.

"If I'd cast that spell, I could have expected maybe three or four hours of exhaustion. Witches are basically human, so she's going to be about as much use as a chocolate teapot, for the best part of a day. It was a huge decision for her to make."

"The local police searched the house that Robert Ellis was staying in," Kurt told me. "It's been abandoned for a few days."

"They're planning something," I advised. "I don't know what it is, but me being here certainly concerned someone enough to get Sarah to try to get rid of me. She originally told me that she'd been told to give me one chance to leave. There's someone else giving the orders; someone told her not to kill me."

"Okay, who?" Petra asked.

"No one good, I imagine," I said.

"So, what's their job?" Tommy asked. "It can't be a coincidence that a witch attacks you just as a bunch of other witches turn up."

"Well, Sarah certainly knew of Mara," I said. "In fact it seems like Sarah likes Mara only slightly less than I do."

"Even so, it'll probably be wise to keep an eye on those witches," Tommy suggested. "There's something off with them, but I can't quite put my finger on it."

"Witches are always weird," Petra said dismissively.

"Do you think Emily might know something?" Tommy inquired.

"I'll talk to her," I said. "She didn't exactly seem to be thrilled to be here. I don't know what it is, but I have this notion that something big is going to happen."

"Surely not in Mittenwald," Kurt said. "Hades's compound is ten minutes away. The last time anyone did anything wrong in this town, Hades's men found those responsible and dragged them back here in chains. You would have to be insane to actively want to piss that man off."

"Insane or very sure of yourself," I said.

"The trip is in a few hours," Tommy said. "We'll talk to Hades and see if he's heard anything. And if Mara and her coven are involved, they've got their own children with them. What kind of parent *purposely* puts her own child in danger?"

Tommy was probably right. Security would be stepped up in preparation for the school's arrival. I couldn't foresee how anyone would want to target the compound—not until security was back to its normal level, which wouldn't be until a few days after the trip ended.

"Maybe a bank job?" Tommy suggested.

Kurt shrugged. "It's possible. There are also many wealthy people in town. Maybe Robert stays in town for a few weeks, scopes out the targets and then, when his people arrive, one of them who's a witch realizes that there's a sorcerer running around the place. They call their boss, who tells them to get rid of you quietly. It all goes to shit because they're human, and they run off to try to figure out their next move."

"It's plausible," Petra agreed.

"No, they knew that I was here," I objected. "Sarah came looking for me in particular; I wasn't a random sorcerer to them." A witch willing to give up her own life just to defeat me screamed of desperation. Maybe she's sick, maybe she needs the money for bills—I don't know. The only thing I know for sure is that if she was willing to sacrifice so much of her own life just to take me out, she must really want me gone from this town.

"So what's your plan?" Kurt asked.

"I'm going with the school to see Hades. After that, I'll see if I can figure out what these people are here for."

"In the meantime, get a shower and something to eat," Kurt suggested.

"I'll go back to the hotel and grab you some clothes," Tommy offered. "I've been away for a few hours, I should probably check on Kase."

"Just in case the second you left they had some huge rave," I said with a smile.

Tommy's face dropped. "That's not funny, man. That's cruel." He eyed the door.

"You have met Kasey before, yes?" Kurt asked. "She doesn't seem like the rave type."

Tommy relaxed slightly. "I know. But I also remember the sorts of things I was doing when I was her age. Boys are bad, Kurt. Bad, nasty little evil fuckers, who need to be stopped at all costs."

I laughed and it hurt my ribs.

"And that's what happens to those who mock me."

"Tommy, your daughter is smarter than you," Kurt said and paused, presumably to think about his statement. "Very much smarter. I think she's a bit more savvy about boys than maybe you're giving her credit for."

Tommy nodded slowly, as if this was new information he needed to assimilate. "You're saying I should just trust in her judgment."

"Which is what we've all been telling you for weeks," I pointed out.

"Yes, but Kurt's older and wiser than you."

Kurt winked at Petra, who laughed.

"Look, Tommy," Kurt said, "let Kasey learn how to deal with what she's going through. Let her make her own mistakes. You can hate boys from afar, and when she brings one home, you just explain that if he hurts her, you'll make him vanish. That's how I did it for our daughter."

"And now she lives in Canada," Petra said.

"Okay, maybe don't tell him that you'll make him vanish," Kurt conceded. "Turns out daughters don't like their dates being threatened."

I laughed again. "This is the oddest conversation I've ever woken up to. Tommy, just let Kasey figure it out. You're there for when she can't. And if anyone ever does hurt her . . . well, you're a werewolf—you'll figure something out."

Tommy smiled. "I love my devious-minded friends."

" 'Never has there been a more wretched hive of scum and villainy,' " Kurt said.

Petra practically launched herself on her husband, kissing him on the cheek. "You quoted *Star Wars*. I love you."

Kurt looked down at his wife and, without smiling, said, "I know."

Petra's smile lit up her face like a firework.

CHAPTER 8

By the time I'd gotten dressed and returned to the hotel, the kids were already being loaded onto the buses. The witches, once again, were being ferried in their own private bus. Mara glanced at me as I got onto one of the buses, a look of anger on her face. She was quickly ignored as the sounds of a hundred school kids took over, and I wished I'd decided to hike up to the compound.

The journey was short, but even ten minutes with forty sugar-hyper kids and someone talking through a megaphone is about five million years in "how-it-feels" time.

We drove away from the hotel and toward the mountains. The road cut through the forest as it snaked away from the lake, eventually leaving the mass of greenery behind as we started the climb upward toward Hades's compound. It took several minutes' drive along steep mountain roads to reach the compound itself, and although the roads were well maintained, it was still a slightly bumpy journey as the smaller rocks regularly fell from higher up the mountain.

After a few hundred yards, the rocky exterior that had been on either side of the road began to change to dense woodland. As we climbed higher, those trees became covered in snow. During previous visits, I'd gone running through the woods that stood all around us on the mountain ridges. They contained enough security that anyone uninvited who was trying to get to the compound would never be able to do it stealthily.

The tree cover only lasted a short distance before the mountains took over and the compound came into view. The sides and back of the place were protected by mountain ranges; the only safe entrance or exit that didn't include helicopters was the main road that we traveled.

The name for the compound was The Wolf's Head. It was named that because one of the three mountains that jutted out over part of the compound gave the impression of the top of an animal's head and jaw—but also because when Hades wasn't around, Cerberus ran it.

"Okay, we're about to stop for a quick search," the head teacher said in a deep voice. I decided that she was definitely part troll. "Once we're given the all clear, we'll go into the compound. Everyone stay together when we exit the bus; *no one* runs around . . ."

I stopped listening at that point, as the bus came to a standstill. Guards in black body armor, with Hades's corporate logo adorning their breast—a raven perched atop a shield—used mirrors to search under it. At the same time, werewolves in wolf form walked around, sniffing at the air. When they'd decided that we were safe, one of the guards signaled for us to go through the main gates.

The Wolf's Head consists of a dozen two- or three-story buildings, dotted around the sizeable compound. The buildings all had different functions: some were barracks or housed administrative staff, but none of them were all that interesting in the long run. On the surface, there was nothing that wasn't in a hundred military installations the world over.

Various helicopters and trucks sat idle outside of a huge workshop, where dozens of men and women fixed and modified equipment as needed. Most of the permanent staff in the compound would have been well versed in war and fighting. Neither Hades nor Cerberus would ever have had fresh recruits in such a demanding job.

The bus doors opened, and I remained seated while the students filed out, their excitement and expectations about what they were about to see almost a physical entity.

As the last of the bus emptied, I got to my feet and followed them out into the cold but sunny mountain morning. In the corner of the compound, several hundred meters away, sat the garage and helipad. I spotted Hades's UH-60 Black Hawk being worked on. It was a heavily modified version of the same one used by the president of the United States of America. I'd been in it a few times and found it to be quite a pleasant experience. Until someone opened the side door while we were in midair. Then it wasn't so fun.

The head teacher continued talking to the now fully assembled group of children, running through the dos and don'ts concerning their time in the compound. I ignored her as a man walked over toward us, a grin on his face, although you'd have been hard-pressed to see it through the massive beard he'd managed to cultivate in the few years since I'd last seen him. He was over six feet tall and looked like he could bench-press a car, which technically he probably could. His muscles bulged under his blue shirt, and unlike the guards at the gate, who were all fully armed with either MP5s or sidearms, he didn't have anything on him that I could see.

"My name is Cerberus," he boomed, silencing the chatter that had moved through the group as he'd approached.

I noticed several people exchange glances, something that Cerberus was clearly used to and saw too. "I do not have three heads," he told everyone. "You can all stop counting now."

Some of the children laughed.

"I am a werewolf," Cerberus continued. "The three heads thing is probably because I can be human or my wolf form or my beast form. Three heads for one body. So that hopefully answers the first question everyone has about me when we meet for the first time. For those of you who don't know, I'm the man in charge of this facility for ninety percent of the year. It's my job to make sure that everyone behaves and that there aren't any massive fuck-ups that undermine the whole reason we're here."

A lot of the kids laughed at fuck-ups. Even I couldn't stop a smile.

"Yes, I swore. I do that a lot, although I'll try my hardest not to do it in front of you. Even so, I'm not exactly the best person at keeping his language bottled up, so if I offend anyone, I'll apologize now. I don't give a shit, but I'll still apologize." He smiled and a lot of the group laughed, although I noticed Mara and several of her witch friends cross their arms and maintain an expression of stern disapproval.

One of the group raised her hand, and I recognized her as the ginger girl who had told me that Mara wasn't very nice to her daughter, Chloe. Kasey and her friends seemed to create some kind of protective wall around Chloe, keeping her separate from her mum, and Chloe appeared to be trying very hard not to glance at Mara.

"Yes?" Cerberus asked.

"Are we really going to travel to Tartarus?"

"That's why you're here," Cerberus told her, and she smiled, but there was a little fear there too.

"Cerberus, are you scaring our guests again?" asked a tall, thin man who left a nearby building and walked over toward us.

Cerberus bowed his head slightly as Hades stood before the group. There were gasps and mutterings of "It's Hades" from several of the teenagers, and even a few remarks like "He doesn't look so tough" from the more stupid of the boys.

"I was just explaining that we will be taking them through to Tartarus," Cerberus told him.

"First, a tour of the compound," Hades told everyone. "The really good stuff is underground, but we couldn't work down there without everyone up here."

Cerberus called several men and women over, none of whom were wearing the intimidating armor of the guards from the gate, and he explained that they would split the group up and go exploring the topside of the facility. As the teenagers very quickly huddled together with their friends, I caught Hades's attention, and we wandered off, away from the group.

"I heard you had some trouble last night?" Hades said.

"Doesn't take long for news to filter up here."

"Kurt called; he wanted me to know about the witches. Do you think those who came with you today are going to become a problem?"

I shook my head. "Only if you're a sorcerer. Apart from being a gigantic pain in everyone's ass, Mara hasn't actually done anything wrong. Sarah, the witch who attacked me, admitted to knowing of Mara, but certainly didn't seem happy about it."

"The guards are on the lookout for anyone out of the ordinary arriving, just in case someone is stupid enough to take a run at us. It wouldn't be the first time."

"Have the Titans been informed that they're having visitors today?"

"I take it you don't mean the kids?"

"Do they know I'm coming?"

"Yes. Most seemed less than interested. Atlas appears to want to tear your head off still. But he agreed to behave, so long as he doesn't have to talk to you or acknowledge your existence in any way."

"Some people hold grudges," I said.

Hades stared at me for a second. "Yes, Nathan, they do."

I smiled. "Is that a dig at me about someone?"

"Hyperion."

I cracked the knuckles on my hands. "He's also free, so it's not like I'm concerned about bumping into him."

Hades stopped walking. "About that: Hyperion is here today, along with a small group of Avalon employees, to do their yearly check."

I pushed down an ever so slight annoyance at the idea of bumping into someone I didn't like. "Odd day to do both that and the school trip."

"They arranged it, and sometimes it's easier to agree and get it done. They're here at the moment, but in the building next to the hangar. There's a possibility you could bump into one another."

Anger bubbled gently inside me; I pushed it down and remained calm. "He's an asshole—"

"Yes," Hades interrupted. "But he's the asshole who helped cost you someone you love. And you haven't seen him since Selene and you went your separate ways. If you meet him, you wouldn't do anything silly, would you?"

"I'm not going to attack him, Hades. He'd rip me in two, for a start."

"That doesn't mean you wouldn't try. I know you too well, Nate."

I placed a hand on my heart. "I promise I won't attack Hyperion."

"Or piss him off in any way."

"Yep, that too. I will be the best guest you've ever had. Besides, Hyperion got what he wanted when he married off his daughter. I'm pretty certain he no longer cares what I or anyone else thinks about him." There had been a concern that Hera's petition to release Hyperion to her care would pave the way for others in Tartarus to be released. There are many down there that should never leave. But thankfully that never happened, although why Hyperion was so important to Hera, no one really knows.

"I assume Hera uses Hyperion for her checks on this place? I doubt very much that Hera herself would be very welcome in Tartarus."

"It wouldn't be a fun visit," Hades agreed. "Hyperion comes about once a month to talk to them. I get the feeling he misses a lot of them. He might be free, but it's on Hera's whim—if she so decided, he could just as easily go back."

"My heart bleeds. What does Hera actually want?"

"Tartarus," he said simply. "She wants everything here. Some of the Titans might want Hera dead, but there are plenty more who would gladly pledge their allegiance to her if it meant freedom and power."

"That would be very . . . bad."

Hades clasped one of his hands onto my shoulder. "And that, my friend, is the biggest understatement anyone has ever uttered."

We caught up with the tour and stayed with the group at the back, which also consisted of Tommy, Kasey, and several of her friends. The whole thing took an hour. I pointed out several nice-looking weapons and showed them the antiaircraft guns that were sitting at either side of the compound, which brought glares from a few of the other parents. Apparently, I shouldn't have been pointing out items of destruction on the tour. Who knew?

Once the groups had finished, everyone met up once again at the courtyard and followed Hades and Cerberus toward the rear of the compound. There were three lifts built into the mountain itself, and we split back into three groups again, to take them underground.

It was a long way down, and the lifts moved slowly, giving the security teams enough time to scan the occupants.

Hades passed metal wristbands to me and the other adults on the trip. Each was painted a different color; mine was deep blue. As the metal had cooled, runes had been carved into it. The entire compound beneath the surface used an updated form of the security system that, among others, Avalon and Tommy used. Without the wristband, occupants would be unable to access their abilities at all. But with it, Hades's system allowed people to still remain conscious of their connection to their power, although they were still unable to actually use it, as any ability used was instantly shut down from completion.

I hadn't been back to the facility since the new system had been put in place, but Hades had been very vocal about how much he loved it, primarily because having your magic—or any ability for that matter—removed from you was like suddenly losing a sense. Having their magic or ability there made people feel comfortable, even if their use was impossible. Even so, I was less than thrilled that for the second time in a day I was being forcibly made unable to use my magic.

When the lift doors opened, we were in a brightly lit hall. Hades's mark was embroidered on the smooth floor, and security cameras watched not only the lift but also the four corridors that exited from this one room.

Everyone followed Hades down the corridor closest to us, passing several doors with names of places, such as Washington, Athens, and Helsinki. They were used as meeting rooms when school trips or dignitaries visited. I'd been in a few of them over the years as an invited guest from Avalon. We stopped outside a room whose sign said "Edinburgh," and Hades opened the door, revealing a sizeable auditorium. He invited everyone to take a seat, and Tommy and I followed those ahead of us to the front of the rows of chairs.

Seating the group took far longer than you'd expect. Apparently some people have to sit next to others, and some want to sit at the back and get told off by teachers for being a pain in their ass. Once everyone had taken a seat, Hades switched on a projector, and the screen behind him lit up.

"As some of you may have heard over the years," Hades started, gaining silence from the auditorium in an instant, "Tartarus is a prison for those who have crossed Avalon or her allies and been deemed too dangerous to allow to stay in this realm. This isn't the whole truth. We used to cultivate the idea that it was the worst place ever created, our very own little hell where we sent only the worst offenders. Telling someone that they were to be sent to Tartarus was enough to gain cooperation through the fear it instilled.

"These trips are an effort to make the truth known. Tartarus is not a prison, nor is it the living embodiment of hell. It's a separate realm to our own, much like Shadow Falls or Olympus. It contains those who do not mesh well with our world; those who seek to usurp Avalon or create their own power, which would upset the balance we've created."

Hades used a clicker, and a bunch of photos all arrived instantly on the screen in front of us. "The first placed in the realm were the Titans. That was shortly after the Titan Wars, in which Zeus and the Olympians raised up to defeat the Titans. There are far too many reasons for why we went to war, but it was prudent to place those who lost in a place that would keep them secure and safe."

Hades turned to face the screen. "These lovely people are the Titans—not all of them, mind you; only nine of the original twelve titans live there. But in there you have Cronus, Rhea, Atlas, and Phoebe. All of these people now live in Tartarus."

A boy's hand shot up.

"Yes?" Hades asked.

"What do they do there?"

"A good question. There are, at last count, over twenty thousand people who live in Tartarus, excluding the guards. Yes, guards. It's not a prison, but that doesn't mean we want people living wherever they like, and also some of the people there hold grudges against one another. An immortal's memory is quite apt at recalling people who have pissed them off."

Everyone laughed, while Hades glanced over at me.

Touché, old friend, I thought. *Touché.*

"The people here live and work as a community. There are farmers, artisans, builders, poets, and people holding jobs that you'd find in any society. They have electricity, clean water, and food, and are completely self-sufficient. We want you, the schools that arrive here, to see that these are not impoverished people, nor are they downtrodden and treated as criminals. They live their lives in Tartarus because they chose to. The other option would have been someone watching them for the rest of their lives. Everyone in Tartarus is there through his or her own volition. In exchange for all criminal charges being removed from their files, they have agreed to live their lives in peace in a place where they can genuinely make a difference."

Another hand shot up, this time a young female teacher's.

Hades nodded in her direction.

"Is it true that any non-humans taken to Tartarus will lose their abilities?"

"Not entirely," Hades said. "The realm of Tartarus is a natural dampener of power, so their abilities are much lessened from what they had elsewhere, but they still are able to access and use them as they wish."

Hades continued to talk for about forty-five minutes. He was a natural with the teenagers and adults alike, all of whom hung on his every word. He spoke about the compound, how the realm gates worked and who and what they would be talking to once through to Tartarus. He warned everyone not to wander off, as anyone left behind might not like some of the nighttime wildlife.

It wasn't until Hades was beginning to wind down the presentation that I noticed Mara stand and clear her throat. Everyone in the auditorium glanced in her direction, and I saw Chloe's head drop into her hands.

"Yes?" Hades asked.

"How many witches do you have on staff, Mr. Hades?"

"Just 'Hades' is fine," he said with an easy smile.

"So, *Hades*, how many is it?"

"Off the top of my head, I have no idea," Hades said.

"What a crock of shit. Clearly you deem us less worthy than the rest of your workers."

"Mrs.?"

"Range," Mara said.

"Mrs. Range. I can't tell you how many witches I employ out of a staff that easily tops five million people worldwide. I also can't tell you how many werewolves, sorcerers, trolls, or vampires I employ. I simply don't know off the top of my head. I do, however, know that out of the few hundred people who work full-time at this facility, six of them are witches. All of them do excellent work."

"And how do you know that?"

"Because along with Cerberus, I personally pick every single employee to work here. I know their names, ages, where they were born, and their children and significant others. I know their abilities and, in many cases, their weaknesses. I know all of these things because it is my job to know them. Every single person who works here is of the highest caliber. If you're trying to suggest that I wouldn't use witches for whatever reason, you're sorely mistaken."

"I think you use them as scapegoats to further your own agenda," Mara snapped as she stormed toward Hades. "Demeter was right about you. You brainwash people into thinking you're a good man, but really you're just a bully and a thug who would even go so far as to manipulate Demeter's own daughter to further your ambitions."

Hades took a deep breath and opened his mouth to speak, but he needn't have bothered.

"If you say one more thing to my husband, I will personally have you hog-tied and flung out of here by catapult," Persephone said as she entered the auditorium alongside Sky and Cerberus. "Cerberus, will you kindly escort this lady out of the facility? If anyone wants to go with her, he or she is more than welcome to follow her out. A word of warning, though: If anyone dares to suggest in my presence that Hades is anything other than a loving father and husband, you will discover why my mother no longer talks to me."

The air in the room turned ice-cold as Cerberus motioned for Mara to leave. A few of the other witches, and their children, stood in solidarity, but most stayed seated. Mara motioned for Chloe to join her, but Chloe looked away, embarrassed either for herself or her mother—it was hard to tell.

I left my seat and walked over to Hades. "Are you okay?" I asked.

He nodded to me. "I am sorry for that," Hades said to everyone.

"It's not your fault, Dad," Sky told him as she joined us, kissing him on the cheek before turning to give me a hug. "Can I go kick her ass?" she whispered.

Sky and I had been close friends for well over a century. For a while, there had been a possibility of something more happening, but that was a long time ago, and we'd settled into a friendship born of mutual teasing and enjoyment of kicking the asses of people who crossed us. "Probably not on a school trip, no," I whispered back.

"I think now is probably a good time to take our trip to Tartarus," Hades said. He smiled, but I could tell Mara's outburst had bothered him. The perception of him as the man who had stolen Persephone away from Demeter and the embrace of the light had always gotten to him. Thousands of years of stories about his evil ways and how he was responsible for the darkness that had settled within the Olympians didn't bother him as much as they probably had when he'd first heard them, but some lies continue to sting, especially when they involve those you love.

The school group stood and got ready to leave. And then the alarms sounded.

CHAPTER 9

A good five minutes of frantic action took place immediately following the alarm. Hades made a call and walked off to the corner of the room to find out what was happening, while teachers and guardians tried to keep everyone calm despite the obvious concern on their own faces.

"What's happening?" Tommy asked as he left his seat and joined Sky and me at the front of the auditorium.

"It's a proximity alarm," Sky told us. "Unauthorized access on the compound."

"Any chance someone just got drunk and staggered through the perimeter?" Tommy asked with all the hope of someone who knows that's not what happened but who desperately wants it to be.

"There's a *situation* above that I need to deal with," Hades told us. "A krampus attacked two guards and got onto the compound."

"A krampus?" I asked, unsure I'd heard him right the first time. "In daylight?"

"It doesn't sound right to me either, but I've been assured that's what's happening. I'll be heading topside."

Persephone nodded. "Go stop whatever's happening. I'll stay with our guests here and make sure people don't start panicking or trying to get up top for themselves."

Cerberus re-entered the auditorium and rushed over to Hades. "There are reports of guards being attacked by other guards," he told us. "We need you up there. Comms are down throughout the complex. Something bad is happening."

"Someone's attacking the compound?" Tommy asked, disbelief in his voice.

"Looks that way," Cerberus agreed.

"Cerberus, take Sky and go to the security room," Hades told him. "I want to know what's going on. I want comms back on, and I want eyes on anything that looks suspicious. On your way, get a squad stationed on this floor. I don't want any surprises."

Sky and Cerberus both nodded and then ran out of the auditorium.

"Ladies and gentlemen," Hades said, his words stopping the increasingly loud chatter in the room. "My apology for the incredibly loud alarm, but there appears to be a fault on the system. My people were running a test to ensure all was right for you on the Tartarus side, and it has unfortunately tripped something. It'll be a short while before it's fixed, but as we now have to complete a full security check, I'll have to ask you all to stay here with my wonderful wife. We'll ensure some refreshments are brought to you, and it shouldn't be long before this problem is resolved. We'll resume the tour once we've figured out which hamster fell off which wheel."

There was laughter at his words, although it was the kind you get when people are relieved that something isn't more serious than they originally thought.

Kasey arrived next to us. "What's happening?" she whispered.

"As I said—" Hades began.

"Don't," Kasey said, her voice soft. "We both know it's more than that. I saw the look on my dad's face when that alarm went off. So, what's really going on?"

"You don't need to worry," Hades told her.

"I only worry when people don't tell me the truth. I'm fourteen, not blind. I can help keep people calm. I *want* to help."

Hades smiled. "Persephone will explain everything, but I really do need to leave." Hades left the room at a slight jog, which I was sure would turn into a full-on sprint once he was out of sight.

Persephone told Kasey about the alarms and possible attack. She left nothing out, nor did she try to give a better account than what we knew.

At the end of the explanation, Kasey nodded and turned to Tommy and me. "Do you need to go?"

We both shook our heads.

"They have it in hand," I said. "We'd only get in the way."

"But you want to help anyway, yes?" Persephone asked with a smirk. "In that case, there will be sandwiches and drinks in one of the other meeting rooms. We were going to have lunch here instead of having to take everyone out just to bring them back. Can you get all the food and bring it here?"

"No problem," Tommy said.

"Glad to help," I agreed.

As we left, Persephone began telling the class that instead of letting them sit around being bored, she was going to put a film on for everyone to watch.

We used the directions that Persephone had given us to find the room in question. Thankfully, the food was still on three massive trolleys, so we didn't need to make multiple trips to carry it all back.

The corridors were empty of people, and only the squeak of the trolleys broke the silence.

"Do you find it odd that Persephone offered to stay behind?" Tommy asked.

"For all of Hades's leadership qualities, Persephone is the one more likely to calm people in a stressful situation. And besides, no one will get through her to those kids unless an entire army gets thrown at her, and even then I'd give Persephone good odds. There's no one better to protect people."

It wasn't long before the squeaky-wheeled trolleys were back at the auditorium.

Tommy went through the door first, to discover that the guests inside were being treated to Robert Downey Jr.'s version of Sherlock Holmes. Hopefully, two hours would be enough for Hades to fix the problem.

I stepped into the auditorium and closed the door behind me. "I'm just going to get an update," I told Tommy, who nodded and had Kasey help him distribute the food and drink.

As I left the room, Persephone was right behind me. "Going somewhere, Nate?" she asked softly.

I nodded. "Just want an update on what's happening."

"I'm sure Hades will update us when he can."

"I know . . . I'm just—"

"Concerned? Unable to sit still? Bored? Which one best describes you?"

"Okay, you got me. I'll feel better if I know what's happening. The fact that the comms were shut off concerns me. And if Cerberus was right and your own guards are involved . . . I just want to check. I'll be five minutes and then right back, I promise."

Persephone grinned. "Good. It means I don't have to do it. Give my husband a swift kick for me; I'd like to know what to do with these people once the film finishes. I think a second movie might make a few people suspicious about what's happening."

"I'll get him to contact you," I promised and then set off toward the main lifts a few corridors away.

As I got closer, I noticed that two guards stood outside the lift that went down to the floor where the realm gate lay. There had been no other guards on the floor, and while I'd heard other people inside the rooms—presumably having been told to stay there—I'd expected to see several more deployed by Cerberus or Hades.

"Are you two it?" I asked them.

Both carried silenced MP5 submachine guns. One was a younger man with a few days of dark stubble, while his companion was much older, although clean-shaven, with some nasty scarring on his bottom lip.

"Can we help you?" The younger of the two asked.

"Are you all that were stationed for this entire floor?"

"What did you expect?" the older man asked, his voice betraying his nerves slightly.

"Hades told Cerberus to deploy a squad here. That's seven people. Where are the rest of them?"

"They're checking all the rooms," the younger man said. "We were told to wait here until they got back."

"Any word on what's happening above?"

Both guards shook their heads. "You'd best go back to your room, sir," the older man said. "We know what we're doing here."

I gave them a thumbs up and turned back the way I'd come, only to hear a radio noise from the guards. I turned back as the younger of the two placed his hand to his earpiece and whispered something back.

"Comms back on?" I asked.

"Spotty," the older man said.

"Best of luck then," I called out and walked off, turning down the next corridor before sprinting the rest of the way to the auditorium.

I burst through the doors, startling those closest to them. They hushed me when I whispered for Tommy, who got up from next to Kasey and joined me outside, followed by Persephone.

"What's wrong?" Persephone asked.

"I just need Tommy's nose," I told them both.

"My nose? Why?"

"I want to check out a hunch. Also, Persephone, why would people be guarding the lift to the realm gate?"

Persephone took a moment to think. "There's no reason. In the event of an emergency, that lift stops at the bottom. It won't go anywhere without authorization from someone with a blue wristband, and each one is linked to someone's genetic code—only that person can wear that wristband. Apart from you, Hades, Sky, Cerberus, and me, there aren't many who have one. Those who work on the realm gate floor do; otherwise, they wouldn't be able to get down there, or leave the floor once they were there."

"How does it work?" I asked.

"You have to wave it in front of the reader next to the lift."

"So my wristband lets me access the lift?" I confirmed.

Persephone nodded. "Yes, but don't go down there unless it's an emergency. That lift is locked down for a reason."

"The lift normally stops on this floor, yes?" Tommy asked.

"That lift goes from here to the realm gate below. That's it— there's no other stop. You have to use the main lift to go between floors."

"So there's literally zero reason to stand guard in front of it. The main lift—sure, I'd expect that—but not one out of use."

"You think something's happening?" Persephone asked.

"I don't know, but I'm going to go find out," I said. "They had comms use. They said it was spotty."

Persephone removed her earpiece from her ear. "This one hasn't gotten anything since Hades went up. It's not spotty; it's off."

"Tommy, can you sniff out people for me?"

"The runes that stop you from using your magic in this place make my senses a little weird, but they're good enough to smell people." Tommy wore a similar wristband to mine, although his was red in color. He still had some of his strength and other special attributes, but wouldn't be able to turn into either his wolf or beast forms.

"We'll be back soon," I told Persephone.

"I'll keep everyone here. You be careful."

Tommy and I set off, walking around the empty corridors as Tommy sniffed out which rooms contained people. There weren't many that had anyone inside, and we opened each room in turn, finding several workers in them. We told them we were just doing a sweep to get numbers of people on this level, and told them to stay put.

We stopped outside a door marked "Tokyo," and a low growl emanated from Tommy's throat. I pushed the door open and found several prone guards inside. We both darted into the room and closed the door behind us. It didn't take long to check all of them, three men and two women, each of them alive, but unconscious.

"How did someone take out a whole team?" I asked. "There were no shots fired; we'd have heard them. And there's no blood or obvious damage to anyone here."

"They all have strong pulses," Tommy said as he checked on the guard in the far corner of the room.

Tommy and I rolled the guards into recovery positions, just in case, and as I finished, I spotted something unusual on the floor. A chrome sphere lay partially under the hand of one of the guards. I picked it up and turned it over. It was about the size of a chicken egg, but completely circular and warm to the touch. It had a ridge around the circumference, about halfway down.

I ran my fingers over the item, trying to figure out what the hell it was. I found another and picked it up, comparing the two. They were almost identical in every way, but I discovered an indentation on the side of one of them. I pushed it and the sphere slid open along the ridge, revealing runes inside, which I instantly recognized.

"Are these concussion grenades?" I asked Tommy.

"Looks like it. New ones, though, pretty state of the art."

"If these are concussion grenades, I've never seen anything like them. There are no serious injuries here." Concussion grenades were designed to be thrown at something. Once one struck, it opened and activated the runes, throwing kinetic energy in a ten-foot radius. They're designed to knock out trolls, giants, and things that usually like to tear the arms off people who get too close to them. I was working for Avalon when the idea was first conceived; that's why I recognized the rune work. Unfortunately, the first grenades created had the slight side effect of causing anyone in the blast radius to suffer some horrific injuries, like losing limbs. Apparently, the item had been perfected, because all the people in the room were still attached to their body parts.

"Avalon has been trying to perfect them for a while now. Apparently someone else got there first. You think they're Hades's own equipment?"

I shrugged. "No idea, but if Hades's own staff are involved, then yes, probably."

"Those two guards you saw—they're not on our side, are they?"

I shook my head. "I think they're probably the other two members of this team. Which means we need to go ask them a few questions."

"They're armed," Tommy said, "and I didn't find any weapons on these guys, did you?"

"No," I had to admit. "We'll wing it."

Tommy grinned. "So, the usual plan then."

"You want to go back to watch the rest of the movie?"

"No, I want to kick the shit out of the people who did this."

We left the room together and walked back toward where I'd last seen the two guards, who thankfully hadn't moved an inch from their earlier position.

"Hi," I said and waved. "We're just coming to ask if you guys want any food. There's a lot left in the auditorium."

"We're not allowed to leave the post," the younger man said.

"We'll bring it here—we just wanted to check first," Tommy said.

We were within arms' reach of them now, but the younger one worried me. He appeared more wired than his older friend, more alert to possible issues. That meant he had to go down first. Hard.

"Go back to your room," the younger man said, and moved his MP5 slightly in my direction.

I dashed forward, pushing the muzzle back at his friend. The guard fired one bullet, which hit the floor by his foot. He tried to jump back, but I'd already hit him in the throat hard enough to incapacitate him, but not enough to crush his windpipe. He started to choke immediately, and this made it difficult for him to put his attention on using his gun, which he tried once again to fire in my direction.

A vicious forearm to his elbow, and the joint broke with an awful sound, followed quickly by the guard crying out in pain. He released the gun and I head-butted him, pushing him back up against the wall before catching him in the side of the head with a kick that almost took his head off. He slumped to the floor unconscious, and a moment later Tommy's guard impacted the same wall with a sound suggesting that if he were human, he'd be lucky to get up again. Ever. He crumpled to the floor, broken and twisted, while pieces of plaster fell on top of both of them.

Tommy passed me an olive-colored Glock 22 along with a shoulder holster. I ejected the magazine to see that it was full of .40 S&W silver bullets. "It was the guard's. You can never be too careful, and now, while you don't have your magic, it may come in handy."

I thanked him and loaded the gun once more before putting the holster on and placing the gun in its new home.

"Nate," Tommy said.

"What's up?" I asked as I searched the guards and placed all of the guns and ammo in a pile beside me.

"You're going down there, aren't you?"

"They were guarding this lift for a reason. I want to know what that reason was. It seems the realm gate would be the more likely destination."

I waved my wristband against the reader next to the lift doors, and the little red light on the panel switched to green. Another panel beside it came to life, and I pressed my palm against it. "These guys are using silver. Be careful. And Tommy, you can't come with me."

"I know. I have to stay with my daughter. I'm sorry, Nate. Should I go get Persephone?"

"Don't be. I'll be fine. But Persephone is needed here, with you. Like I said earlier, no one is getting to those people in the auditorium without going through her. Just tell her what I'm doing. She needs to get hold of Hades and tell him to send everyone he can down there. If I'm right, something bad is happening. Something worse than the attack above, I mean."

"Be careful," Tommy said.

"Why do people always tell me to do that?" I asked.

"Because you always do something stupid," Tommy answered. "And by stupid, I mean reckless and dangerous."

"Thanks, Tommy, it's good to know who believes in me."

"I believe in you, Nate," Tommy said with a faint smile. "I believe in your ability to find trouble like a bloodhound searching for an escaped prisoner." And with that he burst into laughter as the doors closed.

Although there was something to be said for Tommy and Persephone's warning, I had no intention of facing anything that had managed to get out of Tartarus. The Titans were well above my ability to fight if I wanted to maintain all of my limbs.

Hopefully, whatever was going on down there could be stalled, or stopped altogether. I knew that Hades had a squad of highly trained soldiers down there, so with any luck they were already dealing with the problem. The thought didn't manage to make me feel better, though.

There had been precisely one escape from Tartarus in its entire several-thousand-year existence. Pandora. A second break-out within a hundred years was something I was sure Hades and his staff would take personally, but it did raise questions about the security in Tartarus.

The trip down was quick, and I expected to find people running around and dealing with whatever had happened. Instead, as the lift doors opened, there was nothing. I might have been okay with gunfire or shouting, but silence caused the hairs on the back of my neck to stand up.

There were no guards on either side of the lift doors. I stepped out of the lift, removing the gun from its holster as I moved into a hallway that had paintings of various Titans on the walls. I followed the hallway around the nearest corner, to a small reception area. There was no one manning the desk, nor any more guards in the vicinity. There should have been two guards by the lift and two more at the reception. I crossed the floor to the desk, but there was no one behind it.

There were three doors that led off from the reception area. Behind one lay the realm gate, and the other two were holding areas for anyone coming through the gate. I opened the first door. The dark tiled floor was a stark contrast to the white in the reception area, but apart from a few chairs, a water cooler, and a small TV that sat atop a table, it was empty. The second room was across from the first, and the interior was identical except for the bodies it contained.

Three male guards, one female guard, and the female receptionist were all lying on the cold floor. I moved around the room and felt for any signs of life. All were alive, their pulses strong. They were unconscious but otherwise unharmed. Whoever had attacked them had also removed their wristbands, meaning if they woke up, it would be impossible for them to reach the floors above. I searched the guards for weapons but found none. I did, however, find two more of the concussion grenades like the ones that Tommy and I had discovered on the floor above.

I left the room and cautiously made my way to the third and final door, which was behind the receptionist's desk. It was the entrance to the realm gate, a place usually containing half a dozen people—a mixture of guardians and guards.

I saw the first body before I'd even taken a step inside. His uniform suggested that he belonged to the squad of guards for the realm gate. He wasn't dead, and his sidearm had been left holstered on him. I easily discovered the rest of the squad with just a quick check of the room. There was nothing to suggest that they had been aware of any kind of impending attack; they'd fallen where they'd been standing, and none of them had even drawn a weapon.

I doubted they'd been attacked before the security feed had been disrupted, or the whole place would have been notified of the attack. The likelihood was that the comms being taken offline and the attack on the guards had been done at exactly the same moment, to minimize discovery. Whoever had done this wasn't an amateur.

It was only as I finished my search of the room, noticing the two guardians and guards that lay on the floor, that I discovered two more chrome spheres sitting on the floor. They'd rolled all the way to the base of the four steps that led to the realm gate. I dropped the grenades back to the ground; they were of no use to me once they'd been exhausted.

As I turned toward the door, there was a cough from the far side of the room. I quickly made my way over there and found a man trying to get back to his knees.

"You okay?" I asked and offered him my hand, which he took and pulled himself to his feet.

"What happened?" he asked me, shaking his head slightly, his long blond hair flicking across his face.

"I was going to ask you the same thing." I helped him to a nearby chair next to a still-unconscious soldier.

The man noticed my glance. "Everyone else still out?"

"Looks that way. It's lucky no one was seriously hurt."

He nodded and continued looking around, as if searching for something.

"Do you remember anything?" I asked.

He stopped glancing around and looked up at me. "I was working, and the next thing I know, there's a bang and I wake up here. How long before anyone else wakes up?"

"You must have been the farthest away from the concussion grenades when they came in. It's hard to say how long everyone else will be out."

He nodded again as if absorbing the information.

"What do you do here?"

"I'm a guardian," he said. "One of two down here." He looked over toward the realm gate. Realm gate guardians went through a ritual to bond themselves with a realm gate, making them the only people who could operate the gate.

"Was the realm gate activated?" I asked, and at that his glance shot toward me.

"You heard the alarm?" He sounded angry at the information.

It was my turn to nod. "Not for the gate, no. Just the one for the intruder. The gate was activated then?"

"Goddamn it," he snapped. "Do you know who came out?"

"I didn't even know it had been activated," I explained again. "But if it was, finding out who exited is now on my list of things to learn. I haven't seen anyone, though." I was about to ask more questions when the distinct hum came from the realm gate, signaling its opening. The black space in the center of the gate shimmered as someone on the other side activated it.

"You need to get down," I instructed the guardian, and grabbed a Tesla rod from the belt of the nearest soldier. The rods consist of coils wrapped around a carbon fiber, nightstick-like weapon. It emitted a blue hue as thousands of volts of electricity contained within whirled to life. I passed it to the guardian, who gripped it firmly as we both crouched behind the nearest desk, stacked high with computer monitors and equipment.

"I'm not much of a fighter," he whispered.

"That's okay. Just stay there, and only use the Tesla rod if you have to."

Twenty feet away, the dark green runes on the realm gate flared to life, the shimmering mass changing to one of swirling colors, eventually transmuting to show the hills of Tartarus. Two figures, both clad in dark clothes and black masks that covered all but their eyes and forehead, stepped into view. A second later they'd walked into the gate, immediately vanishing from sight. Another moment and they appeared in the control room, allowing me to get a good look at them both for the first time.

They were both clearly male, one a head taller than me, although much more narrow, while his companion was about my size. They both had a dark rune drawn or painted on the back of their bare hands. Although I couldn't tell exactly what the rune was for, it looked incredibly familiar, evoking a shadow of memory somewhere in the back of my mind.

"Where the fuck is he?" the larger of the two men asked. His accent was English, but I couldn't have placed it to one specific place.

"He was meant to meet us here."

"I'm here," the guardian beside me said, and he stood up, holding the tip of the Tesla rod to my throat. "They sent someone down here."

He removed the gun from my hand and tossed it aside before motioning for me to stand. I complied with his order silently, following the guardian to the empty aisle at the end of the computer-laden desk.

The larger masked man watched me intently as I walked, one of his hands balled into a tight fist.

"You picked a really bad day to do this, guys," I told them.

The guardian glanced down for the briefest of moments, but I took the opportunity to knock the rod aside with one hand and punch him in the side of the head hard enough to send him sprawling to the ground. You can't kill guardians when they're near their realm gate, but you can still hurt them.

I turned back to the two masked men and immediately noticed the red glyphs that adorned the forehead and eyes of the larger man.

"How?" I managed before he raised his hand, and the room began spinning until I crashed to my knees.

The sorcerer crouched in front of me. "You're lucky I'm in a good mood."

And then, with another wave of his hand, I collapsed forward to the ground and everything went dark.

CHAPTER 10

"You do realize you should probably get up off the grass?" said a voice that sounded suspiciously like my own.

I opened my eyes and found myself no longer in the control room of Hades's compound, but lying beside a small circular wooden table next to a lake. The sun was shining, and I heard birds chirping. It was both serene and singularly bizarre.

"Um . . . where am I?" I asked aloud without getting up from the grass. The grass was wet. It was at that point that I decided I'd broken my brain.

"Get off the ground," my voice said again.

I did as I was told and sat up. Seated at the table, drinking from a china cup, was me. Except this me had a darkness spilling out from his eyes that covered his entire face.

"You're the nightmare," I proclaimed. The magic inside every sorcerer is alive and wants to be used, but using too much at once makes it easier for the magic to take control and use the sorcerer as it sees fit. There isn't an official name, but they're called nightmares. Mine currently sat across from me, drinking tea. It was a slightly surreal situation.

I looked around the landscape. "And this is . . . different."

"I do wish you wouldn't call me that," the nightmare said.

"What would you like me to call you? Dave?"

The nightmare's eyes sort of narrowed, maybe. It was hard to tell with the darkness concealing most of his face. "You can call me . . . Erebus," he said.

"The Greek primordial deity of darkness personified," I clarified. "Isn't Erebus dead? I'm almost certain he was killed long before I was born."

"He won't mind me using his name, then. Besides, if you insist on giving me a name you can use something more appropriate than 'nightmare.'"

"So is this some kind of weird dream?"

The nightmare, . . . or Erebus, offered me a drink. I accepted, and he poured me a cup of tea from an ornate china teapot, black with swirls of color that changed from orange to white, to purple, and finally to a deep gray color before starting over again.

He poured in a small amount of milk from a jug that matched the teapot and stirred it with a spoon that resembled a tiny battle-axe.

"You're not dreaming," he told me as he passed me the cup.

"So what is this?" I asked, feeling bewildered by what was happening.

"Since you gained more power, I cannot be part of your conscious mind, and your unconscious mind is impenetrable to me, so I exist only here in your subconscious. A place you can't easily traverse. When I was first pushed here, it was a mess. I've tidied it up somewhat."

I drank some of the tea, which turned out to be delicious. Or maybe it wasn't; I wasn't really sure how this worked. "So how am I here now?"

Erebus shrugged. "No idea. *You* don't know the inner workings of the brain, so *I* certainly don't. I am you, after all. I contain all of your knowledge, including that which you've forgotten or decided to ignore, but I can't know things you never discovered in the first place."

"Okay, *why* am I here?"

"That's easier to explain. When that sorcerer used mind magic on you, he meant to knock you clean out, but I managed to grab you as you slipped from consciousness to unconsciousness and bring you here. I felt it was time for a chat."

"About what?"

"About your stupidity."

"In what way have I been stupid?"

Erebus raised his hand and started to count on his fingers. "During that whole mess with Simon Olson and his insane friends several months ago in Maine, you behaved . . . unusually. You were beaten in a fight by someone who doesn't have half the experience you do. You let a vampire take your blood and screw you on the floor after what could charitably be considered a short argument. You knew her power would wear off, but instead of waiting for it, you managed to collapse in front of two policemen after behaving oddly enough to get yourself arrested. You were jumped by that little asshole of a man, Simon Olson, who almost bested you because you were too damn arrogant to realize he might be setting you up. You told a werewolf pack you were Hellequin and then dropped the same information to your friend Galahad, and you have done precisely fuck all about it since then.

"We appear to have run out of fingers." Erebus raised his other hand and started anew. "You got beat up by a witch and some humans. And *now* you're traipsing around Hades's compound like a fucking bull, getting knocked out by a two-bit sorcerer whom you should have torn in half and then stuck the parts on a flagpole for the world to see."

"Are you done?" I asked quietly.

"You are Hellequin," Erebus continued. "People are meant to fear you. So what the hell is going on?"

"Nothing."

"Okay, let me rephrase: I know exactly what's going on. I'm in your subconscious, but in order for you to sort your shit out, you need to come to the realization *consciously*. Right now, three men are standing in the control room to Tartarus after knocking you out cold. You're better than that. Before you lost your memory, you'd never have let a piece of shit like Simon Olson live. You'd have burned any remembrance of him to ash."

"Are you saying I don't kill enough people?"

"Oh, no, that's not an issue. But in the last year, I've only seen sparks of the man you were for centuries. Now, we both know you're not an idiot. But something is stopping you from being the person you need to be."

"*Need* to be?" I slammed my palms onto the table. "People know I'm Hellequin. Hell, all of Shadow Falls must know it by now. Isn't that who I *need* to be?"

"Hellequin is more than a name, Nathan. You are defined by your actions. But it's not just about you. Your friend Roberto gave you information about the man involved in trying to capture Shadow Falls, and you went after him at a nightclub. Not exactly subtle. But then, when you should have killed him outright, you let your prey escape, which could have had dire consequences for Roberto and his family."

"It worked out," I said.

Erebus nodded. "But it might not have."

"I'm Hellequin—isn't that enough to make sure people are safe?"

"What use is being Hellequin, if you're not going to actually *be* him? It happened after the fight in Winchester, didn't it? When you fought the lich. If you keep this up, you're going to get yourself killed."

"That's doubtful."

"How about getting someone else killed? Is that doubtful too?" Erebus's tone was mocking.

"I didn't realize you were my therapist."

He threw the china cup at a nearby rock. The small cup exploded into pieces. "Don't be a fucking ass! Part of your personality is in me, and quite frankly, seeing as how magic strives to be used, and *I'm* the physical manifestation of that magic, I'd really like to see you continue to live and get more powerful. Enough stalling."

I glanced up at the angry embodiment of my magic and sighed. "I lost my blood magic. Having to learn how to heal and increase my power without it made me question a lot of things. It was a magic that maybe I relied on too much."

"Withdrawal?"

"I don't know." I paused. "Maybe a little, but it was more the loss."

"Let's see if I can help. You had to prove to yourself that you could manage without it, but at the same time you felt you weren't quite as good as you had been. You started second-guessing yourself but masked it with arrogance. Something that almost got you killed twice a year ago in Maine and yesterday in a car park. Sound about right?"

I found myself nodding, although I'd never even considered what Erebus was talking about.

"You have your necromancy now. Why are you still hung up on the loss of your blood magic?"

"I had my blood magic for most of my life, and then it was gone. What if one of these marks on my chest vanishes, and I find myself without my necromancy? How do I protect people if I'm not capable of being the man I was?"

"And you think shrouding yourself in an arrogance that almost got you killed will do that for you? Your necromancy is more potent than any blood magic. You'd know this without the need for an intervention, if you stopped and thought for a moment. I wish I could hold your hand and tell you exactly what you're capable of, exactly what is inside this stubborn head of yours, but I can't."

"Why?"

He pointed at my chest. "They stop me. They do more than you realize. More than I can tell you. Once they've gone, you'll know what you were missing."

"That doesn't make me stop worrying."

"You're not capable of protecting everyone. No one is."

"But I should be, damn it!" I snapped.

"You can't protect everyone, but for those you can't save from harm, you find whoever's responsible and, by God, you make them suffer."

I allowed Erebus's words to swirl around my mind. "So, is this what happens every time I start to have problems? I get to come and chat with you?"

Erebus shook his head. "You know there's something happening in the world, and you know it's bad. You can't be flailing around when people need you. And quite frankly, I'd really rather you didn't die. I like it here."

"So we're done?"

"Not exactly. I'm still here, still waiting to take control of your body when the opportunity arises. We will meet again, I'm sure of it."

"Will I remember any of this?"

Erebus shook his head again. "Doubtful. You'll hopefully feel better about the loss of your blood magic and stop using arrogance to mask your concerns about your abilities."

"The witch would have taken me out whether I'd been on the ball or not," I explained. "The *effete* spell was something I'd never have expected."

"That's true, but you walked out into that car park expecting the witch and her friends to cower at the mighty sorcerer. You've been around long enough to know that's not how it works. You were so concerned about your abilities that you rushed head first into everything without even hesitating. That has to stop."

"I couldn't have prevented the sorcerer from using his magic on me either."

"Really? Because we both know the second you saw that red glyph, you hesitated. And I know you can remember the shock in the sorcerer's eyes. He expected you to react immediately."

I thought back and discovered that Erebus was right. "He knew me," I said. "Or at least he knew of me."

"Any idea who he is?"

I shook my head. "I plan on finding out, though."

"Well there lies another problem. You're currently lying on the floor of the control room." Erebus leaned across the table and placed his hand over mine. I didn't flinch; there was no menace or threat in the move. When he removed his hand I had a dark rune mark on the back of my hand.

"What's that? I've never seen it before."

"I explained to you: I only know what you know."

"I don't remember this."

"No, that's true—you don't. Although you will now."

"What does it do?"

"It negates the runes that stop someone from accessing their abilities. In your case, your magic and necromancy will be available to you. It will work in Hades's compound, although as he's modified his security, I can't say for certain how long your magic will last when it returns. For future reference, it will also work in Avalon."

I stared at the small black mark. "How does this exist? I've never even heard of anything like that."

I remained staring at the rune for a few more seconds.

"You don't trust it," Erebus said. "Would it help if I informed you of who taught you that rune?"

"You can do that?"

"You won't remember anyway, so I don't see why not." He stood up and walked around the table until he was in front of me and then tapped me on the forehead. Warmth moved through me as the wind picked up loose leaves and tossed them around.

"What was that?"

"Doing what I can to help you along with a small magic problem you seem to be having. It might take awhile for it to sink in, and I wish I could tell you everything, but I can't."

"Why?"

"Something stops me. I can say little bits and pieces, and access information, but I can't tell you where that information comes from. I really wish I could."

I opened my mouth to speak, and Erebus shushed me before lowering his head to my ear and whispering, "The person who taught you that rune—it was your father."

Before I could say anything, he touched my head again, and I fell back in my chair, tipping over onto the soft grass.

CHAPTER 11

I woke up on the floor of the realm gate control room. I expected I'd been out for several minutes, but apparently the sorcerer who had put me under wasn't as powerfully adept in the use of mind magic as he might think, because I could still hear him, the guardian I'd hit, and the third man talking several feet away.

Part of me wanted to jump up and rush them, but instead I stayed still and quiet, and listened for anything that might prove valuable.

"You could have stopped him before he punched me," the guardian I'd hit said as I heard him get back to his feet.

"Thirty seconds on your ass from one punch was the very least you deserved," one of the other two men said. I recognized the voice of the sorcerer who had used his mind magic to knock me out.

It was good news that I'd only been out for half a minute. Maybe I'd still be able to stop whatever plan they had.

"Have you set the explosives?" the guardian asked, his annoyance obvious.

"We're on it. Unlike you, we did our job." The voice belonged to the third man. He was an unknown quantity, and unknown quantities make me nervous.

"So, how long will this gate be out of commission?" the sorcerer asked.

"A few hours," the guardian said. "You could pile tons of C4 explosives in front of a realm gate, and it would only dent it. They heal themselves—did you know that?"

" 'They'?" the third man asked. "It's not alive—it's just wood and rock with runes on it."

"Actually, it's pretty close to living wood and rock. It can't think for itself, but it does heal when damaged. Although we have no idea why."

"We used enough explosives to screw with the runes, according to your plan," the sorcerer said, clearly ending the conversation. "Will it work? That's all I care about."

"Of course," the guardian said. "Once these things are ready, and detonated, no one will be able to get in or out of Tartarus. Those on the Tartarus side are set to go off in twenty minutes. These will go ten minutes after being set. They should go off simultaneously. It'll give us enough time to get away, and make it harder for Hades and his people to figure out who we let out."

"Excellent," the sorcerer said.

"Who's *that* guy?" the guardian asked after a few moments of silence.

"Nathan Garrett," the sorcerer said. "Although I didn't expect the pause when he saw me. Apparently, he's not the man he used to be."

"Who did he used to be?" the third man asked.

"Pray you never find out," the sorcerer told him. "An old acquaintance of my employer removed his memories a few years ago. I'd heard he'd retrieved them, but from what I saw, he's considerably less of a threat than I remember."

Even with my eyes closed, I would have sworn that I felt their gaze boring a hole into my back. "What if he wakes up?" the guardian asked.

"Kill him quickly or run like hell."

"That's not even slightly helpful," the third man said.

"I'm not trying to be helpful. I just want you to finish your damn jobs and then vanish. You were never here. You'll be paid the agreed fee, and I never want to see either of you again."

"This isn't about the money," the guardian said.

"He's right," the third man agreed. "This is bigger than money."

"I've heard the rhetoric," the sorcerer said. "I think you all have no idea what you're trying to unleash here today, but you soon will."

"So, why are you helping us?" the guardian asked.

"None of your goddamn business."

One of the men snorted in derision.

There was silence for a few seconds, followed by some rustling. "I'm almost done planting the explosives on this end," the third man said.

"The target is now free, so I'm going," the sorcerer said. "I assume you gave him the information he would need to escape this place?"

"He's been told what he needs to," the guardian said. "While you were in Tartarus, I had to make sure he got away as quickly as possible. He knows the plan, which means he knows how to escape. So long as the security people are busy, there won't be any problems."

"If everyone *wasn't* busy elsewhere, we'd be knee deep in Hades and a lot of angry armed guards right now," the sorcerer told him. "Try not to kill anyone. Leaving Hades a big mess to clean up is a lot safer than having him come after us because we killed some of his people."

"Hades doesn't scare me," the guardian scoffed.

"Then you are clearly a gormless idiot," the sorcerer snapped before walking off. I felt his foot brush over my leg as he stepped around me on his way toward the doors.

I tentatively opened my eyes as the door to the room banged closed, and noticed that the blue wristband that Hades had given me was missing. Instead of wondering how I was going to fight without my magic, I grabbed a marker pen that lay beside my arm, and drew a rune on the back of my hand. I had no idea where the knowledge for the rune had come from, but I knew with certainty that it would negate the runes Hades had in place around the facility, restoring my magic.

Ordinarily runes need to be activated with magic; any magic will do, but it needs that spark to begin. The second I finished drawing the rune, the entire thing shimmered slightly, and I felt the access to my magic rush into me.

I pushed myself up to my knees and glanced over the top of the nearest desk, at the two men, who had their backs toward me as they were working on finishing setting up the explosives.

"It's a good thing he's gone," the guardian said. "Creepy bastard."

"You didn't have to go through the realm gate with him," the other man said.

I flexed my fingers as orange and white glyphs spread over the back of my hands and up my forearms, vanishing under the T-shirt's sleeves as they reached my biceps. I stood, making no sound, and stepped into the space between the two rows of desks, watching the men plant their explosives.

"You know, you really shouldn't do that," I said as casually as I could manage.

The two men jumped to their feet, turning to face me, expressions of shock on their faces.

"I'll give you one chance to surrender," I declared.

"There are two of us," the guardian said.

"Congrats on your ability to count. I'll take that as a 'no' then."

"You can't use your magic," the other man said. He was much thinner than I'd recalled, but because he'd removed his mask, I could see his bald head and long dark beard. Tattoos adorned his face around his nose and cheeks, dark swirls that made him look more menacing than his stature alone would have ever conveyed. I glanced down at the rune on the back of his hand; it matched my own.

Instead of showing my rune, I ignited a ball of fire in my palm, spinning it slowly as the two men watched. If there was to be a fight, I didn't want to use too much magic in such a confined place. It was far too easy for the unconscious guards in the room to get hurt.

The guardian dashed toward me.

I threw the ball of fire into his face, which immediately ignited. He stopped running and dropped to the ground, trying to pat out the magical fire. I took the opportunity to kick him in the face with enough force to shatter his nose and probably break a few teeth. He'd heal, but when he woke up, it would hurt. I didn't have a problem with that at all.

The last man scowled at me as he walked around to the front of the realm gate. "I'm not going to be so easy." He ran forward and threw a punch at my head, which was easily avoided. But his fist continued on toward the nearest desk, which exploded on impact.

I put several feet between us as the cloud of dust and wood-chips settled. He cracked his knuckles and smiled as the guardian beside him began to stir. There was an unpleasant sucking noise as he tried to breathe through his broken nose.

The thin man lifted his friend from the ground and started to shiver slightly as a sigh escaped the guardian's lips. I realized what was happening and threw a ball of air at the pair, hoping to break them apart. The thin man darted aside, moving considerably faster than he had only moments ago, and threw the guardian's body toward me, which I pushed aside with a blast of air. The unconscious guardian slammed into a nearby table and bounced over it to the floor.

"You're a siphon," I remarked. "The tattoos depict your tribe, I assume."

"You know of my kind. I'm impressed," he said, although he looked anything but.

"Atlas is a siphon. I've met him a few times. He's about as big an asshole as you are."

"Oh no, I'm much bigger." He darted forward, his mass increasing so that by the time he'd taken three steps toward me, he was at least a foot taller and considerably more muscular.

I threw a blast of fire at him, which struck his now barrel-like chest, but barely slowed him down, forcing me to dive aside before he could attack.

I sprang over the nearest desk, putting at least a little distance between us, as the siphon flexed his considerable bulk, causing his already straining T-shirt to tear at the sleeves.

Siphons absorb the energy of living things, including the life force of any people they touch, so letting the big bastard grab me was only going to end one way for me, and that was badly.

I walked toward the edge of the desk, stepping over one of the still unconscious guards. It had been maybe ten or so minutes since I'd entered the room, and even the older model concussion grenades could knock people out for up to an hour, so there was very little chance of one of them suddenly waking up and helping me.

The moment I got within a step of the gap between the banks of desks, the siphon charged again, batting the monitors and work equipment aside as he tore through the desk as if it were a finishing line in a race.

I jumped back but couldn't put enough distance between us as he grabbed my wrist and dragged me toward him. Siphons need skin-to-skin contact to absorb a person's life force, and I tried to force myself free from his grip. I managed to dodge the punch he aimed at my head and drove a blade of fire into his side, twisting it slightly, which caused him to roar in pain and release me, but at the same time he kicked out to get me away.

The kick hit me square in the chest and sent me flying back ten feet, colliding with a computer monitor, which fell onto the floor beside me as we both crash-landed. I pushed the broken monitor away and rolled to my side, but not in time to evade the siphon, who grabbed my ankle, lifting me from the ground and casually throwing me head first into the realm gate. I managed to twist at the last moment, taking the blow on my shoulder, which crunched.

I yelled out as I dropped to my knees, and gingerly moved my arm. There didn't appear to be anything broken or seriously injured, but it was going to hurt for a while. I was officially done with the "don't use magic" idea and turned to face the behemoth, only to discover that he was almost on top of me.

He grabbed me in a bear hug and lifted me from the ground. I felt my energy ebb from me as the siphon began to drain me, but he hadn't managed to get both of my arms pinned, allowing me to grab a Tesla rod from nearby. I ignited it, and jammed it into the side of his neck.

The siphon instantly began to convulse and released his grip. Unfortunately, as he'd been holding me when I'd electrocuted him, that surge flowed into my body, causing considerable pain as the extensive charge wracked through me.

After what was probably mere milliseconds, but felt considerably longer, I found myself lying on the ground, panting. The siphon was prone on the ground, but I wondered how long he'd stay that way. Probably not long enough for me to get to him and kill him. I pushed the thought aside. I *couldn't* kill him; he had the answers to my questions. Besides, it was incredibly difficult to kill a siphon; they could just use their absorbed energy to heal themselves.

I got back to my feet and readied my magic, the orange and white glyphs igniting in preparation for what I needed to do. I took a step forward and noticed that the glyphs on my forearms looked odd; in places the two different colors appeared to merge so that I couldn't tell where either of them began or ended. I concentrated a little, and the remainder of the glyphs followed suit, so that instead of being orange and white, they were a mixture of the two colors. Lightning leapt harmlessly across my fingertips, and when I glanced up again, the siphon was getting back to his feet, an expression of rage on his face.

With no time to think about what I'd done, I darted toward him. The small amount of magic that danced along my fingers quickly transformed into a blade of brilliant white-blue lightning as I plunged it up into his chest, the brightness of the magic almost too intense to look on. As the siphon screamed out, I created a ball of air in the palm of my free hand, spinning it at an increasing revolution until it was a blur. Then in one motion I removed the blade of lightning and, twisting my hips, plunged the sphere of air into the siphon's chest.

It tore into his body with horrific force, the sound alone enough to stifle the screams that escaped the siphon's mouth. When I'd forced the ball of air far enough into his body, I released the magic.

The effect was catastrophic. With no form to the magic, it exploded, engulfing the siphon and throwing him back through the double doors behind him, with a loud crash. He remained swept up in the maelstrom of air until both he and the magic impacted with the wall in the reception area outside, leaving a huge crater in what used to be solid concrete blocks.

As I walked toward the control room's exit, I noticed the gun that Tommy had given me before I'd made my way down. It sat on the floor next to a fallen computer monitor. I picked it up and replaced it in the holster. I stepped out of the realm gate control room and used air magic to blow aside the cloud of dust and debris that had been expelled when the siphon had met his new temporary home.

"Hands in the air," barked a member of the facility security team as several armed guards entered the reception area, pointing their MP5s in my direction.

I did as was asked, showing I wasn't a threat. "I'm Nathan Garrett."

One of the men walked forward and offered me his hand. The name on his lapel said "West." "Sorry we weren't here sooner. The security floor was under attack too."

A moment of horror dawned on me. "Sky and Cerberus, are they—"

"They managed to subdue the two attackers, although Cerberus was injured in the fight. He's being healed at the moment," West said, from behind the black mask, identical to the ones the sorcerer and siphon had been using.

"Your own people were involved in this," I told him.

He nodded. "It seems some of them let in some outside help. They managed to get some of our gear from the armory. We heard about the concussion grenades. Looks like they were ours. Most of the attackers up top were killed; any survivors ran for it."

"What about the krampus?"

"It ran off back to the woods. We've got people in pursuit. We'll find it. Everything's all gone to shit. You can imagine how keen Hades is to get prisoners who can talk to him."

The image wasn't a very pleasant one. "Well, there are two up on the floor with the meeting rooms, one unconscious in the control room, and one in the hole over there." I pointed toward two guards who were dragging the siphon out of the wall; both had removed their masks beforehand. The larger of the two was female, with short hair and an expression that suggested she was not having a good day. "There's another one, a sorcerer. No idea who he was; he left before the fighting started."

"We didn't come across anyone," the guard said, much to my annoyance. If I'd tried to stop him leaving before I'd drawn the rune on my hand, it would have been the quickest losing fight of my life. But that didn't mean I had to like his escape.

"He won't get far," West said, oblivious of my anger. "What's that on your hand?"

I glanced at the rune I'd drawn. I still didn't know where the knowledge had come from, or why it had decided to come to me at that exact moment, but I was glad for it.

"He's alive," the female guard by the siphon said, gaining West's attention, which I was grateful for. She held the siphon under one armpit while her comrade did the same with the opposite arm, dragging the siphon's feet over the remains of the wall.

The two guards released their prisoner, letting him crash to the debris-littered floor. He'd regressed to his normal size and shape, his dark clothing covered in white and gray dust. There was a dark, raw patch of bleeding skin beneath his torn shirt— whatever energy he'd drawn from the guardian had been used to heal him after I'd plunged the sphere into his chest.

"You okay?" the female guard asked the siphon, who emitted a low groan in reply. The guard moved her MP5 slightly and then smashed its butt into his face, knocking him out.

She glanced up at me and the guard I'd been talking to. "He slipped," she said.

"Yeah, I've heard that's a well-known hazard," I replied with a nod. I didn't care that she'd hit him; I got the feeling he was looking at a lot more of it if he woke up before Hades got a hold of them. But once the siphon was in Hades's presence, I was sure he'd have preferred to be pistol-whipped all day long. Hell, I imagined he'd have preferred being repeatedly shot with one.

I glanced down at my hands. I'd used lightning. I'd used it without much in the way of trying, something I'd never managed before. I had no idea where the knowledge for the rune on my hand had come from, no idea why I was suddenly able to use lightning magic, but it felt as if I'd unlocked something incredible. And very, very dangerous.

CHAPTER 12

Are you okay?" a clearly upset Sky asked as I exited the underground part of the facility and stepped into the sunlight-bathed courtyard again. It had been nearly an hour since I'd fought the siphon. The team who encountered me wouldn't let me go until they'd finished their checks, and they insisted I see a doctor, who thankfully said I was mostly uninjured.

"Yeah, I'm good. Gonna feel sore for a bit, but I'll manage. How's Cerberus? I heard he got hurt."

"He's gone to see a healer. His leg is a bit of a mess, but he should make a full recovery." Sky sighed and rubbed her temples. "One of the attackers on the security floor stabbed him with a silver dagger. Our own guys did this, Nate. At last count, we killed twenty-six people up here, another nine down below."

"How many were caught alive?"

"Five, initially."

"Initially?"

"Two from your fight in the realm gate, one from the security room and the two you and Tommy hurt. One of them managed to grab a guard's weapon and was killed in the resulting fight, and the one Tommy hurt is in intensive care. He had his neck broken. He might live, but he's only an enchanter, so it's touch and go at the moment. So there are currently three people who are able to give answers."

"That's a lot of personnel they've managed to lose."

"Except we don't know how many there are overall." Sky rubbed her eyes with the heel of her palm. "Why would they do this, Nate?"

I didn't have any good answers for that question. "We'll find out." I glanced around the compound. There wasn't a lot of activity. "Where is everyone?"

"After we secured the area, we brought the tour group up. They're in the building by the garage. The dignitaries are with them. Most of the guards are patrolling the facility. Dad is . . . actually, I have no idea. He was talking to several of the dignitaries. They're not exactly thrilled about what's happened."

"Bit too much of a coincidence for my liking," I said.

"You think this was all planned?" she glanced at me for a second longer. "You look like shit."

I glanced down at my dusty, ripped T-shirt. My hands had blood on them, although I was pretty sure it wasn't mine.

"I need to wash my face and change," I said.

We walked toward the building where the school kids had been placed, and I told her about what had happened in the realm gate control room.

"No one of that sorcerer's description came up here," she said when I'd finished. "That would mean that he's still down there."

"Possibly. Do you know who escaped yet?"

Sky shook her head. "But even if our people have given them the blueprints and disabled the security, I don't see how they could have broken to the surface without someone noticing them. It seems crazy to consider it." She waved her arms around. "There's nowhere to realistically hide, and I can't imagine anyone powerful enough to warrant this much trouble being some unrecognizable nobody."

"So, whoever they let out is still in the facility?"

"I didn't say we wouldn't search up here, but they'd have miles of lift shafts to climb up. Could you do that in, what, an hour since the alarm first went off?"

I thought about it. "I wouldn't feel good afterward, but yeah, I probably could if I was motivated enough. And anyone escaping Tartarus with this much help has got to be motivated."

Sky was quiet for a few more seconds until the dulcet sounds of Mara Range's voice broke the silence.

I paused for a moment and glanced at Sky, who sighed, before we both continued on together. The sound of Mara's voice grew as we rounded a nearby building and spotted her screeching at Hades, who was doing his best to try to calm the situation.

"So, there could be some psychopath running around here trying to kill our children, and you refuse to let us leave!" Mara shouted.

Several armed guards were watching the confrontation with interest, probably trying to decide whether Mara was a threat to Hades, and quickly coming to the conclusion that shooting her would be cathartic, but probably not the best idea on a school trip. Or maybe I was just projecting.

"That's not what I said, Mrs. Range," Hades told her, his expression saying that he was in the process of trying very hard to remain calm. "I said, we need to search your bus before you can be allowed to leave. If someone has escaped from Tartarus, we can hardly allow them to use your bus as transport, putting you and your children in harm's way."

"You will not search witch property," Mara snapped. "I will not have strangers going through our things and treating us like common criminals."

Several teachers and children, including Mara's own daughter, Chloe, had left the building and were watching with a mixture of confused interest and concern. Tommy and Kasey caught my eye, Tommy shrugging his lack of knowledge at the situation as Sky and I made our way toward the row.

Mara saw us approach and raised a long finger in our direction. "You will keep her away from me," she demanded. "We've all heard stories of her volatile nature, and quite frankly I don't trust her not to try to scalp me."

Sometimes there are moments when someone says something so offensive that those around them tend to wait, even if only for a nanosecond, for their conscious brain to catch up with what they think they might have heard.

Someone somewhere inhaled sharply, and I glanced aside to find that it was Sky, who had a look of outrage on her face.

I darted forward, grabbing Sky as she made a dash for Mara. "What the fuck did you say?" Sky shouted. "Say it again, you fucking racist bitch!"

"I said she was volatile," Mara said, helping in exactly zero number of ways, her voice full of self-importance. "You'll keep her away from me."

I wasn't exactly certain what happened next, involving those people who had been watching the events unfold around me, or what Hades said to Mara or vice versa. Keeping Sky from kicking seven shades of shit out of Mara was a full-time job.

"Let me fucking go!" Sky snapped at me, trying to get around me. I released her and, making sure not to touch her at any point, I held my hands out toward her, to keep distance between her and me. If I'd laid a hand on her, I was likely to find it broken a few moments later.

"Sky, you need to calm down," I told her. "This isn't helping."

"It'll help when I break her smug fucking face. Move out of the fucking way, or lose your balls," Sky said, her entire body radiating anger.

I sighed and stepped aside, fully aware of Persephone, who had just arrived, and was walking behind Sky.

"Enough," Persephone snapped. Everyone froze, even Sky, whose gaze never left Mara. Hades had anticipated my moving aside and had walked toward his daughter to intercept her. I knew that there was no chance of Mara getting hurt while Hades was still there; otherwise, I'd have never moved, threats to my manhood or not.

"You are my daughter," Persephone said as she reached Sky. "You will behave like it."

Sky's head dropped forward slightly as she searched the ground for something interesting to look at, before turning around and storming off. Hopefully, to calm down.

Persephone didn't even stop walking, although Hades certainly stepped aside for his wife, who laid a hand gently on his shoulder before turning to Mara. A little air magic and her words drifted back over to me.

"Get off this compound and don't ever come back," Persephone said.

"You can't evict me like a common thug! I've done nothing wrong. I've had to deal with incompetent—"

Persephone held up her hand, and Mara's mouth dropped open in shock. I doubted she was used to being shushed. "You have sixty seconds. If you're still here after that, I'll lock you and Sky in a room together and come back in an hour. You are a vile, nasty little woman, and I genuinely feel sorry for the lovely girl you call a daughter, who, quite frankly, has been delightful during this entire ordeal. You, on the other hand, have feelings only for yourself. Now leave."

Mara turned to Hades, who grinned. "I tried to be nice to you," he said. "I really did. You insulted our daughter. My wife has given you a chance to leave by your own power. I advise you to take it. You won't get another."

One of the guards came over and whispered to Hades, although I wasn't using enough magic to pick up the words.

"Thank you," Hades told the guard as Persephone walked off and spoke to the children and adults who had witnessed the whole event.

"Your bus has been searched and declared clean," Hades told Mara.

"How dare you!"

"My dear," Hades said, leaning slightly closer, "if you ever come within my gaze again, I assure you what I dare will become very apparent. As my wife has said, you are a vile, nasty little woman. Your husband is a very unfortunate man."

"I am no longer married," she snapped.

"I assume he's in hiding," Hades said, and I had to place a hand over my mouth to stop from laughing.

"Avalon will hear about this," Mara snapped and turned to walk away.

"Excellent," Hades called after her. "It will ensure they get a good laugh too."

I stopped the magic and watched Mara storm back into the building used by the school trip, just as Chloe snuck around to the side of the building. I made my way after her and found her several feet up the nearby cliff, sitting on a ledge, looking down on the forest beyond.

"You mind?" I asked as I reached the cliff face.

"Be my guest," she said.

I climbed up the cliff ledge, which rose like a stair for about six feet, until I reached the ledge, and then walked along it toward Chloe. "You scaled this pretty quickly," I said as I sat beside her.

"I like climbing," she said. "It's peaceful. A six-foot bit of rock isn't much of a challenge."

Chloe was a pretty girl, with light brown hair that fell to her shoulders and big blue eyes. She wore a silver necklace with a pendant on the bottom of it, a small silver version of a short sword that looked a little bit like a gladius.

"Nice necklace," I said.

She lifted it in one of her small hands and smiled. "My dad got it for me. Mum hates when I wear it around her. But then she hates everything, so fuck her."

"Aren't you, what, thirteen?"

"Fourteen," she corrected. "Why?"

"Because you seem young to be saying things like that about her."

"I heard what she said to your friend, Sky. She was out of order. She does this all the time."

"She always been like that?"

"No. When I was little, she was kind. Then she started to change, become more serious about her witchcraft, screaming at dad and me. Then he left. He should have taken me with him."

"I'm sorry."

Chloe shrugged, but nothing could disguise the hurt in her voice.

"You got any other family you could stay with? Sounds like maybe your mum isn't in the best frame of mind at the moment."

"No one. I spend most of my time at friends' houses. *She* doesn't care."

"You got a lot of friends?"

"Some," she said with a small smile. "Kasey and me hang out a lot. She's cool to be around—smart too. We get in trouble in class for talking. And she's got a badass for a dad."

"That she does," I said with a chuckle. "Tommy's a good guy. You ever need anything, you can trust him. Or Olivia."

"I like Kasey's mum. She's cool. Even if she is a cop."

I laughed.

"I don't know why my mum hates you so much," Chloe said, stopping any laughter dead.

"Weird that someone would hate me when she only met me the day before and then spent most of that time shouting at me or my friends. But I get that some witches hate sorcerers."

Chloe shook her head. "No, she hates *you*. She was furious when she discovered that you were going to be on this trip. She rang some people and demanded that the school remove you from going. She said she'd get Demeter and Hera involved, but the school wouldn't budge. For weeks, she just seethed that you were going and were going to spoil everything."

A few weeks before the trip, I'd been called to the school to have a conversation with the headmistress and teachers there. She wanted to know if I was a danger to her staff and pupils. She'd been made fully aware of my past as Hellequin, which had surprised me. It was hardly a secret anymore, but the information was taking a long time to trickle back to Avalon and its employees. I explained that I had no intention of hurting anyone. She'd already gotten reports from friends of mine in Avalon, including

Kasey's mum, Olivia, so I was allowed to go on the trip. In hindsight, I probably should have fought harder to be told no.

"Spoil what?"

"The trip, I guess. No idea why, though. And then when your room was on the same floor as ours. She didn't stop screaming at me and anyone else who got near. I ended up staying in Kasey's room. Kasey said her dad wouldn't mind."

"Why was she so angry about me being on the same floor?"

"No idea. She stormed off to one of the other adult witches' rooms, and I didn't see her after that except when she'd come in to yell at me about not measuring up and then storm out again."

"Not measuring up?"

"She thinks I shouldn't 'consort with the children of her enemies.' Her exact words. She thinks Kasey is a bad influence on me. She thinks because she knows that, you're going to try to twist my mind against her."

She seems to be doing a good enough job of that all by herself, I thought.

"Can I ask you something?" she said without looking at me.

"Sure, go ahead."

"Kasey said you made a pact with her to be honest about everything."

"A few years ago, yeah. I try to be honest with her, and if it's something I can't tell her, I explain why. She likes to ask me about my life. She's got a bit of an interest in history."

"Can we make the same pact?"

I shook my head. "I made that pact with her because I knew Tommy wouldn't mind. I can't say the same for your mum."

Chloe nodded but looked disappointed.

"I'll tell you what: today, here and now, I'll be as honest as I can. What do you want to know?"

"Is that blood on your hands?"

I'd forgotten about the blood, but there was no use lying. "Yes, but it's not mine."

"So, did someone really escape from Tartarus? Are we in danger?"

"Did someone escape? We can't be certain, but maybe. Are you in danger? No, not even slightly. If someone did escape, they're not going to do something stupid with an army of armed people nearby. They'll try to get out of the compound and as far from here as quickly as possible. It's why Hades checked the buses; it would be a logical place for someone to try to hitch a ride back to town."

"Did you use to work for Merlin?"

"Who told you that?" I asked.

"My mum. She said you were his personal dog or something."

"Lapdog?" I asked.

She nodded. "That's it."

"I did work for Merlin, yes. But I wasn't much of a lapdog. It was my job to try to make sure the world was safer for everyone."

Chloe was quiet for a moment while her mother's shouts echoed across the compound once more. "I'd better go," she said, standing and brushing down her jeans.

"If you ever need a break, talk to Kasey. I'm sure she'd be happy to have you stay over at her place."

"I will." She walked off and began climbing down the cliff, stopping halfway to glance back up at me. "Thanks."

"No problem." I paused for a moment. "Hey, can I ask you something?"

Chloe smiled and nodded.

"Have you ever heard of Sarah Hamilton? She's a witch."

"I know Sarah," Chloe said with a smile. "I've seen her a few times when she's visited the coven my mum belongs to. She's really nice. Why?"

"I met her in town yesterday. She said she knew your mum."

"Yeah, she likes my mum about as much as everyone else."

"Who does she work for?"

Chloe shrugged. "No idea; she works in London for some big company. She said she was in equations."

I had to think about it for a second. "Acquisitions?"

"That's it. She acquires stuff for her boss."

"Sounds important."

"Oh, Sarah is very cool. She taught me some new runes. Just little things, but it was nice to have someone talk to me like I had an opinion."

Mara Range screamed for her daughter.

"I'd better go. Nice talking to you."

"You too," I said as she ran off around the corner. A few seconds later, Mara appeared. Her expression did not lead me to believe that she was happy to have discovered her daughter had been talking to me.

She turned and stormed off as I climbed down from my perch, their bus driving up to the compound gates before I'd made it back to the rest of the group.

"Well, that's probably for the best," Tommy said after walking over to me, Kasey beside him.

"I hope Chloe is okay," Kasey said.

"I'm sure she's fine," I said. "And I think you guys will be going back soon too."

"From that, I take it you won't be joining us," Tommy said.

"I'm going to speak to Hades and try to figure out what's going on."

"This isn't your fight, Nate," Tommy said. "You don't have to get involved."

"It wasn't my fight until last night when a witch and her thugs tried to kill me in a car park."

"Is that your only reason for wanting to be involved?"

I explained about the sorcerer who had recognized me in the control room.

"I'm staying too then," he said. "Don't argue."

"I'll stay too," Kasey said. "It's safer here with you two than it is anywhere else."

"Neither of you are staying," I said. "I'm going to talk to Hades and find out what's happening, and then, if they don't need me, I'll leave. In the meantime, there's a krampus about. So no one leaves that hotel alone."

"Don't worry about that; I'll make sure everyone knows," Tommy said. "You sure you're not coming?"

"I need to know who escaped."

"Because of last time?" Tommy asked.

Kasey immediately latched onto her father's words. "What happened last time?"

"No one had ever escaped Tartarus until Pandora. And now, less than a century later, someone else has managed it. I need to check that the two events aren't linked."

"Why?" Kasey insisted.

"Because Pandora's last escape caused a lot of pain and suffering. And if I get a say in it, nothing like that will happen again."

CHAPTER 13

Berlin, Germany. 1936.

It had been only a short time since I'd left Pandora with Hades and his people, but it felt like much longer. Selene's obvious shock and anger at having her brother, Helios, be part of whatever Pandora's plan was meant she wasn't in the talking mood, and I wasn't convinced she'd have allowed Pandora to leave in one piece had Hades and I not been there.

I was pretty certain that Pandora was immortal and indestructible. Back when she'd escaped and managed to slot herself into the Napoleonic Wars, there'd been an occasion when she'd been hit by a cannonball while walking along a battlefield. I had no doubt about the pain it had caused, but whatever damage had been done was short lived.

Even so, Selene would have more than likely put Pandora's ability to heal to the test if given the chance. Hades had wisely escorted Pandora onto his plane, while I took an enraged Selene outside to the car, where she'd punched a hole in the side of the hangar as the plane taxied for takeoff.

She'd remained quiet since we'd gotten back into the Bugatti. A quiet Selene was never good. Just before we reached the outskirts of Berlin, I pulled the car over onto what appeared to be the start of a dirt road and switched off the engine. "Right, Selene, what do you need to say?"

Selene glanced over at me. "She's enthralled my brother into helping her. Either we stop him, or he kills a lot of people. Are you sure we can't force Pandora to release him?"

"No. She either will or won't. You can't force the situation. People have tried torturing her in the past, and she just endures it. She's been hurt enough in her life; I won't add to that pain."

"It's just, I know what stopping him is going to entail."

"We don't have to kill him, Selene."

"He won't go down without a fight. The only way to stop him will be to do it permanently."

"We'll make sure it doesn't come to that."

Selene closed her eyes and nodded once. "Pandora's right about one thing: he's more powerful than either of us. At least during the daytime. We need to get him during the night, when he's weaker. Even that's going to be hard work. We need to find those people who helped Pandora."

"Jean and Magali Martin. Although we have no idea where they are."

I'd asked Pandora where they could be found, but she didn't know. Apparently, she hadn't been to their house. All we had to go on were that they were French nationals living in Dresden. "When Pandora escaped, I wasn't the only person sent to track her down. Petra and Kurt were sent along too."

"Why only you three?"

"Fewer people for Pandora to use. I'm immune to her, as are Petra and Kurt. It made sense for us to be the ones sent to track her down. They stayed in Dresden, searching for whatever Pandora was up to, while I moved on to Berlin."

"You knew she'd gone to Dresden? You never mentioned it at the airfield."

"We'd tracked her from Mittenwald to Dresden. She'd been in Dresden for a week before she left for Berlin. We had no idea what she was doing while in Dresden, though. Now I'm guessing she was working with the Martins and Helios on her plan."

"Except Pandora doesn't know the plan. Isn't that the whole point? She can just claim it's all down to my brother."

"We can release him from Pandora's grasp. It's been done before."

"With whom?"

"Petra and Kurt were both under her power, although it was done in strict circumstances with Hades watching. Once she releases someone voluntarily, she can't then re-enthrall them. Petra and Kurt worked in Tartarus a lot, so it was necessary to ensure that they wouldn't be taken control of."

"So, how are you immune to her?"

I paused for a second. "Like I said, Pandora has to let someone go."

"She enthralled you?"

I nodded. "Many centuries ago."

"Why did she let you go?"

"Lots of reasons," I said quickly. "They're not important right now."

Selene stared at me for a moment before nodding and turning away. "You don't trust me." It wasn't a question.

I turned to look out of the windscreen. "No, Selene, I don't. And I think there are some pretty big reasons why that is. I'm okay with you helping me track down your brother, but we need to stop him from hurting people. I don't care what Hera's agenda was in sending you, but if whatever your orders are puts people's lives at risk, I'll stop both you and your brother myself." My voice was hard, and I spoke slowly enough to ensure that no emotion would creep in, betraying how hard it was to sit so close to her and talk to her as if nothing mattered.

I felt her staring at me for what seemed like a lifetime. "You've made your feelings perfectly clear there, Nathan." Her tone was sharp, a slither of anger leaking through. "I'll try not to let Hera's *master plan* interfere with saving people's lives."

I opened my mouth to argue and quickly thought better of it. I didn't want another fight.

"I never said our working together would be easy," Selene almost whispered. "But I am on your side."

"And what side are your husband and Hera on? What's their *plan*?"

"Why do they even need to have a plan?"

"I find it hard to believe that once Hera had discovered Pandora's escape and arranged for you to become involved, she didn't have a plan."

I turned to look at Selene, who was absentmindedly rubbing her wedding ring finger, which was bare.

"She wants to remonstrate against my husband for what she considers to be him overstepping his boundaries."

"What does that mean?"

"He pissed her off when he tried to have one of her staff killed after the woman spurned him."

"He cheats on you?"

Selene held my gaze. "We're not discussing this."

"Fine, but do you really think all she wants is to send you here in order to piss off your husband?"

"Well, I guess she'd like to find a way to get control of Tartarus, but she's wanted that for several thousand years, and it's about as likely to happen now as it was when Zeus was alive. So she settles for playing silly games and trying to constantly one-up her own grandchildren and make them feel small."

"Sounds like a fun place to live."

"No, Nathan, it's not. But like I said, we're not here to discuss my personal life; we're here to stop Helios from killing untold numbers of people. I know this is difficult—it is for me too. If I didn't have to be here, I wouldn't have darkened your doorstep with my presence. Now, can we put any future discussions aside until we reach Dresden and talk to people who might be able to help us?"

I started the engine. "Not a fucking problem," I snapped.

For the briefest of moments, I thought I saw Selene deflate slightly as a softness passed over her face, but then she turned away to look out of the window, and I knew there was no point in talking further. I hoped we could find Helios quickly. Not only to stop him from hurting people, but because I wasn't sure how long it would be before Selene or I said something to the other that would cause whatever we'd never said to spill out. We'd never really spoken after she'd left; there had been a lot left unsaid—a lot of anger and resentment that had been left to fester deep down inside of me, where I'd been able to ignore it right up until I'd seen her again.

Damn. It was going to be a hard few days. I was going to be grateful when something came along I could punch. Repeatedly.

We stopped the car outside a four-story town house that sat opposite the river Elbe, which runs through Dresden.

The city itself was beautiful, with stunning architecture, and when you got high enough, views that would stun. I'd always considered it a jewel in Germany's crown, and despite the military presence it was still a hub for artists and scientists to mix and flourish.

It had begun to drizzle as we walked over to the house. The soft, occasional splashes of rainfall and grayness of the sky, a fitting backdrop to the task ahead of Selene and me. Trying to hunt down Pandora was hard enough, even without her talents working on me, but hunting Helios? That was a whole different league of trouble. I wondered how much it would take to subdue him. How many people we wouldn't be able to save before we did.

I forced the thoughts aside as I ascended the steps to the red front door and knocked. It didn't take long for the occupants to open the door, and even less time for Petra to envelop Selene in a tight hug. Petra smiled at me as she held her friend, a knowing smile that bespoke the conversation I was sure we'd have. Again. She appeared determined for Selene and I to resolve our differences, as if Selene's *being married* was just a phase or passing fancy.

Petra ushered the pair of us inside, glancing around the street before closing the door. A woman wearing an ankle length light green dress ran down the nearby staircase, past me, and stopped at the door. She was at most five-two, and her dark brown hair was tied up in a bun. A pair of spectacles sat on her small nose, making her appear much older than her twenty-eight years. Bandages covered part of her arms. They started at her wrists and stopped halfway up her forearms. She pressed her hand against the door, the runes that had been painted on the back shimmering slightly as power was poured into them.

Anything can be used to create runes so long as you have enough power to activate them. But whereas sorcerers and the like need to learn how to use already existing runes, enchanters, such as Lucie Moser, could create and manipulate runes to do a vast amount of things. These ranged from removing the power of everyone in a building, to exploding if tampered with.

"Worried?" Selene asked.

"A natural concern, considering everything that's been happening in this country," Kurt said as he entered the hallway and hugged Selene, then shook my hand.

"Good to see you still have Lucie to help you," I said.

Lucie finished activating the runes and then turned toward me. She was not happy to see me. "You've returned," she said in a tone that suggested she'd rather I hadn't. "I'll prepare some drinks."

I smiled.

Lucie shook her head and walked off, brushing past me with slightly more force than necessary as she did.

"I see you made a friend," Selene said.

"Yes, apparently I'm quite the charmer," I said flippantly before she walked off with Petra into a nearby room. Kurt and I followed a few seconds later.

The room itself turned out to be a library that I hadn't seen on my previous time here before I'd tracked Pandora to Berlin. It was stacked floor to ceiling with hundreds of books, and in the center sat two comfortable red leather couches with a small table between them.

We all sat down and waited for Lucie to reappear. The tray in her hands held several cups and saucers, along with a teapot and small jar of sugar. All of the china matched in color—blue and white—and style; steam billowed out the top of the teapot, reminding me that it had been far too long since my last cup.

Lucie poured and distributed the drinks, glaring as if she'd have preferred to throw mine at me, and when we were all settled, Kurt asked what had happened with Pandora.

I explained about Berlin, the Gestapo headquarters, and the murder of the two men in the alley, telling too what Pandora had told me at the airfield.

"So those people, the Martins, that Pandora was staying with," Petra said. "Any idea where we can find them?"

I shook my head. "She says they're still in Dresden. Thus ends my knowledge. I assume they're helping Helios somehow, maybe by looking around the stadium for a plan of attack."

"They could be working there," Kurt suggested. "I've got a few friends in the police force here, ones I trust. I'll ask around and find out if they recognize the names."

"And if they've changed their names?" Selene asked.

Kurt shrugged. "One problem at a time. It's unlikely they have, though, unless they're wanted criminals, and Pandora wouldn't have used people who couldn't have helped her plan succeed. Besides, if what she told Nate was true—"

"It was," I interrupted.

"Then Magali and Jean have help. Probably a group of people to work with them."

"Has anyone realized that Nathan said these people are opposed to the Nazi regime?" Selene said. "These are the good guys."

I shook my head. "If they're planning on helping your brother kill innocent people just to make a point for Pandora, they're not any good guys I want to work with."

"And killing brothers, you know all about that, yes?"

"Let it go," Kurt said, his tone hard.

"It's fine," I explained and turned to Lucie. "What's done is done. I can't change what happened."

"Do you even care?" Lucie snapped.

I stayed silent.

Lucie flung her teacup at me, which I managed to catch, using a cushion of air magic to stop the contents from covering me. She stormed out of the room, sobbing, Petra in close pursuit.

"You killed her brother, I assume?" Selene asked.

"It's a long story," I said without wish to elaborate further.

Selene never was any good at allowing me to get away without explaining. "What happened?"

I quickly came to the conclusion that hearing it from me might be better than getting it from Lucie. "Her father, stepmother, and younger brother and sister were murdered one night twelve years ago while they slept. Lucie wasn't home at the time. She was sixteen. The police arrived and arrested Lucie's brother, Robin, but he escaped and found his sister. He convinced her it wasn't him, that someone was trying to frame him."

"And you know who that is?"

"I've told Lucie dozens of times there was no one else involved," I said, and cursed inwardly at the lie as it slid easily over my lips. I'd told it so many times it was like second nature now. Lucie didn't need to know about what happened. Sometimes the truth really is worse than the lie.

"And she doesn't believe you?"

"She thinks I framed her brother and allowed the real murderer to escape justice. She thinks the real killer was someone I was told to protect, so I let them go."

Selene didn't ask if I'd ever do such a thing; she was fully aware I wouldn't. "How do you know Lucie?"

"She works for Hades. Her family worked for him too."

"Why doesn't she believe it was her brother?"

"Robin, her brother, manipulated Lucie into believing him innocent. She told the police she didn't know where he would go, and that allowed him to continue killing people. Twenty-six people died before I found him. Hades took Lucie in after that and gave her a job working at his compound. She's always maintained her brother's innocence."

"Any chance he is innocent?" Selene asked.

"None," I promised. "I caught him as he butchered a young girl. He was trying out different runes on his victims, trying to see what effects they had. He carved them into their flesh as they were still alive and then watched them die slowly and painfully as the runes took effect."

"What did the runes do?"

"Various things. Mostly cause pain and suffering. He said he couldn't stop even if he wanted to. He had a notebook detailing all of the killings and what he'd discovered."

"How can Lucie deny what happened if she's seen it?"

"She believes her brother was forced to write the notebook. It didn't change her mind."

"What would?"

I shrugged. "Probably nothing. So she hates me with a fire that can't be extinguished. She's cocooned herself into a world where her brother was her idol, and admitting that he went out and committed horrific crimes would mean she would have to admit that he manipulated her and played her for a fool. It means tainting his memory."

"It doesn't bother you that she hates you?" Selene's tone showed her shock.

I stood and walked toward the door, turning my back on Selene and Kurt. When I'd taken a few steps, I stopped and turned back. "Why should it? People I care about more than her have managed it, and I'm still here, still functioning. One more person hating me doesn't really make much of a difference."

At that moment, Lucie stormed into the library and walked up to me, radiating anger, followed by Petra, who appeared to look concerned. The knuckles on one of Lucie's hands were red from where she'd punched something. "I don't trust you," she said, her voice quiet, as if she were forcing herself to remain calm.

"Okay," I said.

"But this is more important than my personal feelings."

"I'm glad you agree."

"But one day, you'll tell me the truth about what happened. About who killed my family and why you framed my brother."

"Lucie—" I started.

She raised her hand to my chest and shook her head. "Don't you dare deny what I know. My brother was not a murderer; he was not responsible for what happened to my family. Nothing you say can change those facts. But you either know who is and allowed them to flee or they beat you, and you framed my brother to cover your incompetence. Either way, we both know you're hiding the truth. And you'll either tell it to me, or I'll beat it out of you."

"Lucie," my voice was calm and soft. I noticed Selene step around beside me, tension in her shoulders as she readied herself to stop whatever I was about to do. I breathed in deeply and slowly exhaled. "You have no idea who I am. No clue of what I've done in my life and no clue of what happened the night I found your brother. Nothing will change what he did."

I stepped past her and headed for the door, opening it as Petra stepped aside without a word. I paused and turned back to Lucie. "Just one thing: you can hate me for whatever injustice you believe I committed, but the next time you threaten me will be the last time." And I stepped through the door, closing it behind me.

CHAPTER 14

Dresden, Germany. 1936.

It took nearly twenty-four hours for Kurt's friends in the police force to get a lead on the Martins, which basically left me spending a day avoiding Selene and Lucie as much as possible. I didn't want to row with Lucie, and quite frankly, I still wasn't sure about the feelings for Selene that were rattling around my brain.

I was exceptionally happy when Kurt announced they had a lead and asked if I'd like to join them. Unfortunately, they'd also asked Lucie and Selene, so I found myself back driving the stolen Bugatti with Selene beside me, while Kurt, Petra, and Lucie took their red BMW 315.

I followed the BMW out of central Dresden to a small old farmhouse a few miles away, and after driving up a dirt driveway, stopped outside a large barn that had been painted white and red. The roof was made of some kind of metal, and I was certain it would turn the barn into a giant oven on hot days like today.

I exited the car, shielding my eyes from the intense sunshine that glinted off some old machinery that had been dumped at one side of the barn, and looked around. Once the surrounding fields had been used to plant crops, but now sat empty. There was the start of a small patch of woodland on the far end of the several acres of downwardly sloped land, but between here and there were several hundred meters of open land. I was certain that if anyone was at home, they'd already be aware of our presence.

Kurt had parked the BMW outside the front of the large two-story house that sat near the barn. At some point it had been painted white, although the paint had long since started to crack and peel.

Petra wandered off with Lucie to have a look around while Selene and I joined Kurt.

"You sure this is the place?" Selene asked.

Kurt nodded and glanced around. "You know that anyone here is already aware of us."

It was my turn to nod. "You got any weapons on you?"

"Why would I?" Kurt asked. "I'm a werebear; the only way I could be more dangerous is if I were juggling flaming chainsaws."

There was a second of silence.

"Flaming chainsaws?" I questioned as we approached the steps to the house's porch.

"It was a spur-of-the-moment decision."

"Sounds very dangerous," Selene said with a slight laugh. "Probably more for you, though."

The laughter hid a current of anxiety that I felt among the three of us. Anytime Pandora was involved in something, things tended to go from bad to worse very quickly, and despite her relatively quick capture, her influence was still going to be felt in those she'd come into contact with.

Kurt knocked three times on the white door, waited a few seconds, and then knocked twice more. When there was still no answer, he tried the door handle, which didn't budge. He had raised his foot to kick the door in, when it unlocked from inside and opened inward, leaving Kurt looking like he was about to start hopping.

He placed his foot back on the wooden floor and smiled slightly as a woman appeared in the doorway. She was around five feet tall, with pale brown hair that was scruffy. Her eyes were red, big bags under each. She had the appearance of someone who hadn't slept in a while.

"Magali Martin?" Selene asked.

Magali nodded and rubbed her eyes. She wore long gloves that came up to her elbows, where they met the sleeves of her red blouse. Her black skirt covered down to her shins, and her feet were bare. Despite her obvious exhaustion, her clothes looked both expensive and immaculate.

"Are you okay?" I asked.

She glanced at me and nodded slightly. "Haven't slept much for a few days. You'll have to excuse my appearance; it's been a long week."

"May we come in?" Selene asked. "We need to talk to you about Pandora."

I was expecting Magali to object, or maybe even try to flee, but instead she opened the door wider and beckoned us all inside.

Magali led us along a dark hallway and into a room at the rear of the property. It was full of books, littering the floor, and a table had been placed in the center of the room. Paper and pencils cluttered the spaces where the books hadn't encroached, and I had to step over a considerable pile of unused paper to get to the large window, which allowed for a lovely view of the fields behind the house.

"So, you're here to talk to me about Pandora?" Magali asked once we were all inside the room.

"She handed herself in," I said. "But she told me you were working with her. That you and your husband, Jean, were involved in trying to stop the Nazis."

Magali ignored my words and watched me for a few heartbeats. "You're Nathan Garrett, aren't you?"

I nodded.

"Pandora told us that you were dangerous, that you would try to stop us, but that you were also her friend. She said we shouldn't lie to you. That even with the truth, you couldn't stop what was going to happen."

"So, what's the truth?" I asked.

"She came to us and asked for our help to infiltrate the Gestapo. We gave her the name of a soldier who was working with them."

"He's dead now. Pandora killed him."

"Good," she said with no trace of remorse. "He was a monster, like all of them are."

"Why did she need to gain entry?" Kurt asked.

Magali turned to Kurt and pointed at me. "Only he gets answers." She turned back to me before speaking, "Have you ever heard of nerve gas?"

Selene nodded. "The Germans created one called tabun early this year—although I've heard rumors that it was around for a while longer than their official records state. Hera was very interested in its workings."

"What does this tabun do?" Petra asked.

"It kills people," Selene told her. "Horribly and brutally murders anyone who comes into contact with it."

A cold fear crept into my gut. "So, Pandora was after some?"

Magali shook her head. "No, not tabun. There's a second strain, something that's still being developed. It's called sarin. The soldier that Pandora forced to help us told her that the Gestapo were busy trying to get the gas to work, that it was more potent and dangerous than anything anyone had ever seen. They had some working prototypes of missiles stored in a warehouse in Berlin. Enough sarin gas to kill a hundred thousand people. Pandora needed the location, so she had the soldier bring her to the Gestapo. She let them prod and poke her until she found someone who knew where the information was."

"Captain Dehmel," I said. "She was in that Gestapo headquarters to get the whereabouts of the sarin?"

Magali's smile was creepy and unpleasant. "Partially, yes. He, and only he, knew where the weapons were kept. She dredged the information from his mind."

"What do you mean, partially?" I asked.

"I don't know. She didn't tell me."

"Why does Pandora want sarin gas?" Selene asked. "What was she going to use it for?"

Magali shrugged. "No idea. She went to look at it but didn't think it was viable. Besides, she had a better idea."

"Helios," Selene whispered.

"Yes, Helios. He was her new plan. Or rather, she allowed him to do as he wished."

"Do you know Helios's plan?" I asked.

"Yes," she said.

Everyone was silent for a moment. "Where's Jean, your husband?" I asked.

"Dead."

"How?" Selene asked.

"I put a bullet in his skull." She delivered this fact with an utmost calm, as if she were describing pulling up weeds in the garden. "He couldn't accept what was going to happen. Even under Pandora's power, he struggled with the concept. Eventually it broke him, like it has others, and he had to be stopped before he hurt someone or had an adverse effect on the plan."

A shiver crept up my spine. "What is the plan?" I asked again.

"I loved my husband," she said, ignoring another question she didn't want to answer. "We grew up together in Paris, became married at eighteen, and were inseparable. It was a great burden for me to end his life. But we will be reunited in the afterlife, whatever that might be."

"I thought Pandora told you to answer my questions."

Magali shook her head. "That is true, but she also said we were to follow Helios's orders, and he doesn't want anyone to talk about his plan."

"Could you make her talk?" Kurt asked me.

Magali didn't even look fazed that I'd been asked if I could torture the information out of her. I didn't even have to think about the answer. "No amount of persuasion or torture will get the information from her. Pandora's influence will let her mind be torn asunder before she tells us anything she doesn't want to. As she says, she has to tell the truth, because she's been ordered to, but only as far as her own involvement is concerned. Helios is in charge now."

"Then we need to search the house," Selene said. "Can you keep her occupied?" she asked Petra, who nodded. "We'll turn the house upside down if we need to—the barn too."

I glanced over at the table and noticed a book that sat on top of some paper. I moved the book aside and found myself reading the blueprints for the Olympic stadium. I glanced up at everyone else in the room to find them all looking at me, except for Magali, who had turned her back to us all and was staring at the wall.

"What is this?" I asked. "What is Helios's plan for the Olympics?"

Magali turned back to us, removed her gloves, and dropped them to the ground. Lucie was the first to react, as the runes tattooed on the arms of Magali were visible for all to see.

"Enchanter," Lucie yelled and dove at the Frenchwoman, but she was too slow.

Magali placed one hand against her forearm, covering a large black rune tattoo and smiled before exploding.

Magali's entire body turned into a cloud of blood and gore. I'd managed to place a shield of dense air between her and us. The blast hit Lucie first. She was blown backward into Kurt and Petra, and they all crashed to the floor. The explosion drove me to my knees as I tried to keep the shield active. It robbed the blast of its potency, thankfully, leaving all of us hurt but alive. The wall behind Magali and the ceiling above were the biggest casualties, with both vanishing from the blast.

As I stood, I felt a sharp pain in my side and looked down to see part of a bone sticking out of my stomach. I fell back to the floor as smoke and dust filled the room.

Selene was by my side in an instant. "Are you okay?"

"She turned herself into human shrapnel," I said. "Hurts like hell."

She grabbed the bone, causing me to shout, and pulled it out in one motion. Both pain and relief washed through me as my magic set about healing the wound. A burning feeling still blazed inside my stomach, but I had little time to consider the implications.

"Everyone else okay?" I asked.

"Lucie's unconscious," Kurt shouted.

"Other than that, we're okay," Petra continued.

"What about you?" I asked Selene.

"I'm good. You managed to stop her from killing us—or at the very least, making our day much worse."

"Shame I couldn't stop it all, though," I said through gritted teeth as Selene helped me back to my feet. "Exactly what was the point of blowing herself up?"

No one had time to answer as more explosions rocked through the room, tearing walls and the ceiling apart and spraying us with wood, plaster, and pieces of metal.

"Fuck!" Kurt shouted out as something passed through his arm and embedded itself in the wall beside him. "She's put fucking nails in the walls and ceiling. She's turned this whole place into a damn bomb."

Several more of the tiny missiles shot around the room as Petra dragged Lucie over to us, and Kurt crashed to the floor beside me. I created a second wall of air, determined to stop the vicious nastiness that Magali had prepared. The pain in my side made it difficult for me to concentrate enough to stop all of the fast-moving pieces of metal, and when one went through the palm of my hand, my magic ceased.

More explosions sounded from above, and the ceiling caved in. Selene stopped it from covering us with a blast of ice from her open mouth. She created a thick igloo, encasing the five of us in its protective shell as the sounds of collapsing wood and brick created a cacophony of noise in the relatively small, enclosed space.

Selene's eyes had gone reptile orange, and her now scaly skin was the color of silver. Her fingers had elongated, her nails forming razor-sharp talons that could carve through steel as easily as it if were paper.

"I won't be able to redo any of the ice once it starts to crack. The night is too far away," she said. Her voice hadn't changed; it never did, which was always one of the things I found strange about her kind.

Selene was dragon-kin. Long ago dragons roamed the world; enormous and dangerous, they were capable of changing into humanlike form. The resulting offspring of humans and dragons were named dragon-kin. They couldn't change into the huge monstrosities as their ancestors had, but they had inherited a host of their ancestors' strengths and weaknesses. The main one was that dragons and their kin gained their strength and power according to a particular time of day. Some were stronger during the daylight hours; these gained the ability to breathe fire; others, such as Selene, used the night.

Selene couldn't have gone full dragon-kin; the sun was far too strong during the midday, and she'd probably used her reserves of power just creating the dome of ice. But she was strong enough to have saved all of us from having a building crush us.

"We need to leave," I told everyone and noticed that Kurt was still bleeding.

"Silver," he said. "She packed it with normal nails and silver ones. I'm not going to be much use for a while."

I glanced back at Selene, whose skin had returned to her normal color and whose eyes were human once more.

"I'm spent," she said.

The ice above us groaned once more, and drops of water fell onto my hand. The explosions had quite probably created fires inside the house—the igloo wasn't going to hold up for long without Selene's help.

"What are you doing?" I asked Selene, who had crawled over to several scraps of paper that were on the floor.

"We need to know what's happening, what Helios's plan is."

I placed my hands against the exterior wall of the house and concentrated. Pushing the wall out would only result in a large part of the wall above us dropping down into its place, doing none of us any good at all. Instead, I pushed the wall out and up, using my air magic to hold it in place, the weight of the house trying to push it down onto my head as I slowly moved through the new hole.

"Everyone out now," I said and was quickly followed by Petra, who was carrying Lucie, along with Kurt. "Get as far away from here as possible. The second I let the magic go, this whole side of the building is to going collapse."

The strain was immense. I felt my feet slowly pushed into the soft dirt beneath me as several tons of house tried to turn me into wet mush.

"Holding a building up here," I snapped at Selene, who was still grabbing bits of paper.

She glanced up at me, snatched up the last pieces of paper, and hurried out of the building to join the others.

I crept back slowly, sweat running down my back from the effort of holding the building in place, until I was far enough away, and then I released the magic. As predicted, the entire side of the house rushed to fill the void I'd created, collapsing a large portion of the building onto itself.

I lay on the dirt as Petra tended to a clearly angry Kurt, and Selene looked over Lucie, who hadn't moved since the explosion.

"Nate, there are some medical supplies in the car," Petra said. "Can you go get them?"

I nodded and forced myself to my feet. The pain in my stomach and hand was manageable, but it made my movements slow and gingerly. I hoped it was just because of the exertion of using my magic, but it felt as if I'd been stabbed with something silver; a burning sensation tore through my insides, and I wondered if something else had struck me at the same time as the piece of Magali.

I made my way around the side of the ruined house and stopped at the BMW, opening the boot and removing the small medical kit; mostly bandages and ethanol, with some scissors and tweezers. Hopefully, it would be enough to help Petra bandage up Kurt and enable her to take a look at whatever was causing the pain inside me.

I turned to walk back to the group and found myself standing before Helios, who grabbed me by the throat and smashed me up against the BMW, denting the roof and smashing the driver's window.

Before I could fight back, he plunged his fingers into the hole that Magali's bone had made and began to move them around, eventually pulling them out, covered in my blood. Roars of pain filled my ears, while my body screamed at me in agony. He held a small squashed item between his fingers, the remains of a chain dangling down by his wrist. He released me and I fell to the ground, gasping for breath as my body no longer fought against me.

"I knew I smelled something of her in your wound. This was Magali's silver locket," Helios said, his voice calm and matter-of-fact. "I might have let you suffer, but it had a picture of her husband, Jean, inside it. I think Magali would like it back." He tossed it back into the now burning building.

He grabbed me by the throat again, lifting me off the ground once more and throwing me aside. I collided with the barn twenty feet away and crashed back down, looking up in time to see that Helios had fully transformed into his dragon-kin form. Like his sister, his eyes were reptile orange, but his scale-covered skin was a brilliant gold. He opened his mouth, dislocating his jaw as fire roared from it. I rolled aside but discovered that he was aiming at the barn, not me. Where the fire had touched the wood and metal, it had simply melted through, as anything near it burned brightly. Another stream of fire left Helios's mouth, and it wasn't long before the entire barn was engulfed. I staggered back from the inferno, putting distance between myself and the floating figure in front of me.

On Helios's back two huge red and orange wings beat softly, keeping him floating a foot above the earth. Each flap of his wings blew up dust and dirt, swirling it around the front of the barn.

"What am I to do with you?" Helios asked me.

"You could tell me whatever your plan is."

Helios laughed, a deep, rich noise. "No, I shan't be doing that. I can't kill you either. Selene is rather fond of you, I believe, and I don't want this to become a quest for her to gain revenge for your death."

I got back to my feet, wincing as I moved. My hand was almost healed, but the silver wound in my gut would take several hours.

"Whatever you do, get on with it."

Helios smiled. "I will leave you with a warning. Flee from Germany; let me continue my plan, and escape with your life, because if you continue upon your path, I will kill you."

It wasn't even open to consideration. "Can't let you murder innocent people."

Helios sighed. "Selene said you were stubborn. I do not wish to kill you or your friends. But I will if you get in my way. I will even kill Selene if need be."

"You'll find that a difficult proposition," Selene told him as she walked around from the side of the building.

"Ah, little sister, you're in no position to threaten me." He raised his hands to the sky. "The sun is in full bloom. This is *my* time."

"We'll free you from Pandora's thrall," she said.

"Thrall?" he asked and beat his wings furiously, rising several meters above us. "Oh, my dearest Selene. I sought Pandora out. I agreed to help. I'm not in her control; I'm her partner." And with that he flew off across the fields at high speed, leaving Selene and me dumbstruck.

CHAPTER 15

Mittenwald. Now.

Once the buses loaded with school children had left the compound, the guard and guardian who had been involved in releasing someone from Tartarus had been brought up to the outside and marched into a building at the far end of the compound's perimeter. They'd joined a third man, the same one who had stabbed Cerberus.

Hades walked off to talk to them. I can't imagine it would be a pleasant experience for those who'd been caught.

"It's been quite the eventful day."

I turned to see a large, barrel-chested man standing a few feet back. His hair was cut so short to his head that he was almost bald, and he wore an expensive black suit, with a thin black tie and dark boots.

"Kay," I said and stretched out my hand.

His eye twitched slightly before he took my hand and shook it. Kay, as Arthur's brother, was one of the oldest of the Knights of Avalon and, like all knights, was afforded the title "Sir." Most didn't bother using it, but some, like Kay, insisted on its use. However, while I was never a knight, nor afforded the same status as one, I was also in a position within Avalon that meant that we were of equal footing. In reality it meant nothing more than that we were all the same rank, which wound Kay up, as not once did I ever call him anything other than Kay.

Kay was not a popular knight, or a popular person for that matter. He was rigid, tough, and in many cases a bully and tormenter to those who didn't stand up to him. After the Second World War, he was placed in charge of the Shield of Avalon, or SOA. The organization had two main roles: to protect Avalon and its people and to root out internal threats. Kay changed the name to Sword of Avalon and set about making it more proactive, pissing off pretty much everyone in the process. He pushed forward ideas to give the SOA more power and control, losing a lot of trust from those in Avalon and terrifying those outside of Avalon's immediate touch. Eventually, he realized no one was paying attention and changed the name back in the late 1980s, although I'd heard that he'd changed little in terms of policy, just how it was being implemented against the masses.

"You're the dignitary?" I asked.

"Yes, it was my turn. Looks like I picked a bad day. Or a good one, depending on your point of view. You missed Hyperion. Just before the attack started, he was lifted away. Shame—I'm sure he'd have liked to say hi."

I ignored the taunt, my usual course of action when talking to Kay. "Any chance the people who did this knew you were coming today?"

Kay shrugged. "It's not a private trip. I'm sure they could have discovered it. You think this was done at the same time on purpose?"

"Makes sense, although the bigger question is who."

Kay turned to a man standing behind him. His Faceless. The Faceless were officially bodyguards to the more prominent or powerful members of Avalon society. They were utterly loyal in all things involving their masters and carried out orders with a detached coldness. I knew from experience that many did more than just protect their master; some killed or stole for them, destroying their master's enemies or threatening them as needed.

The Faceless are named as such because they all wear a mask that entirely covers their face. Only their master knows their true identity. The design of the mask is up to the master, although all of them cover the entire head, fastening around the neck so as not to be removed, and with a dark material in the eyeholes so that none of the Faceless's features are detectable.

The mask of Kay's Faceless was all black with a red swirl around the right eye. The nose protruded slightly, with two holes for the wearer to breathe normally. The mouth was a smooth piece of polished metal with two rows of three holes in it, presumably to allow the wearer to talk and be heard normally. The mask was raised in certain parts around the eyes and nose, giving it the appearance of a monster. Kay always did like to make people afraid.

I took in the Faceless. He was about a head taller than Kay and almost as broad. He wore dark leather armor, the buckles and straps holding an unknown number of weapons, and his black cape hung to his knees. Faceless capes had a strip of silver sewn into the hem. I'd seen them used as weapons in the past, and they were more than a little useful in a pinch.

"Is there a problem?" Kay asked me as the Faceless glanced my way.

"It's just been awhile since I last saw one in full get-up," I said.

"He's magnificent, isn't he?" Kay said with more than a little pride. "Every ounce of his armor and weaponry is custom-made. He's a one-man army."

"I'm sure he's very imposing. It's almost a shame none of the attackers got out today; he'd have been most helpful in their capture."

"Death," Kay corrected. "He doesn't capture. The standing order is to kill. Unless I say otherwise."

"He's very impressive," a woman said from behind the Faceless, her tone suggesting that she didn't find the Faceless impressive at all.

I moved aside and caught a glimpse of Lucie as she walked toward us. She wore a gray suit and flat black shoes, with her hair tied up in a bun, and looked maybe ten years older than she had when we'd worked together in Germany so many years previously.

"Good to see you," I said as she shook my hand.

"You too," she told me.

"You shouldn't mock my Faceless, Lucie," Kay said with a tight smile.

Lucie turned back to Kay. "Maybe if you had him around less, people would be more inclined to trust you."

"I do not need the weak to trust me, and the strong do not need to fear me."

"Do you have a minute?" Lucie asked, leading me away from Kay, who went back to his hushed conversation with his own personal slave.

"So, you're working for Avalon?" I asked after we put some distance between the others and us.

"Sort of. I work for the SOA as Kay's second."

"Really? You're the deputy director of the SOA?"

"You sound shocked."

"I wouldn't have expected Kay to be someone you'd want to work with."

"Been there for nearly ten years now. I work behind the scenes, mostly doing tours like these and checking internal security protocols. I still haven't found *her*. I came close a few times, but she's always eluded me. I'll get her, though—I promise you that." The tone in her voice gave me no reason to think otherwise.

"So, you work with Kay. That doesn't sound like a lot of fun."

"Mostly I do all the work, and Kay . . . well, you'd be surprised at how much Kay does . . . or rather doesn't do."

"I've known Kay for over sixteen hundred years, and if there's one thing I can say, it's that very little surprises me about him." The last I knew, he spent most of his day drinking, sleeping with attractive women, and avoiding as much work as possible.

"We're not friends, me and you, Nate. Not really anyway. Never will be. Too much has happened and too much has been said, but I trust you. So heed this warning. I've heard rumblings of someone planning to change our way of life. I think Kay knows more than he's letting on."

"You think he's involved?"

Lucie shook her head. "I think he's gotten wind of who it is, and he's waiting to see how that wind blows, to figure out where he needs to be. He loves his brother, and he would never betray him. But that doesn't mean he's against keeping information to himself to aid his own long-term plans."

"You think he knew something was going to happen today? He knew about the attack?"

Lucie nodded. "He didn't agree to come here today for the fun of it. I saw the look on his face when he heard about the krampus. He was as surprised as everyone else, but he never goes to these things unless he thinks something is going to happen that will help him in some way."

"What does he think he's going to gain from this?"

Lucie shrugged. "No idea. I'm just warning you. I heard you killed a Faceless."

"Rumors again?" A few years ago, a member of the Faceless by the name of Reid infiltrated the LOA and got several good people murdered, almost allowing a madman to kill Tommy and Kasey. Reid was dead now. I'd put several bullets in him after he'd challenged me. I'd never liked the Faceless, but after that, I found myself trusting them even less.

"Except, we both know that this one is true, as do several members of their order. You know they don't like it when one of their own is killed. You made some powerful enemies that day."

"They won't attack me without their master's permission."

"That's true, but not all of their masters are your allies. Many in Avalon would gladly see you fall, given a clear opportunity."

"I'll make sure that doesn't happen. Thanks for the info."

She placed a hand on my shoulder. "Take care. Find out who did this and shut him down. Fast." And with that she walked off.

I watched Lucie walk off toward Kay. They chatted for a moment before she wandered away to the offices on the far side of the compound. She was right; any kind of friendship with Lucie was out of the picture, but I trusted her judgment, and if she said she'd heard whispers about something that was supposed to be happening, that wasn't to be ignored. And it meant that Kay probably knew more than he was letting on. I sighed; I really didn't need the added complication of Avalon politics.

I made my way over to the long, single-story building where the three captives were being questioned, and noticed Hades walking back toward the building where the school children and dignitaries had been housed. I considered shouting over toward him, but he was issuing orders to various members of his guard, and I thought better of it. Sky was sitting with her back against a small hut nearby, her eyes closed. She was either asleep or trying to remain calm, neither of which I wished to interrupt.

A guard left the nearby building, rubbing his hands. It wasn't difficult to see that there was a lot of blood on them.

"Did you get anything?" I asked as he walked past.

"No, not a damn thing."

"You mind if I try?"

He glanced behind me and I turned to see that he was looking at Hades, who was several hundred meters away.

"No, that's fine. Good luck."

I thanked him and entered the building, finding it deserted. The building itself was designed to house prisoners and interrogate them. It consisted of a wide corridor with six doors that had been placed at equal distance apart. At the far end of the corridor was a seventh door, a monitoring station that used the hidden cameras and microphones inside each of the other six to record and catalog everything that was divulged or confessed to.

Each of the six cells was of a good size, with no furniture inside and runes inscribed into the very brick to ensure escape was impossible. I'd seen a fire elemental once try to burn his way through them. He'd only succeeded in leaving slight marks by the time he passed out from exhaustion after several hours. Once you're in those rooms, you don't get out unless someone lets you.

The cells all had solid metal doors with a drop-down flap that allowed anyone to check on the inhabitants. With the doors closed, the soundproofing ensured that you couldn't hear anything that was said or done inside. It was an eerie sensation to walk into a building of complete silence when I knew that people were only feet away from where I walked.

I pushed open the first two doors and found both rooms to be empty; the third and fourth were the same. The fifth door opened just as easily as the previous four, but the stench of blood was overwhelming.

I stared at the prisoners as I realized there was no longer anyone to question.

The three men were sitting on wooden chairs in the middle of the room, their feet tied to the chair legs. Their hands were tied to the back of the chairs, making them defenseless against whoever had killed them.

I reached the first man, the guardian from the realm gate control room. As far away as he was from the realm gate, his powers were no longer able to protect him from the brutal assault that had been launched on his body. He'd been stabbed over and over, drenching him in red. I moved his head slightly, and it flopped back. His throat had been slit with enough force to almost decapitate him.

I reached out with my necromancy, hoping to get some answers, but while I could feel his spirit, I could do no more. He hadn't died fighting.

So I moved on to the second man, the siphon I'd fought with, and found him to have been given the same treatment. And the third man, the one Cerberus and Sky had subdued, had received the same as the other two.

I exited the room at a sprint, running down the hallway with magically enhanced speed and bursting out of the building's front door.

"Hades!" I shouted, using my air magic to carry the words across the compound.

I continued to sprint as fast as my body allowed. All the time I watched helplessly as the guard whom I'd spoken to earlier removed a blade from a sheath on the small of his back and launched himself at Hades. For a split second, I thought that was it—that Hades was never going to react in time.

But Hades is always one for the unexpected.

He reached out one hand toward his assassin, and the guard stopped in midair. He snarled at his boss, the words lost well before they could have reached my ears. Hades's expression went from sadness to rage in a second. He flicked his hand slightly, and the guard flew aside, colliding with a nearby wall and crashing through it.

I reached Hades just as another guard pulled the attacker from the rubble of the wall by his hair, dragging him across the compound and throwing him at Hades's feet.

"The prisoners are dead," I said. "He killed them all."

Sky was at my side a few seconds later and was quickly filled in while Hades continued to stare down at his would-be murderer.

"You were one of my people," Hades said. "Why would you do this? Why would you kill them?"

"They knew the end result of being captured. I *will not* betray my liege," the guard snarled.

"How many more of you are there?"

"I will not betray my liege," the man repeated.

"You have to know that if you don't answer my questions, this will end badly for you," Hades told him and crouched down so that he was almost face to face with the assassin. "I am not the monster of legend. I do not wish to watch you suffer while there are more important things I could be doing."

The threat appeared to just wash over the guard. "I will not betray my liege."

Hades stood up. "Last chance. Who sent you, who did you set free, and why are you doing this?"

"I will not betray my liege" was the rote reply.

Hades nodded. "Your name is Wayne Branch. You are married, with two young children. I hope you said your good-byes this morning."

"I will not betray my liege!" he shouted. "There is nothing you can do to me."

"Not me," Hades said and glanced my way. "Hellequin, can you talk to this man?"

Wayne looked over at me. "There is *nothing* you can do to me."

"Yeah, keep telling yourself that," I imparted, and Hades motioned for two more guards to drag Wayne away.

CHAPTER 16

I left Wayne to stew for half an hour. Hades had given very clear instructions that while he was to be searched for weapons and his clothing removed, he was not to be unduly harmed in any way.

"I'd rather Wayne wasn't killed," Hades said when he found me leaning up against the outside of the interrogation building, drinking a bottle of water.

"Why aren't you asking him the questions yourself?"

"He's clearly not afraid of me. I figured maybe he would be of you."

I glanced at my old friend. "Bullshit."

Hades's smile was ever so slight. "I could go in there, tear his soul out of him and force him to answer my questions, but there are runes on his body. I asked Lucie to take a look at him, and she tells me those runes will cause his soul to collapse should a confession be forced out. The three he killed have the same runes. Apparently, it's a good thing I didn't try to take their souls either. From what she tells me, I wouldn't have enjoyed the experience."

All necromancers can absorb souls to increase their power and learn about the person whose soul they absorb. In my case, I can use the soul to enhance my magical power and to heal quicker. Once absorbed, the soul breaks down into pure energy, but the necromancer retains the memories he or she gained from absorbing it. The more powerful necromancers, like Hades, could also use the information to learn something the person knew, like a new language.

Unfortunately, Lucie's assessment made removing the soul impossible without destroying the evidence the prisoner held in his mind.

"That would have to have been created by someone with serious power," I said.

"None of those killed or captured fall into those categories."

"So you want me to take a more physical approach to getting the answers."

"Do whatever you need to do, Nate."

"You sure?"

"Their existence threatens my family and my people. *Whatever* you need to do." He paused for a second before continuing. "Kay and his friends are wandering around my compound. I can't order them to be kept in one place. That wouldn't breed good relations with Avalon. So instead, I'm going to keep them on a very tight leash and only let them see what I want them to see. They want to talk to my staff; Kay isn't convinced that all of the traitors have been routed out."

I mentioned Lucie's earlier comments about Kay.

"Either way, that man in there knows who was involved," Hades said.

"You hope."

"Yes, but right now that's pretty much all I've got. I need to know that my people are trustworthy, and I need to keep Kay from putting his nose where it isn't wanted. Besides, the prisoner said he won't betray his king. We need to know who that is."

"So, why Hellequin? Why not just me?"

"Because, old friend, despite your shouting that you're Hellequin from every tall building you could find over the last few years, it still hasn't filtered through that Hellequin and Nathan Garrett are one and the same. Also, I can tell Lucie that Hellequin was involved, so that when she writes her report she uses your alias."

"Spreading the name Hellequin as an ally of yours just a little further."

Hades placed a hand to his chest as if wounded. "I'm not above using a little manipulation to help in the long run." He glanced at my hand. "Do you know what that rune on your hand is?"

I'd actually forgotten all about it; over the last few hours, the ink from the pen I'd used to draw it had faded, and parts of the rune were now missing. "It lets me bypass runes that shut off my magic."

"How do you know it?"

"I have no idea. I just . . . do. I woke up on the realm gate control room floor and just knew what rune to draw to allow me to access my magic."

He took my hand and stared at it. "We will need to discuss this further at another time. But know this. That is no ordinary rune; use it sparingly. The more powerful the rune, the more energy it takes to activate."

"You mean it might let me bypass security, but at the same time it'll drain my energy from me?"

"If it's what I think it is, yes. It'll drain you dry well before you manage to exhaust yourself."

I was suddenly grateful that the mark had faded. "Thanks for the info. Also, I used lightning."

Hades nodded slowly. "The grimoire worked then."

"No, that's the point. Before I woke up, I couldn't do it—not properly. But I switched it on like I'd been using it for years. How did that happen?"

Hades thought for a second. "I don't honestly know. It was fortuitous; I can say that much. Be careful if any other runes just happen to pop into your head, though." He checked his watch. "It's been awhile now. I think it's time for you and Wayne to have your conversation."

I stood and brushed myself down. "You sure you want this to be me?"

"Sky would kill him in a second, Cerberus is injured, and Persephone is not a woman given to hurting people who can't fight back. She would release him to battle and kill him in the process. There's no one else on base I trust as much as you to get the info we need without killing him. He wants to die. I would rather not give him that privilege until he's of no further use."

I mulled over Hades's words in my head for a few seconds. "Thanks. I think. One question: Hyperion was here; he left just before the alarm went. Any chance he was involved in what happened?"

"Hyperion was only here to be part of the same group as Kay and Lucie. Avalon wanted to send an independent to verify their findings."

"And they sent Hyperion?" I asked, incredulous.

"He's been here many times to visit the Titans. I couldn't refuse him this one time just because Hera arranged for him to be here."

"How many of the attackers today were your guards?"

"A dozen. The rest were external people with smuggled uniforms and weapons. Even so, twelve is far too many."

I turned and entered the building, telling the two guards standing outside room 4 to leave and wait outside.

I watched them go; then I removed my shoes and socks and entered the room.

Wayne was stripped naked. Black swirls had been tattooed over his heart. He'd certainly prepared for the eventuality of being taken prisoner.

He was tied to a chair, as I'd asked. The chair was similar to the ones he'd murdered his comrades in, but I'd also asked for someone to bring in a metal table, which was sitting to one side of the room. Knives and various bladed instruments had been placed on it.

"Well that's very helpful," I said as I took a second wooden chair from the side of the room and turned it around so I could rest my arms on the back as I sat.

Wayne didn't even look my way, just continued to stare at the wall.

"The knives," I said after a second. "It was helpful of them to bring them in here. I didn't ask for it. Hell, I might not even need them, but even so, it's nice that they're so conscientious about our needs."

Wayne was a slight, but hairy man. Thick dark hair adorned pretty much every part of him.

"Not into manscaping then?" I asked with a chuckle. "Seriously, it looks overgrown down there. I always thought the ladies liked a little bit of tidying up, but did your wife go for a more natural look?"

Silence.

"This is an uncomfortable conversation for you, yes? You're probably a little nervous about the fact that I went from discussing knives to talking about your cock. Yeah, I can see why you'd be worried about that.

"Okay, how about the fact that your entire body is covered in blood? I assume you got undressed, killed your friends, and then dressed yourself. Your clothes are spotless, on the outside at least. Nice plan to wear three long-sleeved T-shirts, though; that was good thinking. Stop the blood from soaking all the way through quickly."

Wayne glanced over at me and then went back to looking at his spot on the wall.

"Okay, Wayne. We've established that you can hear me. So, I'd like to know who sent you, how many of you there are, and who you helped escape today."

Silence.

"Do you know why I asked them to strip you?"

Silence.

"It's because it's humiliating. Being stripped naked and tied to a chair. You strike me as a man who doesn't like to be humiliated, who likes to be in control. Is that why you tried to kill Hades? So you could go out on your own terms."

Silence.

"Why did you kill those men? Was it so they couldn't say anything? Did they fail because they got caught?"

Silence.

"As your new friends were tearing your clothes off, I was chatting to those who worked with you. They said you were a bit of a hardass and a stickler for the rules, but that you didn't like being told what to do by anyone other than people you deemed worthy."

I stared at Wayne for a few seconds and then got up, walked over to him, and flicked him on his nose. Hard.

He winced and tried to move back, but couldn't go anywhere as the chair was anchored to the floor. He settled for giving me an evil glare.

I returned to my chair. "Now that I have your attention, we'll continue. You're a sorcerer, yes? A fairly low level one from the sound of things. Nearly a hundred years old and only learned one type of magic. But you've been with Hades's organization for ten years. Before that you were in Avalon. Your record with them is sealed. My guess is you were BOA, the Blade of Avalon. They tend to seal records at the drop of a hat, and you look like the military type. Probably born into it; your father was Avalon too. Pretty high up in the pecking order as things go; not enough to have a say in the running of the place, but well thought of. He died two years ago. As did your mother. Someone strapped a bomb that contained pieces of silver to their car and killed them. Pretty fucked up way to kill someone. So, why'd you do it?"

Wayne glanced up at me with a faint look of surprise on his face. "That's quite the grasp at straws."

I smiled slightly. "The second you glanced at me, I knew that you'd killed them. You didn't have the guts to do it face to face, though. Was it in preparation for this? Something like what you and your friends did today takes a lot of planning. Did one of them figure it out? Maybe they threatened to go to Avalon and expose you?"

Silence again.

"Look, it would be better to talk to me now, when we're on the easy questions. Why'd you kill your parents?"

"They were traitors to the cause."

"What cause? Is that the *liege* you were talking about earlier?"

"They didn't believe as I do. My father was having me investigated. I found out. He had to go, as did my mother."

"And what about your liege—who is that?"

"You're not worthy to know."

"Okay, let's try something easier. How many more of you are there working for Hades?"

We went back to silence.

"Who did you release today?"

Wayne resumed his wall-staring contest.

I reached into my pocket and removed a photo of an attractive woman with short strawberry blond hair and a welcoming smile. She held two young children in her arms, a boy and a girl; neither was older than four, and both were the spitting image of their mother.

"Nice family," I said.

Wayne's attention was suddenly on me, his expression one of rage. "Don't you speak of them."

"Why not? We could get them up here and all have a chat? Maybe I could make you watch as I asked them questions."

Wayne grinned. "Be my guest."

"No, I don't think that'll be happening. I'm not some sort of monster who would hurt children to get to you. Besides, we already know what you did. We sent people to your house and they found your family. I have a question for you: As you went around at night and murdered your wife and kids, were they asleep? Did they know that the man who was meant to protect and love them was about to betray them in the worst possible way?"

I removed a few more pictures from my other pocket. "These were taken earlier. You used your water magic to drown your family as they slept." I dropped the pictures showing his dead family on the floor in front of him.

"It had to be done," he whispered. "I waited until they'd fallen asleep before ending it. They would have been put through hell after my death here. I couldn't have that. They suffered little compared to what Hades and his friends would have done to them. I'm prepared for whatever comes next."

"You selfish little prick," I said as anger flowed through me. "You're not going to die here. Trust me on that. No matter if I have to give you the kiss of fucking life myself, you *will not* die here."

"Then what can you possibly threaten me with?"

"Oh, death isn't scary. We all have to stop at that particular destination at some point. No, death isn't the scary bit. It's the journey that gets you there, that's what *you* should be scared of."

Wayne laughed. "Do your worst."

I walked around to the rear of Wayne's chair and used a blade of hardened air magic to cut through his bindings. He rubbed his wrists as I went and sat back down. "Do they hurt?"

"When I killed my family, for the briefest of moments, I really wished I could have made my wife suffer more. She would have been so shocked to see me there, killing her. Forcing the water to take up all of the space in her lungs."

"Ah, you're trying to piss me off enough that I'll kill you."

"My boy, he opened his eyes as I killed him. He knew what his dad was doing."

And I broke. I snapped forward, grabbing Wayne by his throat and dragging him away, slamming him into the nearest wall, squeezing his neck the whole time.

"I did say I wasn't going to kill you," I said in his ear, the words dripping with anger. "Never said anything about this." I created a blade of fire and plunged it through his wrist, severing the hand. I held the fire against the stump, cauterizing the wound as the smell of burnt flesh filled my nostrils, and Wayne's screams filled my ears. He bucked and thrashed, but my air magic wrapped around him, keeping him still and ensuring he didn't escape.

When I was done, I picked up Wayne's hand and showed it to him as tears fell down his cheeks. "I'm going to take one piece of you at a time until I get the answers I want. Who sent you? Who did you release today? How many more of your friends are there?"

He coughed and tried to get his breathing under control. "None—I was the last," he said at last, cradling his stump in his good hand. He watched in horror as I threw his severed hand across the room.

I squeezed the still raw stump that used to be attached to his hand, and he screamed out, swearing he was the last one. I believed him. "Excellent. One question down. Two to go. Who sent you? Who did you release?"

"You forgot something," he sneered. "Those who sent us here today will want to finish the job. Maybe that werewolf and his lovely daughter. She's about old enough to have some fun with. I'm sure—"

I grabbed Wayne by his hair and dragged him over to the metal table, using my free hand to swipe the blades onto the floor with a loud clatter. I pushed the side of Wayne's face against the cold metal. "It doesn't matter who you threaten. Eventually you'll tell me what I want to know. Who sent you?"

"Hades's whore of a red-skinned daughter," he said with a maniac laugh.

I wrapped a tendril of air around his ear and snapped it shut, tearing part of the lobe off. Blood spilled freely over his face and onto the table.

Once Wayne had finished cursing me, blood covered the side of his face. "My friends are going to find that little werewolf bitch and have their way with her."

I picked his head off the table by his hair and slammed it back down, over and over again. "You dumb fucking idiot. You think I'm playing? You think this is a fucking game? Well, if that's the case, let me know when you want me to stop."

I used air magic to once again make sure that Wayne couldn't wriggle, and then I placed one hand on the table and started to heat it up. It went from cool to the touch to white hot within seconds and soon the sound of sizzling flesh on the side of Wayne's face accompanied his shrieks. He screamed and tried to get free as my magic kept his face pushed down against the heat.

"Don't know!" he shouted after a few minutes of agony. "Don't . . . know . . . who sent us. Not . . . name. Vanguard. Vanguard."

I pulled Wayne away from the table, leaving part of his skin attached to its still hot surface, and dropped him on the floor, where he whimpered softly.

"The Vanguard sent you?"

"We are Vanguard," he managed between ragged breaths.

"You're Vanguard? That's not possible."

"But we . . . we are. I promise you."

"But you're meant to be pro-Avalon. How does attacking Tartarus accomplish that?"

"I only did as ordered. We all did. We don't know why."

I grabbed Wayne's arm, causing him to cry out as I lifted it up and saw the mark of the Vanguard on his armpit. That small shield with two swords creating a "V." He wasn't lying.

"Who gave the order for today's attack?" I asked.

"The siphon," Wayne said. "He was my commanding officer."

"Who did you release today?"

"A god!" he screamed at me, seemingly finding new strength with which to fuel his rage.

I knelt down next to him on the floor, placing my knee on his and pushing down. "Which one?"

"Just kill me," he said, wincing. "I won't tell you. Just kill me and be done with it."

I glanced at the watch on my hand. "I've told you repeatedly that you're not going to die today. But, if you're still unwilling to tell me everything I want to know, I'm sure I can change your mind. We've got a long way to go yet, and you've still got plenty of body parts."

CHAPTER 17

How long were you in there?" Sky asked me as I walked into the mess room, which sat beside the garage. It was usually full of people, but today the mess was empty except for Sky, who sat on one of the many dark-purple sofas, eating a sandwich.

"Is that good?" I asked.

"Got angry. It was either eat this sandwich or punch someone."

"That's an odd set of opposites," I said with a slight chuckle, grabbing a chocolate bar from one of the many trays that sat beside the table where the food would normally be served.

"You didn't answer my question."

I glanced up at the clock above the serving station. "Forty-five minutes."

"Did he tell you everything you wanted him to?"

I tossed the unopened chocolate bar back onto the tray. "No, but most of it."

"You changed your clothes."

"Had blood on mine. These were in one of the lockers and they fit." The dark-blue jeans and orange T-shirt with a picture of an anime-style death on the front were the first things I'd found. My underwear, socks, and shoes were still my own, however. There are some things I'd rather not borrow from a stranger.

"You want to talk about it?"

"He killed his wife and kids," I divulged. "Drowned them while they slept. The young boy woke while his father was murdering him." I paused as my mind replayed the images of their bodies, and I only continued when I'd pushed them aside, "He used his own water magic to drown his family."

Sky was silent for a while. "I find it odd that killing and torturing are just things you do, but that you have problems with the slaughter of innocents."

I turned to look at Sky. "Not in the mood for jokes."

"Wasn't one. If you didn't care when fucking cunts like Wayne Branch murdered their family in cold blood, I'd be a lot more concerned about you."

"In my life I've seen countless people murdered, families torn apart, children . . . horrific things. But hearing that their own dad or mum or anyone who was meant to protect them did it? It always gets to me."

"How badly did you hurt Wayne?"

I opened my mouth to speak, when Persephone stormed in, saw me, and walked over. I stood, prepared for what I was sure would be a fight about me going too far. Instead, she hugged me tightly, holding me against her, her hand pressed against the back of my neck.

"Are you okay?" she asked.

"We've done that bit," Sky said with a smile.

"This isn't a joke, Sky."

"I'm fine," I said and saw Sky take a bite of her sandwich instead of saying whatever retort she'd planned.

"The wife and children will be buried with honors. Hades is arranging it."

"What did Kay and Lucie have to say?" I asked.

"Lucie is still talking to Hades, and Kay has left. He was less than happy that Hades decided to use Hellequin in this matter and was even angrier that he wasn't allowed to see the prisoner."

"What will happen here because of that?" Sky asked.

"That's what Lucie and your father are discussing. When I left them, Lucie was advocating her going to Tartarus to ascertain how he escaped."

The second I'd left the interrogation building and had seen Hades standing there, his guards all nervous and concerned as I dropped Wayne Branch's hands onto the ground, I'd spoken only one word: *Cronus*. Tartarus is a massive place, and the residents there live freely, for the most part. It could have taken days or weeks to figure out who'd escaped.

"I'm going too," Sky said.

"Yes, you are," Persephone told her. "You're going to be Lucie's guide."

"Me too," I said. "I need to see how it happened. I need to know where he's gone and what he plans on doing."

"This doesn't involve you, Nate," Persephone said. "You can walk away."

"No, not anymore."

We stared at one another for a few heartbeats; then she smiled. "I assumed you'd say that."

After I'd spent time with Wayne and heard what he'd done and why, there was no way in hell I was going to just walk away from it. I was going to find the people responsible, and I was going to make sure they paid.

Hades entered the mess room a few seconds later.

"Can we have a moment alone?" Hades asked his wife and daughter, who both got up and left the room.

"I've never seen you do that before," I said.

Hades sat in Sky's vacated chair, motioning for me to be seated opposite him. "Oh, I'll tell Persephone everything later. But right now, I need to know what Wayne told you. And not just Cronus's name."

I sat down and sighed. "He was tasked, along with those who died here today, to keep you busy while a smaller team went in to get the realm gate open. There were other teams too, to ensure that no one tried to use the lift to get to the realm gate, but Tommy and I took them out. Another man he couldn't identify—the sorcerer from the control room, I imagine—took one of the guards into Tartarus and retrieved Cronus. The guardian gave information to Cronus so he could escape from this compound. Wayne didn't know the means of Cronus's escape or even how they got past the guards on the Tartarus side.

"The attackers were supposed to either escape or die here. When three were captured, Wayne took it upon himself to end them so they couldn't talk. He expected you to kill him during his botched assassination attempt. He was given no information about where to regroup, just told that he would be contacted. Presumably with a bullet to the head."

"And who is his liege?"

"No idea. He didn't say, and trust me if he could have he would have. My guess is someone has forcibly ensured that he never utters the man's name. That's a level of power that's fucking scary. We're talking Merlin level of power to remove a person's name but still have that person be referred to as something else. It's usually all or nothing. If someone with less power had done it, Wayne wouldn't have even been able to say the word 'liege,' let alone have any idea who he was talking about."

"You believe he knew his liege?"

I nodded. "He mentioned it over and over."

"So, we don't know why Cronus was released or who ordered it, or what they want him to do? We're not exactly neck deep in information here."

"We know it was Vanguard, which makes no sense. They're pro-Avalon—they're almost zealots in their devotion to them. They normally attack Shadow Falls or someone who has denounced Avalon, but you're an active and powerful member of the Avalon council."

"You think they were being used, like those people in Maine last year?"

I shook my head. "Those in Maine weren't real Vanguard. They were being told what they needed to in order to ensure they'd behave. They'd never set foot in a Vanguard training camp, let alone been allowed to join. The Vanguard are extremists, but they're not idiots. No, these guys are the real deal. Wayne has the tattoo. Ink with liquid silver in it. Burns like hell, but it won't ever fade like a normal tattoo."

"You took his hands," Hades said after a moment.

"He wouldn't give me what I needed. Taking his second hand was what made him give up Cronus. Before then he was just giving me tidbits of info about how long he'd worked for Vanguard or why he was never supposed to get married. They've been planning this for a long time—years."

"That's not why you took his hands and cauterized the wounds to ensure they could never be reattached."

I looked at my old friend, and I knew he wasn't going to let it go until I'd told him why I'd done it. "He used those hands to hold his family while he told them he loved them, to wipe away their tears and share their joys. Then he used those same hands to murder them all in one of the worst betrayals imaginable. He doesn't deserve to keep them. That's why I took them."

"Kay wasn't happy."

"Kay once flayed a man alive in front of his family and forced them to eat their lunch while he did it. Kay can go fuck himself."

"That was pretty much my response too. Still, he was less than happy about the use of Hellequin. I assume Kay knows you and Hellequin are one and the same."

Very few of the knights knew I was Hellequin. Until a few years ago, the fact that we are one and the same wasn't exactly widely known to anyone but a handful of people. Hellequin was the shadowy killer of monsters, someone to be feared, and someone without an obvious allegiance. Nathan Garrett was the guy who worked for Merlin. Sure, people knew that I was a killer, that I'd been highly trained and was capable of taking care of myself, but the two beings were seen as different entities.

"Kay only found out a few centuries ago, just before I buried the name. He just isn't happy that someone else was as feared as he was. But his reputation was down to cruelty and bullying, whereas mine was down to a more primal force. Kay could never do that. He doesn't have the patience. Do you think he was involved, then?"

"I wouldn't be surprised. He comes across as a mindless brute, but he's incredibly smart, with a lot of ears to a lot of surfaces." Hades paused for a moment. "So are you okay?"

"Why is everyone asking me that?"

"Well, you walked out, said one word, and then went for a shower and came in here. You said nothing else to anyone, until, I assume, you spoke to my daughter, who could probably get a conversation out of rock."

"As I've told everyone else, I'm fine. I was angry. Really angry. Angry about what he'd done and how he'd done it, and about the number of dead that releasing Cronus will cause if he's not stopped. I needed to get Wayne's blood off me. It stained me having to be that close to someone who had betrayed so many."

"You want to go to Tartarus, I assume?"

I nodded.

"Good. I need your help on this one. I know the prisoner said he was the only one, but I can't risk anyone else betraying me. Publically, I'm not about to start accusing people of anything, but between you and me, you're one of the few people I trust to find and bring Cronus back without screwing me or anyone else over. You think you're okay with that?"

"I think I'll manage," I said with a slight smile. "How's Cerberus?"

"He'll live, although he's going to have a limp for a few days. He wanted me to tell you that you have his permission to kill whoever allowed Cronus to escape Tartarus. I'm not exactly convinced he was kidding."

"Do you think Cronus is long gone?"

Hades nodded slowly. "Probably. Although I've no idea how he would have gotten across the compound without someone spotting him. I'm hoping someone in Tartarus will give us a clue as to his whereabouts, or at least tell us whatever the hell he's after."

"Rhea's our best bet."

"Agreed. We do have a few plus sides, though."

"Oh, this should be good."

"Well, Mr. Smart-ass, Tartarus limits a person's power, which means that Cronus is nowhere near up to full strength. He's also been gone a long time and so has no idea about a lot of the world around him, which means the second he does something stupid, we'll know."

"Except the second he does something stupid, Avalon and all of her allies and enemies will know too."

"Yes, that's what I consider to be the exceptionally fucked-up part."

"Hera. Once she learns that Cronus is out, she's going to petition everyone in Avalon for her to have a say in running this place. She's been after it for years, and you kept her away with Pandora."

"That's certainly something in my head too. Lucie has agreed not to file the report for seventy-two hours. By then we either have Cronus recaptured, or Hera and her friends will be gearing up to march into this compound and take Tartarus as her own personal playground."

I stood up and stretched. "We'd best make sure that doesn't happen then. How long before we're ready to go?"

"Ready when you are. I've sent guards down to the hotel. Those kids will never know what happened here until they're long gone, and in the meantime, I don't want them or their parents concerned."

"How are Tommy and Kasey?"

"Tommy was pacing around, last I heard, and Kasey is fine. She was talking to a witch by the name of Emily Rowe, a lovely lady who seems to think highly of you."

"That's because I'm a fucking delight."

Hades chuckled. "Ah, my friend, no matter what horrific events take place, you're still able to make me laugh. I shall always value that."

As time was of the essence, we were down at the control room within a few minutes of Hades and me walking out of the mess room, to be met by Sky and Lucie.

Outside the control room itself, a platoon of guards stood, all of whom were being yelled at by a very pissed-off Cerberus.

"Cerberus?" Hades asked.

Cerberus dismissed the guards and, when we were alone, turned to Hades. "Boss."

"Aren't you meant to be in Medical?"

"Don't like to lie down for long," he said, shaking the metal cane he was carrying. "Don't want the men and women under my command to think I'm taking it easy."

"Weren't you stabbed with a silver blade?" Lucie asked.

"Yes, I was," Cerberus said, as if that were no excuse for being lazy.

"Is everything ready for the departure?" Hades asked as we all walked into the control room.

The room held six people who were trying to get equipment working or looking over the gate itself, and another six who appeared to be armed enough to liberate a small country. They stood to the sides of the room and did their utmost to appear not there. It wasn't working very well.

Considering the fourteen heavily armed guards that we'd passed on the way from the lift to the control room, the extra six seemed to be overkill.

Hades walked off and whispered something to one of the guardians looking over the realm gate, before turning to the six guards. "You can all go wait outside, I'm here now, and I think we can let these people work with a minimum of guns pointed around them."

The guards all walked out, and Cerberus looked annoyed.

Apparently, Hades had noticed it too. "Cerberus, you are an incredible warrior and have been at my side for thousands of years, but you're taking out your anger and frustration about what happened by posting an obscene number of guards. I assure you, we're quite safe."

"You'd have said that a few hours ago," Cerberus said as Hades reached him.

"Yes, and I'd have been wrong. But I can't let those who are loyal to us feel like we're constantly waiting for the moment they choose betrayal. We have enough shit to deal with without having my people believe they're not trusted."

"Yes, my lord," Cerberus said, although he clearly disagreed with the assessment.

"And don't call me that; it sounds stupid."

Cerberus smiled, only slightly, but enough to show that Hades had won and gotten his way.

"Are we ready?" Hades asked the guardians around the realm gate.

A lanky woman, with long green and yellow hair glanced back. "Yes, Lord Hades, all is prepared."

"What about the explosives?" I asked.

"They weren't detonated on the other end," the woman said. "No danger to the gate. Looks like we caught the attackers before they could do any serious damage."

"Okay, let's get this done then," Cerberus said and motioned for the guardians to begin.

The tall woman placed a hand against the runes carved onto the wood and rock that made up the gate's structure, and the dark green runes burst to life, bathing the room in color. The mass of emptiness in the center of the gate changed to a shimmering mass of different colors, which shifted and merged before revealing Tartarus.

"I know I worked at the compound, but I've never been to Tartarus," Lucie said. "Not in all my years here."

"Well this is going to be quite the educational trip then," Sky said, and we stepped through the realm gate.

CHAPTER 18

Tartarus does not look like the fiery pits of hell where the eternal souls of the damned are sent to burn for their sins. However, on first entering the realm, it does look ominous and dark. A giant lake sits a little ways from the realm gate, and an almost constant, thick mist rolls over the still waters, coming up as far as the realm gate and blocking out a lot of the brightness from the sun. Once past the mists, though, the realm opens into one of rolling hills, mountains in the far reaches of the land, and immaculate coastal areas where the inhabitants swim and fish. It's pretty close to a lot of people's idea of paradise. So long as you're okay with the griffins.

In mythology, griffins have the head and front half of an eagle and tail and back half of a lion. They walk around on all fours and guard treasure. They're also about as intelligent as your average eagle or lion and tend to eat people who get too close.

The reality is about the same except for two key areas. First, they're smarter than most people I know and can speak without problem, usually in many languages; and second, they walk around on two feet. The top half is all eagle, with beak, feather-covered arms and hands that look like bird feet with talons the size of kitchen knives, while their bottom half is lion, with tail, fur, and paws.

They're an odd sight when you first see them, especially considering they have wings, the span of which would comfortably put two full-grown men in its shadow. It's odder still when you consider that they're the apex predator in Tartarus and often go hunting some of the larger creatures that live in the forests and mountain ranges that are scattered over the landscape. And Hades put them in charge of guarding the realm.

That's not to say the griffins are cruel or particularly unpleasant, but they have a very rigid code of honor and see things in a very black-and-white way. On the one hand, it means that everyone under their charge is treated the same, but on the other, it means that those who cross them are dealt with harshly, no matter the crime. In the thousands of years that Tartarus has been a place to put political prisoners and those who are allowed to live out their lives away from Avalon, there have been three executions. None of those killed received anything close to a good death.

The realm gate on the Tartarus side sat on a small platform beside a large hut made from massive stone blocks and wood cut from the forest behind the gate. Stairs led a hundred feet down into the mists below, where people waited to be taken to the inhabited part of the realm.

One of the griffins stood outside the hut beside us, its golden and silver armor gleaming in the mist. Over six feet tall, and hugely muscular, with dark brown feathers on his top half and an almost caramel-colored fur on his lower, the griffin, like all of his kind, was an imposing sight. The fact that he carried a spear that was in excess of his own height by a few feet, with a razor-sharp blade on one end, enhanced the impressive sight, as did the shiny black talons and bright red beak, both of which could easily have torn flesh from bone.

"Welcome to Tartarus," the griffin said. The first time I'd arrived in Tartarus, I'd expected them to have screechy, high-pitched bird voices, and when they spoke in their own language to one another, it did sound like birds chirping, with the occasional low growl. But when speaking in a human tongue, they copied the accent of the language and spoke in a much lower humanlike tone, which gave the slightly weird side effect of them all having British accents when they spoke English.

Lucie introduced the three of us, and the griffin bowed his head slightly. "My name is hard to say in anything but our own language. But you can call me Lorin."

"What is your language called?" Lucie asked, the interest in her voice clear to hear.

"Ah, we don't have a name for it. Someone once suggested that we name it after the eagles in your land, but we are not eagles, we are something more." Lorin turned to me. "We have not met before, although you did meet my father, Arandi, on your last visit here. Apparently there was some . . . difficulty with one of the residents."

"Atlas," I said. "He's probably not going to be happy to see me."

"He is rarely happy to see anyone, but I've been told he's working at the mine. You should manage to avoid him, unless he discovers you're here and decides to make his presence known."

"And what happens then?" Sky asked.

"We will intervene if necessary, but you will not kill him." Lorin stared at me. "I know of your reputation."

"How's your father?" I asked, quickly changing the subject.

"Good, thank you. I'll let you make your way. The boatman will take you across the lake to the village."

Sky nodded. "Thanks very much."

"I have one question," I said, as Sky and Lucie began to set off. "How'd Cronus escape?"

Lorin appeared less than happy to have to answer the question. "We don't know." His eyes narrowed in anger. "It's being investigated. As soon as we know, a report will be given to Hades."

"Thank you," I said and walked off to join Lucie and Sky. We descended the stairs, the mist becoming thick and obscuring the farther down we went, until you could barely see more than a foot or two in front of your face.

Lit lanterns had been placed every few feet on the journey down, which helped enough to ensure you didn't slip on the uneven steps as you made your way down to the shore of the lake. The farther down we went, the less the sun penetrated the mist, and it wasn't long before the lanterns were the only source of light available to us.

A pier had been built on the shoreline, and a small hut placed on top with a rowing boat beside it. Dozens of lanterns on wooden poles lit the area, but it was still dark and foreboding. I'd been to more inviting crypts. As we got closer to the pier, the sound of the water lapping against the bank of the lake became all you could hear; then a voice, shrouded in the thick mist, called out from the pier.

"Who goes there?" The voice was deep and rumbling.

"It's Sky," she called back. "We need to get across the lake."

"You'd best come here then," the voice responded.

The three of us made our way onto the pier, where we were greeted by a tall, thin man wearing dark leather armor that reminded me of the Faceless I'd seen back at the compound; an identical cloak billowed out behind him as the winds on the pier whipped around us. A long, gray beard obscured most of his face, but his eyes burned the color of molten metal.

"Charon," I said as he looked each of us over.

"Is that Nathan Garrett? I figured you'd be dead by now."

"Sorry to disappoint," I said with a smile.

"Not disappointed, son, just surprised. You had a tendency to piss off the wrong people."

"It's more of a hobby these days," I stated. "You still ferrying souls to and from this place?"

"We all have our penance to pay. This is mine."

"Why does he look so old?" Lucie whispered. "Isn't he the son of Erebus?"

The mention of the name Erebus made me remember something, a conversation I'd had recently, although I couldn't remember the details and wasn't even sure if it had actually happened or I'd dreamed it. I pushed the thought aside. "The water ages you," I told her. "It's why no one swims in it. Even the tiniest bit ingested will cause you to lose part of your life and age you. Charon has done this job for over four thousand years, since the Titans were first placed here. He took their side in the war, so his punishment was to ferry people. Forever."

"And he drinks the water?"

"I started to," Charon said, making Lucie jump slightly. "I'm not deaf, girl."

"Sorry, I didn't mean to offend," she told him.

Charon waved her off. "I'd been doing this job for a millennium when I decided to start drinking the water and take my own life by the natural death of old age. Unfortunately, I learned too late that it takes a percentage of your life, until it can't take anymore.

It doesn't kill you—just ages you physically. So now I'm stuck looking like this."

"I'm sorry," Lucie said.

Charon shrugged. "I still have the energy of someone much younger than I appear. Hades tried to suggest I get someone else to do the ferrying, but I'll be damned if I give someone else my boat."

"What's with the armor?" I asked.

Charon smiled. Maybe. There was a lot of beard in the way, so it was hard to tell for sure. "Hades gave it to me. I needed something better than those old rags I used to wear. I've got a dozen sets. Apparently Avalon keeps giving them to Hades for a Faceless he doesn't have."

Hades had never liked the idea of the Faceless and refused to have one join his organization, despite repeated requests by Avalon members for him to have one. I always got the impression that he found the idea of a masked man at his beck and call distasteful and counterproductive to having people place trust in him.

We all climbed down into the sizeable wooden boat, which could have easily fit twenty people. Charon removed the thick rope used as the mooring line, before sitting in the middle of the boat and taking hold of the grips on the two wooden oars. He used one to push the boat away from the dock, and within a few seconds he'd settled into a slow, deliberate pattern of rowing.

"What's that?" Lucie asked as we moved farther away from the shoreline into the deep waters of the lake.

She was sitting beside me and had spotted something on the shore beside us, just before the narrow neck of the lake opened up into the massive expanse of water between the main town and the realm gate.

I turned my head and immediately spotted the thirty-foot hill nearby. Two huge wooden crosses sat atop it.

"That's Traitors Mound," Charon said, following my gaze. "When Pandora escaped she had two griffins help carry her across the lake and get her through the gate."

"Are the griffins guardians too?" Lucie asked. "Did one of them open the gate for Pandora?"

"A few are," Charon told her. "These two griffins overpowered the guardian there, and one of them opened the gate. Pandora bewitched some people in the control room, which allowed her to escape into your realm. The griffins returned back to town to accept their fate. They were crucified on that mound, their wings nailed to those crosses, their screams easy to hear over the lake as their *questioning* took place."

"Why?" Lucie asked. "Pandora bewitched them too, so why go so far? I didn't hear about any of this after what happened in Germany."

"They weren't bewitched," I said. "Griffins can't be affected by magical or mental abilities. It's why Tartarus was chosen as a place to put the Titans. They helped her of their own free will."

"It's been kept quiet, something that will continue," Sky said, glaring at Lucie. "The fact that two griffins knowingly helped Pandora escape is not something Avalon needed to be aware of."

"They could have helped," Lucie said.

"But they wouldn't," I informed her. "They'd let it slip, and certain people would start to involve themselves, and the whole thing would fall apart. The rest of the griffins hate those two. Not just for betraying them, but for betraying Hades. They'd never work for anyone else—especially if Hera tried to start telling them what to do. Four griffins died because of Pandora's escape; getting Avalon involved would have made things worse."

"Four?" Lucie asked.

"Griffins mate for life. If one mate dies, then normally the other refuses to eat or drink while it mourns. They never take another mate, although sometimes they do recover from that grief."

"And sometimes they don't," Sky finished for me. "The mates of the betrayers died—never recovered from what happened."

"You know I won't tell anyone," Lucie said, "but I still think you were wrong to keep it from Avalon."

"Maybe," Sky said. "But it would never happen again."

"Except maybe it has," Lucie said. "Maybe the griffins helped Cronus escape."

Charon stopped rowing. "Don't even suggest anything of the kind. If any griffins heard you say that, they'd cleave you in two. Unless you know for certain that they were involved, don't even mention the idea."

"Do you have any idea how he got across the lake?" I asked.

Charon shook his head. "The only things I know are that he didn't swim and he didn't fly. There's no way the Griffins knew he was missing. So he had to have avoided them. No idea how, though." Charon resumed rowing, and the only sound for the remainder of the hour-long journey was the oars as they gracefully touched the water.

CHAPTER 19

The mists stopped a few hundred feet before we reached the shore, revealing a green field next to a sizeable pier. Griffins flew over the buildings that dotted the bank of the lake, occasionally landing and entering one of them. The guard barracks were placed there for a very good reason: everyone entering had to walk through them to get to the town, which was about a mile away, next to the coast.

Charon stopped the boat and moored it to a post on the pier, motioning for us all to leave.

"Are you staying?" Lucie asked.

Charon nodded. "I have a hut just over there." He pointed off toward a two-story building a short distance away from the rest. "It's why it takes awhile for someone to arrange to come here. Those on Hades's side have to send word to the griffins to go get me, and then I start rowing."

"Why don't you live with the rest of *them*?" I asked. "I've always wondered that."

"I just prefer the company of the griffins. They aren't good at political bullshit. Just like me. There's too much vying for power in the town. Everyone wants to control their little piece of whatever power they can get. Atlas with his damn mines; Rhea,

the farmland; and Cronus, whatever he's allowed to take. I don't
have the energy for it."

"We'll see you in a few hours then," Sky told him, and he
turned and walked off toward his home, leaving the three of us
on the pier.

The walk to the town took about ten minutes, with the landscape becoming greener every minute. A lush forest bordered
one side of us, and open grassland the other, until we were a
few hundred feet from our destination. The large houses of those
who lived there were easy to spot. Some of them were three or
four stories high and made from carved stone and wood. They
reminded me a little of ancient Roman villas, with immaculate
columns standing at the front of each house.

The grassland faded away, replaced with a golden beach that
led to some of the clearest ocean water I'd ever seen. I wasn't
sure if anyone had ever tried to sail the ocean and see what else
was in the realm. I imagined a few had, but no one ever gave any
indication of wanting to be anywhere else.

"Wow," Lucie said. "You could sell real estate here and
make millions."

We walked under a huge archway that was held up by two
20-foot tall marble columns. The word "Atlantis" had been etched
onto the arch—the name of the town. The Titans had destroyed the
original Atlantis during the war with the Olympians. Hundreds of
thousands had died during the few days of attack, which had led to
the end of the war; Zeus and his forces had been outraged by what
had happened and had retaliated in the most horrific way possible
with the creation of Pandora. After the fighting was over, Zeus had
forced the Titans to take the name as recompense for their crime, a
reminder of how the Titans had brought about their own downfall.

A gigantic golden statue of Zeus had originally stood at the entrance, always looking down on the Titans in their new homes, but Hades had it moved and melted down well before I was born. Ensuring your prisoners were behaving was one thing, but antagonizing them *every single day* with a gleaming thirty-foot statue of the person who had defeated them was only going to end in rebellion and more death.

There were plenty of people living in this Atlantis who had been born and raised here, and even more who had decided that living under the gaze of the griffins was infinitely better than living under the gaze of Avalon. So the town of Atlantis had swelled from a few hundred at the end of the war, to over twenty thousand by the end of the twenty-first century. This feat was even more impressive considering that none of the inhabitants were human and anything that uses magic has a reproduction rate that makes even giant pandas look positively prolific.

The red, brick-paved streets weren't teeming with people, but we walked past several on our way to Rhea's house, which was on the far side of the town, another half-hour walk from the entrance. I'd considered getting horses for each of us but had decided I'd rather not have everyone know of our arrival, and three strangers riding horses through the town would have set tongues wagging.

Each person we passed eyed us suspiciously until they realized that Sky was in our ranks and decided we were no longer a threat. Most of the people in Tartarus would recognize Hades and his family by sight, and their regular appearance in the realm meant that there was probably nothing to be concerned about. Even so, a certain tension was in the air. The fact that Cronus had escaped had probably not been lost on the inhabitants, and they were likely worried about the reaction that it would cause.

We reached a large town square where a number of market stalls had been set up along one side, closest to the ocean. Various foods, some of which I'd never seen before, were being sold and bartered for by dozens of people.

Farther down the street I could see the blacksmith who made many of the weapons used by both the griffins and inhabitants of the town. Owning weapons was not considered a transgression because many people still hunted for meat and fish.

An ornate fountain stood in the middle of the square, water rising up through the blowholes of five large whalelike creatures, the sprays crisscrossing over one another before returning to the basin below to begin their journey anew.

We passed by and I ran my hand through the cool water. From the moment we'd made our way through the fog, the sun had beat down on us, unrelenting, but never unpleasant. A lovely breeze came over the town from the ocean, bringing with it the scent of saltwater, something I'd always really enjoyed.

"You okay?" Sky asked.

I nodded. "I'd forgotten how amazing this place is."

"It is beautiful," Lucie said and smiled at a few teenage children who ran past, shouting to one another in ancient Greek; one of them nearly bumped into her and gave her a nervous grin. Everyone who lived in Tartarus was required to learn some of the modern languages, but most dropped back to their traditional language whenever possible, as though it were a safety blanket made entirely of words.

"What did they say?" Lucie asked.

"'Who's the pretty lady; she must be very hot,'" I said.

Lucie looked at her bandaged hands and arms, and then down at her long dark dress that would soak up heat like a sponge. "It is a bit warm," she admitted with a slight smile.

"The houses are cooler," Sky told her. "They use runes to remove most of the heat."

Lucie's eyes opened wider. "Really? How interesting, I'd love to talk to people about that. Do they have an enchanter in town?"

Sky shook her head. "Apart from you, I've never met one who lived longer than a human."

Lucie shook her head as if that were information she should have guessed, and we started off again.

We'd almost made it to the edge of the square when a deep, booming voice called out, "Nathan Garrett, you goddamn cur."

I stopped walking and turned to see Atlas standing in one entrance to the square. Everyone between us stopped what they were doing and quickly moved aside or dashed past me.

"I knew you'd be back one day, you pissant," Atlas roared. He was well over seven feet tall and probably weighed over four hundred pounds of pure muscle. His gargantuan arms and chest were covered with dirt from the mines he worked in. They were bare, except for a leather strap across his chest that held his battle-axe in place on his back. His brown hair cascaded over his shoulders. He looked every inch the god people used to consider him to be.

He unstrapped the battle-axe from his back and swung it lazily onto the ground with a resounding crunch as it split the bricks the blade touched.

"Can't we do this some other time?" I asked him.

"You'll make time *now*," Atlas roared. "You took her virtue and will pay for your transgression."

"To be fair, her virtue was a distant memory *well before* I ever got near her."

To the shock of no one, that didn't help matters at all.

Atlas roared with anger. "Face me in combat, little man. I'll even tie my hands behind my back if you like."

"Atlas, this is a bad idea," I advised.

The big man laughed. "You think you can take me?"

"If we were back in my realm, I wouldn't have a hope in hell. But here, in Tartarus—well, I wouldn't put money on you coming away unharmed."

"You arrogant little shit."

"You misunderstand," I said and took a step toward him. "You're not at full power here. For thousands of years, you've not been at full power, and while your half-giant side allows you to retain your permanent bulk and strength, you'd be fighting me, a sorcerer who just arrived and whose power hasn't yet been affected by this realm. I think the fight would be a lot closer than you'd care to admit. I think if you took a moment and allowed yourself to consider this, you'd agree that fighting me now would be dangerous."

Atlas took a step toward me, radiating hatred at my words. I sighed and removed my T-shirt.

"Ah, you can't possibly match these." Atlas laughed and flexed his biceps.

"No, I just don't want blood on my clothes twice in one day," I explained as I tossed the shirt to Sky.

"We don't have time for this," Sky said.

"No," I agreed. "We don't."

"Can you take him?"

I shook my head. "Probably not."

"So, why try?" Lucie asked.

"I might not be able to win, but I can lose with style. You two go on and find Rhea."

"I'm not leaving," Sky said.

I turned back to Atlas, who had a big grin on his face. "I'm going to break every bone in your body."

"You're welcome to try."

Atlas dropped his axe to the ground and sprinted toward me, swinging his massive fists—and hitting nothing but air. I used my air magic to increase my speed and dashed around the angry Titan, slamming a ball of fire into his ribs, forcing the flames to engulf one side of his body.

Atlas jumped back, but instead of putting out the fire, he just swung another punch, something I wasn't expecting at all. I didn't move quickly enough, and he caught me on the shoulder with a blow that took me off my feet and threw me back against a nearby wall.

The flames immediately vanished, and a murderous glare settled in Atlas's eyes. He took a step toward me as I readied my lightning.

"What the hell is this testosterone-fueled nonsense?" shouted a woman who'd walked into the middle of the square, between Atlas and me.

"It's my right," Atlas told her.

She spun on the much larger man, and he visibly shrank. "Get out of my sight, Atlas! The next time you feel the need to threaten guests in our realm, you'll spend two weeks working out on the fishing boats."

Atlas shook his head violently. "Rhea, he took my woman's honor!" he shouted and pointed at me.

"Your woman wouldn't know her honor if it came up to her and bit her on the ass. Now get out of my sight before I lose my temper."

Atlas retrieved his axe from the ground, glared at me, and stormed out of the square.

Rhea walked over toward me. Her long, almost white hair fell down her back. She wore a thin blue dress that hugged her figure. In human terms, she appeared to be maybe in her late forties or early fifties, although she was probably close to ten thousand years older than that. "Nathan," she said, "you're a goddamn idiot."

I nodded my head slightly and got back to my feet, wincing slightly as I moved my arm. "In my defense, I had no way of knowing that Atlas would marry the girl a decade after I slept with her."

"Your defense nothing," Rhea snapped. "You antagonized him back then, all those years ago, and he doesn't soon forget. You'll have to fight him one day. And when that comes, no one will be here to stop him."

"A day I'd like to avoid for a while if I can."

"Yes, today we have other matters to discuss." She turned to Sky and hugged her tightly before introducing herself to Lucie.

"Come, the three of you. I assume you wish to discuss my husband's recent absconding. And how I'd quite like him back without him being killed."

CHAPTER 20

We rode horses to Rhea's villa at the far edge of the town limits. Any notion of remaining undetected had ended the second Atlas had decided to single me out.

The villa was a sprawling three-story structure with more rooms than I could possibly think of uses for, and gardens inside which you could have easily fit a football stadium. It was the very definition of opulence, a fact that was even more obvious as we made our way to the side of the building and noticed the view from the cliff top we found ourselves on, looking down at the clear ocean two hundred feet below us.

"This must be the biggest house in the town," Lucie said as we took our seats under the shade of several huge trees.

"One of them," Rhea told her. "All the Titans tried to outdo each other when we first arrived. When the dust settled and everyone decided to behave with dignity, one of the first things we did was create a government. The griffins, our jailers, weren't really up to the task, and we couldn't wallow in self-pity forever, so it was up to Cronus to lead. Toward that end, he decided that our house should be apart from the rest of the Titans' and closer to other groups who had supported us."

"The griffins aren't your jailers," Sky said. "They haven't been for a long time."

"We are not permitted to leave this realm. They stop us. Therefore, they are our jailers. Doesn't matter how pretty the scenery might be; if you can't leave, it's still just a jail."

"Did you help Cronus leave?" I asked, deliberately stopping myself from using the word "escape" instead.

"No," Rhea said softly. "I like it here. We're left alone to live our lives."

"But you just said this is your jail," Lucie pointed out.

"And so it is, but it's also my home. We either deal with that or go mad wanting something we can never achieve."

"Hyperion got out of here; why can't others?" Lucie asked.

"Hyperion was a special case. He had something Hera and her friends wanted. I assure you, Hera doesn't want anything from Cronus or myself. Most of the people who live here would rather tear out her heart than work for her."

"Apparently Hyperion doesn't have that complaint," I said and could hear the anger in my voice.

"So I hear," Rhea said. "You should be careful around him; he's incredibly powerful. Even my husband would have thought twice before engaging him in combat."

"I'm not going to fight him," I admitted. "Doesn't mean I have to like him, though."

"Okay," Sky said, "we need to know why Cronus escaped and where he went."

Rhea poured herself a glass of something that looked like cloudy lemonade and took a sip as blue glyphs appeared on the back of her hand, creating ice cubes that clinked together as they fell into the drink. "I have no idea," she said eventually.

"Bullshit," Sky snapped. "You expect me to believe that Cronus told you nothing about his plans?"

Rhea raised an eyebrow and placed her glass back on the table that sat between the four of us. "If he'd told me his plan, I would have stopped him. I do not know where he is."

"How'd he escape?" I asked.

"Do you want facts or my theory?" she asked me. "Because I have very few of the former, but quite an interesting latter."

"What facts have you got for us?" Lucie asked.

"Cronus had help in getting free. There's no way to cross that lake without taking in at least a little of the water that ages you. Only Charon has a boat. And no, before you ask, Charon did not help my husband escape. Charon is loyal to those griffins and would see it as a gross betrayal."

"Did the griffins help?"

"Not a chance. After Pandora escaped, none of them would dare."

"So, how do you think he did it?" Lucie asked.

Rhea shrugged. "No idea. He wanted out of here long ago, but until Pandora escaped, he was content with his life. Once she got free, he began working in secret. He didn't think I knew what he was doing, but I'd see him trying to figure out how to get across the lake."

"Did he have any visitors recently?" I asked.

"Doesn't Hades keep a log of those who come and go?" she asked me.

I nodded and Rhea smiled; she knew that I just wanted her to confirm what I already knew.

"We don't get many. But Hyperion would visit Cronus fairly regularly. They'd chat away for a while, and then Cronus would seem calmer after. For a few days anyway."

"What did they discuss?" Sky asked.

"I assume Hyperion was telling my husband about his life outside of here and working for Hera. They remained friends even after Hyperion left."

"Could Hyperion have helped him escape?" I asked.

Rhea laughed. "Hyperion works for Hera, who would be the last person on earth to want my husband free. I doubt very much that he helped Cronus do anything except discuss the good old days."

"So, is that it?" Sky asked. "That's all the facts you have?"

Rhea nodded. "But the theory is much more interesting."

"Regale us," I said and drank some of the cloudy drink, which tasted more like strawberry than lemon.

"I think my husband has been working on his plan for a long time, since well before Pandora escaped. I think her escape was what lit a fire under him.

"I think if you walk along the coast for long enough, you'll come to a forest. In there, I think you'll find something that shows how Cronus managed to escape the lake. The answers are there."

"Do you know where he would have gone once he escaped this place?" Sky asked.

"I don't know *exactly* where he'll be, but I'll tell you where you can find him."

"And where might that be?" Lucie asked.

"Wherever that bitch Hera is. She murdered our son, and for centuries we've wanted justice. My husband will undoubtedly be close to Hera, tracking her wherever she might be. That way he can cut her fucking cunt heart out for what she did to our son."

We all sat stunned for a few minutes after Rhea's outburst and her subsequently walking away from us.

Lucie was the first to break the silence. "If that's true, we can't let him get to Hera."

"Don't see why not. Let him have a shot," Sky said. "The world would be better off without her in it."

"You think so?" Lucie asked. "Because I think the world would descend into war without her in it."

"How the hell do you get that idea?" Sky asked.

"Hera has one of the largest and most powerful groups on earth, comprising roughly fifteen percent of all voting power at Avalon. That's only second to the knights. In her group are Demeter, Aphrodite, Ares, Hephaestus, Dionysus, various children of each of those people, and their families, who include people like Selene and Eros.

"Many of Zeus's old allies were merged into Hera's conglomerate when he vanished. In that group, you've got powerful people from the Egyptian, Chinese, and Japanese lines. There's also the matter of the witches, who still get a voting block in Avalon; they're almost always allied with whatever group Demeter prefers. In short, Hera controls a huge amount of power and influence in the world, probably more than any other single person who isn't Merlin. If she dies, it will create a vacuum that will be fought over by everyone who thinks they have a chance of filling it. You really believe that Demeter or Ares would be willing to let someone else get that spot? There would be a massacre the likes of which we haven't seen in centuries."

"When Zeus went missing, there was nothing like that," Sky pointed out.

"There was still a mass exodus of people who didn't trust Hera and a lot more people whom Hera decided to get vengeance on for whatever slight they'd once given her. A lot of people died, and many more were cast away.

"If it happens now, with Hera's organization being so involved in the world market, it would make the recession of a few years ago look like a slight blip. Currencies would cease to exist, and countries would go to war, because any human who has a position of power in a government and who also happens to be Hera's puppet will be very quickly dispatched by those seeking to gain favor with whoever takes over after her death. It might only last a few years, a decade at the most, but in that decade a lot of bad things would happen."

"That's a worst-case scenario," Sky told her.

"We have to stop Cronus," I said softly. "There's no good scenario in which he kills Hera. The only way to stop what Lucie described from happening is to completely replace Hera and her immediate allies, like Demeter and Ares—to take them all out at once and replace them en masse. Cronus won't do that. And if he tries and fails to kill Hera, and she discovers he's escaped from here, she'll petition Avalon to get power in the dealings at Tartarus. She's done it before, and Avalon almost agreed. I doubt they'd be so keen to say no with Cronus running around."

Lucie and Sky stared at me. "Have you been considering how to take out Hera?" Lucie asked.

"When I was with Avalon, it was my job to figure out the weaknesses of other organizations. Hera's weakness is that she has no natural successor. She's privately named Ares, but that doesn't mean shit to the rest of them. You want stability, you remove the Olympians as one and have people you trust placed in their positions. There will still be a time of crisis, but without the constant in-fighting taking precedence over the running of her empire, it won't be so noticeable to the world market or Hera's other enemies."

"It scares me that you think about stuff like that," Sky said.

I shrugged. "It would be impossible to do. Or at the very least, impossible without the help of every other Olympian not tied to Hera, along with a sizeable portion of Avalon. Those groups aren't likely to band together anytime soon. Anyway, back to the problem: Cronus. He's after Hera, but where is Hera? And who helped him escape in the first place?"

"Maybe Rhea's suggestion about taking a walk is a good one," Sky said. "If Cronus had anything from an ally outside of the realm, he wouldn't keep it at his home. Not where Rhea might find it, surely."

"He isn't that stupid," Rhea said as she rejoined us. "He would have destroyed anything like correspondence from outside the realm."

I stood and walked closer to the cliff edge, looking out across the ocean. I turned back to the three women, who were still talking among themselves.

"How long is the lake?" I asked, interrupting them.

"Roughly a five-mile radius to get from any point here to the realm gate," Sky told me.

"How deep is it?"

"Just under two thousand feet," Lucie said. "Why?"

"I think I know how he managed to get across the lake."

"You care to share?" Rhea asked.

"Sure, I think he dug himself a tunnel to get there."

There are people in the world who like to be right all the time. They're the same people who, when you tell them something, immediately google it to see if you're right. And if you correct them, and they discover that you're right, they'll come up with an excuse as to why they're wrong. Those people are a real pain in the ass.

I've never been all that concerned with being right. If I'm wrong, someone will correct me, and if I'm right, then no one will. Being wrong is how we learn; it's how every species—human, sorcerer, or otherwise—has managed to survive without imploding. We learn from our mistakes. Saying that, I did feel a slight twinge of pride when Sky, Lucie, Rhea, and I found a hole some distance into the forest, exactly where I thought it would be.

It had been created at an angle; the hole at the surface was only big enough for someone to crawl into and was covered by ferns and branches. Once I got inside and ignited my night vision, I saw that it opened out considerably to allow someone to stand, with headroom to spare, after a few dozen feet in. I'd managed to walk about a hundred feet when I realized that the almost steplike earth beneath my feet had carried me down a considerably steep trajectory.

I tapped the wall beside me, which felt like concrete, and made my way back to those waiting for me; Sky offered me her hand, and helped me out of the hole.

"He dug himself a tunnel. My guess is, it's steep enough that it goes right under the lake. It must have taken him years to do this. The trial and error alone would have been infuriating."

"How did he do it?" Lucie asked.

"Like myself, my husband can use earth magic," Rhea told her. "But how did he keep it from collapsing?"

"And where did he put all the dirt?" Sky asked.

"You'll probably find that the earth was just pushed around," Rhea said. "The likelihood is that the lake is now considerably less deep at this point then it was when he started."

"It looks like he hardened some of the earth to create pillars and buttresses," I explained. "Some of that earth is a few feet thick. It probably had to be, to stop the water from ruining it."

"Can I assume you don't want to walk all the way through the tunnel to the other side?" Sky asked me.

"I'd rather not. Although if anyone just collapses this tunnel without doing it correctly, that lake is going to be a bit less full afterward."

"Why don't the griffins fly overhead here?" Lucie asked.

"Because I don't think anyone ever believed that some-one would actually try to tunnel under the lake," Sky told her. "Besides, even if anyone could have made it all the way through, they'd still have to get through the realm gate, and there's no one here who will open it. Not after Pandora anyway."

"Someone told Cronus exactly what time to be outside that realm gate, so when the people who attacked the facility got it working, he was right there waiting for them."

"And we're back to Hyperion," Sky said. "That's the only external visitor for anyone here who wasn't working for my fath . . ." She trailed off, pausing for a second. "Oh, shit. My father's employees come and go all the time. They're tracked through the gate, but they wouldn't have been monitored once they'd actually arrived here."

"So, one of those who attacked the compound today could have been feeding information to Cronus about what time to be outside the realm gate and what was going to happen."

"Cronus met with Hades's guards often," Rhea confirmed. "There's nothing out of the ordinary about that. It would have been easy to get information from them."

"We need to get back to the realm gate," Sky said. "We need to find Cronus, and my dad needs to be told what we've found out."

Lucie and Sky set off toward the town, but Rhea took my arm as I went to follow them, forcing me to stay with her. "Please bring him back to me," she said. "He won't have anywhere near his full power. He's been here for too long. It would take months, maybe years, for him to get his strength back to what it should be. If he tries to hunt Hera, she *will* kill him."

"I'll do my best, I promise. But he won't come easily."

"Then don't give him a choice. If he won't come back here under his own power, *make him.*"

CHAPTER 21

It felt like it took ages to get back to the town, find Charon, and make our way back across the lake toward the realm gate. The crossing was done quietly, as Sky, Lucie, and I were all deep in thought. Cronus had escaped to go after Hera. It was something that needed to be stopped. Quickly.

"Nathan," Charon said as everyone disembarked.

I stopped walking and turned to the old necromancer.

"Be careful. Cronus is not a man to cross without expecting retribution. If you're going to hunt him down, you're going to have to make sure you're on your best. Anything else, and he will kill you."

"I plan on trying my best to make sure that doesn't happen," I assured him.

"He's gone after Hera, hasn't he?"

"It certainly appears that way," I admitted. There was no point in lying—who was he going to tell?

Charon nodded. "I figured as much. He's not thinking right when it comes to her. It's a blackness in his soul that threatens to consume him. He blames her for getting Zeus and the Olympians to rise up against the Titans all those years ago, and on top of that he believes she murdered Zeus. Hell, everyone I know believes she was involved in his murder."

"Disappearance. There's nothing to say he's dead."

"You don't believe that."

"No, I don't. But there's no evidence to say Hera did anything wrong. No body, no witnesses—nothing. And until that changes, Avalon won't do fuck all."

"Which is why Cronus will do it for Avalon."

"I'll bring him back," I declared.

"Good. I'm not his biggest fan, but I'd rather see him here than know he's in Hera's clutches. I don't think he'd enjoy that visit too much."

"Take care," I said and ran after Lucie and Sky. They had ascended the stairs and were standing next to Lorin, who had already opened the realm gate.

The women saw me arrive and stepped through the gate. I paused for a second and looked at Lorin. "Cronus did this himself. I'm guessing if you search the area, you'll find the entrance to a tunnel he created under the lake. Everything was planned, to avoid alerting the griffins."

Lorin appeared relieved. "Thank you."

I stepped through the gate and was descended upon by Hades, who had a million questions, most of which were explained by Sky, Lucie, and myself as we made our way back up to the outside of the facility, only to discover that darkness had crept over the sky above us.

"I assume you're now involved," Hades said to me as we entered the still empty mess room.

"Without question. Although we need to know where Hera is so we can figure out where Cronus has gone."

"I'll check into that," Sky said.

"I need to go back to Avalon and make some inquiries," Lucie said, "You can't keep this secret. Not now. Kay is going to be the first person shouting from the rooftops that someone escaped here. He might not know it's Cronus, but I can't keep that to myself. I have to file a report."

"I know," Hades said. "I won't ask you to delay the report."

"The thing is, though, Avalon's a big place. Lots of people working there, lots of rules and regulations. Kay is going to have to take it to Merlin and the rest of the council. That's going to take a few days. If you can get Cronus back before that happens, there's going to be less of an immediate need for Avalon to take action. Most in Avalon don't want this place in anyone else's hands. Don't give them a reason to consider it."

"How long?" I asked.

"Seventy-two hours at most. If Cronus isn't caught by then, Avalon will intervene."

"We need to inform Hera too," Hades said. "I'll do that myself." He offered his hand to Lucie, who shook it. "Thanks for your help."

"Find him. Find him fast." Lucie turned to Sky and hugged her. "It was good seeing you again."

When she came to me, Lucie offered me her hand, which I took. "Good hunting," she said.

I nodded a thanks, and she walked out of the mess room.

"She still doesn't trust you," Hades told me.

"She never will. Not totally. I killed her brother. That's a difficult thing to get over."

"She understands why you did it," he said. "She just doesn't like it."

I stood and stretched. "I'm going to go try to get a few hours' kip at the hotel, unless you need me for something."

Hades shook his head. "I'm going to try to contact Hera, and on the off chance she doesn't take the threat seriously, I'll find out where she is and arrange for discreet security. I'll contact you when I know more. In the meantime, everyone go get some rest. You're going to need it."

I said my good-byes and decided to walk back to the hotel. It took about an hour, but it was relaxing, and the cool evening air gave me time to consider all I'd learned in the previous hours.

As I got closer, I saw a commotion outside. Several people appeared to be looking around for something. I wasn't a hundred percent certain what was happening until I heard one of them call out, "Chloe!"

I began jogging until I reached the hotel's front door, running inside, trying to find someone I recognized to ask what was happening. Fortunately, I ran into Tommy first.

"Didn't you get the messages?" he asked, a frantic tone to his voice.

I shook my head. "I walked back from the compound. Why are people looking for Chloe—has she run off? I said no one was to go out of the hotel." It wouldn't have surprised me if she had; she'd appeared considerably upset about her mother's behavior and probably needed time away from her.

"Don't worry. I told everyone that outside was off limits until the krampus was caught, but she's missing. She snuck outside with one of the other girls, who turned around for a minute and Chloe was gone."

"Did she walk off?" I hoped that the answer was yes, but I doubted it very much.

Tommy shook his head. "The other girl doesn't think so."

"Where is the other girl?"

"In the bar with a bunch of witches, including Mara."

"Okay, let's go talk to her."

Together, we walked into the bar to find a clearly terrified ginger girl sitting in a chair surrounded by adults, all of whom were either talking to one another, while ignoring the poor girl, or looking very concerned. Emily Rowe held the girl's hand and occasionally whispered to her. As one, they all turned toward Tommy and me, and their conversations ceased.

"What are *you* doing here?" Mara demanded.

"I'm here to help find your daughter," I told her.

She held my gaze for a moment and then nodded, stepping aside for me to talk to the ginger girl.

"Hey," I said to the girl on the chair. "We met before, right?"

She nodded. "You're Kasey's dad's friend."

"That's right. My name's Nate. I want to know what happened to Chloe tonight."

She glanced behind me at the witches, just for a fraction of a second, but it was clear that they made her uncomfortable.

"Can you get rid of them?" I asked Emily.

She nodded and then spoke to Mara, whose glare I was almost certain I could feel on the back of my neck. But I heard Mara begin to argue before Emily shut her down, and then Mara quickly agreed to leave. Soon after, the only people in the bar were Tommy, Emily, the ginger girl, and myself.

"So, what's your name?" I asked her.

"Donna Preston," she said softly.

"You want to tell us what you saw?"

"We snuck outside with some of the boys. We know we were told not to, but Chloe's mum had forbidden her to go outside, and that was like a red flag to a bull. Chloe was flirting with the boys, being all giggly and stuff."

"Do you know the boys' names?"

"We've already spoken to them," Emily said. "They told us they left the girls and came inside about an hour before Chloe was taken."

"What happened after the boys left?" I asked Donna.

"We sat and chatted. She wanted to talk about her mum."

"Anything else?"

Donna shook her head too quickly.

"Donna, whatever you say here won't get Chloe into any trouble. We just need to be able to find her. So, if you're keeping something back, it would be best if you could just tell us what it is."

"Well, are you sure she won't get in trouble?"

I nodded. "Promise."

"We were smoking," she almost whispered. "Her mum found out a few weeks ago and went mental, like totally freaked out and everything."

"But Chloe kept smoking?" Tommy asked.

Donna glanced behind me, at the exit to the bar, before nodding. "Said she needed it to deal with her mum."

"Did you have any?"

Donna glanced at Emily.

"It's okay; you're not in trouble," Emily told her.

Donna nodded again.

"Do you have any on you?" I asked.

Donna reached into her pocket and pulled out two cigarettes, which had probably seen better days, and passed them to Tommy's waiting hand.

"Can you track her with those?" I asked.

Tommy took a big sniff of the cigarettes before nodding. "I'd prefer something of hers, though. Something with a stronger scent."

"You can find her?" Donna asked, her delight obvious.

"I hope so. But is there anything else you can tell us? Did she talk to anyone she doesn't know? Did you see anyone around?"

Donna thought for a moment. "I didn't just turn away for a second," she confessed.

"What did you do?"

"I left Chloe alone for longer than that. Maybe five minutes. I went back inside to talk to one of the boys."

"That's okay," I said with a smile. "You've done nothing wrong. Did you see anything when you got back?" The girl hesitated.

"So what did you see, Donna?" I asked again.

"Chloe was gone. I thought she was just messing around, so I looked about and called her name, but I couldn't find her. I walked into the woods a little." Donna paused; all of the children had been expressly forbidden to enter the woods without an adult—there were plenty of places in the woods that were dangerous if you didn't know where you were going, and the denseness of them made it easy to get lost.

"I won't tell anyone," I said and turned to Emily and Tommy. "You guys keep that to yourselves, okay?"

Both nodded, which seemed to make Donna happier. "I heard something. Like a bell."

Horror dawned on me in an instant. "A bell, are you sure?"

Donna nodded vigorously this time. "Definitely, a bell. Although it sounded like there were a few of them all ringing at once. Something about them scared me, so I didn't go in any farther and just ran back to tell everyone that Chloe was missing."

I turned to Tommy, who instantly knew the creature that Donna was describing. The krampus was in the woods, and it had more than likely taken Chloe.

"Anything else?" I asked, as the rest of me was itching to sprint out of the hotel and chase down the monster that had snatched Chloe.

"Nothing, I promise."

"Thanks," I said. "You've helped a lot. I'm sure your teachers will want to talk to you, but we're going to go find Chloe now."

Emily took Donna out of the bar, and Tommy's need to do something immediately became evident. "We need to go—*now*," he snapped.

"You need to change first," I mentioned. "And we've only got those cigarettes to go on. We need something of hers for you to get a scent from too."

"I can help," Kasey said as she entered the bar.

"How much did you hear?" Tommy asked.

"Everything. I was hiding outside the bar, under a table. And I know you won't let me go, but I want to help. She's my friend. I got you this from my room. She left it there from last night."

Kasey threw a small T-shirt to her father, who caught it in one hand. "I need to change to my wolf to get a better scent off this. Thank you, Kase."

Kasey smiled and her dad kissed her on top of her head as he made his way past.

"Can you find her?" Kasey asked me.

"Almost certainly."

251

"Before whatever has her hurts her?"

I was silent for a heartbeat, but it was long enough for Kasey to realize I might lie to spare her feelings. "The truth," she demanded.

"I don't know," I admitted honestly. "But your dad and I will do our damnedest to make sure she isn't harmed."

Emily arrived behind Kasey, who turned and smiled before walking away. "I'm coming with you," Emily said. "I've spoken to the teachers and confirmed we might have an idea where Chloe is."

"Good, we might need your presence there once we find her. It'll be better if it's someone she knows and trusts. Are the teachers or hotel staff sending anyone with us?"

"They've got almost every available adult out scouring the forest now. They offered to send people to help us, but I figured they'd only get in the way."

"Probably true. If Chloe is with the krampus, the fewer people it can see as targets, the better. Besides, the three of us will make a lot less noise than a few dozen. What about the witches?"

"Mara and the witches have gone to their rooms. I think they believe that witchcraft might help."

"Will it?" I asked.

"Witchcraft created a krampus; I very much doubt it's going to do an awful lot to make this situation any better."

My smile was slight. "Once we have the girl, I'll find out who created this krampus. Then we'll deal with them too." I already had an idea about who was responsible, but couldn't be certain.

"You mean you'll kill them? I won't help you kill witches."

Kasey reappeared. "Dad's in the woods, says he's ready."

"You stay here," I instructed, and then I walked off with Emily toward the hotel's exit.

"You never answered my question," Emily said as we left the hotel and made our way south to the forest beside the lake.

I didn't look at Emily as I spoke. "Tommy's ready. Let's just go get that little girl back. We can discuss the rest later."

CHAPTER 22

The full moon and clear skies gave more light than would have been usual at this time of year. Even so, I used my magic to start my night vision well before I reached the forest where Tommy was waiting for us.

Werewolves, like all weres, have three forms—human, animal, and beast. The beast was the strongest, and most dangerous, of all the forms. In his beast form, Tommy stood on two legs, was easily over six feet tall, and probably weighed double his human weight. He was a machine designed to kill and fight. The monster inside him was closer to the surface, and once fighting started, it was more likely to try to convince Tommy to ignore his humanity and give in to the urge to kill.

Fortunately, as a gray wolf padded toward us, it was clear that Tommy had decided to use his wolf form. It was a harder form to maintain, but better for tracking and stealth. There was also less likelihood of the monster inside gaining any kind of leverage. Probably a good idea when dealing with what I was sure would be a very scared fourteen-year-old girl.

"You got a scent?" I asked Tommy, who nodded.

I enhanced my use of air magic in preparation for keeping up with Tommy. In his wolf form, he was faster than anyone in a human form could possibly be, certainly much faster than a natural wolf. The only way to keep up was to use my air magic to increase my own speed and agility, one of the benefits of air magic, just like earth magic users can increase their strength.

I turned to Emily. "You going to be able to keep up?"

She'd drawn runes around her eyes in pen. I recognized the runes as a way to let people see in the dark. It was old, and usually pretty unpredictable, rune magic; either whatever ink you used faded, along with your night vision, or it left you with permanent night vision until you got rid of the runes, sometimes screwing your vision up even more if you were exposed to bright lights before you got rid of them. But it was better than running head first into a tree. Witches tended to have whole books of runes, most of which they kept with the same level of secrecy as sorcerers did their grimoires.

"Let's go," Emily said, ignoring my question and motioning for us to get started.

Tommy didn't need telling twice, and with a quick sniff of the air, he bounded into the darkness beyond and started running at speed. Even with being able to use my fire magic to create a sort of night vision and air magic to increase my speed, it was still difficult to keep up with Tommy, who seemed to avoid branches and trip hazards as if they weren't even there.

I'd been running with Tommy a lot over the years, and normally it was a fun, exhilarating experience. But this time there was no joy in it. This time I expected the worst but prayed for anything other than that.

After about two miles of running at a speed that would have put Olympic runners to shame, Tommy slowed to a stop. I followed suit and crouched beside my friend, whose breathing had barely changed at all. Two or three miles was a short trip for him, even at full sprint.

I wanted to ask what he'd seen, but didn't dare interrupt him as he tried to figure out where Chloe's trail led. After a minute, he motioned toward something to the east of us and began trotting off, his movements slow and deliberate.

Another few hundred feet and he stopped again, sitting down and sniffing the air.

"What's he doing?" Emily asked from behind, as she caught up with us.

"Tracking," I said and turned to look at her. "Good run?"

Emily nodded and raised a finger for me to wait a moment. "Bloody knackered," she whispered and sat beside a large tree.

"You made good time, though," I whispered back.

Emily raised the leg of her trousers, showing the dark rune on her ankle.

I frowned. "You're going to exhaust yourself. You're not an enchanter; you keep on painting runes on yourself, and it's going to have serious repercussions; and I don't just mean the amount of your own life force you're using to power them."

"I'll crash after we get Chloe. She's more important than my immediate health."

I shrugged. It wasn't really my concern about how much witches burn themselves out by using runes to access magic. Witches usually only added a few runes to themselves, unlike most enchanters, who tattooed dozens over their bodies.

Tommy growled slightly and moved forward past some thick bushes. I followed at a crouch, and then Tommy just stopped as voices floated through the darkness.

"The girl okay?" a man's voice asked.

"I think so," a second man said. "She's quite the fighter. We couldn't have done this quietly without the big ugly bastard to distract her."

"You're telling me. My jaw's gonna hurt like hell tomorrow."

"Oh don't be such a pussy," the second man said with a chuckle. "How long is she supposed to stay here?"

"Couple of hours. Then she'll be miraculously found."

"And that creepy bastard isn't going to kill her?"

There was a brief pause. "No. It can't kill her without the witch's say-so."

"She's a creepy bitch too."

"Yeah, no shit. Holds a grudge like no one's business. You ever get the feeling that this is all personal for her?"

Another pause. "It's something. She's not part of the Vanguard, though. I don't trust her. I didn't like the fact that she made the krampus escape the compound, leaving our guys behind. Did you hear? None of our people got out of Hades's compound."

"Yeah, but that doesn't really matter anymore, does it?"

"Right, let's go," a third man said, and shortly after I heard the three men walk off into the forest, chatting quietly among themselves.

Tommy growled, low and menacing.

"Follow them," I said.

Tommy shook his head.

"Look, of the three of us, you can track the best. Just follow them and see where they go. Emily will grab Chloe, and I'll take care of whatever else is there. But this is our one chance to track whoever is behind this."

Tommy made a noise that sounded like grudging acceptance. He nudged my hand with his maw, the best way he had to wish me luck, and then slunk off silently into the dark forest once again.

I moved forward until I reached the edge of a clearing that contained a huge rock formation that stretched fifty feet into the sky. The mouth of a dark cave sat directly in front of me, and an orange light flickered inside. Someone, or something, was in there.

"What's the plan?" Emily asked as she crouched next to me. Her perfume was slight, but still noticeable; it was probably a good thing she'd not been able to keep up with Tommy and me.

"I'm going to go get Chloe out of that cave, and then you and she are going to run back to the hotel."

"You're sure she's in there?"

"We won't know until we look, but it certainly sounded that way."

"Can you beat a krampus?" Emily asked. "You could come back with us instead."

"Can't leave it out here, where it could hurt someone else. It seems to be under the control of whoever was behind the compound attack. Maybe I can get more details." I turned to glance at Emily. "Right. You wait here, and I'll either come out fighting a monster or have Chloe with me. You ready?"

She nodded, and I stood and walked into the clearing, remaining quiet and low as I made my way toward the mouth of the cave. The smell of blood and animal was overwhelming as I got closer and closer, until I was able to peer into the cave.

The cave consisted of a fairly narrow pathway that opened up into a huge cavern about fifty feet in. I crept down the pathway and crouched beside some rock that jutted out of the wall, to survey the cavern.

A large fire burned in the center of the open space, to one side of which sat Chloe. She sat hugging her knees and resting her chin on them, and kept her gaze firmly locked on the ground in front of her. In the far corner, half-concealed in darkness, was the whiteness of bone. I was too far away to see what the bones had once been a part of, but their very presence sent a shiver up my spine.

I kept looking around, trying to pinpoint the exact location of the krampus, but couldn't see it. I moved out of my hiding place and immediately spotted the monster at the far side of the cavern, opposite Chloe. It was a tall, well-built creature with a long face the color of an infected wound, and two huge, goatlike horns on top of its skull. Its mouth was full of tiny razor-sharp teeth and two massive canines, which it was currently using to tear into the flesh of the cow leg it held in one of its dark fur-covered hands, on the ends of which were long talons. The krampus's entire body was covered in thick, black, shaggy fur, although it had a long white beard of fur that stretched down from its jaw.

The unexpected crack as the krampus's strong jaws crunched into the bone made Chloe look up quickly. She moved her arms, and I could see the chains connecting them to the floor beside her.

The krampus tossed the bone toward the large pile, causing several to spill onto the ground, before selecting another piece of cow and tucking in once again.

I crept toward Chloe, sticking to the shadows that stretched along the sides of the cavern, and made it to her without being spotted. I placed a hand over her mouth, and she glanced up at me, the fear in her eyes softening as she realized who I was.

I removed my hand and created a blade of fire that I used to cut through the chain, catching it as it fell to ensure it made no noise louder than the krampus's.

Chloe slowly got to her feet, but as she took a step forward, she stumbled, kicking a rock and catapulting it across the cavern.

The krampus glanced up, saw me, and roared in anger.

"*Run!*" I shouted to Chloe.

Chloe froze, her gaze fixed on the monster getting to its feet.

"*Run!*" I shouted for a second time, jolting Chloe out of her trance.

She sprinted toward the exit, followed quickly by the krampus, but a blast of air magic slammed into its side, throwing it against the cavern wall and giving me time to run after Chloe.

I found the young girl outside, beside Emily.

"No time—*go!*" I shouted to them both, and to their credit, they quickly moved off into the forest as a roar of anger, accompanied by unmistakable bell ringing, resounded from the cave behind me.

I turned to see the krampus emerging from the mouth of the cave, the bells that were grafted to its flesh ringing with every step. Protruding from each of its wrists was a four-foot-long silver whip; it grabbed one in its hand and smashed the whip against the ground, causing dirt and grass to rain down around itself.

At one point, the krampus had been human, but dark magic had been used to transform someone with a wicked soul into a monster of pure malevolence. In the past, witches had almost always performed the ritual, usually as a form of punishment against someone who had wronged them. They'd transform the person and then send him off to feed on the children in nearby towns and villages, usually places the witch had been expelled from.

The fact that the krampus hadn't taken or hurt Chloe was a surprise. Whoever had created it had expelled a huge amount of power to do so, which meant a lot of people would have died in its creation. Using magic to change a person's form requires the darkest form of blood magic—human sacrifices. Sorcerers could use such means to create monsters such as the one before me, but there are other creatures that are easier to control, so sorcerers don't bother with a krampus.

The krampus stamped its hooves again and again, roaring at me while I stayed between it and the route Emily and Chloe had taken.

"You're not going to get them," I said through gritted teeth.

It rose to its full height, a good foot taller than my own five-eight, and flicked its whips in the air, slamming them into the ground several times.

"I can do that too," I said and created two whips of fire that trailed down from my hands, burning whatever ground they touched.

The krampus darted forward; the speed at which it moved was at odds with the size of the creature. It brought one of its whips down toward me, but I moved sideways, extinguishing one of my whips and blasting the krampus's hand aside, opening the creature to my other whip across its belly. The krampus dodged back in time for the whip to only kiss its toughened skin, causing the beast to roar in pain, but not doing much damage.

The krampus backed off, and I extinguished my whip. It was too fast to fight with whips, and I didn't want the confrontation to be long and protracted, if possible. Apparently, the krampus felt the same way, as it scuffed the loose dirt with its hooves and charged toward me.

I dodged aside, but it managed to grab me around the leg before a blast of air took its own legs out from under it and sent it tumbling into the nearby thicket.

I didn't have time to capitalize on the situation because the krampus exploded back into the clearing and aimed itself at me. Another blast of magic threw loose dirt into the air, blinding the creature, but it managed to flick one of its whips around my leg and, with enormous strength, pulled me off my feet and flung me into a nearby tree.

I surrounded myself with a dense shield of air, which took the brunt of the impact, and I dropped to the ground, sore but in one piece. The krampus stood in the center of the clearing, its dark eyes trained on me with ferocious intensity.

I took a step forward, and the creature charged once again. When it was close enough, I darted forward and to the side, dropping to my knees and driving a blade of air through the krampus's thigh, using my own momentum to get back to my feet in one fluid motion.

Thick black blood spilled from the injury, but the krampus made no noise; it didn't even show any sign that it had been injured. It just turned back toward me and began stalking forward, seemingly ignoring the wound as its whips flicked around it in a blur of deadly motion.

It snapped both whips at me, but I dropped to my knees, allowing them to sail harmlessly over my head; then I sprang upward, my fist wrapped in dense air. I caught the krampus under the chin, snapping its head back with vicious force. I followed up with a right hook to its jaw and a kick to the chest that sent it sprawling in the dirt.

I moved forward, creating a blade of fire in one hand and intending to finish the job, but the krampus moved quickly, putting some distance between us. I extinguished the blade, and the creature watched me closely, maybe trying to figure out what was going wrong for it. After a few seconds, it paused and retracted its whips. It then moved forward slowly, watching my every move, like a predator stalking its prey. Well, if there's one thing I've learned over the years, it's that I make for pretty awful prey.

I dashed forward, avoiding the powerful swipes of the beast's claws, and went to drive a blade of air into its ribs. But the krampus smashed its arm down on my back, knocking me to the ground and then kicking out with a hoof, which I blocked with another blast of air, putting some distance between us. I threw a ball of flame up at the monster's face. The krampus moved back, avoiding it, but not avoiding the blast of fire that hit it in the chest.

All but ignoring the fur burning on its chest, the krampus charged me once again. I threw out tendrils of air, wrapping them around and around it, tightening them until I heard something crunch. The krampus roared in pain and rage. I tried to stop it from moving, but it kept stepping forward, despite the obvious difficulty in doing so. Eventually, the strain of keeping the magic in place was too much, and I had to release it, which allowed the monster to dart forward and catch me across the chest with one of its newly extended whips.

The pain of the silver whip cutting into my flesh and the burning sensation that followed forced me momentarily to one knee. But a moment was all the krampus needed.

It wrapped the whips around my arms and raised me to its eye level as it growled, a low rumble that seemed to echo around us. It threw me the length of the clearing. I managed to create a second shield of air before I hit the rocks, but couldn't stop myself from landing in a heap on the ground, knocking the air out of me and giving the krampus enough time to grab me by the back of the head and smash my face into the nearest rock before throwing me aside once again.

Blood flowed from a new cut on my forehead as the krampus moved slowly and with purpose. It was like a force of nature; no matter what I did to it, it just kept on coming. I wrapped my air magic around its legs and pulled, taking the monster off its feet with a crash and giving me time to wipe the blood from my eyes.

The krampus was incensed, and once back on its feet, it tore free part of the rock cliff and threw it at me with ease. Despite the size and weight of the piece, the speed with which it reached me made dodging it much harder than it should have been, and also put me back in the path of a charging krampus.

I got back to my feet and tensed as the beast almost reached me, before I ignited my magic, creating lightning that crackled over my fingertips. I grabbed one of the silver whips and used it as a conductor, pouring my magic into it, which tore into the krampus. The monster fought back, grabbing my hand and pulling me toward it. I saw my opportunity and placed my other hand against its head, throwing as much lightning magic into the creature as I could possibly muster.

It released me and I kicked it away, putting distance between us as it convulsed on the ground for a few seconds and then returned to its feet.

I created a sphere of air in my palm and ran at the monster, burying the magic in the side of the krampus and then releasing it. The krampus flew back against the rock wall with a sickening crunch and crashed back to the ground—but despite coughing up blood and having more of the dark liquid stream from various cuts on its body, it refused to die.

I walked toward the krampus, a blade of brilliant flame in one hand, and plunged it through the monster's heart, expecting that to end the fight. But the krampus remained on its knees, swayed slightly, and then growled and tried to fight back, taking swipes at me that forced me to move away.

"Stubborn bastard, aren't you?" I said and wondered exactly what it took to put a krampus down for the count. A large, shimmering blue *jian*, a Chinese sword, appeared in my hand, one of my two soul weapons—a manifestation of my necromancy. They don't leave a mark on the body of the attacked, but instead damage the soul. I stepped back within striking range, avoiding the monster's weak swipes, and plunged the blade into its heart. I twisted the sword and dragged it out. The krampus, finally succumbing to its injuries, crashed down to its knees.

I kicked the monster onto the ground and replaced my *jian* with my second soul weapon, a large battle-axe. The krampus took one last halfhearted swipe in my direction with its whip, and I used my air magic to pin the weapon to the ground before driving the battle-axe down into the krampus's head.

With the creature finally dead, I extinguished the soul weapons and resisted the urge to collapse to the ground. I searched the cave but found that the bones I'd seen had belonged to various animals, and there was no sign that any other abductions had taken place. Whatever else I'd learned, at least I knew for certain that no mere bullet was going to kill a krampus—not unless it was attached to the end of a nuclear bomb. The fact was that it was Sarah's friend who was meant to have killed the krampus, and from what I'd overheard from the two men leaving the cave, it sounded like Sarah herself was responsible for the creation of the krampus. That meant she was also involved in the kidnapping of Chloe, and by extension, for what had happened with Cronus's escape from Tartarus.

I made my way back outside, thankful that the krampus was truly dead. The last twenty-four hours had been fairly exhausting, and I was unsure how much more I could have done against it. Even so, I kept glancing over to check that it hadn't moved.

I placed a hand just above the krampus's body and concentrated. A second later I sensed the soul inside the krampus. A dark and twisted mass, full of corruption. Part of me didn't want to bother trying to absorb a soul that dark, but another part of me wanted the power it would undoubtedly give me. The words of Hades as he was training me to use my necromancy months ago flickered to the front of my brain, telling me that the corruption wouldn't carry into me, so I set about taking the krampus's soul.

Absorbing the soul only took seconds, but once I'd consumed it and felt the power inside me, it was almost too much. It forced me to my knees as I coughed and spluttered. It felt like something was trying to break me open from the inside. I placed my head against the ground and allowed the sensation to pass, as the ground beneath me began to crack. Power leaked out of me while I tried to control the soul. A soul belonging to something as powerful as a krampus would be useable for a long time. I wouldn't need to worry about having sufficient reserves of necromancy to power my magic or heal myself if I became injured. But, at the same time, it was the single most powerful soul I'd ever absorbed, and the shock was a lot to take.

As the sensation finally subsided, I mentally prepared myself for the memories that came with absorbing a soul. Unlike most souls I'd absorbed, the krampus's crashed into me like a wave, and in an instant I knew everything about the man who had eventually become the monster beside me.

His name had been Ben Anderson, a career criminal from America who had moved to Germany. He was forty-six years old and had spent his life murdering and stealing from many. I saw Sarah Hamilton as she tortured and killed people in front of him, until she used a huge amount of blood magic to create the krampus. She was a serial killer and had created a creature of evil. She had to be stopped. But first my body protested that it had suffered enough, and I passed out on the soft ground, next to the dead krampus.

CHAPTER 23

I was more than a little surprised when I woke up in bed. In my own bed at the hotel, to be more exact. I wasn't particularly happy that three times in the last twenty-four hours I'd either passed out or been knocked out, and on two of those occasions I'd woken only to discover that someone had dragged my sorry ass to safety. On the plus side, waking up in bed was probably better than waking up next to the corpse of a . . . well, anything.

I flung my covers aside and glanced at the clock on the bedside table: just after 7:00 a.m. The memories of the previous night came flooding back. Sarah Hamilton and her friends were responsible for what was happening. I didn't know why, but I intended to find out.

Someone knocked on the door; then it opened, and Sky walked in, waving a keycard at me. "Glad to see you're up and about," she said.

"Who dragged me back here?"

"Emily, that witch friend of yours. She went back for you when you didn't return. Used your mobile to call me, and I rushed right down to mock you."

"Thanks for that—it means a lot."

"Yeah, I like to get my mocking in before breakfast if possible. Tommy was a bit concerned about you, but he's downstairs stuffing the equivalent of a whole pig's worth of bacon into his mouth."

I smiled and stood up, ignoring the fact that I was only wearing a pair of boxer shorts. "I need a shower," I explained to Sky.

"Go for it," Sky said and sat on an armchair by the window. "I'll wait."

I didn't bother arguing and instead had the hottest shower that I could manage to get without using my magic to heat the water. Once finished, I dried off and, with a towel still wrapped around my waist, opened the bathroom door.

"You're still here," I said.

"We need to talk," Sky said, her tone serious. "I'm worried about you."

I sat on the bed. "You want me to put some clothes on first?"

Sky shrugged. "Don't change the subject."

I grabbed a clean pair of boxers and put them on, throwing the towel over the top of the door. "I'm not. Why are you worried?"

"You threatened a few other people yesterday. Almost beat one siphon to death, tortured a man. Oh, and let's not forget that you killed a krampus."

"It was a big day," I said with a smile.

"Not now, Nate."

I sat on the bed again and nodded. "I'm fine. I actually feel pretty good. For a while, I was more concerned about the loss of my blood magic than I let on, but for some reason I'm now okay with it. Also, I took the soul of the krampus last night, so I know that Sarah Hamilton created it."

"We'll talk about that later. I'm more concerned about you. What's going on in your head?"

"Those four marks on my chest are still there. One has been fading for the better part of a year, but it hasn't gone yet. I don't know what any of the remaining ones do. Once they started vanishing after my little escapade with Mordred a few years ago, and I got my memories back that he'd taken from me, I expected to get *all* of my memories back. But those first eight years of my life, before I woke up outside Camelot, are still blank. I can go back to any point in my life and pick up traces of memory. But right before that day is a giant black hole. There are no sensations, no memories—nothing.

"It made me wonder exactly why someone would go to the trouble of removing them while at the same time putting these marks on me. Does one of these blood curse marks hold those memories, or do they do something else?

"Other than that, I'm good. Really good, actually. I got knocked out in the control room, and I woke up feeling refreshed, like my worries about my necromancy and blood magic had been dealt with."

Sky got to her feet and walked over to the window, propping herself up on the small ledge. "You don't find that odd? And what about that rune on your hand?"

"I do find it a bit odd, now that you mention it, but it doesn't really concern me, so I'm taking that as a good thing. As for the rune . . . I don't know. I just knew how to draw it—and knew it would do what I needed. How'd you get rid of your blood curse mark? Back in Montana, when we first met, you saw my marks. But you can't see them anymore. You've asked me about them twice in the last few years."

"I didn't realize you knew about them," she said and then sighed. "About a decade ago, I found some of the people who'd put the curse on me. They did it when I was ten years old, considering me someone they could possibly use because of my parentage. One of them was a sorcerer. I used him to kill the others who'd been involved in my family's murder and used their sacrifice to remove the curse from me."

"Did you let him live?"

"He assumed I would. He assumed wrong."

"What did the curse do?"

Sky was quiet for a moment, and when she spoke, it was almost a whisper. "It made me forget that they were the ones who had my parents murdered. They didn't do it themselves, but they manipulated people within the tribe to do it for them. Once they heard that my father worked for Hades, they brought me back to those who had murdered my parents and then scattered. They not only murdered my family but allowed my family's entire tribe to be wiped from existence."

"You never told me any of that."

Sky shrugged. "Bad things happened. Eventually, I tracked down and killed some evil pieces of shit. Not much to say."

"You okay?"

"Yeah. The curse fucked around with the memories of my parents. I knew who they were but couldn't remember anything about certain people in the tribe, like they'd been erased from my memory. Anyway, we're slightly off track. My dad asked me to talk to you about the rune. The other stuff was just me; I wanted to make sure you were okay."

"It's just a rune. Maybe something got dislodged when that sorcerer used his mind magic on me."

"My dad says it's not just a rune. It's one of the original Norse dwarf runes."

The Norse dwarves didn't like to write a lot down, as they believed that words held literal power. To be fair, in their case, it was true, as runes were a big part of their written language. All runes currently used, no matter what they do, come from the original twenty-one runes that the dwarfs created and then modified as needed. Each original rune was an exceptionally powerful version of those that followed.

These original runes were lost to time millennia ago, or so the legends say. Certainly, not even enchanters know what they look like, and since the dwarves disappeared a few decades after I was found in Camelot, no one has ever been able to ask them about the runes.

I glanced at the back of my hand. "One of the twenty-one? Are you sure?"

Sky nodded. "Dad said he's positive."

"It let me bypass the security restrictions to access my magic and necromancy. Hades said that if I keep wearing it, it'll just drain any of my magic that's not being used."

"Dad said it ignores any kind of dampener runes placed in its vicinity. Apparently, it only works for a set period of time, based on how advanced the runes are that it's trying to override, but it would basically let you bypass any rune-based security anywhere on the planet. At least temporarily. And when it's not actively working, it absorbs energy anyway to ensure it's always on."

I glanced at the back of my hand. The rune had come off some time ago, but I could still recall the image in my mind with ease. "How am I able to remember it?"

"Dad doesn't know. He thinks someone must have put the knowledge deep inside your subconscious. If my curse mark fucked around with my memories, I'm sure one of yours could easily have hidden some information about runes."

"Except none of the four marks have faded completely away, which would have been necessary for me to retrieve anything it had hidden."

"Then I have no idea. Dad's worried there are more runes hidden inside that head of yours. Some of them are insanely powerful. People would quite literally kill to have access to them. He doesn't want you to make yourself a target, and quite frankly neither do I."

"I'm always a target," I countered. "But he has a fair point. If my brain starts throwing out more rune knowledge, I'll go see him before I start writing them on my body."

"I guess that'll have to do. He's not too happy that you found a way to bypass his security with one rune, though. He had to make some pretty important phone calls to see if he was right about the rune being dwarven and to find out whether it could be counteracted. He's going to have to change his security."

"If it makes him feel better, I'm not going to go around telling people about this rune. If someone buried it deep inside my head, they did it for a reason."

"You think it was done before you ended up at Camelot?"

I nodded. "That would be my guess. Now, can you let me get dressed?"

"Oh, yeah, that was the other thing: Tommy spent most of the night hiding in some woods near the house he tracked those men to. A big place about a mile outside of town. He said there are guards patrolling the perimeter, four or five of them. They were there this morning when he left. Kurt, Petra, Tommy, you, and I are going to go pay them a little visit."

"Sounds like a plan. What happened to Chloe?"

"Oh, they're gone."

"Who's gone? Chloe?"

"All of them. The witches all left en masse this morning. Can't say I blame them. From what some of the other guests said, that Emily woman brought Chloe back, and she was rushed up to her floor, and none of the witches or those with them left the floor till they all packed up and departed at first light."

"I had questions," I said.

"Yeah, a lot of us did." Sky's tone didn't suggest she thought the witches innocent in all that had happened.

"Well, one thing at a time. Hopefully, Sarah Hamilton and her friends can tell us where Cronus is. Or at least give us more information than we have right now."

"I'm sure we can persuade them," Sky said as she opened the room door. "Are you sure you're up for it?"

"They kidnapped a fourteen-year-old girl and gave her to a krampus for reasons only they know. Even if the fact that they'd aided Cronus's escape was unknown to us, I'd still want to kick some people's teeth in."

"Put some nice boots on then," Sky said and closed the door.

CHAPTER 24

I found Tommy downstairs, waiting for me in the hotel's foyer. He was unshaven and looked tired. A werewolf's metabolism was a scary thing to behold, but even werewolves needed sleep after spending time in one of their other forms.

"You okay?" I asked him as we made our way toward the hotel's exit. "Where's Kasey?"

"She's with some of her friends. That kid Donna and a few others. I don't want to leave her alone right now, but on the other hand"—he paused and glanced back at the children who were running around the hotel—"I'm surprised that only the witches left."

"The teachers did a good job of keeping people calm."

"Yeah, they did. But while they're doing that, it means I can do my part: finding the bastards responsible." He took another step and stopped. "Oh, and I'm fine. Just tired and irritable. So punching someone in the face will probably do me a world of good."

I patted Tommy on the shoulder, and we walked out into the crisp daylight to meet the rest of our hunting party. Sky was still in jeans and a dark-purple hoodie, with comfortable trainers, pretty much mimicking my own look apart from the color of the hoodie; mine was black. Tommy didn't even bother with a hoodie, despite the cold morning. When about to go into a fight, the less clothing a werewolf has to remove, the better.

"Yeah, we're meeting Petra and Kurt just outside the forest to the south," Sky said. "They've got whatever we need."

We all climbed into Sky's 4X4 Land Rover, and she took us the short distance to a secluded spot where a second Land Rover—this one blue to Sky's black—waited for us, along with Petra and Kurt. Both wore combat trousers, big boots, and body armor, and carried SCAR-H MK17 rifles.

"We invading a country?" I asked as I exited the car.

"You mock," Kurt said, "but the last time we went to a confrontation with you unprepared, we got blown up."

Kurt moved aside, showing the additional sets of body armor and guns in the rear of their Land Rover.

"You're a werebear," I said, catching one of the sets of armor as he tossed it to me. "You healed."

"It still hurt. Don't fancy doing that again."

"We go in there, all magic and teeth, and we might set off some runes," Petra said. "I'd rather not have a house fall on us again."

"Technically, I *stopped* that from happening," I said as I buckled up the armor. "Do I get a SCAR too?"

"We've got one of these," Kurt said and passed me an MP5 and some ammo. I immediately loaded and slung the gun over my shoulder.

The MP5 was a good gun. Actually, it was an excellent gun and something I was very happy to be using when dealing with people inside an enclosed property.

"I assume we're on foot to the house?" Sky asked as she loaded shotgun cartridges into the Benelli M4 Super 90 she'd been given, an identical weapon to the one Tommy held.

"That's the plan," Tommy said. "It's a half-hour jog, but I figure it'll be better than driving and triggering any runes. If these guys are Vanguard, they're military trained to a very high degree and will have ways to try to ensure we can't track them. I found three in the woods last night; one was sitting up a tree with a rifle, a hundred yards from the house."

"How'd you know about the wards?" I asked.

"Saw some woman preparing them. These guys aren't slouches. It's not going to be an easy morning."

"Tell me again why Hades isn't helping?" I asked Sky.

"My parents are in Tartarus, dealing with the fallout of Cronus's escape."

"I think we got the better deal," Petra said.

"From now on, if we have to talk, it's done over these," Kurt said, and he passed around some small headsets, which we all immediately put on. They only covered one ear and had a thin microphone that sat close to one's mouth.

Without another word, Kurt and Tommy set off at a jog toward the same tree line I'd gone into only a few hours earlier, with the other three of us following close behind. We even passed by the site where I'd killed the krampus. I slowed noticeably for a moment when I realized that the body was gone, along with any blood, although evidence of the battle that had taken place still littered the area; the gouges in the ground and trees would take longer to disappear.

Tommy stopped moving just as the house that contained our targets came into view through the thick trees. It was a huge log cabin, with several trucks and 4X4 vehicles parked outside.

"Blood," Tommy whispered through his headset, and Petra immediately sniffed the air, followed quickly by Kurt, both of whom nodded their agreement.

"Fresh?" I asked as I crept up beside them.

Tommy nodded. "Up there." He pointed to a massive tree a hundred feet away. "He's not there anymore."

I made my way over to the tree and quickly scaled the trunk, using air magic to hold on as I climbed. When I reached the carefully hidden platform thirty feet above the ground, it was easy to see why Tommy had smelled blood. The man's throat had been slit from ear to ear while he was still lying prone on the platform. Someone had stood over him and done this without him ever moving. I wasn't sure how that was possible, as I couldn't imagine how a spotter would have missed seeing someone who stood over him. Even if it had been someone he trusted, he must have been suspicious when the person climbed the tree. There was only room for one up here.

I returned to the rest of them and told them what I'd found.

"There are two more bodies in the bushes over there," Kurt said. "I went to have a look."

"Everyone wait," Sky whispered and took a deep breath before closing her eyes. "Eight souls are out here, all of them recent deaths. I can't tell about the house; the wards stop me from finding out."

"How'd the two in the bushes die?" I asked Kurt before we all set off toward the house.

"One had a puncture wound at the back of the neck that looks like it went up into the brain; the second had a hole in his forehead. I'm guessing a blade of some description."

The five of us made our way toward the front of the house, careful to keep low and avoid open areas as much as possible. I paused by some runes drawn onto the doorframe.

"You know what they are?" Sky asked.

I shook my head.

"There's no one inside that room," Petra said. "I can smell death, though. Recent death too."

"I smell it too," Tommy said. He readied the shotgun and tried the door handle, which moved easily, eventually clicking softly before he pushed the door open.

The next few seconds passed in silence. Kurt took point, and all five of us moved into the house, guns ready to remove whatever resistance faced us. The reception room was obviously empty, and Petra and Kurt elected to stay behind in case anyone decided to try to catch us by surprise while we were clearing out the rest of the house.

Tommy, Sky, and I remained silent, relying on one another to do our jobs and watch each other's back. Each room we came to was searched in the same way; Sky stood watch at the entrance while Tommy and I entered the room and did a sweep. If we discovered it was clear, we each pressed the button on our headset, creating a clicking noise. Once all three of us had clicked, Tommy would come over and tap me on the arm, then Sky, and we'd follow him to the next room. We continued this exact same pattern of movement for the first three rooms, which were empty of anything but furniture, but as we got closer to the rear of the building, the smell of death that Petra and Tommy had noticed became all too apparent. At the rear of the one-story house, we found bodies. Lots of them.

We ignored the dead around our feet and continued to check every hiding place we could; getting surprised by someone when your guard is down because you didn't check the building properly is a very good way to end up dead.

Tommy clicked clear, followed by me as I closed a large cabinet at the end of the room, and then Sky, who was searching behind long flowing curtains that could have easily hidden a grand piano, let alone a man or woman.

I counted five dead, all male, all wearing guns, although few had been drawn. The attack had been fast and accurate, giving little time to retaliate or escape.

"Someone fired through these windows," Sky said, and Tommy and I found ourselves looking at the holes that perforated the glass.

"Five smashed windows," Tommy said. "Someone's a good shot."

The trajectory of the bullets coordinated with where three of the bodies lay. Two more had obviously figured out what was happening and tried to flee, but hadn't made it out of the room.

I pushed aside one of the curtains and looked out at the forest a hundred feet behind the house and then at the bullet holes in the glass. "They were in those trees," I said.

"Kurt," Tommy said into his microphone, "the trees at the south of the house. Can you and Petra check for a sniper position?"

"Will do. You sure there's no one in the house?" Kurt asked.

"This house is clean. If anyone was going to pop out, they'd have done it by now."

"I assume whoever took the shots is long gone now," Sky said. "I would have felt them if they were still there."

"Any ideas about how long these guys have been dead?" Tommy asked.

Sky was quiet for a second. "Fifteen minutes before we arrived. Maybe thirty. Not longer. And that one isn't dead, although he might be wishing he was." She pointed toward a couch that had several bullet holes in it; the stuffing tumbled out where it had been torn into.

I glanced behind and found Robert Ellis, one of the men who had attacked me outside Petra and Kurt's restaurant and the man who had claimed to have killed the krampus with a bullet. He coughed slightly and brought up blood. He'd been hit once in the stomach, creating an awful smell as the small piece of metal had torn his insides open. He'd die—no two ways about it—but it wasn't going to be quick.

"You look like shit," I said and tapped him with my foot to make sure he realized I wasn't an hallucination caused by what I was sure was an incredible amount of pain he was going through.

He coughed again and focused on me. "I fought you."

"You did," I told him.

"You were tough."

"That's what people tell me. Who did this?"

He coughed and spluttered some more, probably causing more pain to wrack his body, but he didn't appear to want to answer the question.

"Why did you break Cronus out of Tartarus?"

"Told to. I'm Vanguard; we do as we're told. Can I get some water?"

"No," I said. "You were told to help free Cronus?

Robert nodded, although the movement was weak and appeared to cause him discomfort. "We were sent to work with Sarah. It was her plan. All of this—her plan."

"Who is Sarah Hamilton? Who does she work for?"

He coughed and choked again, gasping in pain once he'd finished. "Go fuck yourself."

I didn't have time to make him talk. Besides, I doubted he'd live even long enough to sit him up. "Fine. Why attack me?"

"Sarah knew you'd be here. Knew she'd need to remove you from the picture." When he spoke, he sounded weaker; his words appeared to be harder to get out.

"Why?"

"She was working for someone. Kept calling them. Don't know who."

"Do you know how Cronus escaped from the compound?"

"Witches. All I know is witches were involved."

"You sure?"

He tried to nod. "One of them brought Cronus here last night. She said she wouldn't be missed because everyone was out looking for that girl we stuck with the krampus."

"Sarah created it, didn't she?"

Robert nodded again and coughed more blood onto the floor. "Before I got here. She said we needed it, could use it as a scapegoat. It grabs the kid and everyone searches, letting Cronus get to us without problems."

"Why hunt it and pretend to kill it?"

"It broke free of the cave, ran through town. Had to get it back and have everyone think it was dead. Worked out well, as we needed to be seen around town without suspicion."

"Someone made the townspeople think you were the right choice to do this; someone soothed the townspeople's emotions."

"Empath." Robert's head pointed to one of his dead friends. "Clive was a good soldier."

"How'd you know the krampus wouldn't kill Chloe?" Tommy asked.

"Sarah said it couldn't without her say-so, unless it was attacked." He started coughing again, and for a second I thought the pain was going to end him. "She said the girl was safe so long as she was quiet and didn't bother the krampus."

"She was a young girl, you fucking asshole!" I almost shouted and barely resisted kicking him in the bullet wound.

"I didn't like that part of the plan. Using young girls just to smuggle Cronus out was too much." He said it as if holding on to just one part he found distasteful would redeem him.

"Were all the witches involved?"

"The witches knew—some, all—I don't know. But those who were involved knew about using the girl."

"Do you know who killed you?" Sky asked.

"The witches have an enforcer," he said. "Never met him . . . but he did it. We were set up after Sarah died."

"Sarah is dead?" I asked. "Where's Cronus?"

"Cronus killed Sarah with some dagger she carried and ran for it."

"Where's her body?"

"Cellar."

"The enforcer was cleaning up your mess," Sky said.

Robert nodded, which caused him pain. "Proud to die for the cause."

"You died for nothing," I snapped. "I promise you that."

Robert was silent for a moment as his breathing became shallower. "Cellar outside."

Tommy and Sky had heard all they needed to, and they made their way toward the room's exit. I stepped past Robert, who reached out and grabbed me by the ankle. "Don't leave me like this," he pleaded.

I glanced down at the dying man. His face was pale, and blood saturated the floor beneath him. He didn't have long left. I walked over to his friend, Clive, and removed the Glock from his belt before dropping it on Robert's chest, making him wince. "You use that to take a shot at me, and I promise I'll keep you alive only long enough for you to regret it."

Robert glanced down at the gun, and I knew by the look in his eyes that he wouldn't be able to pull the trigger. He looked up at me. "Please."

I crouched down beside his head, making sure to avoid the expanding puddle of darkness that crept out from under him. "Did Chloe plead when you took her? Did she beg for you to let her go?"

Robert's expression told me I was right.

I picked the gun up. "You terrified a young girl just so you could make it easier to get Cronus free." I placed the gun in his hand and pointed it at his temple. "Go fuck yourself." And then I stood and made my way out of the house, leaving him to die.

I caught up with everyone else outside, just as rain began to fall in steady streams. Tommy and Sky were speaking with Kurt and Petra, who'd completed their check of the area.

"There's nothing there," Petra said. "No scents or anything. I'm not sure how that's even possible. Even if a person could remove their scent, there should be the scent of the gun, the powder—something."

Everyone was silent for a moment. Someone had killed the people in the cabin but hadn't left any scent. I didn't have a good answer to how that was possible.

"How can we be sure they've gone?" I asked.

"We can't," Kurt said. "We've checked all of the sniper positions, and there's no one there, but someone could still be out there. What would you do?"

"I'd run," I said. "The second I was done, I'd get as far from here as possible. You don't stick around."

"My guess is they didn't either," Kurt agreed.

"Let's go search the cellar," I said as I tried very hard not to turn to look at the trees around me. The mystery of the scentless assassin could wait until we'd finished.

The five of us moved around to the rear of the building. Beneath the broken windows, beyond which the dead lay inside the house, were two cellar doors. There was no lock or chain on the rusty handles bolted to each door, so I pulled them open and peered down into the darkness.

"Death," Tommy growled. "There's a light switch," he continued and touched something just inside the gloom, bathing everything beyond in a soft glow.

I was first into the cellar, taking the steps down slowly, just in case some of Robert's friends happened to be around, hiding while the others were slaughtered above, but the cellar was empty.

Tommy, Petra, and Kurt walked over to a sizeable cupboard at the far end of the cellar, and Tommy and Kurt each pulled one door opened, revealing the corpse inside, which fell out onto the floor with a loud thud.

We all quickly surrounded the body, and I turned it onto its back, revealing Sarah Hamilton. She looked very different from when I'd last seen her standing above me in the car park of Kurt and Petra's bar. Her skin was gray and stretched tight against her bones, giving her face an almost skeletal appearance. She wasn't just dead; she'd been drained. I'd seen that kind of thing once before, on victims of vampires who had gone too far, but here there were no obvious bite marks.

"How did Cronus do this?" Sky asked as she lifted Sarah's thin, bony arm. A ring on the dead witch's thumb fell off and rolled across the floor.

There was a tear in her blouse, just above her stomach, stained with a tiny amount of blood. I lifted the fabric, exposing her sunken ribcage, along with a stab wound.

"There's no blood," Tommy said as everyone stared at the wound. A blackness on the skin around it stopped after a few inches, forming a perfect ring of darkness. "How can that be possible?"

I moved away from the body and searched the cupboard, looking for the dagger that had killed Sarah.

When the cupboard yielded nothing, we searched around the rest of the cellar. It was a sizeable room, with a double bed and some more cupboards. A small TV sat on top of a chest of drawers at the end of the bed. Black carpet had been laid on the floor, and two electric heaters were turned on, keeping the room warm. The space had clearly been designed to house some-one for a while. There was even a small fridge in the corner; I opened the door and found it stocked with milk, bottles of water, and various packages of ham and chicken. A half-empty loaf of bread sat on top.

"There's a toilet back here," Tommy called from beside the stairs. "Shower too."

"Cronus stayed here," Sky said, picking up the top book on the bedside cabinet and showing me the cover. It was about the last twenty years of world history.

There were also an assortment of British tabloid newspapers, some German newspapers too, and a few porno mags. All in all, it wasn't the classiest table of literature I'd ever seen, but then what do you get the man who's been kept in another realm for several millennia?

"Well, he certainly had fun," I said.

"So, where was he meant to be taken?" Kurt asked. "Robert said Cronus killed Sarah and ran off. What would he have to fear from a witch and a bunch of Vanguard thugs?"

Eventually, I discovered the dagger underneath a small chest of drawers, lodged at the back. I pushed the furniture aside slightly and retrieved the weapon.

The dagger had a five-inch blade, which curved slightly from the wide base to the considerably thinner tip. A thin groove sat in the blade, moving from tip to hilt, where a small black hand guard sat. The hilt was black with red and white runes carved into it, and a small spike sat at the bottom. I hefted the knife in one hand. It felt much heavier than a blade that size should have, although maybe I was imagining things, giving weight to what the dagger had been used for.

I unscrewed the spike and glanced inside the hilt, tipping it up and allowing the small vial concealed inside to drop out onto my palm. The small oblong object was about two inches long and had barely the same circumference as a pencil. It was green and gold, with no obvious markings. On the top sat a small, razor-sharp spike with curved grooves carved into it.

"She was stabbed with this," I said and showed everyone the dagger.

"Oh shit," Sky said; the rest appeared slightly confused about what I was showing them.

"What is it?" Tommy asked.

"It's a dwarven dagger," I said. "It's called a Kituri dagger, and it's probably a few thousand years old, although it could be even older. It's named after one of the dwarven gods. The god of chaos."

"What does it do?" Petra asked.

I showed them the small vial. "This is used to cut someone and collect their blood. It's then placed inside the dagger." I unscrewed the top of the vial and tilted the bottle as if to pour a little blood onto my hand, but it was empty. I pushed the vial back inside the hilt of the dagger and closed it. "The runes carved into the dagger transfer the life force of someone stabbed with the dagger to the person whose blood is inside the vial. Once the victim is dead, the blood in the vial, and that in the body of the victim, evaporates.

"The dwarfs used to settle blood feuds and serious crimes by having two champions fight. Inside each blade would be the blood of the person they were fighting for. As the fights continued and both sides sustained wounds, their masters or the person they were fighting for, would get stronger or weaker accordingly. Eventually, one champion would die, and his entire life force would travel to his opponent's master, making him strong enough to kill his rival without too much trouble. It was used in matters of war mostly, because only two people had to die to settle the conflict and stop the fighting. Occasionally, it was used during criminal proceedings too."

"Why hide it? Why not just take it with him and use it himself?" Tommy asked.

"It's not a quick way to get energy," I explained. "The runes inside the vial and the blood have to be allowed to infuse for several days."

"But Cronus definitely stabbed her with this . . . blade?" Kurt asked.

I nodded. "Anyone killed with this ends up looking like"—I pointed to the body on the floor—"that."

"Are knives like this rare?" Tommy asked.

"Very. I know of only five people who owned one. Zeus—or now Hera, Merlin, Hades, Galahad as the ruler of Shadow Falls, and Pandora. There are probably a few more out there I don't know about, but there can't be too many. The dwarfs weren't exactly keen on handing them out to people."

"So why hide it?" Petra asked.

"My guess is he either threw it aside and that's where it landed, or he figured if he couldn't use it, no one else should be able to. He was probably in a hurry, didn't really have time to think things through."

"How'd Pandora get one?" Sky asked.

"No idea. But I saw it in her possession a few centuries ago."

"One of these days you'll have to tell me what happened between the two of you," Sky said.

I ignored her probing suggestion and removed the vial for a second time, placing both it and the dagger on the table beside me. It was too dangerous to leave it intact. The link between the dagger and owner of the vial's contents was severed once the blood had evaporated, but someone who knew what they were doing could always use it again.

"Do you know whose that is?" Tommy asked.

"I wish I did," I said softly and used my necromancy to try to find Sarah's spirit. If I could find her, I could ask what happened. "She didn't fight," I informed everyone after a few seconds. "I can feel her there, but I can't interact."

"I'll try," Sky said and dropped to her knees, silently using her own necromancy to get the answers we needed.

"You still can't talk to spirits then?" Tommy asked.

"I can sense them easily enough," I explained. "I know Sarah's there, but I can only contact those who died fighting. Not sure if I'll ever be able to speak to those who didn't."

"Sarah was supposed to kill Cronus," Sky said. "She was meant to take him somewhere that would have ensured his magic was back to full capacity, and then use the dagger on him. She went to a lot of trouble to make him believe they were allies. I doubt he considered they'd go to the trouble of getting him out of Tartarus just to kill him. But when Cronus saw the dagger, and knew exactly what it was, he panicked, killing her in the process."

"Where was she going to take him?" Tommy asked, but then his mobile phone rang, so he left us alone and exited the cellar to take the call.

"Not sure; somewhere in England," Sky continued, still kneeling on the floor. "She was meant to get him to London and receive new instructions from the person employing her."

"We have a problem," Tommy said as he almost jumped down the stairs. "That was Olivia. Hera and friends are in the UK. They had to get clearance from the LOA, so Olivia was notified. They're staying in a mansion in London."

"That can't be a coincidence," Kurt said.

"Who employed Sarah?" I asked Sky.

"That's a bigger problem," she said as she got back to her feet. "There's a weird mental lock on her spirit. It'll take days to get through it. When you ask about the plan, she just keeps sprouting words and names—krampus, Mara Range, and a bunch of others that belong to our dead Vanguard friends above. But one name popped up that I found interesting: Brutus."

"That makes no sense," I said. Brutus was the king of London. Brutus had made it difficult for any representative of Avalon or its allies to access London without his permission. London, like Shadow Falls, was exempt from Avalon's control. "Why would Brutus want all of this to happen? He's a bit of a pain in the ass to Merlin, but for the most part he's an ally of both Avalon and Hades, and while he's certainly no friend of Cronus, I can't imagine he'd want him dead."

"Looks like we're off to London, then," Tommy said.

Petra had been searching Sarah's body and now found something interesting. A small mark was visible on Sarah's hip, about the size of a pound coin. It was a little yellow crown with a tiny green leaf behind it.

A deep pit of worry settled inside me, and everyone in the room fell into a hushed silence.

"Hera," Tommy whispered. "The mark of Hera."

All of Hera's employees who worked in the upper echelons of her organization bore her mark; it was a way to control everyone who was loyal to her. Sarah had evidently been considered a loyal worker of Hera's.

Everything had just gotten a lot more complicated.

CHAPTER 25

On returning to the hotel, Tommy had informed Kasey of her future travel plans. That meant that I felt really uncomfortable about being in the same room as them both as they argued about whether she was going to be sent back to London to her mum. Tommy wanted her back home; Kasey wanted to be with her dad and try to help.

I left them to their increasingly loud discussion and went for a walk around the floor as my mind drifted back toward what had happened in the last few hours. I hadn't thought about it until we'd all gotten back to the hotel, but Mara and Sarah had certainly known one another, even if they hadn't been friends.

I opened the door to Tommy's room again, just as Kasey told her dad she would rather walk home and slammed the bathroom door closed. Tommy used his thumbs to massage his temples.

"Anyone searched the ninth floor?" I asked.

"The one the witches stayed on?" he shrugged. "No idea."

I eyed the bathroom door. "Just tell her we'll take her with us," I suggested. "Hades is sorting out a private jet, so she doesn't have to go back with everyone else and gets to stay with you. She's just worried about you."

"I know," he whispered. "But . . ."

I waited for him to continue. When he didn't, I said, "You don't know how to finish that argument, do you?"

"No," he admitted. "I'm her dad; she should do as she's told."

I laughed. "Yeah, because you're such a rule follower. Face it, you have a stubborn daughter who takes after her stubborn parents."

"Go check the witches' rooms," he said with a sigh that made me smile.

I left Tommy to his parenting troubles and took the staircase up to the ninth floor. After opening the door, I found myself in a small foyer with the lift doors opposite me and a hallway door to either side. Each door had a plaque depicting the room numbers that were beyond.

I removed my phone from my pocket and dialed the reception desk. My call was answered by the hotel manager who had tried to calm Mara down after she accused me of wanting to kill her. His voice reminded me that I had a bottle of scotch in my bedroom that I hadn't even gotten around to opening.

"Mr. Garrett," he said in a tone that suggested he hoped I wasn't going to cause trouble. "How can I help you?"

"Has the ninth floor been cleaned yet?"

There was a silence as he probably considered whether this was information he could give me. "No," he said eventually. "That floor is not due to be cleaned for a few hours."

"Can you tell me what room Mara was in?"

"I'm sorry, sir, but that's not information I can give out."

I really didn't want to be a dick, but needs must. "Look, you know that Mara's daughter was kidnapped last night, and that she was brought back safely, but I figured I'd take a look at the room just in case there's any *incriminating* evidence about what happened to her. No one wants what happened to her to get out. Maybe a keen but disinterested set of eyes can spot something so it can be removed before the cleaners get here."

The manager paused for a moment once again. "Room 907," he almost whispered. "This goes nowhere."

"Promise. I just want a look around. Can someone bring me up a key card?"

"Give me two minutes," he said and hung up.

True to his word, by the time I'd looked around the corridor for anything out of the ordinary and then made my way to room 907, the manager appeared, handing me a key card. "This never happened. I'm only doing this because something weird is happening here. The key will access every room on this floor."

I waited until the manager had left the corridor before using the key on the door, which opened without incident. I'd been concerned that the witches might have used runes to rig the doors to explode or some such, but doing so would probably have given them more attention than they'd wanted. So after a quick check, I figured the door was safe to open.

I stepped into Mara's room and immediately noticed how tidy everything was. For a room that hadn't been cleaned by the hotel staff, someone had certainly made sure that the room was spotless. Freshly polished surfaces gleamed, and even after checking everywhere I could think of, there was nothing to say that anyone had even stayed in the room for the previous few days.

I left Mara's room, then proceeded to check every room along the corridor, searching the bedrooms and bathrooms for . . . well, to be honest, I wasn't sure—anything out of the ordinary. Sarah and Mara had known one another, and despite Sarah's dislike of the other woman, I doubted that their being in the same place at the same time, while Cronus was escaping Tartarus, was coincidental.

I got through eight of the sixteen rooms before I found my first evidence of something weird. I had no idea whose room it had been, but while looking through the bathroom I discovered the bathtub had a tidemark-like ring around it. It was an odd substance that seemed to catch the light in just the right way as to make it invisible to the naked eye. But when not quite looking directly at it, it was apparent there was something not quite right.

I touched the substance with a rolled up piece of toilet paper. It felt a little slimy through the paper, but after a few seconds the part of the paper I'd used appeared to vanish. I held the paper up to the light, the normal white color changed slightly as I looked at it from different angles. I went back to the bedroom, looking for something else to use, and grabbed a pen from the bedside table, taking it back into the bathroom and rubbing the blue lid along the shimmering mass in the bath, ensuring that the lid was fully coated in the substance.

It took a few seconds, but the lid simply disappeared from view. My mouth dropped open in shock, and I found myself quickly tapping where the lid would be to ensure it was still there. The lid was still attached to the pen, but it was now almost invisible to the naked eye. I moved the pen slightly, and the movement made the lid visible for a short time, but once the pen ceased moving, it became concealed once more.

I removed my phone from my pocket, without taking my eyes off the pen, and dialed the manager. "Whose room is 914?" I asked him.

There was no pause this time, no concern over whether he was doing the wrong thing. He'd already given me the keycard; he could hardly say no now. "Emily Rowe's."

"Thanks," I said and hung up. So, Emily *was* involved. I found it hard to believe that the rest of the witches could have brewed a potion in her bathtub without her knowledge. Potion making isn't a stealthy pastime. It's also not like the stories; there's no eye of newt or such rubbish. It's all about using items that have been placed in rune-marked, or magically enchanted containers. The contents take on the property of whatever the rune or enchantment might possess. The contents are then mixed with water or some other liquid. Hence baths and the like are the usual place for such things to be created. The idea is a bit like when someone makes a drink from concentrated fruit juice and puts water in to water down the flavor. Same with concentrated rune-enhanced liquid. It needs to be watered down, or it would be unstable at best, but incredibly dangerous at worst. Potions take a long time—months, if not years to get the concentrate right—which is why few people bother. Most people want a more immediate effect, and with potions if you get one of the ingredients wrong, or the rune even slightly incorrect, you risk either ruining everything or killing everyone.

I dialed Tommy, who answered immediately. "Apparently, Kasey will be joining us on our journey back to England," he said.

"That was quick, but you can tell me later. Get to room 914. I've got something to show you." I hung up and went back into the room, opening the door so that Tommy could get in.

"Hey, Nate," Kasey said, almost skipping through the door a few minutes later.

"I hear you got your own way," I said with a smile.

"I'm an idiot, that's why," Tommy said as he appeared in the doorway. "I hope this is as thrilling as I'm expecting."

I passed him the pen.

"A pen? Be still my beating . . ." He stopped for a second. "What the fuck?"

"Dad!" Kasey snapped.

"Sorry, Kase, but what did you do to this pen, Nate?"

I told them about what I'd found in the bathroom.

"A chameleon potion," Tommy said. "Wow, that's pretty heavy stuff. Certainly not the kind of thing witches should have. For a start, you need an enchanter to make the container."

"Couldn't they make it themselves?" Kasey asked.

I shook my head. "Rune-marked stuff like this needs to be done by someone with a lot of magic to use, like a sorcerer, or someone who works with runes exclusively, like an enchanter. Witches usually get a friendly enchanter to make the containers for them. The magic used is very powerful; any witch doing it would have used up a lot of energy. Much like Sarah and her *effete* spell. Witches could do this if they didn't care about their own life."

"Dying for the cause," Tommy said with a shake of his head. "They'd have to be fanatical. Or insane. Or more probably, both."

"This is how Cronus escaped," I imparted. "The bath's tide line shows it was easily deep enough to soak some clothes in. Give them to Cronus after he escaped, and he could get out of the compound without being detected. So long as he moved slowly and carefully."

"He was on the bus the witches took," Kasey said.

I nodded. "Probably hiding under it. He stays still and no one sees him. Which is why Mara and the witches were in such a hurry to leave the compound. If this potion was good enough, it would hide Cronus's scent and any heat from his body too. It also explains why Petra found only the scent of the gun back at the cabin in the woods. My guess is whoever shot the Vanguard soldiers wore clothes and had a gun that was covered in this stuff too."

Tommy took a deep smell of the pen's lid. "Yeah, there's nothing here; it's like it's been removed. Even a normal pen has scents on it from those who used it before, or even from just the ink. This has nothing."

"This means that Mara and the witches were involved with Sarah and the Vanguard. It was all one big job," I said.

Kasey made a horrified noise and placed a hand over her mouth. "They knew about Chloe."

I nodded. "Mara used her own daughter as bait. I doubt any of the kids knew—too much uncertainty. As the coven leader, Mara would have to have been involved; it's probably why, when we were out searching for Chloe, they were up here scrubbing the whole place clean. They couldn't risk anything being found once they'd left."

"They didn't do a great job," Tommy pointed out.

"That's the trouble with lots of people cleaning in a hurry; someone always leaves something."

"I'm surprised by Emily's involvement," Tommy said. "Actually, 'saddened' is a better word. I figured she'd be less inclined to help someone hurt a young girl just to create a distraction."

I didn't say anything, but I echoed Tommy's feelings. I'd thought Emily was better than that; I'd thought she would do anything for those kids. She certainly came across as someone who cared about them. But I guess I'd been wrong, and she was lying. Despite the fact that I barely knew her, I'd liked Emily, and I couldn't help but feel stung by the revelation.

"So, what do we do with this information?" Tommy asked. "After we call Hades and let him know about how Cronus escaped, I mean."

"The witches will be on their way back to England, and apart from some leftover potion in a bathtub, there's very little connecting them to what Sarah and the Vanguard did. I say we notify Olivia, get her to keep an eye on them while we go get Cronus back. We can deal with the witches after that."

My mobile rang. "Hey, Nate," Sky said, "We're ready to go when you are."

"We'll make our way up to you. How are we getting to London? I assume we're flying."

"We're taking the Blackhawk."

I could practically hear her smiling.

"Great," I said, with all the enthusiasm of being told you were about to be repeatedly kicked in the bollocks, and hung up.

"From the way you sound, I guess we're flying," Tommy said.

The word stuck in my throat a little: "Blackhawk."

"A helicopter? Wow, how you doin'?" There was no mocking in his voice.

"You don't like helicopters either?" Kasey asked.

I liked helicopters *even less* than airplanes. I'd crashed three times in a helicopter, twice from being shot down and the third time from someone trying to kill me while we were both on-board. I'd ascertained that while I disliked helicopters immensely, they appeared to actively hate me. "I need to go get myself some whiskey," I said.

CHAPTER 26

The journey took several hours, with a small stop in Paris for refueling despite the extra fuel the Blackhawk had on board. I sat and drank the bottle of whiskey the hotel had given me, while Tommy, Kasey, and Sky all did their best to ignore me. It was probably for the best; I doubt I'd have made good conversation.

Sky informed us all that although Hades had tried to get hold of Hera, she hadn't taken any of his calls. He'd left messages with members of her staff, but whether they told her that her life was in danger, he couldn't say.

We landed in London at a heliport on the southern bank of the river Thames, a large open space with several helipads, opposite Chelsea harbor. Once out of the helicopter, we found Olivia waiting for us.

Kasey ran toward her mum and hugged her tightly, only moving so that her parents could kiss. Eventually, Olivia nodded toward Sky and me.

"Are you causing trouble again?" Olivia asked me as the noise from the rotor blades died down. When the director of the southern England branch of the LOA asks if you're causing trouble, it's probably a good idea to stop doing things that bring you to her attention. Unfortunately, as she was Tommy's partner, that was never going to happen.

"I think *technically* I'm trying to stop trouble," I pointed out.

"Well, Hera won't be happy to see you."

"She rarely is, but we'll leave her for after we've seen Brutus. Hopefully, Hera will never need to be warned of Cronus's plans."

"Do you really believe that?" Olivia asked, as we all walked away from the helipad.

I shook my head. "No, but I like to have some optimism."

"While Sky can leave London whenever she wishes, her father is going to be another matter. I managed to call in a lot of favors a few years ago to get him access to Tommy's security firm after what happened with the lich, favors from people I'm unconvinced I can call on again."

"That's okay," Sky said. "Dad's trying to see who owes him what. He wants to be there when Cronus is taken down. I don't think he trusts anyone outside of his organization at the moment. He's worried about people using the situation to their advantage."

"With good reason," Olivia told us. "There's already a smattering of talk about something having happened at the facility. It's only going to grow with time."

"We've got about forty-eight hours to get Cronus," I said.

"Lucie, I assume," Olivia confirmed. "She mentioned something to me about her sitting on her report. She's good people."

I nodded when it became apparent that everyone had turned to stare in my direction.

"Does Brutus know we're coming?" Sky asked.

It was Olivia's turn to nod. "By 'we,' you mean all of us," she said. "I'm coming with you."

"What about Kasey?" Tommy asked.

"She's coming with us," Olivia told him.

Kasey's grin could have been seen from space.

Olivia didn't even look in her daughter's direction. "Young lady, if you do anything except what we tell you, I'll have you sent back to Winchester to sit in my office, guarded by very professional people who will shadow every step you take." Apart from being an incredibly influential member of the LOA, and Avalon as a whole, Olivia was also a powerful water elemental. When she tells you to behave, you behave.

"Yes, mum," Kasey conceded, although her smile had now changed into a subtle smirk.

Olivia stopped and leveled her gaze at her daughter. "I mean it, Kase. No messing about. You do what we say, when we say it."

"Okay," she said softly.

Olivia kissed Kasey on the forehead and we all set off again, leaving the heliport compound, where we were met by half a dozen agents standing beside three black Mercedes SUVs. Four men and two women of various shapes and sizes, all of whom were wearing immaculate dark suits, which did little to hide the holsters they wore underneath their jackets. As we reached the cars, Olivia, Kasey, and Tommy climbed into the middle one, while Sky and I were motioned toward the last in the line.

It was incredibly comfortable inside, and I would have happily had the ride be ten times as long. Unfortunately, time was not a luxury we had much of, and the trip was over quickly.

Sky and I exited our car while the two agents remained in the driver and passenger seats. I looked up at the massive building that towered above us. The Aeneid wasn't too far off, five hundred feet tall, and was by far the tallest building in the area.

Sky and I waited while Tommy, Olivia, and Kasey left their SUV and joined us, along with a young female agent. The three vehicles drove off, presumably to the underground parking area, and we made our way into the expansive foyer of the building. From the outside appearance, it seemed the building had offices on the first ten floors and then housing for the top twenty-five, with the twenty-sixth being an exclusive penthouse that took up the entire floor.

An unassuming, middle-aged woman sat behind the reception area, which was in between two corridors, each with a sign saying either "Office" or "Residential." Olivia walked over and spoke to the woman while I glanced around, noticing the three guards standing at various points around the well-lit area, and a fourth who was sitting on an orange chair reading a magazine.

"Nate," Tommy said, getting my attention and then pointing toward Olivia, who was walking over to the corridor labeled "Residential."

As I walked past, one of the guards nodded a greeting at me, which I returned as the lift doors opened and we all stepped inside. The lift was all floor-to-ceiling mirrors, with a golden dragon painted on the ceiling.

Olivia pushed the first number on the panel, 11, and there was a small jolt as the lift took off, the doors opening seconds later to show another large, open area. If the guards in the foyer were meant to be intimidating without seeming overly threatening, the half-dozen men on the eleventh floor beyond simply didn't care how menacing they might appear. This was a declaration of power and a promise of what would happen to those who misbehaved. It wasn't subtle, but then it was almost certainly not meant to be.

We walked past them without comment or incident; despite the presence of the weapons, we all knew none of them would even consider using them so long as we gave them no cause to consider us a threat. A couple of them even put their weapons away once they saw Kasey.

At the far end of the room was a mazelike corridor that split off into several smaller corridors, all with doors along both sides. If you didn't know where you were going, it would be easy to get lost. Brutus had once told me he'd based its design on the Minotaur's lair near Knossos, although whether that was true or simply one of Brutus's many twists on the truth, I was unsure.

Eventually, we reached two massive, ornate doors that were guarded by two equally massive men. They nodded toward us and opened the doors, which led to another room with a few dozen more guards, all sitting on comfortable couches scattered around the large room. Light spilled in through the huge floor-to-ceiling windows that ran down one wall, and in the center, on a raised platform, was a golden throne.

"Is that real?" Kasey asked, pointing toward the throne.

"Yes, my dear," a voice boomed as a man appeared from behind the platform.

He wore a sharp black suit, which was clearly of the highest quality, and carried a walking cane, although I doubted he actually needed it.

"Brutus, you dressed up," I said as he walked toward us and shook my hand.

"Well, Olivia called and told me you were arriving." He glanced at Kasey. "Although she didn't mention you'd be bringing her daughter along. My apologies for the armed guards; I do not wish to frighten you."

"I wasn't frightened," Kasey said. "I've been around enough people with guns and swords. Also, my dad turns into a giant werewolf. Guns are much less scary."

Brutus laughed, followed swiftly by several members of his court, who stood around the throne room.

Brutus was a large man, easily over six and a half feet tall, and built like a heavyweight boxer. He cast an imposing figure. His dark hair was cut short, and he was clean-shaven, both of which were very different from when I'd last seen him. He was the kind of man you'd enjoy having a drink with, but you'd never want to do it too often. He had a personality that flickered from calm and warm to hostile in moments. I'd had both aspects pointed directly at me on more than one occasion. I didn't exactly consider him a friend, but I had to admit I liked the guy. Sometimes.

"So, why are you here?" Brutus asked after he'd shaken hands with Tommy, Olivia, and Sky, lingering slightly before releasing Sky's hand. He'd always had a bit of a thing for her, and she'd always turned him down, making him want her even more.

"Is there somewhere we can talk in private?" I asked.

"I would, but my advisors don't like it when I discuss things without them," Brutus said, motioning over his shoulder to three men and a woman who sat watching us.

Two of the men were twins, not quite identical, but near enough, although their names eluded me. They were tall and thin, with shaved heads, and each wore a gray version of Brutus's suit. The woman's name was Diana; she was the Roman goddess of the moon and hunting, and I think birth, although I never really understood that part. To be fair, I don't think she did either.

"Nathan," Diana said and walked over to hug me tightly. She smelled of strawberries. She wore a pair of jeans and a red T-shirt with a picture of The Beatles on the front. Diana was the kind of woman who turned heads wherever she went;

roughly my height, although in the heels she was wearing, she was a few inches taller, with a face and body most super-models would kill for. Her dark hair was tied back in a braid, and since she was also half-werebear, her long elegant fingers contained enough strength that she could crush me like a bug if she so desired.

"Diana, you're looking wonderful," I said as Brutus continued to talk to the rest of the group.

"I don't believe in dressing up for guests," she said with a smile. "Not friendly ones anyway."

"Not sure how friendly we'll be after this visit," I admitted. "It's not good news."

Diana's smile never wavered. "I have your back."

She meant it too. Diana and I had gotten along since the day we'd met when I was a young man working for Merlin and he'd sent me to talk to Brutus. I was never really sure why Diana stayed with Brutus; she certainly had the charisma to have her own organization, but she'd never been interested in politics, preferring to help Brutus and his people.

The third man, who had watched me intently from the moment we'd all arrived, chose that moment to get involved. "I hope this is important," he said, as he got to his feet. His voice was low, and in those few words he managed to convey his unhappiness at our—or more specifically, *my*—presence.

"Licinius," I said with a forced smile.

There are two types of sorcerer in the world; those who are happy to share information and experiences to better themselves and others, and those like Licinius. They see other sorcerers as automatic competition and treat them with disdain and suspicion because they're too hung up on the possibility of giving away some huge secret about magic that they can do and assume no one else can. Licinius is a good few centuries older than me and likes to point out his ability to use Omega magic at every available opportunity, but in a way that suggests he's somehow figured out something no one else possibly could. In short, Licinius was a wanker. A giant, colossal, fucking idiotic, arrogant wanker.

"Nathaniel," he said, intoning the word with the exact right amount of disdain and apathy at my presence.

I also never understood why he refused to call me Nathan. Probably more stuff relating to his being a jerk. Diana placed a hand on my shoulder in a gesture of solidarity, a gesture that didn't go unnoticed by Licinius, whose features darkened.

"Maybe we *should* discuss this elsewhere," Brutus said, finally noticing the tension surrounding us. He looked over at the twins, who shrugged but didn't move. They were clearly quite happy to stay where they were. "Follow me," he said to the rest of us, and we all followed him out of the throne room and back down the corridor to the lift, where Brutus took us up to the twenty-fourth floor.

After exiting the lift and going through the only door available to us, we found ourselves in Brutus's living room. The entire floor was his, and it was furnished with ancient pieces of art, pottery, and weapons. Two full suits of ancient Greek armor sat beside the windows that gave a wonderful view of the city hundreds of feet below us.

Brutus motioned for everyone to sit on one of the two large black couches. A young blond woman, wearing some sort of gray and blue uniform, appeared out of nowhere, and Brutus sent her away to get drinks.

"You have a maid?" I asked.

"Several. I have butlers too," he told us. "I'm a king, after all."

"How can you be king of England?" Kasey asked with all of the innocence that only someone can possess who has no idea of the minefield she's just placed herself right in the middle of.

The maid brought back a tray of drinks.

"To answer your question," Brutus said, selecting one of the glasses of what appeared to be lemonade and settling onto a leather chair, "I arrived here after being forced to leave the battle of Troy. England was ruled by giants, who didn't appreciate the interference I and my people brought with us, so we defeated them and I crowned myself king. Unfortunately, Merlin had already claimed this country as Avalon territory, and we had a disagreement. We settled on the idea that I could keep London for myself, so while I'm not king of England, I am the king of London."

Brutus's *disagreement*, was basically a fight between him and a still young Merlin, one Brutus lost handily. Over the years, Merlin regretted giving Brutus London, which had still been a tiny place at the time. Brutus doesn't involve himself in the day-to-day city dealings but does require anyone from Avalon or one of the big organizations to ask his permission to enter the city limits. Although on the flip side of that, Brutus can't leave the city without permission from Merlin, permission my old teacher was rarely eager to give.

"We've got a problem," I said and began telling Brutus about Cronus's escape. Concern shot over his face as I described the involvement of the Vanguard and the krampus.

"You think I was involved?" he asked. There was no anger in his voice, once I'd explained that Sky had gotten his name out of Sarah Hamilton's spirit.

I shook my head. "I think you know who Sarah Hamilton was, though." I removed the Kituri dagger from inside my jacket and placed it on the table before us.

Licinius, who'd stood behind Brutus, almost leaped over the back of the couch to protect his boss. "You brought a weapon in here?" he demanded.

"Oh sit down, it's not like they're going to kill me." Brutus lifted the dagger and began examining it. "It's dwarven steel. Explains why none of the metal detectors in the foyer downstairs spotted it. You know how much this is worth?"

"A lot," Tommy said.

"That is an understatement. A dagger of this kind, you're looking at millions of pounds."

"I don't think it's for sale. Do you know who it belonged to?" I asked.

Brutus shook his head. "Did Sarah Hamilton have this in her possession?"

"Before Cronus murdered her with it, yes," Sky told him. "Nate says Pandora has one."

"Well, she might have, but she's hardly allowed weaponry where she is. So if she did own one, and this is it, then Sarah must have retrieved it from somewhere outside of Pandora's current whereabouts."

"Even so, we'd like to speak to Pandora," I said.

Brutus glanced over at Licinius. "Can you arrange it?"

The sorcerer glared at me but left the room nonetheless. "He really doesn't like you," Brutus said.

"He clearly saves all of his sparkling personality for the ladies," I suggested, which got a laugh from Diana.

"Sarah Hamilton was a witch," Brutus told us. "A good one too. She worked for me. Started here about eight or nine years ago."

"What did she do?" Olivia asked, the cop side of her taking control of the conversation.

"She was a guard for Pandora. Yes, I know what you're thinking," he added quickly. "But Pandora did not have that dagger in her possession."

"But she could have told Sarah where it was," Olivia suggested.

"That's possible. Because Sarah was a guard, they had plenty of opportunity to talk to one another. But Pandora couldn't have enthralled her, so if Sarah did retrieve it, she did it under her own power. None of the guards are permitted entry to the cell, and as Pandora can only enthrall those she's in physical contact with, Sarah was never under her spell. It's the only way to ensure the guards are loyal to me and not Pandora."

"Can they fake not being enthralled?" Olivia asked. "Maybe a few of them get sloppy and she makes contact."

"No, they all undergo a weekly psychic examination. Any hint of control and it flags up. I pay a lot of money for those examinations; independent contractors do them. It's foolproof. Besides, there are always guards watching the guards. Anyone screws up and someone will notice."

"How long did Sarah work for you?" Olivia asked, moving the conversation back to the topic for which we needed answers.

"She was a guard here for three or four years, and then she came to me with an idea. The head guard for Pandora's security is Justin Toon. Sarah and Justin had this idea where . . ." He paused for a second. "Look, what I'm about to tell you is very confidential. I'm only saying anything because, quite frankly, having Hades as an ally and in charge of Tartarus is a lot better than not. Besides, Cronus running around fucks things up for everyone. But this goes no further. Agreed?"

Everyone nodded.

"It was a few years back, and Hera was starting to buy up land in London, something that concerned me. Her asshole of a son, Ares, created that Mars Warfare place."

"That was Ares?" I asked. Memories of the atrocities I'd seen there flashed into my mind. People murdered, experiments run on children. Mordred behind it all, torturing me, tearing out my memories that took me a decade to recover. And then, only by going back into that hellhole so he could torture me all over again. He'd murdered people I cared about, forced another to sacrifice her life to save mine.

A dull anger grew inside me. Mordred was dead. But I knew he'd been working for someone who hid in the shadows. I'd made every effort to look into that, but it was a dead end. To discover it was Ares . . . he would have to pay for what he'd wrought. One day, even if it took centuries from now, he'd find me being the last thing he saw.

I probably should have figured it out, but it seemed too obvious and brazen for even Ares to call a place he owned after the name he'd adopted for the Romans, *Mars*.

"Have you seen that place? Word is, someone . . ."—Brutus glanced at Kasey—"messed up a huge chunk of it a few years back. It's been pretty much unused since."

"Yeah, I had the honor," I said sarcastically as everyone glanced my way.

"Is that where Mordred took your memories?" Tommy asked.

I nodded. "If Ares was bankrolling Mordred, then Hera knew about it." I took a deep breath. "Keep going."

"Well, Sarah knew someone on the inside of Hera's organization, although I can't say who because I don't know. The three of them got Sarah inside as a spy to feed back info to me about Hera's operation. Sarah got noticed by Demeter, who introduced her to Hera, and then Sarah became a member of Hera's trusted advisors."

"Hence the marking," Tommy said.

Brutus nodded. "I thought Sarah was in too deep, and I was apparently right. If she helped Hera get Cronus free, then I was wrong about her."

"Wait, why would Hera want Cronus free?" Sky said, echoing the question we'd asked earlier. "Cronus will try to kill her. He might succeed. Why would Hera want that?"

No one could come up with a good explanation.

"Maybe that's the point," Kasey suggested. "Maybe she wants Cronus to try."

"Your daughter is a genius," I declared to Olivia who shared Kasey's smile. "What if Hera does want Cronus to try? If Sarah was working for Hera, then they arranged for him to escape and go after her. Sarah gets Cronus to the right place for the attack to take place, but Hera would already know where and when Cronus was going to be and so, after making it look good, they kill him with the dagger so Hera can absorb the enormous amount of power a fully powered Cronus would possess. She then goes to Avalon and says—"

"Look what happened at Tartarus," Sky finished. "Hades has made it unsafe. It needs more eyes on it."

"She'd cause an escape just so she could petition Avalon to get control over Tartarus?" Tommy said and then paused. "Actually, that's exactly how she'd do it."

"So Hera used the witches to get Cronus free?" Diana said. "Why can't more of their kind see the sort of person they've thrown their hat in with?" Diana held a special place for witches, and they for her. Over the years she's managed to show a lot of them why Hera and Demeter were not helping, but many more just ignored her.

"Sarah knew Mara," I said. "Sarah goes to Mara and says, 'I need your help.'"

Tommy shook his head. " '*Demeter* needs your help.' That would work better."

"Agreed," I said. "So now Sarah has a group of witches on her side, willing to help her get Cronus away from Hades and his compound. Sarah involves the Vanguard to actually break Cronus free—although we still have no idea why they'd agree to something like that—and then uses the witches to get Cronus away from the compound and to the house in the woods."

"You still think Pandora might be involved?" Brutus asked.

"Probably not," I agreed. "But what if this isn't Hera's Kituri dagger? She's not going to want anything to link back to her, just in case. So if Pandora let slip that she's got a stash of stuff somewhere, and Sarah went to get it, there could be more weapons like that one out there. There's no telling what else Pandora accumulated over the years."

"Then we'd best go see her. I think it would be best for your daughter to stay here," Brutus told Olivia. "Diana, would you do the honors of entertaining our guest?"

Diana stood and took Kasey's hand. "I have a collection of weaponry and armor I think you'll find very interesting," she told Kasey, whose apprehensive expression melted in an instant to a broad smile. Unfortunately, I couldn't say our afternoon was going to be as much fun.

CHAPTER 27

Pandora is housed in the very top floor of the citadel that Brutus calls home, the roof of which opens up to the outside with the push of a button. Her cell sits in the middle of the floor and consists of a large, apartment-sized block with the entire ceiling akin to a gigantic sunroof that opens on command. When both the roof and the ceiling are open, it allows Pandora some measure of the outside. There was a concern about her ability to escape, but it is a twenty-foot jump from the top of the ceiling to the roof, and she's watched all the time.

The walls of her apartment are made transparent from the outside. I don't know exactly how it works, but it's made of an almost indestructible substance that feels like concrete, but can't possibly be. Brutus has never told anyone, except maybe Hades and a few at Avalon, who made it or how. All people need to know is that Pandora is monitored twenty-four hours a day by a rotating shift of twelve guards. Two guard the door of the cell; two sit in the control room; and two stand at each corner: one on the same level as the cell and one on a raised gantry that runs around the cell at a few feet below roof height.

Pandora has not once tried to escape. Her cell has a bedroom, bathroom, kitchen, and library, all of which are fully stocked with whatever she needs. The bathroom is the only room where the walls aren't transparent, but then only a bath, toilet, sink and shower are in there, and it's searched weekly, so one minor concession to keep Pandora happy wasn't seen as a big deal.

"There's something you all need to know," Brutus told us as we stepped out of the lift and made our way through the security checkpoints. "Only Nate can go in."

"Why?" Olivia asked.

"He's the only one who's been enthralled and then released by Pandora. She can't take control of him after willingly letting him go."

Olivia stopped walking. "Wait a second. Pandora enthralled you?"

"About a thousand years ago," I began. "Pandora had escaped yet again, and she was trying to make her way across Europe. I went to intercept her. Unfortunately, she enthralled me." It's a weird sensation being enthralled. It's like your decisions to do anything are automatically what Pandora wants. The only time you get a piece of yourself back is when you sleep. That's when your subconscious starts screaming that things are wrong.

"What did she do?" Olivia asked, nervous.

"She took me to a cabin in the middle of what is now Austria and spent three months with me there. She didn't ask me to kill anyone, or try to kill me. We spent a lot of time talking. She told me about her life and how she was created and why she felt so angry about what the Olympians had done to her, just discarding her as a mistake because they were too ashamed to deal with her properly.

"Every time she's escaped since she was tossed aside like she was nothing, she's created chaos: World War II, the Napoleonic Wars, and even the Black Death. She thrives on it. Like she's punishing the world for what happened to her. Each and every prison we found for her, she escaped from. Even Tartarus. But for those three months, she just lived with me in that cabin. It was peaceful, and at the end she released me and allowed me to take her to Avalon, who arranged transport for her."

"That's why they always send you after her?" Sky said. "Because she let you go?"

I nodded.

"Why did she keep you at all?"

"I think she saw something in me she liked. Something she trusted. At least that's what I choose to believe. She's not evil, but she is dangerous and uncontrollable. When Hope's in charge, she can be reasoned with, but with Pandora, it's more about trying to minimize casualties." Once Pandora enthralls someone, she can manipulate that person at will from anywhere on earth. The link she creates doesn't have a time or distance limit.

"You sure it wasn't Hope with you in that cabin?" Sky asked.

"Hope doesn't have access to Pandora's abilities. She's just along for the ride, so to speak."

"Nate, you go down there," Brutus said, pointing toward a set of double doors at the end of the corridor, guarded by two armed men. "The rest of you come with me to the control room. A word of warning: There are no abilities used beyond those doors, Nate. We use a similar system to Hades. It's why the guards are armed with guns. I won't make any exceptions to that rule."

"Not a problem," I said and walked toward the two guards, who stopped and searched me, the second time I'd been searched since arriving on the floor. They found the dwarven Kituri dagger, but Brutus had already explained to them that I needed Pandora to see it, and they allowed me to continue through the doors.

The cell was an imposing structure, even if it was transparent. I glanced to my left and right and saw two of the eight guards who were watching the cell itself. Both looked my way for a brief moment before returning their gaze to the central structure. The gantry was ten feet above my head, putting it just below the open roof. The wind whipped in from above, meaning the room was a good few degrees cooler than the rest of the building.

Being inside a transparent house is a little on the weird side. Mostly because although the walls were transparent, none of the furnishings inside were. It meant that all of the kitchen and bedroom fittings were quite visible, as was the couch, TV, and every piece of wiring and plumbing. It was a very odd thing to view.

Pandora was in the room closest to me, where dozens of book cases, floor-to-ceiling high, obscured two of the guards from her view. There was a small stepladder so that she could reach the books on the very top shelves, but she was currently seated in a red leather armchair, reading.

The immediate urge was to shout out to her, but the substance that makes up her cell is the same as any normal house building material, and besides she couldn't see me from inside the cell. I walked up to the door and knocked once.

I watched as Pandora got up from her seat, and still carrying her book, made her way toward me, where she opened the door. "Nathan," she said with a smile. "What a lovely surprise. Please, do come in."

I walked down the hallway as Pandora closed the door behind me. "Tea?" she asked.

"Green, if you've got it."

"Always. It's loose leaf too. Can't be drinking that bagged shit; there's no telling what stuff gets put in there."

I followed her into a sizeable kitchen and glanced up at the removed ceiling, giving her a view of the sky above. "How do you get used to it?"

She followed my gaze. "We like it. Not as much as, say, being free, or even in Tartarus, but it's a nice middle ground. It's peaceful too, and we get lots of visitors. Usually dignitaries from Avalon or people who are looking to write things about us, but it's better than being in a pit somewhere."

Pandora poured some water in a kettle and then, just before the water was at boiling point, she poured it into two cups with tea leaves inside. She passed me a cup and inhaled the aroma on hers. "It's mixed with cherry blossom," she told me. "Smells lovely."

"Yeah, it smells great," I agreed.

"You're not here for a social call are you?"

"No, I'm here because Cronus escaped from Tartarus."

Pandora started laughing. "Holy shit! The old man finally did it. Good for him."

"Not really, someone broke him out with the intention of killing him. With this." I placed the dwarven dagger on the kitchen counter.

"That's ours," she said immediately. "Do you know whose blood is inside it?"

I paused.

"Oh, don't look so shocked. No one is going to try to kill Cronus with any kind of dagger unless it's powerful enough to get the job done. And we know full well what our dagger can do."

"Blood magic would be able to tell us the species the blood belonged to maybe, but not the specific person. And I can't use blood magic anymore."

Pandora's eyebrows raised in shock. "When did that happen?"

"A few years back," I said, not wishing to elaborate further on how it had been replaced with my use of necromancy. "You sure this is your dagger?"

"Yes, we've used it several times in the past, so it's something we'd remember. Only ours has this yellow gem on the side, just under the hilt." She picked up the dagger and turned it slightly, showing it to me. "It's one of a kind."

"So, how did Sarah Hamilton get hold of it?"

"Well, that's sort of our fault." She walked past me back into the library, and I followed without interruption as we both sat on identical leather chairs. "She used to work here, and we got on pretty well. She used to come and chat during the evenings. On one occasion, we mentioned that small cabin you spent time in with us, and how we used the basement to hide stuff. We assume she went there and took this."

"Anything else there I should know about?"

"Money, mostly. Some old books, maps, probably a few old pieces of weaponry. Nothing else that presents this level of danger. We're not even sure why she'd have gone to the bother of getting it."

I paused for a second. I knew that Pandora couldn't lie to me, but I wondered whether she'd known that giving Sarah the dagger would cause chaos. Chaos that Pandora couldn't be blamed for, but one she certainly would enjoy hearing about. "Sarah was also working for Hera," I said, taking the subject to more immediate matters. "Originally, as a spy for Brutus, but it looks like she got into her inner circle, and from there she helped formulate a plan to help Cronus escape. We think Hera wanted Cronus to try to kill her to give her an excuse to get more access to Tartarus."

"That would mean the blood in the vial is Hera's. We'd have liked to get hold of some of that. Can you imagine the horrible things we could do to her?" She smiled and a flicker of anger was noticeable behind her eyes.

"The dagger was used to murder Sarah," I finally admitted, after making sure Pandora wasn't involved. "The blood has evaporated."

"Sarah's dead?"

I nodded and explained what we knew about Sarah's involvement.

"A krampus?" Pandora asked when I'd finished. "That's actually quite impressive."

"She never mentioned anything about Tartarus or Cronus to you?"

"No, never. We usually spoke about books and old artifacts. In fact that's why we were telling her about the dagger. She had a marked interest in it." She paused for a moment and took a drink of her tea. "Cronus will almost certainly try to kill Hera. He hates her for helping Zeus start the Titan Wars, and even more for killing Zeus."

"No one knows what happened to Zeus." It was a sentence I'd been finding myself saying a lot recently.

"Do you really believe that?"

I shook my head. "What I believe and what I can prove are two different things. Cronus needs to be stopped."

"We agree," Pandora said, and she must have noticed my obvious surprise. "We don't want anyone else but us killing that bitch Hera. One day we will get our vengeance on her and her evil fucking clan, and Cronus will not take that vengeance away from us. The same goes for anyone else who tries to stop us, for that matter."

"Do you know where Cronus would go once he reached England?"

"He's not going to go after Hera until his power is increased. He doesn't plan on doing a suicide run. He's not the type."

"Okay, so where does he go to get power then?"

"A magic well?" she offered immediately.

I opened my mouth to speak and stopped for a brief moment. "Oh, shit," I finally managed.

"We assume you didn't think of that."

I was silent as I contemplated the implications. A magic well is a place where magic is naturally occurring in the environment. Where a sorcerer who knows the right runes and the right way of using them can tap into that magic and draw it into himself. The problem is that the United Kingdom has tons of the things all over the place. Most humans would just walk around such a place and say they could feel reverence or that it gave them goose bumps. But sorcerers would be able to make themselves more powerful, albeit temporarily, by tapping into the magic itself.

"Any idea which one he'd use?"

Pandora laughed. "Seriously? We can think of maybe twenty places off the top of our head that he'd think were viable."

"All of them will have an Avalon presence, though."

"You really think that's going to stop Cronus? All it'll do is give him more chances to kill people. You want our advice?"

I motioned for her to continue.

"You go find Hera and warn her that there's a reckoning coming. Because Cronus is single-minded at the best of times, and once he gets within arm's length of killing her, there's nothing that's going to stop him short of his own death."

I stood and realized I hadn't touched my tea.

"It's okay," Pandora said, noticing my gaze. "Go save the bitch; make sure she's nice and secure. Because we want her healthy for when we get our own chance to tear her fucking head off."

"Shit, shit, shit, shit, shit," I said as I returned to the control room, where all the others sat in silence. "I assume you heard all of what she said?"

Everyone nodded at once.

"I've made some calls," Olivia said. "All LOA staff are on high alert for anything unusual. I've said we have info that someone is going to try to get to a magic well, but nothing more than that. Any ideas where he might go?"

"I'd have guessed outside of London, but I've got no idea of his frame of mind. He might go to the biggest one in London and use it as a massive 'I'm here' to get Hera's attention."

"I'll get my people to keep an extra eye on the Tower of London, then," she said. "But once Cronus turns up at a magic well, any hope of keeping this quiet is gone. Magic wells are not made for stealthy use."

"We'll cross that bridge when we have to," I said. "In the meantime, we need to go see Hera. She's got to be warned of Cronus. He won't be able to kill her *and* everyone else, but she's his priority, and she needs to be made aware."

"I'll come with you," Olivia said. "She might be more respectful to the presence of an LOA Director."

"Thanks," I said.

"I'm staying here," Sky told everyone. "My parents are on their way here. One of them is going to need access to whatever magic well Cronus decides to fill up on."

"I'm coming with you," Tommy assured me. "What with Brutus, his people, Sky and—when they turn up—her parents, it's almost guaranteed that Kasey will be safe here."

"We'll be happy to keep her company. Nate, if it was Hera's blood in that dagger, she'll be more powerful now," Brutus said. "Sarah might have only been a witch, but she was exceptionally talented and not above using powerful magic."

"Yeah, I remember," I said as the memory of the *effete* spell bounced to the front of my mind. "Any idea where Hera is?"

"She has a place to the north of here. She's with all of her allies," Brutus told us. "That means it's going to be more than a little frosty for you and your friends. You might be better off finding Cronus and stopping him."

"One thing at a time."

"I heard Sarah was murdered," said a man as he entered the control room. He was about my height and build, but with a shaved head with several scars on top. He wore jeans and a shirt, with a holster for two revolvers.

"Justin," Brutus said. "You heard. I'm sorry. Everyone, this is Justin Toon, our head of security."

Justin nodded curtly in our direction. Somehow Justin was the man whose connections had placed Sarah inside Hera's operation. A move that had eventually gotten her killed. I could forgive a little curtness in his situation.

"I did tell her not to get involved too deeply with Hera," Justin said. "You're going after Cronus for this?" The question was directed at everyone.

"Yeah," I said. "But Sarah was a willing participant. She created a krampus, murdered people. She wasn't an innocent."

Justin rubbed his eyes and shook his head sadly. "She was a good person, but working with Hera changed her. She became more focused on helping Hera and her people and began to forget that she was there to spy, not help them. They twisted her to their own vision. There's no other explanation."

I could think of a few, mostly involving money and power, but decided that bringing them to his attention would do little to help the situation.

"She was thrilled when Demeter started to notice her and took her to see Hera," Justin continued. "Even more so when Hera started asking for her personally."

"When did you last hear from her?"

"About four months ago. She said she was dealing with some plans of Hera's. That it was going to be big."

"I guess we know what that was," Sky said.

"I can't believe she'd fall so far as to murder people for Hera. It's just not something I'd ever imagined."

"We need to go," Tommy said.

"Yeah, we need to help some people who hate us stay in one piece," I said sarcastically.

"Well, to add to that list of shit things," Brutus said, "my sources say that Selene is going to be there with Hera too."

My entire body deflated with one massive sigh. "Well that's just fucking wonderful, isn't it?"

CHAPTER 28

Dresden, Germany. 1936.

It took me the better part of a day to fully heal from the injuries sustained by an exploding Magali Martin, not to mention the beating I'd taken at the hands of Helios. Magali's silver locket, which had embedded in my side and caused so much damage, was the last thing to heal and a constant reminder that Pandora's thralls were fanatical in their commitment to her needs.

Selene had dealt badly with her brother's involvement in Pandora's plan when she'd first discovered it, but the realization that her brother was not only helping but was also the architect of everything was a massive blow. For some reason, our escape from serious injury—or worse—had made her want to discuss our past relationship, a conversation I was unwilling to have.

It was an odd sensation, wanting so much to talk to her, but needing to push her away. Selene was not someone who allowed herself to be seen as weak more than once, so from the second I'd walked away from her request to talk, Selene had thrown herself into finding anything that would reveal her brother's plan. She went out with Kurt to talk to his contacts in the city while Petra helped an injured Lucie.

I found myself sitting in the house's library, reading some information that Kurt had uncovered about the availability of sarin gas in Berlin. I was certain it was part of Helios's plot, about which all we knew for certain was that he was going to try to kill Hera at the opening of the Olympic games, only a few short days away.

"I need to thank you," Lucie said as she entered the room, bringing me out of my concentration. "You probably saved my life."

"Not a problem. You may not like me, or trust me for that matter, but I'm not the monster you think I am."

Lucie stood silently for a few seconds before turning and leaving me alone in the library. I sighed. There was always going to be uneasiness between us. She clearly believed her brother hadn't been responsible for anything that had happened and that I'd killed and framed him as some sort of scapegoat.

I rubbed my eyes. It had been a very long few days, and the constant need to avoid both Lucie and Selene had been much more tiring than I'd expected it to be.

As if on cue, Selene opened the door and stepped inside. "We need to talk."

"About what?" I asked.

"My brother."

"Your brother is involved, and he's doing this of his own volition. Whether he sought out Pandora or vice versa doesn't really matter."

"Agreed," she said and sat opposite me. "My brother has made his bed and must be stopped. That's not what I'm talking about. I mean us. When I saw you hurt—" She paused, breaking off for a second. "My heart stopped."

"You left me," I said softly, so as not to betray my still raw anger at what had happened so many years ago. "You left me for Deimos. A man you'd always told me you hated. Obviously, hate wasn't enough to stop you from marrying him." As the words left my mouth, I regretted them, but I was too stubborn to actually say anything of the kind to Selene, who physically recoiled from them.

"Will you ever stop hating me?"

I opened my mouth to say something hurtful, anything to make her feel the same pain I did, but I couldn't. "I don't hate you," I whispered. "That's the damn problem."

She reached out and touched my leg, but I stood and walked off, turning away from her. "Don't."

I heard nothing else until the door opened, and I turned to find myself alone once more.

I sat in quiet for a few moments. It had taken a lot to tell Selene no. I wasn't certain I could do it a second time.

"Why did two women come out of here in a hurry?" Kurt asked as he opened the door. "I assume you've been your usual charming self."

"Who knew a library could be so busy?" I said with a forced smile.

"My people in Berlin found something you might be interested in." He walked over to a table nearby, where he placed several photographs.

I picked up the one closest to me; it was of a warehouse's front door. There was a lorry standing outside, and several Nazis stood around, either guarding it or keeping watch on the warehouse. Two more Nazis—officers judging by their uniforms—were talking off to one side.

"What was in the lorry?" I asked.

Kurt passed me another photo showing the Nazis' bodies littering the ground and a smoking ruin where the lorry once was.

"Helios, I assume."

"My contact said that the Nazis removed something like artillery shells from the back of the lorry. He couldn't get a photo of it because they were very nervous at that point and making sure to watch all around them. But once they'd finished, he said that a winged god landed on the vehicle, and it exploded."

I flicked through the photos, but there was nothing there that Kurt hadn't already told me.

"They were working for Helios, and he killed them all," I said.

"Looks that way. I guess he didn't want any witnesses, or maybe someone figured out what he was going to use it for and then threatened to pull the plug."

"Either way, we need to go look at that sarin."

"Hold your horses; it gets worse." He removed a map from his back pocket and unfolded it, laying it out on the table. Red crosses dotted it at certain points, and I realized that they were all clustered around where the Olympic stadium stood.

"This is where the sarin is being placed, isn't it?" I asked.

"We tracked down someone who worked with Magali and her husband, Jean, who live in another part of town. They eventually admitted that the sarin was going to be used in bombs placed around the stadium, and gave us the locations. Selene is very persuasive when she needs to be."

"We're sure of the placements? This person wasn't enthralled by Pandora to hand out false information?"

"He was hired help. He'd never met Pandora, so it's doubtful. He could have been lying, but I didn't get that impression. Besides, we've checked the areas in question and they're undoubtedly the best places to put the gas if you want to kill everyone in that stadium."

"So, what's your plan?"

"According to our man, the gas will be in place tomorrow night. There's a team of lackeys just itching to help Helios kill Nazis. They think they're freedom fighters."

"So apparently 'freedom fighter' equates to the murderer of innocent women and children now?" I asked, my words dripping with sarcasm.

No one spoke for a moment; apparently, I'd stopped the conversation in its tracks.

"So, what's the plan?" I asked again.

"I'll get everyone else, and then we'll go over it." He left the library, and I continued to study the map until he returned with Petra, Selene, and Lucie a few minutes later.

"Okay, Kurt, let's hear it," I said.

"Selene, Petra, and I are going to go around tomorrow evening, defusing any bombs and stopping any people we find there. In the meantime, Nathan and Lucie, you're going to the warehouse." Kurt grabbed a photo from the table and pointed at something on the building's external wall. "You see this rune? No idea what others are going to be there, so, Lucie, I hope you're up to making sure they're not a problem. Nathan, you're there to provide muscle. My contacts say there are no guards in the area, but if there *is* anyone there, they'll need to be removed. From what we were told, a lot of the sarin is out being used in the bombs, but there's still plenty left in that warehouse to hurt a lot of people. Hopefully, the building is empty of people, but we can't risk letting any of this gas get into anyone's hands, let alone it going to a group of people who will actually use it."

"Wait a second. Only the enchanter who put the runes there can remove them. So how is Lucie going to manage that?" I asked.

"I have my ways," Lucie said with a sly grin. "Besides we don't know what put that rune there, and it's only an enchanter's runes I can't remove. Maybe luck will be on our side, and I can just wipe it away without trouble."

I let it drop. "Okay, so how do you know that none of the other explosives will have runes on them?"

"Their enchanter is the same man we interrogated. Helios hired him to do the job. He doesn't really want to kill tens of thousands of people; he just wants to get paid. He'd already put the runes on the bombs before Helios's friends took them away for safekeeping until they were ready to be used. We have him tied up in his hotel room. We're going to fetch him, and then he's going to remove the runes."

"Or I'll remove parts of him," Selene said.

"How are we going to remove any sarin left in the warehouse? We can't just carry it out and hope for the best. For that matter, where are you going to put the stuff you find when you defuse the bombs?"

"I've contacted Hades," Petra said. "He's going to be on his way up here with a containment team. They'll arrive tomorrow night too, but they're coming to us first to take whatever sarin we find, so you need to sit on that warehouse and make sure no one gets in or out until they arrive."

"Any idea where Helios is going to be?" I asked.

"He'll be wherever his base of operations is," Selene said. "Probably going over plans in his head. He's very detail oriented. He'll be holed up somewhere once the sun starts to dip. He won't want to risk anything happening to him that could disrupt the plan."

"Any idea where his base is?" Lucie asked. "I don't want to run into him at the warehouse."

"We don't know," Kurt admitted. "Somewhere in Berlin is our best guess. If he *is* at the warehouse, you're going to have a hell of a fight on your hands. Just contact us on the radio—there's one in the back of your new car. We'll come running."

"Basically our plan for dealing with Helios is to hope like hell he isn't there," I said.

Selene smiled, and Kurt rolled his eyes.

"Good—just checking." I turned to Lucie. "Bring some weapons because I guarantee you Helios will now be at the warehouse."

"How can you possibly know that?" Lucie almost snapped.

"Because I can't think of anything that would piss me off more than having to fight Helios while making sure a bunch of exceptionally deadly nerve gas doesn't explode all over us. And if the last few days are any indication, whatever pisses me off the most is exactly what will happen."

I spent the rest of the afternoon trying to burn off the nervous energy I felt coursing through me. There were only twenty-four hours until Kurt's plan was due to be placed in motion, and I wanted to get some sleep before then.

After a few hours spent working out in the sizeable garden behind the house, I showered and then tried to relax. Grabbing one of the many books from the library, I returned outside to read, trying to dislodge my thoughts about what was, in my mind anyway, the impending fight.

"We never finished talking," Selene said as she sat on the chair beside me, drawing my attention away from the book.

I placed the novel on the small glass table beside me. "We did. You ran off."

"Okay, let me rephrase: I don't want to leave it like that."

"How should we leave it, Selene? Am I meant to want you to drop everything and divorce your husband, so I can take you back with open arms? You left me."

"I had no choice. There's more to it than I can tell you."

"So, someone physically forced you to leave me and marry your asshole of a husband?"

Selene remained mute.

"Good old dad, marrying off his daughter so he can get out of Tartarus. He made a deal with Hera and used you as collateral. I don't know what makes me angrier: that they arranged it or that you let them."

"Believe what you like, I guess," she said and stood. "It was stupid of me to come here and expect to change your mind."

"Yes, it was," I agreed. I closed my eyes and leaned back in the chair.

After a few seconds of silence, I opened my eyes to discover that Selene wore an expression of hurt, and my anger subsided.

"I think about you all the time," she said. "We were perfect. I wish every day that I could tell you why I left. I can't, though. And I'm sorrier about that than you can possibly understand."

Words caught in my throat. "*Were* is the word you should focus on." I stood and picked up my book, catching a whiff of

Selene's perfume. It made my heart beat faster, but I was damned if I was going to let her win.

I inwardly cursed myself. *Win*—what a fucking stupid notion. As if this were all some game being played. In my mind there was no winner. No matter the outcome, I had still lost someone I cared for.

"I'm angry at you," I found myself saying. "Not because you left me, although, that's certainly part of it, but that you come here to work with me and let your feelings show for me. I could deal with this if you were cold, if you kept your distance. It would mean I wouldn't have to deal with this shit. But when we were in that house, and you saw me hurt . . . I saw in your eyes how worried you were about me, and that was more than I wanted to take."

Selene took a deep breath and stepped toward me.

"Don't," I told her. "When you left me, when you just walked out without explanation, except from what I managed to piece together from rumors and hearsay, it fucking broke me."

Selene stopped and her eyes became moist.

"So don't," I continued, the words just spilling out of me whether I wanted them to or not. "Don't come back here and try to reclaim something between us, because I can't do halves with you. I can't think I have you, only to watch you walk back to a man I refuse to believe you even tolerate let alone feel any kind of affection for."

Selene took another step, tears beginning to fall.

I shook my head. "Don't, Selene. My feelings aren't something you get to toy with. This isn't something you can start up without consequence."

She reached me and placed a hand on my chest, making it feel as if my heart were about to burst free from it, before taking my hand and placing it against her own.

"I want you," Selene whispered and kissed me softly on the lips. She tasted like peach.

"You're married," I whispered back.

"Why should that matter?"

"Because it's *you*." I pushed her back slightly, although I still lingered for far too long before doing so.

"Are you sure?" she asked and stepped toward me once again. "I know we shouldn't. But I don't care about that. I just want to be with you."

Selene kissed me again, and whatever resolve I had shattered. I held her against me as emotions and memories swirled through my head.

She kicked off her shoes and led me barefoot through the grass to the large guesthouse that she'd been using at the bottom of the garden. I'd like to say I put up a fight—hell, I'd like to say I had thoughts in my mind other than being with her again, but I didn't. As she led me through the front door and we stumbled up the stairs to her bed, there was only one thing on my mind: Selene.

CHAPTER 29

Dresden, Germany. 1936.

The sex was, as it always had been between the two of us, amazing. Selene brought out the best in me in a lot of different ways, and I knew it. But once we'd finally succumbed to sleep, my dreams were fitful, full of betrayal and anger. Full of death.

I woke with the nagging doubt that our actions had been wrong. Not because she was cheating on her husband: when push came to shove, he was a nasty little asshole, but because I wished I could believe that Selene would leave Deimos, but I didn't. I expected her to go running back to him for whatever reason she'd left me for in the first place. Generally, I'm neither naïve nor stupid, although I'll admit that those qualities wavered whenever Selene was concerned. So, though the doubts were there, I *wanted* to believe otherwise.

By the time we were both up, washed, and dressed, it was getting on to early afternoon. Selene was acting as if no one would ever come between us, as if we really were newly in love. She kissed and touched me, but we didn't talk much. There was no discussion of the past or future; only the present existed. It made me even more wary.

Once we were dressed, her in leather armor and me in combat fatigues belonging to the German army, we left the guesthouse and walked back into the main house, only to be greeted by Petra, Lucie, and Kurt, who were making preparations to leave.

"Glad you could join us," Kurt said to us both. "Hope you got that out of your system."

Selene smiled and walked off, leaving Kurt and me alone.

"Do you have any idea what you're doing?" he whispered.

I shook my head.

"I hope it works out for you, my friend," he said and clasped me on the shoulder, passing me a silver dagger. "No guns."

"I think I'll manage," I said and attached the dagger's sheath to one of the loops on my belt.

A few minutes later, everyone was ready. Kurt went over the plan once more, and then we left the house. Lucie and I climbed into a newly stolen 1935 black and red Audi Front. Lucie wore a military officer's uniform, while I was meant to be her driver, something I think she enjoyed a lot more than was probably considered normal. Every time we passed soldiers at a checkpoint, she handed over fake identification that someone Kurt knew had created, and took great delight in telling them how much of an idiot I was, which, if I'm honest, probably helped us. More than once I got a glance of sympathetic understanding and was let through before they'd even seen her papers.

We reached Berlin and noticed the excitement in the air and the sheer number of people on the streets. It was obvious that any attack from Helios and his helpers would cause nothing short of a massacre.

I took the car along the city roads, getting closer and closer to the warehouse and wondering just how accurate Kurt's information was. But as I pulled the car down a dark side road and entered the group of buildings that held our target, it became apparent that there were no guards. Not even the booth and checkpoint to allow people onto the site was manned.

"Looks like Kurt's information was right," Lucie said, as I did a lap of the entire complex, which contained six more much smaller buildings. Then I returned to our target and stopped the car. Lucie got out, and I followed suit, noticing that the sun was just beginning to dip down, the day moving toward dusk.

"This is odd," I said. "I'd have expected someone to be here."

"Surely that just makes our job easier."

I shrugged and walked over to the closest building, a one-story structure with blacked-out windows that stood out against the white-painted walls. I tried the door, which was locked, but a swift kick to the lock ended that barrier. The building was about fifty feet long and contained chairs and tables, along with several mountains of paperwork. I walked over to the nearest pile and picked up the top piece, a delivery note. It was dated the day the photos had been taken, although it said nothing about the contents of the delivery other than "Ordinance."

I left the building and found Lucie standing, arms crossed, beside the car. "You're supposed to be helping me," she said.

"I'm making sure we don't get any surprises. If you like, you can help check. We'll be done quicker. Then we can check the warehouse."

"Fine, let's get this done." Lucie walked over to a building, identical to the one I'd just exited from, but to the left of the car, and opened the door.

I didn't wait around to see what she'd found, but made my way to three more buildings. They contained nothing of interest, although they showed that people had been working here recently. In one, a cup of now stone-cold tea sat on a desk and a half-eaten sandwich on another. People had left in a hell of a hurry.

After flicking through a particularly large file, I discovered that I'd been right about Pandora trying to learn how to take control of Hope's body. The memory of Pandora using "me" roared to the forefront of my mind.

"Nathan," Lucie shouted, and I ran out of the office as she jogged over toward me. "This whole place was Gestapo."

I gave her the file I'd been reading. "They were trying to find a way for Pandora to gain total control of Hope's body, pushing the human soul aside. It looks like they wanted to take Pandora apart to figure out how she worked. That's probably when she killed all of them at their headquarters. Hades needs to be told about this, and sooner rather than later."

Lucie read part of what I'd given her. "There's more in the other office. The Gestapo quite like their paperwork about all the evil shit they're doing. Any idea who attacked this place?"

"Helios probably. Pandora wouldn't have wanted anyone to be able to re-create her, I'm sure of that. That leaves the question of why all this research wasn't destroyed."

It appeared that neither of us had an answer, so we made our way to the final building. It was a two story, red-bricked office that gave off the smell of death well before we reached the door, and by the time we'd made it there, the stench was overpowering. The door opened on the first try, and I immediately closed it again as the stench of the dead inside threatened to overpower me.

"You okay?" Lucie asked, using a handkerchief to cover her mouth and nose.

I nodded. "Let's go look at those runes. I want to see how you think you're going to remove them."

I followed Lucie back to the warehouse and kept watch while she went and looked at the runes. She knelt before the hand-sized rune on the wall, in between the door and a massive shutter for a loading dock, and concentrated.

"You know I've never understood something about enchanters," I said.

"And what would that be?" she asked without glancing my way.

"If I have to use a rune, I need to know it. I need to have studied it and figured out what it says. But you don't. I've always wondered why that was."

"Sixteen hundred years old and you never asked before?"

"In case you haven't met any others of your kind before, they're not exactly forthcoming about what they can and can't do."

"Because sorcerers are so well known for being free and open with their magic?"

"Good point," I conceded.

After a few seconds of silence passed, I'd come to the conclusion that Lucie had no intention of telling me anything, and I began to wonder how long this day was going to feel.

"We think of the word we want to create, and the effect it will have, and if we have enough power, then the rune is created. The words have to be simple." Lucie pointed at the rune on the wall. "This says 'Explode.'"

"So how do we remove it?"

"Well, as you pointed out yesterday, I can't remove any runes created by another enchanter, which I can tell this one was. However, I can add to it, making it far too complex, therefore either collapsing the rune or changing it enough to make it less effective. I've just added a second rune to this one to say 'Explode down.' In theory it should tear through the wall, but not go back into the warehouse or come out toward us. I could try to add more to it and collapse the rune, but the effects can be unstable, and if there is sarin gas in there, I can't say it would end well for us."

"How do we activate it?"

"The easiest way is opening the door."

I paused. "How *powerful* is this rune?"

"Someone put enough power into it that anyone opening this door without disabling it would probably be vaporized."

"You're not exactly selling the idea of opening the door."

"You could try to destroy the door with magic. But if you get it wrong and there's anything behind there that's going to hurt us, we'd soon know about it."

"You sure your rune works?" I asked. "If you're wrong, I'm going to be very upset."

"Noted."

I walked up to the door and readied a dense shield of air magic all around me before grabbing hold of the door handle and pulling the door toward me. The runes did their job and exploded down through the wall, gouging a massive hole in the concrete.

I released the shield as Lucie stepped up beside me. "Told you it would work."

"That you did," I said. "Sorry I doubted you."

Lucie paused as if she was going to say something, before deciding against it and walking through the door into the warehouse, which as it turned out, was empty.

"This is unexpected," she said as I picked up some wiring from the floor near a wooden pallet.

"They cleaned the place out. It was probably used as a staging area."

"Then why the runes?" I asked.

We walked the length of the warehouse but found nothing of interest until we came to a door about halfway along the hundred-foot side of the building. The door was next to another loading dock. There were no runes, so I opened the door—and immediately wished I hadn't.

The room wasn't big—maybe a hundred square feet—but the rear of it was stacked floor to ceiling with pallets, each containing several massive artillery shells. Most of them had been opened and their internal parts removed, but several were still intact. I moved to the closest shell and read the German writing on the red label affixed to the wood beneath it: "Warning! Sarin gas."

"The sarin was in the shells. They extracted it from these open ones to make the bombs. That's a lot of gas. This is what was unloaded from the truck. I wonder why they'd bring it here. Why not somewhere more secure?"

"I don't know," Lucie admitted. "But we need to make sure that those shells don't go anywhere."

We closed the door to the storage room and walked back to the front of the warehouse, where we found two chairs and sat. There was little else to do; neither of us was versed in the art of defusing sarin gas–filled military shells.

I wondered how Selene, Kurt, and Petra were doing; hopefully, they'd stop the bombs before anyone got hurt. I glanced over at the room with the sarin. There wasn't a lot of gas left unused, but what was there made me uncomfortable.

CHAPTER 30

Berlin, Germany. 1936.

Why Hellequin?" Lucie asked after ten minutes of silence between us as we sat together inside the warehouse.

"What?"

"Hellequin, why? What does it mean? Hades told me you used to go by that name."

"I buried that a long time ago," I said, feeling slightly annoyed at my past being discussed.

"Sorry, just making conversation."

"Merlin came up with it," I said. "It's an old dwarven word. It means 'he who brings death,' although it was probably a lot less cliché at the time."

"Nice name to have," she said dryly.

"Merlin wanted a name that people would sit up and pay attention to. It sort of fits."

"But isn't the Hellequin also a French character?"

"Ah, the play? Yes, a few hundred years after I started using it. A French writer, who'd seen me fighting a group of soldiers, wrote a play using the Hellequin name. He dressed the character in black and red with a black mask and wrote that I took the souls of the evil to hell. At some point in the fifteenth century, that changed to become 'harlequin.' Which was, I guess, more of a comedic character who flips and flops around the stage."

"Must have been odd, seeing people dress up as you, in a way."

"That whole century was weird. Seeing people dressed in a manner that was based on me took some getting used to. Although I didn't take it personally."

"So, you're responsible for one of the most recognizable characters ever."

"I think I'd rather not see it like that. I don't think wearing tights and prancing around a stage is something I'd be very good at."

Lucie's chuckle was good to hear. "Maybe you're not the monster I thought you were for so long. But I still want the truth about what happened."

Any hopes of us getting along vanished. The fact that I'd been the one to kill her brother, whether warranted or not, was always going to be between us. "Your brother killed dozens of people. I caught him in the act, there was a fight, and he died. That's what happened."

"I don't believe you."

"He confessed to killing your family before he died," I told Lucie, ignoring her disbelief.

"Lies!" she shouted and leaped to her feet, her face full of sudden anger.

"Lucie. I didn't frame him for murders he didn't commit. He killed a lot of people. If you want more information, you'll have to talk to Hades. I've told you all I can." I opened my mouth to say more, but closed it again. She didn't need to know the rest. Even telling her she should talk to Hades was a slip of the tongue I shouldn't have made.

Lucie's hands balled into fists, and she took a step toward me but stopped as she glanced out of the still open warehouse door. I followed her gaze and noticed the hooded figure walking toward us. He stopped by the car and gazed inside the window.

I stood and exited the warehouse. "Sorry," I said in German. "This is private property."

The man reached into the car and with a loud crunch removed the radio, dropping it to the ground. He took a few more steps toward me and tossed back his oversized hood, revealing Helios's smiling face. "Now, Nathan, we both know this property isn't yours."

I cracked my wrists; violence was inevitable. And Helios had some payback coming for what he did to me outside of Magali's house. "You've come for the sarin, I assume. I don't think there's enough left for you to bother with."

"Oh, that's rich. You think that little cupboard in there was where all the sarin was stored? Regardless, it's mine. I paid for it. Well, technically I paid for the Gestapo to bring it here so I could kill them all in the same place, but it's still mine."

"There's more of that dammed stuff," I whispered, and glanced at Lucie. "Fantastic."

I turned back to Helios. "Why'd you leave out everything about Pandora gaining control of Hope's body?"

"Ah, you found out about that. I was supposed to destroy it all. But I got so tired from killing all of these people that I thought I'd save it until tonight. Now I can burn you all with it."

"The bombs will never be detonated!" Lucie shouted.

Helios laughed. "Yes, you're probably right. But they won't stop me from walking into that stadium and butchering Hera and her friends in front of the world's eyes. The first live televised massacre. It'll be quite the eye-opener for those watching. The sarin—well, that's just the icing on the cake."

I walked toward Helios, with Lucie following just behind. "This won't be easy for you," I informed him. "It's almost night." As a dragon-kin powered by the sun, the night would leave him depleted and, in theory, easier to defeat. In theory.

"Then I'd better hurry, hadn't I?" A roar of fire escaped his mouth, causing me to dive aside, dragging Lucie with me. The fire followed us until we reached the office building, which gave us some cover, although the smell of burning paper inside the office suggested it wasn't going to be cover for very long.

"Can you buy me time?" Lucie asked.

"To do what?"

"A 'yes' or 'no' will suffice," she told me as she unbuttoned her jacket and let it fall to the floor, exposing the bandages wrapped around her arms.

"Sure—no idea how long, though."

I left Lucie alone and walked around the side of the burning building.

"Decided to join the fun?" Helios asked as I walked toward him.

"Sure, let's try that fire trick again."

Helios opened his mouth to breathe fire once again, but I threw a bubble of air at his open maw, which caused him to stop suddenly lest he inhale his own flame. He crushed his jaws together; creating a huge amount of pressure that destroyed the magic.

Helios grabbed his hooded coat and tore it free, throwing it onto the ground as two large wings unfurled on his back. They weren't the brilliant red and yellow they'd been when I'd last seen them outside Magali's house. Due to the fading sun, their color was now a dull yellow, but they were still impressive.

He beat his wings once, avoiding a jet of flame that shot from my hands. I turned the jet into a whip and threw it up at a hovering Helios, but he avoided it with ease and roared more fire at me, causing me to move back.

"Are we done with this?" Helios asked. "This feeling-out process?"

"Sure," I said and created a shield of air that covered my entire body. "Let's see what you've got."

Helios dove at me, his wings driving him forward with enormous power. I didn't move until the last moment, when I used a blast of air to throw myself up over Helios, who couldn't turn around in time to stop me from landing, wrapping a tendril of air around his feet, and giving it a giant pull, which stopped his ability to fly.

Helios crashed to the ground and tumbled into the side of the nearest building. "You're beginning to try my patience," he said as he got back to his feet, just in time for me to smash a column of air magic into his face.

He dropped to one knee but then suddenly launched himself toward me, catching me with a punch that sent me flying back through the air until I struck the side of the still-burning building at an awkward angle and felt at least one rib snap in protest.

I dropped to my knees as my breath left me, and pain shot up and down the side of my torso. I used the building to pull myself to my feet but wasn't quick enough to avoid an incoming Helios, who swept me off the ground and into the air, holding me by my throat as I struggled to break free. Two swift punches to my ribs ended my fight. He found the dagger that Kurt had given me, and tossed it aside.

"I did tell you to leave. I said I'd kill you if I saw you again," Helios said with no trace of malice or anger, just disappointment.

I tried to plunge a blade of air into his chest, but scales now covered his entire body, an effective armor against such weapons. I didn't have the strength to drive the blade through them.

"My sister will have to get over you." With that he threw me at the burning building.

I wrapped a dense shield of air around me, which probably kept me alive, but didn't soften the impact of a forty-foot fall much more than to stop me from turning into a paste. I crashed into the side of the building with enough force that I didn't come to a stop until I'd gone through the opposite wall and impacted with the concrete beyond.

"You okay?" Lucie asked as she ran up to me.

I coughed up blood and tried not to think about the pain in my body. I managed a nod, although it was hardly what anyone would have called enthusiastic. I glanced up at Lucie, who had removed the rest of her clothes and was busy unwrapping the bandages that covered her body. For the briefest of moments, I wondered how hard I'd hit my head.

I shook my head and took another look. Lucie wasn't naked; she wore some sort of skin-tight shorts that stopped mid-thigh and a bra-like top that appeared to be more functional than sexy. The rest of her body that I could see, from her neck to her bare feet, was covered in tattooed runes. Dozens and dozens of them adorned her body. Only her still bandage-wrapped hands and feet remained covered.

"You done staring?" Lucie asked. "Lots of women have these."

"Not them, the runes. I've never seen an enchanter cover so much of their skin in runes before."

"The runes give me different powers, once activated: strength, speed, thicker skin, increased healing. They have to remain covered, though; they take a lot of energy to keep active. I only use them when I must."

She unwrapped the bandages on her hands, showing more runes on wrists and fingers, before tearing off the bandages on her feet to reveal the same. Apart from her face and her covered breasts, there wasn't any part of her that wasn't tattooed.

"You sure you're ready?" she asked.

"Pain," I said. "Body is healing. I'll be fine."

Lucie placed her left hand on her right arm and shivered slightly before doing the opposite with her right hand. Then, no matter that I wasn't with her, she walked around the building.

"Ah, I don't believe this is the sort of thing a woman should be wearing in public," Helios said, his tone mocking. "Maybe that's the sort of thing you should wear once you find a nice husband to settle down with." He began to laugh.

Helios's laughter was cut off by the sound of flesh striking flesh, once and then a second time, before there was a loud thud as someone struck the building that I'd just impacted with. A second later Lucie emerged out of the hole. "You helping, or what?"

I stood and walked through the ruined building as Lucie rubbed her cheek. "He's got a good left hook," she told me with a smile.

She sprinted out of the building back toward Helios, who dodged out of her way and right into a jet of fire that leaped from my hands. He shielded himself with one of his wings, and Lucie caught him in the jaw with a punch that sent Helios tumbling to the ground.

Helios scrambled away, lifting up off the ground and not stopping until he was thirty or forty feet above us, which is when he unleashed another roar of flame, which slammed into the ground between Lucie and me, separating us. Some of the fire splashed onto my jacket sleeve, immediately burning through the fabric and forcing me to tear off both it and my shirt in frantic haste before the fire could touch my skin.

I flung missiles of hardened air at Helios, who dodged them with ease, but it gave me time to get back to the warehouse, where I found Lucie unhooking the chain that would allow her to pull open the shutter for the main loading dock.

"What are you doing?" I asked.

She appeared to notice me for the first time. "Why are you topless?"

"Fire hot," I said, my words oozing sarcasm. "Why are you giving him an easier way to hit us?"

"You're going to throw me at him."

The words took a moment to sink in. "What?"

"Use your air magic to throw me. At him. Can you do that?"

"It's not a question of 'can'; it's more a question of sanity." Part of the ceiling above my head clattered to the floor beside me and sizzled.

"He's going to get in here eventually. We might as well take the fight to him in the air."

"He won't come in here—not enough room to fly—but he will have an easier time of hitting us from outside."

"Even more reason to help me move this chain."

I cleaved through the steel chain with a blade of fire, and the shutter flew up a second later. I wrapped my air magic around

Lucie, pouring more and more power into it in the hope that it would carry her far enough and with enough speed.

I wrenched the magic back, creating tension, and the second I saw Helios hovering, I released it. Lucie was thrown upward toward Helios at incredible velocity, and for a second I wondered if I'd miscalculated. But once I saw that smug grin on Helios's face melting away, I knew I'd gotten it right. He tried to move out of the way, but Lucie had taken the remains of the chain with her, and wrapping it around her wrist she lashed out with it like a whip, wrapping it around Helios's arm, using her own momentum to travel behind Helios and land on his back.

I watched with a mixture of awe and fear as she held on, raining punch after punch down on the back of his head while he tried in vain to claw at her with his deadly talons. I couldn't do anything to help her—any blast of magic had an equal chance of hitting her, instead of him, as they spun and twisted in the air.

Helios screamed in rage as Lucie wrapped the chain around his neck and pulled back with all her force, but he grabbed the chain and yanked it forward, forcing Lucie to let go before she flew over his head. She grabbed hold of one of his wings, and for the briefest of moments everything appeared to be silent . . . until the quiet was ruptured by the sound of Helios's wing being snapped, followed by his screams of agony, which echoed around the complex.

The next thing I knew, both of them were tumbling toward the ground at high speed. I sprinted from the warehouse and created a cushion of air in the hope that it might save Lucie's life, but they both impacted with the ground so hard that my magic vanished in an instant.

I ran over as Helios was struggling back to his feet, their crash having left a small crater in the concrete, and knocked him away with a column of air that sent him spiraling into a nearby wall. It wouldn't stop him forever, but hopefully it would be long enough.

Lucie made a soft moaning noise as she moved toward me; she was covered in cuts that drenched her in blood. She managed to get to her knees, then pitched forward, although not before I saw the five puncture wounds just above her waist on the right side. Thick blood poured from the holes, and her blood stained my arms and chest as I lifted her up and carried her back into the warehouse, stopping only to pick up Helios's discarded jacket on the way. Mine was a charred mess and of zero use to anyone.

I laid her down near the rear of the building and checked for a pulse, which was slow but steady.

"Is he dead?" she asked, almost making me jump; she'd been limp since I'd picked her up, and I'd assumed she was unconscious.

"I doubt it. Stay here. You'll be fine."

"I know." She moved slightly and winced with pain.

I tore a strip off the jacket, using it to wrap around Lucie's abdomen. "You need to press hard here," I explained.

She pressed one hand against the makeshift bandage before I laid the rest of the jacket over her. "I'll be back soon."

I walked out of the warehouse, watching Helios as he leaned against a wall. He smiled, which infuriated me more than him trying to breathe fire on me.

Blood magic allows me to use not only my blood, but also the blood of others to power me. In this instance, that meant Lucie's blood. My blood magic flared to life, the black glyphs running along my palm and arms, and immediately mixing with the air magic I threw at Helios. The power was incredible, certainly more than I'd ever managed to feel from using the blood of an enchanter before. It coursed through me. It was as if Lucie's blood contained an almost endless supply of power. Lucie was no mere enchanter; there was obviously more to her than she first appeared to possess.

Helios tried to dodge the blast, but with one broken wing he wasn't fast enough and had to settle for using his working wing as a shield. But even then he was thrown back into the building behind him.

I walked toward him while using my air magic to pin him in place. The nightmare inside me made its presence known for the first time. I felt a need to use more and more magic, to push myself further. I ignored it, hoping it would stay quiet while I ensured that Helios felt the full brunt of my fury, and after a second it fell silent.

I increased the pressure of the air magic as I walked toward Helios, causing him to cry out in pain. I took another step forward, and he roared fire directly at me, causing me to drop the air magic to use it to protect myself. It was all Helios needed, and pain shot through my arm, swiftly followed by the burning sensation of silver. I turned to see a small blade protruding from my shoulder. I grabbed hold of it, but the entire shaft was just one giant blade, and it sliced into my fingers and palm.

"Hurts, doesn't it?" Helios quipped while he walked toward me, carrying more blades in his hand. "You didn't think I'd come unprepared, did you? I know your power, Nathan. I know what you can and can't do. And you can't pull that blade out without causing even more pain to yourself."

He threw the second blade and it struck my thigh. I dropped to my knees. "Lucky you," I said with a grimace.

I started using my air magic, forcing myself to ignore the pain as I wrapped hardened air around the dagger in my shoulder in an effort to pull it free, but Helios made a tut-tutting noise. "Now, don't do that. I can see you using your magic. Just stay there like a good boy. Maybe Selene won't have to mourn you after all."

As he walked off, I used my blood magic to push the blades out of my body. It was incredibly painful and caused me to shout out, but by the time Helios realized what I was doing, the blades had already clattered to the ground.

I turned as he sprinted back toward me, his mouth agape, ready for another blast of flame, but I threw air at his face, which he had to move to avoid, putting him right in the path of my blade of air. It caught him under the rib cage, between the scales that protected his body, and he sagged forward as I twisted the blade before extinguishing it.

He crashed to his knees, blood pouring from the wound. "Selene will never forgive you," he almost hissed.

I paused for a nanosecond—not even long enough for a humming bird's wings to beat once, but that split second was all he needed as he pushed himself up toward me, pinning my arms behind me in an astonishing display of speed for someone with his injuries. He used his good wing to encircle me and keep me still. I ignored the searing pain of my injured ribs being crushed, and head-butted him on his nose, again and again with a crunch, but he still refused to release me.

I inhaled, heating the air up inside my lungs and then breathed it directly into his reptilian eyes. The contact made

Helios roar in pain. He released me, and I fell to the ground, my ribs screaming at me to stop making things worse. Helios began pawing at his eyes, rubbing them with the heel of his palm in a desperate attempt to stop the burning.

I scrambled away as Helios started flailing around, trying to keep himself from being attacked again, although my entire focus was now on learning how to breathe again. After a few seconds, my magic began to heal me, and I was soon getting back to my feet, but Helios had stopped moving and was looking right at me, despite his injured eyes.

"I can smell you," he said and grinned horribly, showing bloody teeth and lips. "I'm going to feast on your heart, you little fucker." He ran right at me, swiping at my chest with his deadly talons. I avoided them in enough time to miss being torn in half, but not enough to avoid the talons from still ripping at my flesh.

He was faster and stronger than me, but he was also really, really angry and not thinking straight. I dodged more blows, using a blast of air to push him off balance with each punch, until I'd backed up against the wall, dropping to my knees to avoid a blow that tore through the brick like it wasn't even there.

I shot up from the ground, with my fist wrapped in air, and caught Helios under the jaw with a punch that would have killed a human. His head snapped back, and he staggered away, but he kicked out at me, catching me in the chest and driving me through the wall.

I fell to the floor inside the building, covered in dust and bits of brick and wood, pushing part of a table off me and trying to take a moment to ready myself for continuing the fight. Helios dove through the building, almost landing on me in the process. He grabbed me by the throat, and I threw a punch, but he blocked it easily, caught my hand, and before I could do anything, he'd crushed the bones in my fingers like they were kindling. This time it was my own screams of pain that filled my ears. There was no use in blocking out the agony, so I took a deep breath and drove one thin blade of air into his eye. Helios cried out and threw me aside with enough force to send me flying back through the wall to the outside. I hit the ground at an awkward angle, with only my magic stopping me from breaking an arm or worse.

I was crippled and exhausted, with a creeping sense of the nightmare's darkness settling inside me as the dusk turned into night outside. I needed to finish this fight, and quickly. I stood and discovered that Helios's claws had also raked my stomach, producing a steady stream of blood, which I used to draw a rune on the back of my ruined hand, with only moderate pain. Using my broken hand to draw on my good one, however, was such an incandescent agony that I had to force myself to finish. Finally, I used my blood magic to charge the spell and waited for Helios to reappear, which he did a moment later, destroying the remains of the wall and narrowly missing a large section of roof that crashed down, almost landing on him.

He roared in rage at me. I calmed myself, raised both hands, and said, "*Effete.*" Energy left me in one huge, agonizing rush, and I crashed to my knees. I'd marked Helios before he'd thrown me back through the wall, and while the spell managed to drop him to his knees, he was powerful enough to ensure that it didn't completely take him out of the fight. He was soon moving back toward me, albeit at a slow stagger.

I forced myself back to my feet. The curse had taken everything I had left, and I knew it, but I was not about to die kneeling. Helios was going to win. I was furious with myself as he moved slowly toward me, blood streaming from one ruined eye. The one I'd burned would heal; the other, the one I'd stabbed, probably not so much.

I doubted he had much left either, and I motioned for him to hurry up. I didn't have long before the effect of the curse would start on me, and I wanted to get this done.

He was six or seven steps away from me when the blast of ice smashed into him, taking him off his feet and propelling him up against the burned-out office. Helios roared in defiance as the stream of ice just kept coming, covering him from his feet up to his neck. The combination of our fight and the time of day had left him with nothing to fight back with, and he soon fell silent.

Selene floated to the ground in front of me, her eyes locked on her brother. Her wings, silver in color and matching her scaly skin, gleamed in the night.

"Do you really think you can kill me, little sister?" Helios demanded to know as he used his incredible strength to begin breaking the ice. Even when the sun had settled for the day, he was still a threat.

"Probably not. But I'm almost certain that *they* can."

She pointed behind her as a huge werebear, in its beast form, walked toward us, his eyes firmly fixed on the still-frozen Helios. This one was followed by a werewolf in her beast form, only slightly less imposing, but no less capable of tearing flesh from bone.

"Sorry we couldn't get here sooner," she said to me.

I raised my good hand and opened my mouth, but no words came out, so I lay down on the ground as the effects of the blood magic curse finally took their toll.

CHAPTER 31

Berlin, Germany. 1936.

"Ouch," I said as I opened my eyes and sat up, finding myself on a gurney in the warehouse. The silver wounds in my arm and leg were still painful. My fingers, once crushed and unusable, were mostly pointing in the right direction, even if they were sore as all hell to move.

"Three hours," Petra said as she came out of the room that had contained the sarin, and walked over to me. "I wondered how much longer you were going to sleep. You snore, did you know that?"

"Thanks for the information. I'll get right on not doing it." I swung my legs over the side of the gurney, and Petra was beside me in a moment, helping me to my feet.

"You need rest," she cautioned.

"'Need' doesn't really get a say right now," I explained as we walked together toward the front of the warehouse. Someone had closed the shutter, presumably after repairing the chain I'd destroyed. "Is the sarin gone?"

"They found the stuff in the warehouse as well as in the entrance to the complex beneath here. Looks like the Gestapo was stockpiling the stuff. It's all gone, setting their chemical warfare back a few years. A lot of dead down there too. Helios certainly did a good job of killing everyone involved in the creation of sarin. Hades is getting rid of it. You should know something, though."

"Hera's here?"

"You knew?"

"I knew Selene was going to tell her mother-in-law about what happened here. Whatever happened between us, it wasn't enough for her to stay with her *family*." I almost spat the last word.

"I don't think that's it, Nathan," Petra said as she opened the exit door.

The outside was awash with people, most of whom I recognized as working for Hades. A massive lorry was sitting up against the warehouse loading area.

"How's Lucie?" I asked.

"Recovering in the ambulance over there," Hades said as he joined us. "The sarin is being taken to my facility. I assume you're wondering about it."

"I trust you," I said.

"How are you?"

"Sore," I admitted, "but I'll live. There's a lot of information here about Pandora. About how she could take control over Hope's body on a permanent basis. You need to get that information to Brutus. If Pandora is trying to erase Hope, that could make her more dangerous. There could be stuff about the Gestapo trying to create their very own Pandora too."

"We found the information after Lucie told us. We got it all cleared away before Hera and her people arrived. No one will be making a second Pandora, and she's going to be watched very carefully for a long time."

"Good. What are you going to do with Helios?"

"Helios is not my problem. Hera has claimed him as an enemy combatant. He's in that black van over there."

I set off in the direction Hades had indicated, to find out what was happening. No one tried to stop me, although someone probably should have. I wasn't sure what I was going to do or the reception I was going to receive when I arrived.

Several of Hera's guards watched me approach, but no one tried to intervene as I walked up to the back of the van. Helios sat in the rear, his head bowed, his hands tied together with what looked like some sort of modified sorcerer's band.

I wanted to say something but wasn't really sure what. I wasn't sorry for what I'd done to him, and I certainly wasn't sorry that we'd stopped tens of thousands of needless deaths, but as these thoughts drifted through my head, only one question sprang to mind. "Why?"

Helios shifted to look at me, or at least in my direction. One of his eyes was covered with gauze. "Nathan. You have disfigured me."

"You tried to kill me."

"I did this to destroy Hera. To gain vengeance for all those lives she's torn apart."

"You did this for yourself," Selene said as she stepped up beside me. "And you're an idiot for it." She closed the van doors before turning to me. "Nathan."

"Cram it, I'm not interested," I snapped. "I see Deimos and Hera over there, watching us intently."

"I work for Hera. I couldn't *not* involve her."

"You could have done nothing, but you just chose to involve her."

There was a silence between us. I wanted to ask if she was going back to Deimos, but what I wanted more was for her to admit it to me.

"You want me to say it? That I'm not leaving him?"

"Yes," I whispered, placing all of my anger into one word.

"I was never going to leave Deimos. I can't."

I began to turn away. "Well, you've clearly made your choices in life, so good luck with them."

"Nathan." She reached out to touch my arm, and I moved aside.

I leaned toward Selene. "Your husband is over there," I whispered. "You know, the one you cheated on last night? Twice." Despite my having assumed she was going to go back to her husband and his family, the realization that I'd been right hurt. My heart felt heavy. I'd wanted to be wrong so badly I could taste it. Being right made me angry. I knew I wasn't blameless in what had happened—I knew I was being an asshole, but once I started, I just couldn't stop. "I wonder, was fucking me part of the plan? Was that your job all along? Because if it was, you should get a bonus; you were excellent."

Selene slapped me hard enough that I needed to place my hand against the rear doors of the van to stop myself from falling over.

"I should never have done that with you. It was a mistake."

"Lucky me," I seethed. "Go back to Hera and her friends—to your husband. I don't care why you left me anymore. I'm just grateful you did." I walked away, noting Deimos's anger as he moved to intercept me.

Deimos was like a smaller picture of his father, Ares. He was about my height, but even wider. His long blond hair fell over shoulders that strained to be contained within his gray suit. Everything about him was designed to intimidate. He'd grown a long beard since I'd last seen him, but the same arrogant, malicious, little bastard still oozed out of every part of him.

"She's mine now," he said, his accent British, something he'd clearly worked on over the years. "If you ever touch her again, I'll tear your eyes out."

Movement from the corner of my eye caught my attention. I turned slightly, to see Hera watching Deimos and me. She had a slight smirk on her face. I got the feeling she was enjoying this whole show a lot more than her grandson was.

"That's the difference between you and me, Deimos," I said, returning my full attention to him. "When Selene was with me, I never felt the need to tell anyone that she belonged to me." I walked past the angry man and toward Hades, who had quite probably been watching intently everything that had happened.

"You okay?" he asked.

I shrugged. "Define 'okay.'"

"Well, I'm about to make your day worse. He slipped a shoebox-sized box into my hand. "It's time," he told me.

"You sure?"

"Yeah, she needs to know the truth."

"Why now?"

"Petra and Kurt convinced me to let her know the truth. Apparently, her anger at you has gotten the best of her a few times in the last few days. I promised her dad I'd watch over her and keep her safe. Lying to her doesn't do that. She needs to know the truth. She needs to decide how to deal with it."

I took a deep breath and walked over to the ambulance where Lucie sat, telling those inside it to give us some time. "What are you?" I asked when I saw that the wounds on her stomach had vanished. "You're not just an enchanter."

"My father was a siphon," she said. "I got his long life and ability to heal and use energy. Without it, I might not be alive."

I passed her the box that Hades had given me.

"What is this?"

"This is the truth about what really happened with your parents and brother. This is what's been kept from you."

I let Lucie look through the contents of the box, and when she looked up at me, there were tears in her eyes. "Is this real?"

I nodded. "The first letter is from your father. He wrote to Hades, asking for his help because someone was turning your brother against him and your family. When I got to the house with Hades's guards, it was too late. Except your father wasn't dead yet. He told us that your brother was responsible and that he'd left a tape recording in the house for proof. His last words were to ask that you not know anything about who helped your brother. He knew what your response would be. Everything is in the box."

I turned to leave the ambulance.

"Tell me. Tell me all of it."

"Why?"

"Because I don't want to read cold words about what happened. I want you to tell me the truth. Please."

I sat back beside her. "Your brother did murder your stepmum and father, but someone else killed the others. Your brother escaped and began doing experiments on people, trying to see how runes affected different people in different ways. When I found your brother, there was no fight; he simply gave up and asked to be executed. The person who had twisted him and shaped him into the man who helped murder your family had set him up. You were that person's real target. You were the only one to be kept alive; that's why it was done on a day you weren't there."

"Who helped him?"

"Your mother," I disclosed. "She contacted your brother. The letters about it are in there. But your brother discovered her plan too late. He was killing people with runes in the hope that he could find one that would protect you from her. He just went about it in the most horrific way possible. He wrote a confession—that's in the box too. It explains everything he was doing. The tape from your father asks Hades to keep you safe, to keep the truth from getting out."

"Where is she?" Lucie asked, her words full of barely contained emotion. "I haven't seen my mother since I was four years old. Where is she?"

I shook my head. "I don't know. No one does. She vanished soon after the murder of your family, when she realized that your brother wouldn't give you up. You're under Hades's protection, and she's evil, but not stupid. All we know is that she managed to find a way to extend her life, even though she's an enchanter. I'm sorry for lying to you all these years, but no one wanted you going after her."

"I'm going to find her," Lucie said with iron determination. "Thank you for telling me."

I left the ambulance and found Hades sitting on the steps to the warehouse, eating an apple. "You think telling her was the right thing to do?" I asked.

"She needs to know. Deserves to know, if nothing else. I'm not sure she'll forgive me or you or anyone else who was involved in keeping it quiet. She might go work for Avalon. Depends on how much she wants to find her mother."

"So, this sarin? Where are you taking it?"

"Well, thanks to Kurt, Petra, and Selene, we've got all of the sarin and the explosives they used to create the bombs. The warehouse is now empty of the rest of the sarin too. We'll dispose of it all in a secure facility I run north of here. It's evil stuff. I'll be glad to no longer have it near me. You and Lucie did a good thing here today."

Kurt and Petra walked past, Kurt slapping me on the shoulder before they continued on.

"What about Pandora?" I asked Hades. "Is she settling in to her new accommodation?"

"Pandora's housing in London is considerably nicer than Helios's will be."

"Do you think Pandora will stay this time?"

"She'll stay put for as long as she needs to, and then she'll escape and we'll go through all of this again."

"Except next time we might not get so lucky as to avert a war."

Hades shook his head. "We've averted only one war, Nathan. Mark my words: there's another one coming, and there might well be a day when you think to yourself, *'What if I'd just let Helios succeed in killing Hera?'*"

CHAPTER 32

London, England. Now.

I got out of the SUV and walked toward one of the two guards standing outside the lengthy driveway that curved up toward Hera's mansion in St. John's Wood. The large metal gates, and a nearly ten-foot, red-brick wall with spikes on top, stopped people from gaining easy entry to the property; the guards were just a nuisance, albeit, if their jackets were any indication, an armed one.

I stood well back while Olivia spoke to them, showing her credentials. One of the guards, a large man with a South African accent, made a call on the radio and nodded as the reply came back in his earpiece.

"You can go in," he told us and opened the gate without another word.

We walked up the drive to the massive white house that sat in an elevated position above the main road we'd pulled up on, as if the owners wished to be able to look down on everyone around them. A lofty goal in a place with as many million-pound properties as St. John's Wood.

Two more guards met us at the front door, and once again Olivia showed them her ID before they allowed us inside. We were immediately surrounded by opulence and grandeur. The reception area held only the finest of furniture and artwork. A large spiral staircase sat at the end, with two doors behind it and two more on either side of us.

A man appeared from one of the doors behind the staircase. He wore a black suit and white shirt, with a black tie. "Please come this way," he told us.

We followed without question, through the door he'd arrived from and down a corridor to a door at the end. The man knocked on the door and then opened it, motioning for us to go inside.

We all did as we were asked, and I felt a slight trepidation as he closed the door behind us with an audible click.

The room was some kind of living room, with a large TV in front of a couch that could probably sit a dozen people comfortably. A cabinet behind the couch held enough bottles of alcohol to drown the sorrows of a substantial number of people.

Tommy walked over to some doors that led out to a patio and stared at the immaculate garden outside. "How much do you think this place is worth?"

"Lots," I said. "Lots and lots."

"I thought my house was impressive, but this is a GDP-of-a-small-country kind of price."

"Hera will be glad you like it," said a woman from the side of the room.

I turned to the direction of the voice and found myself smiling. "Eos," I said as I crossed the room to embrace her. "It's been a long time."

Eos's smile was a sight to behold. It lit up her face and put a sparkle in her eyes. In many ways she looked a lot like her sister, Selene, although her skin was slightly darker and her hair cut shorter. Unlike her siblings, she wasn't dragon-kin. She was a dusk walker, someone who could use shadows as a method of transport.

"It's good to see you, Nathan. I've missed our sparring sessions."

"You've had no one's ass to kick in the last few decades, I assume?"

"On the contrary. I just preferred kicking yours."

I moved aside and Eos embraced Tommy before being introduced to Olivia, who went to shake her hand but was dragged in for a hug anyway.

"I hope you're prepared for this," she whispered to all of us.

Eos led us through the door into a large room with windows along the rear and a large meeting table between the windows and us. Around one side sat Hera, Demeter, Ares, Deimos, Aphrodite, and Selene. It took everything I had not to glance her way, not to acknowledge that she was even there. It was made easier when another door opened behind them, and Hyperion walked in.

Eos instinctively grabbed my wrist hard enough to remind me where I was. She could have broken it if she'd desired, and I took the hint: *Behave.*

Hera looked as attractive as ever, in a long green dress, with her natural light-brown hair highlighted with blond and cascading down her back to just above her tailbone. The dress hugged her in all the right places, and it was easy to understand why Zeus had fallen for her. It was less easy to understand once you'd actually *met* Hera, but Zeus never had thought with his brain when it came to members of the opposite sex. She stood and embraced Hyperion, offering him a seat at the table. I didn't point out that she hadn't even offered *us* a seat yet, but decided it probably wasn't the time.

I glanced at Aphrodite, who sat next to Hera and could have easily graced the front cover of every magazine and newspaper in the world ever. Hell, *Gardeners World* would have put her on the cover to sell a few copies. There was something about her that wasn't quite right, though, as if the beauty you were seeing was so total that it couldn't be real. But most people ignored that aspect and settled for being intoxicated by her presence. She'd dyed her hair a bright red since I'd last seen her. It matched the rubies in her dangling earrings and the lipstick on her full lips, and her black, low-cut dress clung to her curves in a way that made my internal man do a little happy dance. I dug a nail into my palm; as a succubus, she could have made me take my clothes off and dance around a little if she'd really turned on her power. Reminding yourself of the viper hiding behind the façade was a pretty good way to stay alive.

Ares sat on the other side of his mum, Hera, and my anger rose considerably at his presence. But I knew that diving over the table to grab him for his backing of Mordred's twisted experiments would get me killed.

Ares had married Aphrodite years ago, after her last husband, Hephaestus, divorced her when he caught them going at it like rutting dogs in his bed. Word was that the much smaller man scared Ares. For all of his biker-looks, his huge physique, and imposing personality, it made me wonder what had really happened between him and Hephaestus. Because ever since then, Ares will happily prove just how manly he is to anyone who questions it, usually by beating the guy so badly that he can't talk for a few days.

The fact that Hephaestus wasn't at the table wasn't a surprise. He'd never been much of a politician and had preferred to work with his alchemy, creating things for himself and those he cared about. I always thought that he was a creepy bastard, but anyone who scared Ares couldn't be all bad.

Demeter sat on the far side of the table, her gaze at me full of evil intent. To suggest that she didn't like me was probably akin to me saying that being shot isn't much fun; I'd need a lot more adjectives. Demeter looks a lot like her daughter Persephone, but her face is harder, and her eyes are full of menace. You know people say that if your heart is filled with evil intent, your face will start to reflect that evil. Well, Demeter looks like she wraps herself up in that shit and never wants to leave.

I risked a glance back to Deimos, who sat on the other side of Aphrodite, and caught him looking down her top. He saw me watching him and quickly averted his gaze, glancing instead at me with total disdain and an anger that appeared barely in check, while Aphrodite smiled. Deimos still had the same beard as when I'd last seen him, although now he had tattoos on his arms, one of which appeared to be a strand of barbed wire wound around his tense bicep, noticeable because of his skintight red T-shirt that showed off every single muscle in his upper body. It also made him an even bigger dick than I'd originally thought.

I glanced at Selene, who was looking away. I hadn't seen Selene since I'd walked away from her in Berlin in '36. She'd grown her hair out since then and changed the color to a dark red. She looked elegant in a red and black dress, and a mixture of anger and the need to be with her flowed through me, neither one winning that particular skirmish. Deimos placed his hand on her forearm and nodded in my direction. Eos held onto my hand as if it were the only thing stopping me from exploding.

Hyperion sat on the other side of Selene and took a deep breath. He looked to be in his mid-fifties, with short graying hair and a few days of stubble. He looked a lot like his son, Helios. I wondered if he'd stopped whatever awful things Hera would have had done to Helios once he was in her custody. Hyperion glanced up at me once and held my gaze, although he ignored everyone else in the room apart from Hera and his daughters.

I wanted to punch him in his face. Even after all these years, that was the overriding desire. Instead, I turned back to Hera, who was having a chat with Ares.

"Hera," Eos said when it became apparent that Hera didn't give a fuck about our being there. "You need to hear what these people have to say."

Olivia stepped forward. "My name is Olivia Green. I'm the director of the Winchester branch of the LOA."

Hera actually yawned, and I saw Tommy tense.

"Why should I care who any of you are?" Hera asked, almost bored. "I was enjoying an evening with my family and friends. Exactly what was the point in your removing me from my pleasant time?"

"Cronus has escaped," Olivia said.

"And?" Hera asked, as if it weren't something she needed to concern herself with. "I got the message from Hades. If I didn't want to talk to him, why in the world would you believe I would talk to you? Cronus has wanted me dead for a long time." Hera laughed. "You think he'd manage to succeed? Because I'm certain he won't get through the gates."

"He won't do it here," I said.

Hera's eyes narrowed in my direction. "Did I say you could speak?"

"I'm not sure," I said. "Maybe I imagined it. Cronus is coming to kill you. He thinks you murdered his son and wants revenge."

"You know nothing about Zeus," she snapped, and an angry expression crossed Ares's face.

"I didn't suggest you did anything to Zeus," I said. "But Cronus doesn't care. He won't kill you here; he'll wait to attack somewhere where you're less safe. Do you have any public engagements in the next few days?"

"The book fair," Aphrodite said, managing to make the words "book fair" sound sexy, a feat that had probably never before been achieved in the history of humanity.

"You have a book fair?" Olivia asked.

Hera glared at Aphrodite, who barely seemed to register the other woman's feelings. "Yes, the London Book Fair. We'll be going to have some meetings with investors. As you know, Aphrodite owns one of the world's biggest publishers of romance books. But I assure you, we have our own security, and there will be thousands of people in Earl's Court. Cronus would not try to attack us there—it would be suicide."

Earl's Court was a massive building in London. It was usually the place to hold huge conventions and the like. It meant there would be thousands of people inside that building when Cronus attacked. Thousands of potential victims.

"I don't think he cares about such things," I said.

"What you think doesn't matter!" Demeter snapped. "Now, you came here to give us a message and you've given it. You may leave."

"So, that's it?" Olivia asked.

"He's barely going to be a match for a human," Ares said. "He's been in Tartarus for too long; his power will be tiny compared to ours. We'll destroy him—hell, I'll welcome the fun."

Aphrodite giggled, actually fucking giggled, like she was someone's damn groupie, and Ares grinned like an idiot. From what I understood, Aphrodite held the power in that relationship, even if she liked Ares to think otherwise.

I turned to leave.

"Nathan," Deimos called out.

I stopped and turned to face him as he walked around the table. "I just wanted you to know something," he said loud enough for everyone to hear. "Every night when I'm inside the woman you used to love, when she closes her eyes and arches her back as she comes so damn hard . . . Oh, actually that's it, I just wanted you to know what she does *every* night."

I glanced at him and returned his grin with one of my own. "You seem to be under the false impression that I care about who she sleeps with, but I can assure you, that ship has well and truly set sail. Enjoy your married life together."

Hera glanced over at Selene and grinned. Selene, on the other hand, had turned away from watching her husband and me talking.

"We both know you can't stand that I won," Deimos snapped as I walked away. "Selene is mine, not yours. As it will always be."

I paused at the door and turned back to the room. "Deimos, exactly who do you believe Selene's thinking about when she closes her eyes? Because it sure as fuck isn't you." I walked out of the room without another word.

We'd left the mansion, and I wanted nothing more than to let Cronus come and try to kill Hera. She was so damn certain of herself and how safe she was that it was infuriating. She couldn't see any possibility that her life was genuinely in danger. And the word of three people she considered beneath her was hardly likely to change her mind anytime soon.

We'd reached the SUVs when Eos called out from behind us. We all waited by the cars as she left the security of the mansion's grounds and walked over to me.

She hugged me tightly and grabbed my hand, leaving something that felt like paper inside. "This address in thirty minutes," she whispered. "There are things you need to know. Do not be late." Then she turned and walked back past the gates, which closed after her.

Once I was at the car, I opened the paper, making sure I kept my back to the gates. The address written on it was for a bar not too far from where we were. I told Tommy and Olivia.

"What do you think she wants to talk about?" Tommy asked.

"No idea," I said. "I guess we'd better go find out."

Tommy took the car with me on the short trip, presumably because Olivia had her phone out and was talking on it before we'd even reached the cars.

"So, that went better than expected," Tommy said once we were on our way.

I turned toward my friend. "In what way is that true?"

He ticked the reasons off on his fingers. "One, you didn't try to tear Deimos into tiny bite-sized chunks. Two, no one died. And three, I managed to keep my temper when that fucking asshole spoke down to Olivia like she was something found on the bottom of her shoe."

"I noticed that," I admitted. "I was very proud of you. Being all grown up and everything."

"I've been practicing. So far I've gone a few years without tearing anyone's head off for pissing me off. It's going well."

I laughed. "Glad to hear it. You know Hera could have killed us all if she'd had the inclination."

"Oh, yeah, the woman terrifies me. I wonder if she really did kill Zeus. If I were him, I'd have gone into hiding long before she got the chance."

"Don't know. My gut tells me he's dead. But I've thought people were dead before, and they popped right back up. If Zeus isn't dead, he's somewhere far away from anyone who knows him. Either Hera killed him or removed him from the picture. Either way, something bad happened to him."

"So, how was seeing Selene again? You managed to embarrass Deimos. Again."

"Everyone needs a hobby."

"Pissing off that psychotic little prick is probably one that will come back to bite you in the ass, though."

"He can get in line; I'm busy."

Tommy was quiet for a few seconds. "Do you think Kasey is okay?"

"She's fine; certainly she'll be enjoying herself more than we are. But if you're worried, call her. Brutus wouldn't let anything happen to her, and Diana certainly won't. Would you want to go up against Diana?"

"I'd rather fight Cronus." He took his phone from his pocket and dialed, talking to Kasey a moment later. When he'd hung up, he turned to me. "Kasey said that she wants to go back to Brutus's place at some point in the future. Diana said there's loads of stuff she probably won't get to see."

"Glad to hear she's enjoying herself."

"Living with a teenage girl is like walking through a tiger-infested forest; you're pretty sure you know where the trouble's coming from, and you try to avoid it, but just as you think you're scot-free, a big fucking mass of trouble jumps out at you."

I laughed. "But I guarantee you: you wouldn't change it for the world."

"Nate, I've considered shooting her with a tranquilizer dart, just so she'd stop being a moody shit. But, no, I wouldn't change it for the world. She's my little girl. Always will be."

I patted him on the shoulder. "Plan on having more?"

"Fuck no!"

We both laughed as the car pulled to a stop, and were still laughing as we got out and met Olivia. "What's so funny?" she asked.

"Nate wanted to know if we were going to have more kids."

"Fuck no," Olivia expressed, making Tommy and me laugh again.

"Every day I wonder if I behaved toward my mum the way Kasey does," she said as we waited by the cars.

"Did you?"

"Almost certainly. I think the only difference is that my mum was more apt at throwing stuff at my head when I did."

"Did that make you stop?"

Olivia shook her head. "I think the days of pelting our children with stuff are sadly behind us."

"Parents these days," I said with a grin.

"Very funny," Olivia said. "We'll send her to stay with you for a week, see how you take to having her roll her eyes at you every time *you* say something."

I laughed, and it felt good to remove some of the anger and tension that had built up inside me.

The bar was off the main street and appeared to be a fairly classy establishment, with very few people in there. The area was quiet, and there was a park nearby with two policemen walking through it.

"You can go in, you know," Eos told us from the darkness that sat at the edge of the building. She stepped into view, under one of the nearby streetlights attached to the wall overhead.

Tommy held the door open for Olivia and Eos, who both nodded a thanks. He even held it open for me.

"Good job that, man," I said in my best upper-class accent.

"No tip?" Tommy exclaimed. "Fucking cheapskate."

I flipped him my middle finger, which caused Tommy to laugh, gaining the notice of everyone in the quiet bar.

"Are you two done?" Eos asked. When we nodded, she spoke to an older man behind the horseshoe-shaped counter, and he pointed to a booth in the corner.

"You want anything to drink?" he asked Eos. She asked only for a jug of water and four glasses, but left a fifty-pound note on the counter, which vanished a moment later.

"What was that all about?" I asked as I sat at the booth opposite Eos while the jug and glasses were placed between us.

"I didn't want us to be interrupted," she told me and turned to Olivia. "Are those guards of yours just going to stay outside all the time?"

"Yes," Olivia said. "Nate, if you say anything about them not being housebroken, I will kick you in the ballsack."

Tommy had poured himself some water and found it difficult to laugh and drink at the same time. He gagged, then coughed violently.

"That'll learn ya," I said. "Why are we here?" I asked Eos.

"Because you're a fucking idiot."

That wasn't quite what I was expecting. "You probably could have told me that without all the secrecy," I pointed out.

"Your turning up at Hera's tonight went down about as well as a fart in an elevator, but that isn't actually what I'm referring to. You have this anger against my dad and sister, and it blinds you. It's time you knew what happened and why she left you."

"We don't have time for this," I said and tried to move, but Tommy wasn't budging, so I sat back down.

"You listen to my words, and maybe they'll enlighten you. You do it without comment, and then I'll tell you what I know about Cronus and Hera."

"Do you know where Cronus is going?" Olivia asked. "Because if you don't tell us—"

"You have a few hours before he arrives. More than enough time to listen to me and still get there. I don't wish to have anyone's death on my conscience, but it's time for Nate to listen for a change. Because everything that's happening here links back to you."

"Ummm, how in the hell is that possible?" I asked.

Eos looked between Tommy and Olivia. "You sure you want them knowing?"

"Tommy knows everything about me, so no problems there. Olivia knows more than most, and being together with Tommy, probably more than she should. I think we're okay."

"Before I get to that part, you'll want to know about my father, Hyperion. A few centuries ago, Hera visited Tartarus and asked Hyperion for him to join her group in exchange for getting him out of there. He turned her down. Pretty emphatically, I'll add.

"A century ago, while you were with Selene, she repeated the offer. This time she threatened to kill Selene, Helios, and me if he disagreed. He still refused, and she left disappointed. There was no way she was going to kill the three of us; it would have cost her dearly both in terms of manpower and Avalon's ire. It was all bluster and she knew it. So, because she's really bad at accepting defeat, she decided to be a colossal douchenozzle and go through his children in the hope that one of us would convince him to help her.

"She came to me first and asked me to help her. I told the hag to go fuck herself with her own broom, and she left."

"You have a beautiful way with words," I confessed to her.

Eos smiled. "I'm not done yet. Hera tried the same trick with Helios and Selene, each of them telling her which short pier to take a long run off. I believe Selene was *dating* you at the time—that's probably the right word, yes?"

"I guess so."

"Hera retaliated by threatening to kill Selene, which we all knew was bullshit, so she laughed in her face. And then Hera threatened you. Apparently, Selene laughed even more at that. Threatening you when you were still with Merlin was insane; Merlin would turn the fucking bint to molten thundercunt. And Hera knew it."

She paused while Tommy and I stifled a chuckle. "It was 'thundercunt,' wasn't it?"

We both nodded.

"It's an apt term for her. Anyway, you two done?"

We composed ourselves and motioned for Eos to continue. "By this point, Hera was getting desperate. We didn't know what she wanted my father for, but it was certainly enough for her to go after his children, a fact that wasn't lost on him. She wanted to get us to work for her so she could show him how dangerous it would be for us if he continued to say no to her requests.

"She got my attention when she threatened my children. Just told me what she'd have some of her people do to them; make me watch it all. I was furious, but I also knew that she would follow through with that threat. I couldn't risk it, and I caved. I admit it, I wanted to tear her fucking head off and stuff it up Demeter's ass, but I caved. I had no choice.

"I sent them away to be with their father, and they grew up not knowing me. They had new identities, new lives. I'll never forgive Hera for that." Eos stopped and took a deep breath. "The last few years I've made contact with them in secret, and they've become powerful. I hope that one day I'll be able to leave Hera and never have to watch my back for her assassins. But until then, I remain in exile from my own family."

Eos took a drink of water and settled herself, while we remained silent. "Sorry. It's a raw spot."

Olivia placed a hand on Eos's. "I'm sorry you had to go through that."

"I never knew," I said. "I mean, I knew you had kids—hell, I met them loads of times, but I was told you broke up with their father and you shared time with them. I'm sorry, Eos."

A low growl emanated from Tommy. "No one should have to go through that."

Eos smiled. "Thank you, but I'm not done yet. Once Hera realized that threatening our loved ones had the desired effect of getting us to work for her, and with no retort from Avalon or anyone else—which was the reason she'd waited for so long to use them against us—she went after Helios. He'd run off by that point. He had no one he cared about save himself, so Hera had no leverage. But Selene was a different matter. She wasn't fazed by threats to her or you or her father; she just didn't care.

Then they stopped threatening you with harm and threatened to expose you if she didn't join their organization. Deimos had Hera force Selene to leave you and marry him. If she ever spoke of the reasons, she would die, and the leverage they had on you would be public knowledge. Not even Merlin could have put that genie back in the bottle."

"Why are you telling me, then?"

"Because this is the first time I've seen you in decades, and I'm sick and tired of living under the rules that bitch placed on me. My children are grown and are powerful in their own right. Now that Cronus is free, I do not think we will be quite as . . . *needed* by Hera as we were before her plans came to fruition."

"So what were they going to say about me? That I was Hellequin?"

"Your wife, Jane, was murdered by soldiers," Eos continued.

"I hope this story has a really good point," I said slowly, my words coated in anger and pain.

"You found her body," Eos said, ignoring me. "And then went on a sort of rampage for a year, killing whoever you could until you found those responsible and murdered them all. Then you buried the Hellequin name. It's a touching story, Nate, and it's the official story too, from what I can find out. Even Merlin admits to you hunting down and killing your wife's murderer before moving out to America. And all the while, people are still using your Hellequin name and attributing it to more acts of violence against the evil people who lived at the time. But it's a lie, isn't it?"

I thought hard about my answer, and certainly from the expression on Olivia's face, she expected me to deny everything and tell Eos to go fuck off under a bus or something. "Yes," I said. "I lied."

Olivia reacted as if she'd been slapped.

"Jane *was* murdered, and I did track down her killers and take my vengeance. And Merlin *did* send me to America to deal with Washington after the Revolution. But I didn't bury the name Hellequin. I kept using it. I became it." I'd told Olivia about Jane after Kasey and Tommy had been kidnapped by a maniac seeking revenge. I'd told her that I'd buried the name of Hellequin when I'd killed the man responsible. I'd lied to her.

"What does that mean?" Olivia snapped.

"After Jane's death, I started to feel resentful toward those who were still alive and using their life to inflict evil on others. So, I removed them."

"What does that mean?" she repeated.

"I snapped," I admitted. "I went after people who abused others: rapists, murderers, those who hurt innocents. I used the name Hellequin to instill fear wherever I went."

"Was any of it sanctioned?"

I shook my head. "Humans, sorcerers, people whom Avalon would not have wanted me to kill—I didn't care. I went after anyone I deemed unworthy of living. I hurt people, a lot of people, in my quest for . . . hell, I don't really know. For a few years it was fine, but then Merlin started to notice that the Hellequin name was being attributed to a lot of deaths in America.

"Eventually, he sent Tommy to track me down, and Tommy managed to stop me from getting worse. It was at that point that I buried Hellequin, after I'd taken the lives of a few hundred people in sixteen years."

"So you murdered a large number of evil people, most of them humans?" Olivia asked. "I can see why that would need to stay quiet. I mean if you'd killed a few, even a few dozen, but a few hundred—to do that much damage. That's some Mordred-level shit."

"It gets worse. While I was doing these killings, I was still working for Avalon. Still carrying out Avalon duties. And some of the people I killed were members of Avalon or other important groups, although I made sure not to attribute the Hellequin name to those murders."

Olivia exhaled. "Fuck," she whispered. "You were acting as an unsanctioned executioner while working the entire time for Avalon. Why haven't I heard about this before?"

"It was kept quiet. Only a few knew I was Hellequin at the time, so it was easy to brush it off as murders committed by someone with no affinity to anyone. And then, over time, the tales got embellished and the truth got lost somewhere in it all."

"What you did, that's exactly what Mordred used to do."

There was a time, many centuries ago, when Mordred was the darling of Avalon, when he was seen as its protector and was someone I considered a friend. Then he went crazy, murdered a bunch of seemingly random people and attacked Arthur and me, almost killing us both. After the public displays of crazy, we discovered that for decades he'd been murdering people who didn't fit with his view of right and wrong. I was well aware of how close I'd come to losing myself to the same madness.

"What would have happened if that had become public knowledge?" Eos asked.

"Well, by the time Selene left me, I'd already left Avalon, and the deaths had taken place well over a century ago. Even so, it would have forced Merlin to investigate me and my dealings at the time, including those with George Washington and his new government. Questions would have been asked about whether those I'd killed were in any way people who would have helped create a free America. At the time of the Revolution, a lot of people were throwing their hat into the ring and trying to carve themselves out a piece of territory. Any indication that I stopped that from happening would have had some pretty serious consequences.

"I'd have probably been excommunicated from Avalon as a whole. Merlin might have even decided I was an enemy of the state and sent people after me like he'd done with Mordred."

"What would happen now?" Tommy asked.

"Avalon would almost certainly deny all knowledge of his actions," Olivia said. "It would either stir up some deep-seated feelings of anger for people who didn't get what they wanted after the Revolution, or create questions about whether America was truly a free country or was ruled from the shadows by Merlin without Avalon's knowledge. Either way, he'd have been thrown under the bus. The friends of those he'd killed might want retribution."

"Does she have proof?" Tommy asked. "Because anyone who isn't her ally won't just rush to believe her. Nate has friends in high places. They'll back him."

"She knows that Hellequin and Nate are the same," Eos told us. "She has for a long time. Not everyone you killed was attributed to Hellequin, but she has a list of people she believes you murdered. It includes Avalon members and those of her allies. If enough people kick up enough trouble, Avalon will be forced to investigate. If they find that even one of them was your doing, it'll open the floodgates."

"So, *were* any of your victims people involved in the creation of America?" Olivia asked.

"Probably," I had to admit. "Members of Avalon wouldn't have been there for anything less than negotiations or taking things by force on behalf of their masters."

"You really fucked up, didn't you?"

I nodded. It wasn't my finest hour. Killing people in the line of my duties for Avalon or, once I'd left their employ, disposing of enemies, was fine. In fact, so long as I'd disposed of the bodies well enough and didn't kill anyone of note, I doubted Avalon would have paid much attention. But purposely tracking and killing high-ranking members of Avalon, would have been far too much like Mordred for many people's liking, and any thoughts that someone would be going down the same road as he did would have ensured swift retribution on Avalon's part.

"Selene left me to protect me from Hera?" I said after several seconds of silence. My voice was quiet. I'd pushed all of this behind me so long ago. But there's no time limit on an offense against Avalon and its allies. "Why me and Selene? Apart from Hera getting Selene to work for her and, by extension, Hyperion, what do we have to do with any of it?"

"Hera originally couldn't care less about you or Selene. She wanted Hyperion and used whatever she had to ensure she got his help. You were both just the easiest way to ensure that happened. Now, she keeps us around to keep our father in check; it's why she married Selene off. None of the others wanted to marry me; I think they believe I might stab them in their sleep."

"Selene should have told me," I said softly.

"Selene left you to spare you what was most probably a death sentence," Eos said. "She left you because anything else was unthinkable to her. My father had nothing to do with it. In fact, he only left Tartarus because Hera turned up and told him what she'd done and how Selene and I were now under her control. So you see, if you'd never murdered those people, Hera wouldn't have had leverage to use against my sister, meaning my father wouldn't have joined her cause, and Cronus wouldn't have been able to escape."

The revelation was a lot to take in, and I asked Tommy to move aside so I could go outside and get some air. The idea that Selene had been coerced into leaving me and marrying Deimos made me very, very angry. But not as angry as I was with myself for what I'd thought of Selene since it happened. I sat on a bench by the park, and a few seconds later Eos sat beside me.

"All of this isn't my fault, Eos," I said. "That's a bit of a stretch. I'll accept responsibility for giving Hera the information she used to blackmail Selene into joining her, but Cronus escaping isn't on me. One doesn't necessarily have anything to do with the other."

"Maybe you're right, but I needed to make sure you shut up and actually listened to me. Telling you it was your fault seemed like a good idea at the time."

"You should have told me decades ago, Eos. About Selene and Hera."

"I'm sorry," she said. "Selene forbid us all from telling you the truth. She'd rather you hated her than that you went and got yourself killed trying to free her from Hera's clutches."

"Does Deimos force her to do anything?" I asked.

I didn't need to elaborate; Eos knew exactly what I meant. "Selene hasn't spent more than ten minutes in his company since their wedding. If he tried anything, she'd tear him in half. The little shit is more scared of her than of Grandma Hera. And he's plenty scared of Hera."

"Selene told me something about Deimos being punished back in '36 because he tried to kill someone."

"Yeah, the dick tried to kill one of Hera's favorite aides, but failed and got caught, so he was punished spectacularly. Do you know how Hera hurts those close to her? She humiliates them at every single opportunity. For centuries. Every day, she reminds Deimos that he can't even fuck his own wife. That he has to hire whores, that he's less of a man for letting the man his wife loves walk around without retribution. It's one of the reasons he hates you—because he's reminded by Hera every single day how much better than him you are in Selene's eyes."

"And the other reason?"

"Selene loves you. She will never, *ever* love him. And there's sweet fuck all he can do to change her mind."

"This is a lot to take in, Eos," I repeated. "I had no idea that anyone knew about my past. Only Tommy and Merlin were meant to have any knowledge about it. Apparently, I can add at least Hera to that list. Tommy stopped me before I took things the next step from killing scum to killing people who might possibly turn into scum. It's probably the darkest point in my entire life."

"I wasn't about to let you go full Sith, Nate," Tommy said, as he placed a hand on my shoulder. "Olivia wants a word. Probably several."

I nodded, expecting it. I'd told Olivia a lie, and she wasn't the kind of person who took being lied to well.

I found her leaning against the rear of one of the SUVs. "I have a very real desire to shoot you, or arrest you, or something," she told me.

"Okay—" I started.

"Shut up and listen. I should knock you on your ass. You told me something dark and personal and then lied. To find out that while you were working for Avalon you also murdered a large number of their people is not something I can just forget or get over. All the good you've done before and since goes some way to making sure that I don't take you to Merlin myself and press him to charge you with something.

"The fact is, whatever these people had done to deserve your wrath, you've never shown any indication to me that you're anything other than someone I can trust with my daughter. I understand why you and Tommy kept this information to yourselves. I don't pretend to understand what you were going through back then, or how finding your wife affected you, but Tommy assures me that it was a horrific time in your life.

"If you'd just kept it to killing pieces of shit no one cared about, it wouldn't have mattered, but killing Avalon members, some of whom would have had real influence and who were in a country that the majority of Avalon was trying to carve up between themselves. Jesus, Nate that was bad. If Tommy hadn't gotten to you first—if someone else had—you'd be dead, or on the run. You would have hurt Avalon, your friends, and yourself. But it happened a long time ago, and if I was judging people on acts committed centuries ago, half of Avalon would be in jail or dead."

"I'm sorry for lying to you."

"I know." She hugged me. "If you ever do it again, I'll shoot you."

"Deal."

"This can never be made public. The proof that Hera has on what you did—we need to get it. A problem for another day, but it's a serious concern to think that someone in Avalon gave her the info."

"I thought the same thing."

"You shouldn't have kept this from me, Thomas Carpenter," Olivia said as Tommy met up with us.

"Wasn't my tale to tell," Tommy said. "Nate did a lot of good by removing those people from the earth. No matter how far into darkness he traveled, he never went after people who didn't deserve it."

"Avalon wouldn't have seen it that way," Olivia said. "Do you know who the people you killed were?" she asked me.

"A vampire lord, a bunch of low-level thugs for some high-level Avalon members, a Blade of Avalon general who enjoyed hurting women, and a few others."

"Avalon would have gone nuts for the general alone," Olivia said.

Eos joined us, ensuring the conversation between Olivia and I was over.

"So where is Cronus?" I asked Eos. "And how can you be sure?"

"He's been in contact with my father. They're like brothers. My father's job was to help him escape and get to Hera."

"Why did Hera send someone to kill him?" I asked.

Eos looked confused. "She didn't. She wanted Cronus to get to her so she could make a big show of killing him. My father told Cronus this, but he didn't care. Cronus just wanted the chance to kill her. He's going to power up before he comes after her, though. A magic well."

"We assumed as much," Olivia said. "Which one?"

"Stonehenge. He'll arrive there at just after 1:00 a.m., according to my father."

Olivia was immediately on her phone, mobilizing agents, while Tommy called Kasey and told her what was happening.

"You know when this all goes to shit, your father will be the scapegoat," I told Eos.

"He knows. He's got a contingency plan for that."

"Sarah Hamilton was found with a dwarven dagger. A Kituri dagger, to be exact. If Hera didn't want Cronus dead, that means the blood inside it wasn't hers. Who else wanted to take Cronus's power enough that they'd send Sarah to kill him?"

"I can't say, but Deimos was the one who introduced Sarah to Hera. Maybe he knows."

"When we get back from Stonehenge, I'll make sure someone goes and asks him," I said.

Eos's grin was full of mischief. "And I'll make sure that Selene and I are in attendance for it. I'm aware of your ability to piss off the wrong people, but if you ever go after Deimos, make sure he can't come back the next time with an army. You put him down hard and fast, and you make sure he knows never to try again."

It was my turn to grin, although what I was sure would turn into an impending battle with Cronus had receded from the front of my mind, replaced with *Did Eos say that Selene still loved me?* I pushed the thought aside; my love life would have to wait. First I had to stop someone who had once been considered one of the most powerful beings in the cosmos from destroying a well-known chunk of Britain's natural heritage.

CHAPTER 33

The journey from central London to Stonehenge is roughly two hours, factoring in traffic and observing pesky little rules like speed limits. Fortunately, we didn't have to. Within half an hour, we were halfway there, hurtling down the M3 motorway. There really isn't anything quite like a flashing light and lack of other motorists to ensure you get to your destination in record time.

My phone began to ring, breaking the silence that had settled in the car. "Hi, Sky," I said after answering it.

"My parents are here," she said. "Brutus told us you're on the way to Stonehenge."

"Let me put you on speaker," I said and switched my phone over so that Olivia and Tommy could also hear. We'd all decided to take the same car so we'd arrive together. The LOA agents hadn't been thrilled that only one of them was in the car with Olivia, but none of us had time for arguing, and they'd decided to follow in the second SUV.

"Any good news?" Olivia asked.

"Lucie is trying to get permission for my father to leave London," Sky told us. "She says that someone's blocking his permission to leave."

"Any idea who?"

"No, but Lucie hasn't mentioned Cronus once, so whoever it is has no reason to actually do it. Even at short notice, it shouldn't be as much of an issue as it's become. Not unless they have an ulterior motive about keeping Cronus active."

Someone of Hades's stature had to ask for permission from Avalon to set foot on English soil, not including London. It was the same for all of the more powerful beings who had a stake in Avalon but didn't have anything to do with running its day-to-day operations. It was a fairly standard request, although it usually took a little while to process, because it went to the Shield of Avalon for any objections. It was why Hades had sent Sky to help us deal with the lich problem we'd acquired a few years ago.

Some things can be arranged on short notice, but this usually requires favors being owed. With Lucie's help, and considering her standing within the SOA and Avalon, Hades's request should have been pushed through within a few hours, bypassing a lot of red tape. The fact that it was being blocked meant someone with serious power, well above Lucie, was ensuring it didn't happen. They couldn't block it forever; any request has to be seen by the highest-ranking SOA members, whether it's initially turned down or not, but that can take a few weeks.

"I'm not sure I can call in *favors* this time," Olivia said. "If someone higher than Lucie is involved, I doubt I'd make any difference."

By favors, she meant threats. She'd told a few people they didn't want her as an enemy, and they'd allowed Hades to visit me at Tommy's place of business.

"That's fine," Sky said. "But someone in Avalon didn't want my dad helping with the lich, and now they're stopping him from leaving London to help with Cronus."

There was some muffled whispering. "You're on loud-speaker," Sky said a second later.

"Nate"—Hades's voice came through the phone's speakers—"you need to keep Cronus occupied. Someone will be there as soon as possible to help."

"I've got LOA agents en route too," Olivia said.

"Good," Hades said. "But even with their help, someone will have to go into the well and ensure that Cronus doesn't keep absorbing magic. Someone has to keep him distracted. And by someone, I mean you, Nate."

"And how exactly should he do that?" Tommy asked. "By the cunning use of bad language?"

"And why me, exactly?" I chimed in. "Why can't we just throw everyone at him?"

"Have you ever used a magic well before?" Hades asked.

"No," I admitted.

"Right, well, the person performing the ritual opens the well, and the magic goes into them, and for the most part, only that person. Anyone else walking in there will have zero abilities. It's the natural equivalent of my security system."

"The rune," I said softly. "I need to use it."

"Yes. And drawing it on a bunch of people won't work either. If they're not as powerful, or not compatible with it, there could be dire consequences."

"Like people dying?" Tommy asked.

"Like people dying in the most horrific manner possible."

I began to understand why these runes were hidden, why they had been changed to less powerful versions before being sent into the world. "Anything else I need to know?"

"Once the well is operational nothing nonorganic can get in or out of it without being attached to something organic. So the clothes you're wearing will be fine, but firing bullets won't work. The well will just act as an impenetrable barrier. Even taking the gun in wouldn't work unless you were touching each of the pieces individually."

"Okay, get into the well and stop him," I repeated. "Not sure I can. I only used the rune for a short time earlier, so didn't feel any adverse effects. If it needs energy to keep going, then it's going to start feeding off me. I don't know if I can stop Cronus before it drains me."

"Once in the well, you'll start to absorb excess magic automatically. That should keep the rune activated, but you won't have long. You need to put Cronus down. Hard. He can only maintain the ritual when stationary and concentrating. Just keep him moving."

"Okay, will do," I said.

"And Nate, be very careful. Cronus isn't someone to underestimate. When he was at full power, it took the combined might of most of the Olympians to stop him."

"That's not reassuring, Hades; that's the opposite of reassuring."

"If it helps, we were very young at the time, and Cronus was at full strength."

"Not even a little bit," I let him know.

There was silence for a heartbeat.

"Nate," said Sky. "Please be careful. Dad's worried. He doesn't like to show it, but I know when something is concerning him. Cronus won't go down easily. He's got too much invested. He wants too much."

I said good-bye and the phone went dead just as we began the drive toward the Stonehenge visitor center. In the distance, where the henge itself stood, a column of green light rose high into the clouds above. Cronus had already started the ritual.

The car stopped and we all got out, with three LOA agents who were already at Stonehenge, moving up to talk to Olivia. All wore combat armor and carried SA80 combat rifles. "He's surrounded by armed men," one of them reported to her. "We've tried engaging, but there's no cover for about a hundred yards from the road."

"We need to create a space for Nate to get into the well," Olivia told them.

"Ma'am, no offense, but I'm not sure why anyone would willingly go in there. From what I understand, the only person who could be in there and still have access to their abilities is the person performing the ritual."

"Do you have a pen?" I asked. "Permanent ink, like a Sharpie, would be better."

The LOA officer opened a pocket on his armored jacket and removed a small pen, passing it to me.

I drew the rune on the back of my hand and passed the pen back.

"Right, I'm good to go," I said.

"It's a five-minute ride to the stones," the officer told us.

We climbed back into the SUV, and the three officers stood on the running boards and hung on to the car. We waited for a few seconds before we were off once more, and I mentally prepared myself for what I was about to do.

"You'll be fine," Tommy said.

"Sure, it's just one little guy who people used to worship as a god. No biggy."

The car stopped beside some sort of visitor center, and we all piled out. There was a steep slope beside us, and well over a dozen cars sat in a semicircle around a large number of LOA agents.

"So, what do we know?" Olivia asked.

An agent with the name "Scott" embroidered on his breast walked over to us. He had a balaclava pulled up to show his face, which was thin and hadn't been shaved in some time. He looked angry about something. "It started twenty minutes ago. Cronus appeared and simply walked through the few men who'd arrived by then. By the time we'd got here, he'd already had ten minutes to set up the ritual without interruption. We engaged and were attacked with small arms fire. There's a ring of heavily armed people surrounding Stonehenge. From what we've heard from witnesses, they were already here, waiting for Cronus."

"Those people with Cronus are most likely Vanguard," Tommy told him. "Although I'd expected them to run off when Cronus escaped."

"Frankly, sir, I don't give a flying fuck who they are," he said. "They opened fire on my men and seriously hurt two of them. If I have to sit here all night, that's something they're going to pay for." He turned to me. "You're the one who needs to get in there. You capable of stopping him?"

"No idea. But if I don't try, a lot of people are going to die before the next few days are over."

"That'll do, I guess."

"I assume you have a plan," Olivia said.

The agent brought us to a nearby table, which contained a large map of the immediate area. "The Vanguard members have placed a barricade of cars between us and the well. Also, once you're in that well, what's stopping them from just shooting at you?"

"The bullets can't pass into the well," I explained. "And any Vanguard trying to get in there will die. Just get me in there; I'll do the rest. You guys just need to take the Vanguard out. If all of this works and I stop Cronus, that well will collapse. I don't want to be a sitting duck for a lot of pissed off, heavily armed nutcases." I spoke with about as much confidence as I could muster.

Something in my tone must have sounded a little off, because the agent raised an eyebrow in question, but he soon looked back at the table. "If we can create enough hell, you can sneak in here." He pointed to two spots on the map.

"I have another idea," Tommy said with a grin that meant it was not an idea I would enjoy.

"And that would be?" Olivia asked.

"I noticed you have a helicopter," Tommy said to the LOA agent.

"I'm not jumping out of a helicopter," I told everyone. They all completely ignored me and instead started working out exactly *how* I was going to jump out of said helicopter.

I'm sure I've said it before, but my friends suck. They suck hard enough that when I was getting fitted with a parachute and loaded onto a helicopter, no one listened to me as I pointedly reiterated the fact that I did not wish to jump out of the fucking thing.

I watched as the second part of Tommy's glorious plan came to fruition, namely the part where the agents stood well back and shot at the Vanguard from the relative safety of being on the ground.

"You done this before?" asked an agent who was sitting in the rear of the Eurocopter with me.

"Once or twice. Not in one of these, though."

"The EC145 is excellent. Loads of room back here."

Indeed there was tons of room in the back of the helicopter, plenty to put five or six people without too much trouble. He glanced out of the window and then turned back to me. "We're just over a thousand feet high, got a bit more to climb. You'll be jumping at fifteen hundred feet."

"Screw you, Tommy," I whispered, which caused the agent to laugh as he heard it through my microphone.

"Not a fan of heights."

"Mostly I'm not a fan of hitting the ground at speed *from* a great height."

"You'll be fine. By the time you reach the ground, you'll be gliding in beautifully. Now, this won't be like a normal jump. You've got only a few hundred feet before you need to deploy, or you'll hit the ground too hard. When your altimeter says it's time to release the chute, do so. Don't fuck around with this; you won't have long before you reach the height you need to be at, so pay attention." He tapped the altimeter strapped to my wrist. "You're wearing a base-jump parachute, it should make things smoother from this height. You're lucky we have them."

Lucky! I didn't bloody well feel all that lucky.

"We also can't take you too close to the landing zone," he continued, "because we'd crash once we touch that magic well. Same for you. If you go into it too early, you're going to drop like a stone. Try to avoid the gunfire. I think everyone below is keeping the Vanguard busy, but if any of them look up they might see you, despite the outfit."

I'd been given some black armor similar to that used by the Faceless. Hopefully, the fact that it was touching my skin would mean it wouldn't vanish the second I hit the well. I didn't really want to fight Cronus in my boxer shorts and socks.

The agent pulled open the helicopter's door and motioned for me to come close, which I did as my stomach decided to flip up and down. *Do not vomit,* I demanded of myself.

"You ready?" the agent shouted.

Am I ready? Am I fuck! Instead, I raised my thumb, although the middle finger almost popped up too.

The helicopter began hovering in place, and I sat down, my legs dangling over the precipice. Far below I saw the fighting that was happening around Stonehenge.

"Do not launch up," the agent said and pointed to the rotors not too far above my head.

"I'll try to remember," I said with as much sarcasm as I could manage, and wondered if it were possible to tie a werewolf to one of the rotors and fly up in the air.

The agent placed his hands on my back. "One."

I pitched forward slightly, ready for the drop that was coming. "Two."

I released my hands from the strap on the side of the door.

"Three." And he pushed with just enough force for me to move forward, out of the helicopter. And then I was falling very fast, from a great height, toward a fight with a god. When this was done, if I survived, I was going to get so fucking drunk.

CHAPTER 34

It's impossible to realize how fast a person falls until you're actually the one falling. I kept my eye on the illuminated altimeter, and the moment it hit the required height, I released the chute and began gliding toward the towering green light.

It was temping to use my magic to make me move faster toward my target, but I was by no means an expert parachutist, and if I used magic while concentrating on not crashing into the green light, there was a pretty good chance that was where I'd end up. Hitting the ground from a few hundred feet in the air might not outright kill me, but it would damn well hurt, and I didn't really have time to sit around and heal.

The closer I got to the ground, the louder the gunfire from below became. One of the cars being used as a barrier by the Vanguard was on fire, and another was smoking away. A few bodies lay on the ground. Although I couldn't tell if any real damage had been done to the LOA forces, it appeared that the Vanguard were the ones having a harder time of the situation.

I was two hundred feet above the ground, and coming in to a landing just outside the light, when the first bullet hit the canopy. I pulled hard to the side and tried to pick out my assailant from below, when a second bullet hit the strap above my hand, tearing through it and causing me to dangle, like a fish on a hook, as I began to fall at an increased speed.

I pulled hard on the remaining cord and swung myself toward the green light as hard as I could before using magic to cut through the last strap and a little more magic to propel me into the light as more and more bullets tore into the now empty chute.

I hit the light and felt an enormous tug on my chest and shoulders as the remains of the parachute were ripped from me and remained outside the light. Bullets tore at the well, but I had other concerns—namely, the hundred or so foot drop onto very large rocks.

I spotted Cronus kneeling in the center of the henge and was incredibly grateful when he didn't budge as I threw huge amounts of air magic in front of me in an effort to slow down. When I was thirty feet above the ground, I whipped a tendril of air around one of the giant stone lintels and let my momentum carry me down and under it, my feet almost brushing against the grass, before I released the tendril and flew toward Cronus.

When I was several feet away, he catapulted himself backward, using the earth to throw himself away from my trajectory. I hit the ground pretty hard, using air to help slow and stop any injuries, but I managed to tear a massive crevice in the ground as I did so.

"I did wonder how long it would take for someone to get here," Cronus said as I glanced up at him. He was naked from the waist up. On his muscular chest and arms were several large runes.

"I assume those are for activating the well." I got back to my feet and brushed myself down. "You're not going to just shut this thing off and come with me, are you?"

"What do you think?" He stared at me for a moment. "I remember you . . . Nathan, that's your name. You knew my son."

"We met a few times."

"He spoke highly of you—both he and Hades. They seem to think big things are in your future. If you stay here, I'll make sure your future is very short. Leave."

"Can't," I said. "I can't let you go after Hera. I can't let you get your power back. You killed Sarah."

"She had a Kituri dagger," he said. "She was going to bring me here, let me get my power back, and then murder me. Couldn't let that happen. Zeus needs justice."

"This isn't justice—you know that."

"Vengeance then; if the stories I heard about you are right, you're not going to tell me vengeance is wrong."

"No, it has its place. I've killed my share of people who have wronged me or someone I love. Can't say I didn't. But this—this will hurt countless more than just Hera. That's why I can't let you go. I can't let the people I care about down. I won't."

"Then you're going to die here."

I shrugged. "Then I die fighting."

Cronus darted toward me and struck out with a plume of fire from his open palm. I stepped aside and responded with my own plume, which he stopped by pushing my arm away. We went on like that for a few seconds, punches and palm strikes powered by magic, each one deflected or blocked as we each tried to gain the upper hand.

I struck out at Cronus's head with a jet of fire, but he moved at the last moment and tried for my ribs. I stepped into the attack and changed the jet of fire into a whip, bringing it down toward Cronus with incredible force. Cronus blocked the strike with a magically created rock above him, his glyphs turning green as he used his earth magic, before throwing himself back, putting distance between us.

The combat had been fast and brutal. I'd been burned on my arms and ribs, but so had Cronus, and he looked really angry about it. Although, whether that was due to the pain I'd inflicted or his inability to beat me quickly, I was unsure.

"You're not at full strength," I said. "This isn't a fight you can win easily."

"I won't be beaten by a child." He spat the final word, as if the notion that someone as young as sixteen hundred years could possibly better him was unthinkable. I aimed to prove him wrong.

He grabbed a huge rock, which probably weighed several tons, and threw it at my head. I stopped it by pushing up with a massive gust of air, giving Cronus the chance to throw a second rock at me from the opposite direction. I released my magic and aimed more at my feet, propelling me up and over the rock. When I was halfway past, Cronus changed the direction and flung it up toward me. I brought down a whip of air, which cracked the rock, but didn't break it. Instead, the rock plowed into me, knocking me to the ground and then rolling to turn me in a squishy mess.

I drew in a portion of the krampus's soul that I'd taken in Germany and used it on my air magic, pushing a column of air up at the rock, which exploded from the impact. The fact that Cronus managed to keep the magic together and turn the remaining rock pieces into tiny missiles was a testament to how powerful he was. A blast of air in his chest robbed him of his concentration, and the small chunks hit the ground harmlessly.

I got back to my feet. My continued existence and refusal to just lie down and die had etched an expression on Cronus's face that was similar to the one on the face of someone who'd found their trash bins knocked over, spilling rubbish everywhere. I wondered how much longer I could keep pissing him off before he went nuclear—probably not long. Cronus wasn't known for his ability to keep his temper in check.

Cronus walked over to one of the massive vertical stones that littered the Stonehenge circle we were inside and, with a crunch, grabbed hold of it, his fingers digging into the rock. He picked it off the ground as if it weighed nothing, and threw it at me. A little air magic to make me quicker allowed me to dodge the block as the rock struck the ground and tore a lengthy trench into the earth. Earth magic allows its users to increase their strength, much in the same way that air magic allows me to increase my speed and agility.

The second the massive stone came to a stop it was joined by a second one, forcing me to use my air magic to deflect its trajectory, taking it straight into a third rock. The noise was deafening as little pieces of rock began to pepper the hastily assembled shield of air I'd created. Stonehenge had stood for thousands of years, and Cronus had destroyed a sizeable portion of it in less than a few minutes of fighting me.

I wrapped air around Cronus's feet and yanked back, forcing him to drop yet another stone. He used his earth magic to shield himself before part of Stonehenge connected with his skull, but a second yank back on my air magic forced his head to smash into part of the stone anyway.

He threw a ball of fire at me, which turned, slowed, and changed direction when I avoided its first pass. Trying to control any magic in such a way is hard work, but doing it during a fight meant Cronus had to put his attention elsewhere, which let me sprint toward him and tackle him to the ground. It wasn't pretty, or particularly impressive, but it made him lose his concentration, equally so when I slammed my air covered fist into his jaw a few times, drawing blood.

The ground around us sprung to life as Cronus drew on his earth magic, smashing into me and throwing me off him with enough force to knock the wind out of me, despite my air shield. I dove behind a stone pillar and waited for my breath to return. I kept an eye on Cronus, who'd gotten back to his feet and shouted something in Latin that I didn't pick up. I guessed it wasn't anything nice when a boulder the size of a hatchback was hurled at me with enormous force. It crashed into the stones I'd been using as a shield, tearing my makeshift cover to pieces, but I was already on the move, using my air magic to sprint toward Cronus faster than any Olympic runner could have managed.

I threw a ball of flame at him. He stopped it with a shield of earth, which appeared across his arm. But with my power still increased by the soul of the krampus, the whip of fire tore through Cronus's shield with ease. He threw himself aside and countered with a jet of almost white-hot flame. But I'd moved beyond where he'd expected me to be. Dodging more jets of flame, I raced within striking distance and drove a blade of fire up through his side, twisting it slightly before tearing it free through his back.

Blood cascaded from the wound, but I couldn't follow up as four huge slabs of earth shot up around him, protecting him from further harm.

I released my magic and stopped my use of the krampus soul. I'd been traveling at much higher speeds than I'd ever have been capable of without it, but I doubted that Cronus was finished. I didn't want to be without one of my most powerful weapons when he rallied.

I threw a ball of fire at Cronus's earthen shield, which simply absorbed it, the wet muck moving as if to take the flame for Cronus to consume.

I wasn't sure if Cronus could still absorb magic while practically encased in mud and rock, but it wasn't a risk I was willing to take. I created a sphere of air in my palm and began rotating it, faster and faster until it was almost a blur, and then I ran at the rock and drove the sphere into it before releasing the magic. An entire side of the shield vanished from the impact, but the cloud of dust that was thrown up allowed Cronus to crash into me, taking me off my feet and driving me into the ground, where more of his earth magic leapt around my hands and throat, keeping me pinned down.

"You're stubborn and strong, but not strong enough," he said, slightly out of breath.

He got up, and I kicked him in the knee, hitting it just right to dislocate the joint and force his magic to vanish. I was up and on him in an instant, raining blows down with fist and elbow across his body, but he would not go down. He used his earth magic to ensure he stayed rigid and upright as he blocked a blow to his jaw before slamming a pillar of solid earth up into my face.

I didn't move in time to shield myself. The best I could do was move enough to take it on the shoulder. The impact was sufficient to lift me off my feet and dump me several meters away from Cronus. Pain wracked my shoulder, and I knew it was, at the very least, dislocated. I touched the limb and found the arm free of the socket. I smashed my shoulder into a nearby stone, which caused me to cry out.

"I'm done playing now," Cronus said, and when I looked up at him, his fire and earth glyphs had merged over his arms.

I scrambled to my feet as lava flowed over Cronus's hands and up to his forearms, a constant stream of molten heat that he was preparing to use. I didn't have to wait long as a stream of lava headed toward me at an astonishing rate. I didn't even try to use my magic to counter it, but just ran, the lava incinerating everything it touched as Cronus followed me in an attempt to turn me into a barbecued version of myself.

I'd made a whole lap of Stonehenge before Cronus realized he couldn't keep up and just decided to destroy everything. Huge stones and boulders hurtled at me with every step, and it was all I could do to keep moving, to keep the krampus soul burning inside of me to ensure I was quick enough. But I couldn't do it forever. The soul would extinguish at some point, and then I was as good as dead.

I threw a jet of flame at Cronus, who created another block of earth in front of him to stop it, but by the time the flame was extinguished, I was already on my way toward him. A huge rock appeared in front of me, but with some air assistance, I leapt up onto it and onto a second rock that appeared as if out of nowhere. Every time I cleared a rock, a new one appeared, forcing me to go higher and higher above Cronus and the battlefield below. After the fourth rock, I created a sphere of air in my hand and poured part of the krampus's soul into it, creating an orb of incredible power. I cleared yet another rock, but there was nothing below me but dozens of feet of space.

Cronus must have seen the sphere, because a massive column of rock tore out from in front of him and up toward me. Just before it hit me, I activated my fire magic, merging it with the air and forcing lightning into the sphere. Electricity crackled from within it as I put my arm out before me, the sphere now containing traces of yellow and red.

The sphere hit the top of the column like a bomb, destroying the first ten feet of solid rock as if it were paper. It took me through the next ten feet with barely any resistance, although the sound it created as the rock was torn asunder was deafening. Just releasing the magic wouldn't have worked; it would have destroyed the rock, but left Cronus standing. Instead, I focused the hand-sized sphere into something smaller and smaller, until it was the size of a golf ball. When it was the exact size I wanted it, I pushed it into the rock and then released it.

There was no big explosion or catastrophic failure of the rock. The sphere bore through it like a mole through soft earth. I fell to the ground, managing to use enough air magic to keep me from making a splat, but not enough to stop my ribs and wrist from breaking. I glanced over at Cronus just in time to see the sphere exit the rock near his chest. The Titan didn't stand a chance. It struck him as if it were a sniper rifle round, tearing into his body and through the other side with enough force to lift him off his feet and throw him twenty feet back into one of the giant stones. The barrier of the well stopped the sphere; otherwise, I had no idea where it would have ended up.

The massive stone column crumpled to the ground before Cronus and shook the earth beneath my feet. Cronus had fallen to his knees. I was almost out of my krampus soul, and my body was beginning to tell me that enough was enough. I remembered reading something in Zeus's grimoire, a piece of magic he'd used time and again with devastating results, but a trick so dangerous that one wrong move would cause him terrible pain. Considering I was already in pain, I figured there wasn't a lot to lose and stood up.

I raised one hand to the night sky and concentrated, creating a blade of lightning that stretched up five feet above my head. I gathered my magic inside me and pushed it out toward my extended fingers. I held the magic in place with incredible concentration and hoped to whatever gods happened to be around that I knew what I was doing, and then I pushed the magic out of my hand, up toward the sky.

The rumble of thunder was deafening to the point of making me want to clamp my hands over my ears, although with one hand being broken and the other covered in magical lightning, it probably wasn't a good idea. Lightning, natural and terrible, flew down the magic well toward my fingers. I'd anticipated the power surge, but it was like nothing I'd ever felt. The lightning mixed with my magic, and power grew inside of me, a dark, horrific power whose sole purpose was to destroy. There was no creation in the mixing of real lightning with magic, only ruin and chaos. I extended my broken hand toward Cronus, and the lightning left my body in one giant agonizing push.

It destroyed the stone that Cronus had been kneeling in front of, pretty much vaporizing a large portion of the surrounding area too, and I crashed to my knees. I was as close to spent as possible. Using the lightning had taken a huge amount out of me. I'd used the remainder of the krampus's soul to ensure it didn't fry me on the way through, and I was pretty certain it was a trick I wouldn't be trying anytime soon, but it had worked. Cronus was no more. It was a shame he'd had to die, but there'd been no other—

Cronus stood up out of the wreckage of stone and earth.

Heat poured off him. Parts of his clothes were melted to his skin, and other parts were on fire. His skin was bright pink, blisters formed around his mouth and forehead, and one arm hung loosely by his side, the skin barely recognizable as belonging to anything that was once human in appearance.

He took another step and stopped. The skin on his arms began to heal before my eyes. His face returned to normal, and the look of rage in his eyes stopped me from opening my mouth.

"You *dare*!" he shouted. "You dare use my son's own magic against me?"

I'd taken an idea from Zeus and thought I'd won the battle, but all I'd done was make it much, much worse.

CHAPTER 35

There are times in my life when I just wish I hadn't bothered. Kneeling before an exceptionally angry Titan who'd just gone from looking like someone who'd been strapped to a sun bed for six months, to his normal healthy glow, was probably not going to bode well for me.

I was pretty much spent. The lightning had taken almost the last of my reserves, and the only thing I had left was to pour as much magic out of me as possible in the hope that the nightmare took over before I died. It wasn't exactly the best plan, but I'd skipped over "best plan" some time ago and was now happily settling for "desperation."

I got back to my feet, ready to fight, and created a blade of fire. If I was going to lose, I was going to fucking well give Cronus something to remember me by.

The fist-sized rocks hit me in the chest with the speed of an aircraft, flinging me back to the ground. I scrambled up, but a second squadron of the little bastards smashed into me, and my shield of air only managed to deflect half. The rest hit me in the chest and head, knocking me silly for a moment. I felt blood flow into my eye, half-blinding me. I was unable to stop the pissed off Titan from grabbing my throat and head-butting me on the nose, breaking it.

The next few minutes were a blur as Cronus kicked the shit out of me in the middle of Stonehenge. I tried to fight back, but every time I used magic, it was weaker and he was somehow stronger. I crashed to my knees in front of a stone column and wondered how much longer I had to wait.

"Magic wells are wonderful things," he said and lifted my hand toward me. The hand that was supposed to have my rune inscribed on it. When I'd fallen from the column, just before the sphere had struck Cronus, something had cut through my hand, severing the rune.

"You understand now, yes?" he asked. "I was amazed that you even had enough magic to access the lightning. By the way, for that, I'm going to kill you. I can't have people use my own son's magic against me."

I spat blood onto the ground. "You're healed."

"The well—again, you kept piling on the pressure, but you never severed my link to it, and the whole time you were fighting me, I was getting stronger and stronger. The sphere was a nice touch, though. I've never seen that before. Maybe Zeus and Hades were right about you. Either way, it doesn't matter."

Cronus picked me up off the ground and held me by my throat, my feet dangling helplessly.

"This was fun," I wheezed. "We should do it again sometime."

"No." Magma covered his hand again, extending out to form a blade of pure lava. I struggled slightly, but it was no use. "I'll make it quick."

"Release him," said a woman's voice from somewhere behind Cronus.

Cronus sighed and let go of me. I fell to the ground coughing and hacking, but otherwise okay.

"Persephone," Cronus said. "This isn't your fight."

I rolled away, finally stopping by a small group of rocks near the edge of the well. Persephone wore a pair of Lycra shorts and a loose T-shirt. Both appeared to be dark in color, although to be honest, I wasn't really paying much attention.

Persephone wasn't wearing shoes. As she was an earth elemental, it was something that should have struck Cronus too. It should have been enough for him to run like the damn wind, but he was arrogant and stubborn and had just kicked my ass, so he probably thought very highly of himself. He was about to be proven wrong.

"Look, woman, go back to being Hades's trophy wife and let me do what I need to do."

Persephone put herself into a fighting stance, and I noticed the rune on the back of her hand for the first time. She'd come here to fight, and Persephone was not someone who did that lightly. I tried to get to my feet, but my body protested, and I collapsed back to the ground.

Cronus threw a ball of fire at her in a halfhearted way, but she just swayed to one side and avoided it. It was then that I noticed that wherever Persephone stood, the grass actually appeared to grow and was brighter in color, curling up over her feet and ankles.

"You sure you want to do this, *girl*?"

Persephone stretched one arm out in front of her and moved her hand so that the back of it was facing her opponent, and then she motioned for Cronus to come get some. Cronus created a massive bolder of rock and threw it at Persephone with no care for whether she lived or died.

Persephone didn't even move. She just turned her hand around, and the ground leapt up and grabbed the rock before it was even close, vanishing back under the dirt as if it were never there. Cronus's smile faltered just a little bit.

The big difference between sorcerers and elementals is that sorcerers use a magical version of the element they're throwing around. We create it from nothing, and it molds to our will. But once we've created it, it's as real as any other element. Elementals are *one* with the element. They're part of it, the real thing. And that means any sorcerer who throws an elemental's own element against them is basically pissing in the wind.

Persephone shifted her foot, and the grass grew around Cronus's feet. The first he knew was when they tugged him into the ground itself. He tried to use his earth magic in desperation, but elemental trumps magic when it comes to commanding non-magically created nature.

Cronus tore himself free and charged, throwing balls of fire at Persephone, who blocked each of them with rocks pulled from the ground. When she'd finished, over a dozen rocks, each about the size of my head, spun slowly in the air. And then they rushed toward Cronus in an instant, forcing the Titan to dive aside after he finally got free of the ground. Persephone shifted her foot again and vanished from view before jumping out of the ground beside Cronus and catching him in the jaw with an uppercut that almost took his head off.

Cronus fell back onto the ground but was on his feet before Persephone's stamp reached his head. He punched up with a lava-wrapped fist that Persephone avoided by head-butting him as hard as anyone could possibly be head-butted. Another uppercut to the jaw and Cronus staggered back, blood streaming from his ruined nose. He threw another punch, but Persephone vanished once again, reappearing an instant later at his side. She broke his arm in one fluid movement, stepped around him, and snapped his knee with a vicious kick before driving her own knee into the mask of blood that was his face, as he dropped forward.

I would have cheered her on, but it was probably inappropriate.

Cronus threw a plume of fire at Persephone, who was forced to move aside, into a second plume, which engulfed her. Just as I thought that she'd been hurt, she appeared out of the ground, behind Cronus, who caught a punch to the jaw when he realized where she was and turned to look.

From there it was only a matter of time. Although the magic well was helping him heal quickly, there was no way his body could keep up with the excess of punishment that Persephone was dealing out. A few more punches—her fists wrapped in solid rock— and one particularly nasty kick to his head ended Cronus's fight.

Persephone grabbed his legs and dragged him to the edge of the well. He couldn't be taken out of it while the marks connecting him to it were still on him, so she created a blade of stone in her hand and cut through the runes across his chest. The well spluttered for a second and then vanished.

I struggled back to my feet as my magic rushed back into me. Several LOA agents placed on a semiconscious Cronus a sorcerer's band—a small band with runes carved into it designed to stop a person's access to their abilities, and rigged with magical napalm to go off should anyone try to remove it. Then they transferred him to a spinal board and carried him away. Persephone came over and offered me her hand, which I took.

"You know I warmed him up for you, yes?" I said with a smile.

"Oh, heavens, yes," Persephone said, grinning. "Clearly you did all the hard work. I just stepped in and finished it. A bit like when someone tries to open a jar. You just loosened it up for me."

"See? I'm glad we're in agreement."

Persephone kissed me on the forehead. "Are you okay?"

"Magic is fixing me." My hand was completely healed, although the rune was still incomplete.

"I saw what you did with the lightning."

I paused, unsure what to say.

"You need to practice that if you plan on using it again. Using real lightning to power your magic is dangerous. Just like using real magma would be for Cronus."

"I know, but I didn't have an abundance of options." The idea of practicing with real lightning over and over until I was good at using it was a fairly scary thought. The fact that I could use my magic to call it was more than enough for me at the moment. "Did you kill him?"

Persephone shook her head and sat on the remains of one of the stones. "No. He'll live—just not feel too good about it. He always did think women were inferior. Now he'll remember what happened to him when he mouthed off to one."

I sat beside her and watched the scurrying of agents as they moved the deceased Vanguard and arrested those still capable of moving under their own power. "You know we sort of trashed a national monument. We destroyed some ancient stones today."

"You do realize that, by their very definition, quite a lot of stones are ancient. As for the destruction—well, I guess that's a good thing I'm an Earth elemental. I'll have all of this back together before morning. No one will ever be able to tell the difference between my creation and that done by those crazy druids."

"How did you manage to get out of London, by the way?"

"Turns out someone above Lucie was stopping Hades's entry, but never thought to stop mine. Shockingly, I got a call just before

I landed to say that Hades's entry was allowed. He was about to join Sky on his way here."

"Whoever stopped it figured there was no point in keeping Hades out now that you'd been allowed through."

"Someone in Avalon is working against us."

"Kay?" I asked.

Persephone shrugged. "If it was, I'd imagine he'd be a lot less subtle about it. He's got the subtlety of a . . . well, one of these rocks."

Tommy and Olivia came rushing over, both asking how I was at the same time. I explained very nicely that I was fine and that the next time Tommy had the idea to make me jump out of a helicopter, I was going to use him as my parachute.

"So, what now?" I asked.

"Now, you rest," Persephone said. "Because Hades should be on his way, and he's going to have a million questions."

"This still doesn't make sense," I said, ignoring her incredibly subtle attempt to make me go lie down somewhere. "It wasn't Hera blood in the vial; we know that much. She didn't want Cronus dead, not until he'd tried to kill her so she could finish him herself. So, who benefited from the power when Cronus killed Sarah?"

"Didn't Eos mention that Deimos was punished for trying to kill someone in Hera's employ?" Tommy asked. "Maybe he's decided to go after the matriarch himself. If he introduced Sarah to Demeter, then he could have been using Sarah as a spy of sorts."

"Deimos is a bully and a thug, but he's not a smart one," Persephone said. "He'd have tried to blow Hera up or something. Patience isn't his strong point either."

"So, someone else? Maybe one of the other big players working with Hera is making a move?" Olivia suggested.

"Demeter wouldn't dare," Persephone said. "Ares is a momma's boy through and through. Aphrodite, though, yeah, she's possible. There are a few others who would take a shot given a chance too."

"She always has surrounded herself with the most pleasant of people," I said as a helicopter came in to land by the visitor center.

"How'd you get here, by the way?" I asked Persephone.

"Helicopter," she said. "Brutus keeps half a dozen of the things for getting around."

"Who owns half a dozen helicopters?" I asked. "Isn't one enough?"

"Someone rich enough to own a percentage in pretty much every part of London," she said. By now, the helicopter had landed, and Hades got out, accompanied by Diana, Sky, and Kasey, who ran the few hundred meters to her parents. Olivia was first to receive a gigantic hug, followed by Tommy.

"Heartwarming, isn't it?" Hades said as he reached us.

"I'm not having kids, Dad," Sky said with a slight roll of her eyes.

Hades laughed and kissed his wife. "I hear you helped Nate take down Cronus." The way he said "helped" made me think he was fully aware of what had happened and was humoring me.

"He did all the heavy lifting," Persephone said with a chuckle.

"Cronus won't forget that in a hurry," Diana said.

"Maybe he's mellowed with age?" I suggested.

"It only took him, what, millennia to get over being beaten in the Titan Wars?" Diana said. "I'm sure a minor skirmish like this will only take a few centuries."

"I'll add him to the list of people who are angry at me," I said. "How come you're here, anyway?"

"I flew the helicopter," Diana said. "Besides I wanted to say good-bye to my little warrior over there." She pointed at Kasey, who ran over and gave her a hug.

"You enjoy yourself?" I asked Kasey.

She nodded. "I even got to meet Pandora."

Olivia glanced at Diana. "Really?"

"She was perfectly safe," Diana said. "We did it via Skype."

"So, what did she have to tell you?" I asked.

"I said I'd never been in a helicopter until today, and she told me that maybe Brutus would let Diana take me, Hades, and Sky to mum and dad once Cronus was captured."

I paused. "It was her idea for all of you to leave Brutus's building?"

Kasey nodded. "When I said that Persephone had just left to help, she told me that we should leave too. She said it would be a once-in-a-lifetime experience to see a magic well in action."

From somewhere in my mind, something pinged. "The well."

Tommy glanced at me. "Eh?"

"When I asked her how Cronus would get his power back, she went straight to the magic well. She didn't say anything else; that was her first and only guess."

"You think she knew?" Hades asked.

"Once in a lifetime," I said. "Those were her exact words. How many people in this world would have said 'magic well' if my question had been how do I increase my power? Blood magic, runes, and artifacts; there are lots of other, quieter ways that it can be done. But Cronus was told about the well by whoever set him free. They were going to bring him here and then kill him once he'd finished. What if it was Pandora who told them about it?"

"If that's the case," Diana said, "then I need to get back to Brutus."

"I'm coming," I said.

"We are too," Hades said.

I shook my head. "Hades, if she manages to enthrall Tommy or Sky, I can deal with it. She does the same to you and a lot of people could get hurt. Same goes for Persephone. Everyone's best served with you two staying here."

"I'll stay with Kasey," Olivia said. "I need to coordinate all of this anyway." She kissed Tommy before he ran off with Sky, Diana, and me to get in another helicopter. If nothing else, all this flying about was getting rid of my phobia. Silver linings and all that.

CHAPTER 36

We landed on the roof of the building beside Brutus's tower and quickly made our way down to the lobby of the Aeneid, which appeared no different than it had when we'd last entered.

"Anything strange happen?" Diana asked one of the guards.

"No, ma'am," he said quickly.

"Brutus on his floor?" she continued.

"Yes, ma'am, we've heard nothing from him to say different."

She thanked him and took us toward the lift, ignoring the ones that we'd used before and instead using a small key on a lift at the far end. The doors opened to an identical interior as the other, except a fingerprint and retina scanner replaced the numeric pad.

After the system confirmed Diana's identification, she spoke: "Twenty-fourth floor." The doors closed and we were soon headed up.

After a second of silence, Diana motioned for us all to move aside, and she used the key to open a compartment in the floor. It contained several handguns, a shotgun, and an MP5, along with an accompaniment of bladed weapons. Diana grabbed the shotgun and a dagger, tucking the sheathed weapon into the belt of her jeans. She opened a small box of shotgun shells and loaded the weapon.

"You guys take what you need."

Sky immediately grabbed two knives, and Tommy the MP5, leaving me with a Glock 19 and a silver dagger. Like Diana, I tucked the dagger in the back of my belt, pulling my T-shirt over it and keeping the gun visible.

The doors opened, and we were greeted with silence as we moved out of the lift. The floor search was done quickly, with Diana on point, until we found Brutus and Licinius lying on the couch. Brutus was face down, his wounds unknown, but Licinius had two bullet holes in his chest. Blood spatter patterns across the wall indicated they'd been shot and then fallen on the furniture.

"Brutus is good," Diana said and pulled him over onto his back. "He's got a strong pulse. "These are tranquillizer darts, and it's not his blood."

"Licinius's pulse is weak, but it is there," Sky said. "Why try to kill him, but not Brutus?"

"Brutus was nice to her," I said. "Check the other floors."

"And where are you going?"

"Pandora. She can't enthrall me; she can you."

"And what if the people who shot Licinius are still around?"

"I don't plan on letting them shoot me."

"And if Pandora has already escaped?"

"She won't have," I told them. "She won't go until she's sure she has my attention. I'm one of the few people who can track her without fear of her power. If she's after Hera and company, she'll try to persuade me to side with her. If that doesn't work, she'll threaten me—tell me she'll hurt me if I come after her. She's done it before. She wants people to know why she does the things she does."

"You're counting on a lot," Tommy said.

"I know, but I'm certain of it. She's waiting for someone she can tell her story to. She knew I'd be forced to come back here when she gave everyone the idea to leave here. She didn't want people I care about in harm's way. We've always had mutual respect. If she hurts my friends, she knows it'd be all over. I'd come after her with everything I have. I'd bury her in a hole so deep the light could never find her. It's why she always eventually allows herself to get caught, and why, when she's out, she never hurts people who are innocent. Hope won't stand for it."

"Best of luck then."

I left everyone to it and took the lift up to Pandora's floor, stepping to the side of the doors as they opened and waiting for whatever was about to come. I might have believed that Pandora wouldn't hurt me, but I wasn't so sure of the people helping her escape.

The immediate area outside of the lift was empty, as were the corridors and rooms I walked past. In fact, I wasn't given any trouble by anyone the entire way to the cell. The doors, normally guarded, were open, and there was no one in sight as I stepped into the cell room.

Part of the roof of the building had opened, allowing the ferocious wind outside to create a fair bit of noise in the enclosed space. Pandora sat in her library reading. I walked up to the door and knocked.

Pandora got up, walked over to the door, and opened it without pause. She held no visible weapons and wore a plain black jumper and blue jeans. She was barefoot and didn't exactly look like someone who was planning to escape anytime soon.

"How are you, Nathan?" she inquired.

"I assume you'll be wanting to escape soon," I said.

"Soon, but not just yet. You want to come in for a drink?"

My magic had cut off the second I'd stepped onto the floor, and although I'd considered using the rune, I wasn't sure about the effect it would have after my fight with Cronus. Besides, with the gun and knife, and with no one else able to use their abilities either, I was fairly assured of my ability to hold my own for the few seconds it would take for me to draw the rune. It was then I remembered that I didn't have a pen, or pencil, or—hell—even a piece of chalk. I sighed. It had been a long night, and that one tiny thing I'd overlooked was going to bite me on the ass, I just knew it.

"I'm good, thanks," I said, declining her invitation.

"That's a shame. Please, come in. We need to talk."

"You know, I think that's a bad idea."

Pandora sighed. "Let us spell it out for you. Our people have planted explosives all around this part of London. If you don't get in here with me in the next ten seconds, we're going to signal for them to detonate. There are only four or five packages, but how many people do you think that might kill? A hundred? Two? A thousand? It's quite late, so probably it wouldn't wreak quite the devastation it could cause earlier in the day, but even so, people will die. Get in here. Now."

I did as was asked, and Pandora closed the door behind me. I walked into the library and paused.

"We haven't got explosives in here," Pandora said from behind me. "You're safe."

I sat on the same chair I'd used last time, and Pandora left the room again, returning with two cups and a pot of tea.

I glanced at the china teacups as she poured the amber tea from the pot into them.

"Seriously, Nathan?" she asked when she saw me stare at the drinks. "We haven't poisoned them." She took one of the cups and took a drink. "As you know, we can't lie to you. Not ever, remember? Drink."

I took a sip of the tea and waited for her to begin.

"Just so we're all on the same page, the lifts have been locked out of use, and no one is coming for you. We have about ten minutes before we leave, so we figured it was only fair that you got to ask us questions."

"Justin Toon, the head guard, he works for you," I said.

"Indeed. The entire security staff does. Justin hired them all from someone he knows. We didn't even need to enthrall them, although occasionally we do so just to ensure loyalty. We don't know who they are, but they're very bad people."

"Are they Vanguard?"

"No idea. They were pretty good cannon fodder, though; we can't say we're unhappy with their ability to die and leave no one to answer questions."

The words of the traitor I'd tortured in Hades's compound sprung to mind. "Who is their liege?"

Pandora shrugged. "Not a clue."

"You got Sarah to work for you."

"We enthralled her. Justin let her in; she had no idea what was happening until it was too late. Had her in my palm for years. She went to Hera's to spy for Brutus, but she fed us the info we needed. Well, she fed Justin, and he told me. It was our information about how Cronus could escape that she gave to Hera; it was our plan to get Cronus out and have him try to kill Hera so that she could kill him and then claim a stake in Tartarus.

"Unfortunately for Hera, Sarah was meant to kill Cronus at Stonehenge. That was how you figured out we were involved, yes? We explained about the magic well. It was a gamble, but we're glad it paid off."

My body felt heavy and I couldn't move, as my eyes started to lose focus.

"Ah the drugs—excellent. Don't worry, it's not lethal. We just needed you to be out of it for this bit. You see, we've been lying to you. While we were in Tartarus, we found this book about souls and their use. It's very interesting, but the gist is that instead of enthralling someone's mind, we can enthrall his or her soul. It doesn't register on any psychic scans, and it means that anyone enthralled who breaks free can be enthralled again and again. Unfortunately, we discovered this after our time together, so you can't be made to do anything. But it does mean that *I can* lie to you.

"We're a camel. See, a great big lie and we can say it. So, we want you to know, we lied about the tea, about the Vanguard and who employed them, about it being our blood in the vial— because it obviously was. We lied about a lot. Helios started our plan so many years ago, but you stopped him. You can't stop *me* this time."

I slurred something in response, and Pandora rubbed my cheeks before removing my gun and placing it in the band of her jeans. "Try again, slowly," she said.

"You said 'me,' not 'us.'"

Pandora clapped. "You noticed that. The Gestapo had some very interesting information about how to merge the two souls into one. Then they decided to dissect me, so I killed them all, but I did learn a lot from them before they had to die. I realized

I'd slipped up a few times back in Berlin, and I was worried you'd picked up on it. I was very careful not to do it again, until just now. Obviously."

"Hope gone."

"Oh, yes, Hope is well and truly a thing of the past."

"Helios's plan *was* your plan."

"That's very good. Yes, Helios's plan was to kill Hera and her friends on the first ever live televised event. That was all me. The sarin gas—I heard all about that after—was his idea, which was stupid when you think about it, but Helios is an asshole. Besides, there's no accounting for brains when you don't have a lot of choice."

"All about revveeeallll."

"About what?"

"Reveal. Revealing us . . . all. To the world."

Pandora clapped her hands together. She was certainly enjoying herself. "That's exactly it. I don't just want Hera dead; I want to out the whole fucking lot of you. They took an innocent girl and fucked her life up. I think letting the world know that you've been behind their entire lives for centuries should go some way toward me feeling better about myself. Once humans realize they're no longer the top of the evolutionary ladder, at least some of them will do something stupid. They'll force Avalon to take action."

"Many will die."

"So? Many die every day. At least they'll die knowing the truth. Admittedly, that's not much of a consolation for them. But I don't care—it's going to be glorious."

My head sagged forward.

"The drugs will wear off in a few minutes. Just long enough."

"How'd . . . you . . . know . . . know . . . Germany?" I asked, taking a guess at something.

"How'd I know you were in Germany?" she asked.

I attempted to nod.

"Mara had been bitching and moaning about your presence in Germany for weeks before the trip. She was furious, according to Justin. She told Sarah, who told Justin, who informed me. And what's a girl to do? So I told Sarah to track you and convince you to leave. I didn't want you throwing a spanner in the works, now did I? But Justin wants you dead, either out of jealousy of the bond we share or because he felt that was the best idea—I don't know. But while I'll be sad if he kills you, I can't have you coming after me."

"Witches."

"The witches were all Sarah's idea. She really didn't like that Mara woman, so she arranged to have her be the fall guy. But unfortunately for Sarah, she got sloppy and then she got dead. I felt her power rush into me, which I can tell you for a witch was some serious mojo. A fully powered Cronus would have been better, but you take what you can get when you're in a jail cell."

"Kram—"

"The krampus." Pandora bounced around with glee. "That was a brilliant touch. Sarah went to go use some criminal idiots, really vicious little bastards who deserved to die. She found some glorious souls to take, and then, even better, she found the exact person to become the krampus. It was beautiful. I assume you killed it."

I couldn't manage a full nod anymore. It was too much hard work.

"Figured as much. You've grown stronger in the last few decades. Killing a krampus is no mean feat. Part of me hopes you live through what's about to happen. It's a small part, but enough. I genuinely like you, Nathan. But needs must. And you must be sacrificed for my needs to come true."

"Can't just walk out," I said as my brain began to feel less fuzzy.

"Walk? Oh, dear Nathan, look up."

I glanced up as part of the ceiling to her cell just moved aside, showing the stars through the opened roof above, which were quickly replaced with a lowering helicopter. I was really beginning to hate those damn spinning bastards.

A rope was dropped from on-board, and Pandora placed one foot on it and tugged slightly. "I'm sorry it had to finish like this, but finish it must. Good-bye, sweet Nate. Just so you know, I lied about the bombs too. I'm a lot of things, but I'm not going to kill innocent people." She paused for a second. "Unless I have to."

I watched her ascend quickly while my faculties began to clear. People were coming to kill me. I shambled down the hall, using the walls to ensure I didn't fall over, and fell through the bathroom door, slamming it shut with my leg. I wasn't going to have long; I had to prepare for whatever Justin and his guards had planned. I fished the dagger out of my belt. Well, if they were going to come for me, they'd better bring their best.

CHAPTER 37

The wooden bathroom door was about as useful as asking really nicely, in terms of keeping out anyone Justin sent to kill me. I was pretty certain that anyone he'd hired wasn't going to be some gung-ho idiot and would probably behave in a professional manner. That also meant that I wouldn't hear them coming. They weren't going to make any flippant comments about coming to get me; they were just going to get in position and open fire.

I searched the bathroom for anything that might help. While I wasn't entirely sure how thick the walls were, the odds were good that they weren't going to be bulletproof. I needed something to ensure the bullets didn't tear through me like paper. The bathtub was a possibility, but bullets shatter enamel, turning it into shrapnel.

I opened the medicine cabinet's mirrored door, in the vain hope that there'd be something useful, although it was probably too much to hope that she kept a tiny chain gun in there. Instead, I found some makeup, a toothbrush, and toothpaste, along with various feminine products that probably wouldn't do me a huge amount of good in a gunfight.

I took one of the many lipsticks and removed the cap as the sounds of feet trampling along the hallway filled my ears. I drew the dwarven rune on my hand and my magic sparked to life.

A second later, I had a shield of air pushed out in front of me as hundreds of bullets poured into the bathroom.

The sound was deafening. I poured more and more magic into the shield. The bullets deflected off the shield, striking everything else around me. Within a few seconds, the toilet and sink had been destroyed, spraying water into the room. A few seconds more and I had to extend the shield when a piece of bath enamel sliced through my cheek and embedded itself in the wall.

Using so much magic to keep the shield in place was exhausting my already diminished power. I'd used an enormous amount in the last few hours, and I wasn't too sure how much longer I could keep it going before the nightmare . . . Erebus decided to come out to play. And I'd really rather not have to deal with passing out once he'd left. Every second I was here, Pandora was getting farther away.

After a ten count, the bullets stopped, while the water continued to pour into the room, creating a small pond that had began to flow under the ruined door. I removed my magic and then moved as quickly and quietly as possible behind the door. I kept the rune in place, just in case, but I knew that I wouldn't have long before it started to take more energy than I had available.

I removed the dagger and took a breath as the door was pushed open. The muzzle of a carbine was the first thing I saw, but I waited as its wielder took another step, and then I snapped to the side, pushing the muzzle away and driving the dagger up into the throat of the man.

He pulled the trigger on the gun, which destroyed more of the bathroom, and I twisted the dagger and pulled it free, stepping to the side to avoid the shower of blood that accompanied it. I caught the guard by his bulletproof armor and spun him round, toward the hallway, dragging his sidearm free and putting two bullets in the head of the closest guard. I pushed my shield to one side, intercepting a bullet meant for my head, and put two in my next would-be attacker. Three dead in less than ten seconds.

I dragged the corpse farther into the hallway and dove aside, into the bedroom, as automatic gunfire slammed into it. I shut the door. It didn't have a lock, but then it would have been useless against automatic gunfire. I considered barricading it, but thought better; anyone outside of the cell could see me anyway, so they'd know I was out of options, even if I couldn't see them.

I put two bullets through the door, on the off chance someone was behind it, and then rolled over the bed, rubbing off part of the lipstick rune, and making me magicless once more, when a shotgun blast tore through the door handle. A second hit the bed I'd rolled over, and a third took out a lamp as the gunman stepped into the room. I lay on the ground and fired into the knee of my assailant, and he cried out in pain, dropping to the ground and releasing his hold on the shotgun. I fired a second bullet as I stood, striking his forehead, and he didn't move again.

I left the shotgun and moved toward the door, firing blind down the hallway in a hope-filled attempt to either flush out more attackers or maybe get lucky and hit one. When no one fired back, I stepped out into the hallway, keeping my body low so as to be a smaller target. I crept along, hugging the wall, but when I reached the library and glanced into it to make sure I was free, someone fired at me from the still-open roof. I dove aside, firing up as I moved, and was thankful that I hit my target in the throat. He dropped through the ceiling to the floor, his noises disturbing and awful as he died. But the distraction had been enough, and as I got back to my feet, someone charged into me, smashing me up against the nearby wall and knocking my gun free. I tried attacking with my dagger, but he deflected my arm and struck me in the joint, causing me to drop the knife on the floor between us as pain radiated up the limb.

He grabbed me by the throat and started choking me, forcing me down to the floor, but stopped once I punched him in the knee with everything I had. The padding he wore around his legs softened the blow, but he backed off, putting distance between us and allowing me to see him for the first time. My attacker was huge, nearly seven feet tall, and probably weighed twice what I did. He was an imposing figure, even without the body armor and combat fatigues.

"You're going to get killed by a human," he said with a slight smile. "How many of my kind get to say that they killed a sorcerer?"

"You're human?" I said, rubbing my neck. He was massively strong and, because my own natural abilities were unattainable for the moment, someone I probably didn't want to go hand-to-hand with.

He stalked forward, limping slightly when he put weight on his knee. I moved back into the kitchen, forcing the large man into a much smaller space than we'd had in the hallway.

"Nowhere to run," he said with a grin.

"You too, dumbass," I said and flung open the fridge door, right into his face, before kicking out again at his injured knee. He staggered back as the door swung closed, but regained enough poise to throw a punch. I grabbed a paring knife from the kitchen counter and dodged the blow, pushing the blade up into the larger man's forearm, twisting it, and pulling it out.

Blood poured from the wound, and he roared in pain. He was lucky I hadn't nicked an artery. He staggered back and I moved toward him, grabbing my dagger from the ground and throwing the paring knife at him, which he dodged with ease. There was a look of rage in his eyes; he wasn't used to being on the business end of an ass kicking.

As he stepped back, he removed his belt and tied it around his arm, making a makeshift tourniquet so he wouldn't bleed too much. His left arm was useless, though. I thought about charging forward, taking the fight to him, but there was no way he wasn't expecting it, so I turned the dagger so that the blade was pointing to my elbow and settled into a fighter's stance while he took out his own combat knife.

The serrated edge of his knife was black, and it had a slight curve at the top. It was an evil-looking blade, designed purely to cut and hurt as much as possible. He kicked aside the chair I'd been using earlier and motioned for me to come get him.

I'd checked both sides of the hallway before entering the library, and had discovered it was all clear, but as I took another step, the man grinned, and I felt the hairs on the back of my neck stand up. I ducked just in time to see a blade come hurling at me from the roof above. I spun and threw my dagger up at him, catching him in the eye. He pitched forward, landing face first on the carpet behind me, with a noise I'd have rather not heard, as his orbital bone shattered from the impact of the dagger's hilt against the floor.

The momentary distraction gave the larger man the time he needed, and he shot forward, low and fast, swiping the dagger up at my throat. I moved aside, pushing his arm away with the palm of my hand and striking him in the throat with the other. He whipped the knife back toward me, barely missing a beat, and once again I blocked the knife, but he switched his grip and pushed the blade across my palm, causing my hand to burn from the silver his blade contained.

He followed through, plunging it toward my stomach, but I moved aside, putting a little distance between us as I edged back toward the end of the hallway. I flexed my fingers. My palm hurt, but it wasn't a deep wound. I was certainly losing less blood than my opponent.

No magic, no weapon, and fighting a much stronger opponent. I had to admit I'd been in better situations. And then half a dozen more armed guards entered the house. "For fuck's sake," I said to no one in particular. "Guys, you really don't want to be here right now. I'd run."

I placed my index finger against the blood on my opposite palm and then drew the dwarven rune on my opposite forearm. Magic flowed back into me, and I smiled. I wasn't sure how much I had left, but I either used it or I died. And I was damned if the second choice was even an option.

"Too late." I extended my hands and lightning leaped from them. White-hot, terrible lightning that destroyed whatever it touched, turning my knife attacker into a smoking hunk of jerky in seconds and turning the hallway into one long killing floor. The other guards died before any of them even got a shot off. The magic sprang between the walls, tearing the cell apart until I stopped it.

I stepped over the sizzling corpses of the guards as I made my way toward the front door, where I was greeted by a burst of machine gun fire, tearing through the open front door. I was about to launch myself through the door when the bullets stopped, replaced by a gurgling noise. I risked a glance through the holes that now littered the door and saw Justin face first on the floor. A pool of blood was spreading out from beneath his head, which had an arrow sticking out of the back of it.

Diana walked up to the body, placed a foot on the back of his head, and with a terrible squelching noise, removed the arrow, taking a chunk of something unpleasant with it.

I stood and walked around the door as she cleaned the arrow on Justin's back.

"Thanks," I said.

"Was that lightning coming out of the doorway?"

I nodded.

"Wow, look who got all grown up," she mocked with a smile.

"Pandora's gone. Someone in a helicopter came and picked her up."

"Any idea where she is?"

Tommy and Sky came through the door, Tommy in his full werebeast, the fur on his paws covered in blood. Sky had no blood or injuries on her at all and barely looked like she'd been doing anything, although the idea of Sky sitting a fight out was unimaginable. And then I saw her knuckles and knew the blood on them wasn't hers.

"You got cut?" Sky asked, pointing to my hand. "And you're covered in blood."

"This will be fine," I said, lifting my hand. "And the blood isn't mine. Most of it, anyway."

"Any idea where she's gone?" Tommy asked, his voice deep and accompanied by a low growl.

"Yeah," I said. "She's gone somewhere public where Hera and everyone she values will be."

"The book fair that Aphrodite mentioned," Sky said. "When does it start?"

No one had a clue.

"Let's find out," I said. "And get Hades—we're going to need him."

"Why? I thought you didn't want him near her," Tommy pointed out.

"Yeah, but that was here, when he could have been enthralled. There are going to be thousands of people at that book fair, and the four of us can't control that many. We need some big guns to keep the people she enthralls from killing anyone, or themselves, while I deal with Pandora. Preferably before she decides to end our way of life and start a fucking war."

CHAPTER 38

Sixty-four people died that night. Twenty-two of them were innocents in the wrong place at the wrong time. The rest were traitors. Brutus had trusted Justin to employ and manage his security staff, and he'd been rewarded with a group of people who were just waiting for the signal to turn on their supposed employer and kill those they worked with. No one dared explain the irony of that statement to a man who'd been on the other end of the betrayal in quite spectacular fashion in the past.

To suggest that Brutus was livid was an understatement. Once the tranquilizer had worn off, he'd destroyed his flat, tearing the furniture to pieces. Diana had eventually calmed him down, and after an hour we all found ourselves sitting in a meeting room on the third floor. Brutus sat at the head of the lengthy table. Diana sat between Sky and Tommy. Hades and Persephone, who'd both been flown in by Avalon, sat on the other side with me. Licinius had survived his attack and was apparently less than happy about being left out of the meeting, but seeing that he couldn't walk or even talk for long, it was probably for the best.

Everyone had cups of tea or coffee. It was still dark outside, but I doubted anyone was going to be getting much sleep for the next few hours. There wasn't long until the book fair took place, and we had to prepare.

"So, you're sure the book fair at Earls Court is her target?" Brutus asked me.

"Aphrodite told us that they were all going to be there. It's a big deal for them. And there will be a lot of people for Pandora to use as cover. Clearly some parts of the Vanguard are helping her, so we can expect armed resistance. Pandora knows we're not going to want a bloodbath."

"How long has she been lying to you?" Hades asked.

"I don't know. Maybe decades. She's figured out a way to enthrall a person's soul, instead of their mind. She told me those who are enthralled don't show up when scanned by a psychic. Pandora seems more powerful, so expect her to use that against the civilians inside Earls Court."

"It's a risk to bring us," Persephone said.

"It's a risk not to," I replied. "You two will be providing ground assistance. Pandora is mine, but I can't deal with several thousand people in the way."

"Can you take her out?" Brutus asked.

"She can be hurt, therefore she can be subdued. We have no way of knowing if anyone other than the Vanguard is helping her. And we don't know who got the Vanguard involved. There will almost certainly be unknown quantities inside the building."

"You say she wants to show the world that Avalon exists," Tommy said. "How?"

"Ten thousand people will be in that building. Authors, agents, journalists—all with camera phones. Someone in there is going to get evidence and write about it."

"We can suppress a lot," Olivia said from the loudspeaker of the phone on the table in our midst. "But that many people— it's going to be too much to stop everyone from talking about whatever they see. If the world finds out about us, there are gonna be some pretty serious repercussions. Humans won't like learning that they're not the top of the food chain."

"There'd be pandemonium," Tommy said.

"I thought you people controlled the media," Brutus said. By 'you people,' he meant Avalon.

"We don't rule the Internet, Brutus," Olivia said, and to her credit she didn't rise to Brutus's comment. "And we're not a communist state. People can find out about Avalon and the like, but the second anyone broadcasts that knowledge, they get shut down. We make up what—one percent of the entire world's population? Maybe a little more? Someone in the crowd at the book fair will get it out, and then there will be trouble. My LOA agents will be on hand at Earls Court to contain everyone there and ensure nothing we don't want leaked gets out. It's all dependent on you getting Pandora subdued, though."

"You know, I don't understand why we just didn't stick a sorcerer's band on Pandora centuries ago," Brutus said. Clearly his temper was getting the better of him again.

"She burns them out," I explained. "Which you know."

Brutus gave an exasperated sigh. "So, what's the plan for containment? She's not coming back here, I assume."

"Do you want her?" Sky asked.

"No. She can fucking burn for all I care."

I noticed a glance between Persephone and Hades.

"What's the plan?" I asked them.

"Nevada. There's a facility there where she'll be kept isolated and away from anything resembling the public. She was threatened with being taken there back in Berlin, but she chose to cooperate. Now she has no choice."

"You mean Area 51?" Tommy asked. "You're taking her to an underground prison?"

Area 51, despite various alien theories popular among humans, is actually a giant underground complex where people whom Avalon deems too dangerous to remain free are placed. It's been up and running for a few decades, and it houses just under a hundred people, most of whom are unable to shut off their dangerous abilities. They're made as comfortable as possible, but the fact is that the inhabitants are kept mostly isolated and underground.

"I don't see why you didn't do that before," Brutus snapped, seemingly forgetting that it had been his decision to take Pandora back in 1939.

"Because she's not a mistake we can throw away and forget about," Hades replied. "The Olympians created her, and it's our responsibility to ensure she's dealt with in a humane manner. You seem to forget that Hope is along for this ride; she's done nothing to incur our wrath. Pandora said that Hope is gone, but I don't want to believe that."

"I don't see Hera or Poseidon around here helping out. In fact, you're the only one, and if memory serves, you weren't even involved in her creation."

"Yes, well, someone has to stop her. If not me, then who?"

"Those responsible for her creation?" Brutus snapped.

"This isn't getting us anywhere," Olivia pointed out. "We need to ensure that Pandora gets inside Earls Court before we go in. We can contain the building once she's inside. We can't lose the opportunity to take her down. If she escapes—"

Everyone was silent while we contemplated the damage Pandora could do in the modern world. No one wanted that to happen.

"So, the plan's set," Hades said. "We'll wait for Olivia's word that Pandora and her people are inside the place and then intervene. She won't run; I assure you of that. She wants Hera and her people to pay. She won't go anywhere until that happens. And she won't afford them a quick death either. She'll want to tell them why they're dying. Once we're inside, we'll provide cover for Nate, who will go find her." Hades turned to me. "If you have to kill her, do it."

I nodded. I really hoped it wouldn't come to that, but I knew Pandora wasn't going to stop her plan without some serious, possibly very final, convincing.

Five hours later, it was 9:00 a.m., and the doors to Earls Court had opened, allowing the beginnings of a huge line of people into the massive building. By 10:00 a.m., thousands of people had gone in, and there was still a massive queue.

"Anyone seen her?" I asked into the microphone attached to the top of my T-shirt.

"Not yet. You sure about this?" Hades asked.

"Positive. She wants lots of witnesses and coverage. Anywhere else won't work."

"What if she knows we're waiting and decided not to bother?" Tommy asked from beside me. We were both, along with Sky, Hades, and Persephone, in a building above the tube station directly opposite the front of Earls Court.

The empty room we were in was one flat in a block currently under construction. Brutus had made a few calls, and suddenly everyone who was supposed to be working there had a day's holiday. The wall on one side wasn't entirely built, and there were no doors or glass in the windows to keep the wind and drizzle out, but the plastic tarpaulin over the wall meant no one could see us, while we could see out after a few adjustments were made to its position.

"She won't care that we're here," I explained. "By now she has to know that Justin didn't make it out of Brutus's building, so she's down several accomplices. She'll have to assume the worst: that we got the information we needed before disposing of him. She'll expect people to try to stop her. She just believes she's better than everyone else. There's no part of her plan she's considered where she doesn't win. She isn't wired to think otherwise."

"So at best we're an annoyance to her?" Sky asked.

I nodded. "We always have been. It's why when she's caught she doesn't fight to escape; it's why she let the Gestapo take her. She wants to see what we'll do to her next. She can't die, so any pain inflicted is only fleeting. She knows eventually she'll escape, kill everyone who wronged her, and go through the whole thing again. But this time, she finally has specific knowledge of where Hera will be and when. She's not going to wait another four thousand or so years for a second shot."

The three of us returned to watching the street below for a few minutes until Tommy broke the silence, "You need to name that sphere thing you do in your hand."

"I assume 'spinning sphere of magical destruction' isn't a good name?"

"It's not exactly catchy, Nate. It should be one word."

"I'm not trying to market it, mate," I pointed out as Sky chuckled. "I think a toy of me with a real spinning sphere of death, is an unlikely action figure."

"It just feels like it's begging to be named. There's a show that Kasey watches—it's an anime—and one of the characters uses something similar to it."

"I think Rasengan might be too on the nose," I said.

Tommy's mouth dropped open in shock as he stared at me.

"Yes, I've seen it. Yes, I know what it is, and no, I'm not calling it that."

Sky's chuckle broke into full laughter. "Tommy, you're the geekiest person I've ever met. Looks like you're dragging Nate down with you."

"We're moving slowly," Tommy said. "The anime was a nice surprise, though."

"Kasey made me watch a bunch of stuff the last time I looked after her," I explained.

"How much is 'a bunch'?"

"About two hundred episodes in three days. I sort of got into it," I admitted.

"Geek," Sky coughed into her hand.

I turned to Sky. "If I remember correctly, you cried when Spock died."

Sky stopped laughing. "We need to keep an eye out for Pandora. This is serious stuff—no time for joking around."

She walked to the window while Tommy tried to stop himself from laughing and failed miserably, earning a glare from Sky.

"He sacrificed himself for his friends, damn it," Sky said. "It was heroic."

The three of us started to laugh, until Olivia's voice came through the radio. "Got her. You guys ready to go, or do you need some more bonding time?"

The laughter stopped immediately, and I grabbed my jacket from the back of a nearby chair. "Let's go catch Pandora."

We left the construction site and ran across the busy road to a waiting Olivia, Hades, and Persephone.

"My men are trailing her," Olivia said. "It looks like there's no one with her, but that doesn't mean she won't have help in there."

Brutus had allowed Olivia to bring her LOA agents into the capital for several reasons. The one he told us was that Avalon needed to capture Pandora because he simply didn't have the room to store her. But Diana told me before we left that he couldn't trust any of the guards who were left and wasn't about to make things worse. He had a lot of pieces to pick up when this was all over.

We crossed over to a heavyset man in a suit, standing near the entrance. He nodded at us, and we followed him inside. He couldn't have been more obviously an agent of Avalon if he'd had it stamped on his forehead, but this wasn't a stealth mission.

After running up some stairs, we entered the main area of the building, and I was immediately taken aback not only by the size of the place and the number of people there but also by the sheer level of noise they all made. It took a few seconds to get my bearings as I searched the crowd.

One of the LOA agents, wearing plain clothes, came over to us. "She's gone down the middle aisle."

"Thanks," I said and began to walk in the direction the LOA agent had pointed.

The hall contained dozens of stands of various sizes, all advertising a different publisher. Some small publishers had tiny stands with only one or two people there, but the larger companies had huge stands, with dozens of people all talking or looking at the books that were sitting on shelves.

"The meeting rooms are upstairs," Olivia said. "If Aphrodite has business to take care of, I imagine she'll want privacy. The entrance is over there." She pointed off toward one side, several hundred meters away.

The six of us spread out as we got farther down the spoke-like aisle, while more agents took the other aisles. We'd made it about halfway down when I spotted Pandora at the bottom. She was watching us advance, with a wicked smile on her face. She said something that we were too far away to hear, but then abruptly everyone down the aisle fell silent. There was no gradual drop in noise—it went from loud to quiet in an instant.

"Apparently, I can do more than I thought," she said. "Enthralling a few thousand was quite hard work, although it got easier when I volunteered to be the one stamping everyone's hand as they entered."

I looked around at the statue-like group that surrounded us. They all had their eyes on us.

"You've been here awhile then?" I asked.

"Broke in last night. Prepared myself until I was ready for you, then used the corridors under the building to get out to the street above. It was simple really."

There was a bang behind us as the doors were closed, followed by a jangle of chains as they were locked shut.

"You plan on killing us?" Sky asked. "It didn't work so well for your men last night."

Pandora shrugged. "I assumed they were all dead. Nice to know for sure, though. So, I'm now left without my Vanguard helpers. Come get me, Nate. I dare you."

She turned and ran off, and I took a step after her only to be clouted in the head with a laptop wielded by a middle-aged woman in a suit. I grabbed the erstwhile weapon and threw it aside while she tried to claw at my face. A second later she went limp and then fell to the floor, as all around us those controlled by Pandora woke up to do her bidding.

"Don't kill any of them," I shouted.

"Just go," Tommy replied as he threw one man into a group of others, knocking them all to the floor.

A few hundred people blocked the way forward, but before I could ready any magic, they all stopped moving and collapsed to the ground in unison.

"Go," Hades told me. "I'll keep them still for long enough."

I wondered how long he could keep the souls of hundreds of people tampered with. Probably not long enough to be able to help subdue anyone else. As much as I wanted to stay and help, I left everyone and sprinted after Pandora, dodging anyone who got too close or tried to stop me, and blasting a few with air to make sure they left me alone.

I rounded a corner, watched Pandora run through a door at the far end, and hurried after her. I was about a hundred feet from the door, with several dozen controlled people in front of me and an unknown number behind, when someone shouted, "*Stop!*"

Everyone did as they were told.

"He's mine. Go find someone else."

The people did as they were told, walking away as Deimos stepped out from behind a pillar.

"I don't have time for this," I explained. Fighting anyone would take time I didn't have, but especially fighting an empath as powerful as Deimos.

"Yes, you do," he said. "Pandora made sure that all of these people would obey my commands. She's going to kill my bitch of a grandmother and everyone else with her while I make sure no one stops her."

I took another step.

"Well, if you're going to be like that," he said, and suddenly terror crept up inside me.

I took another step, determined not to let Deimos affect me, but the emotion overcame me, and I crashed to my knees.

"Now we get to have some fun," he said and kicked me in the head.

CHAPTER 39

I woke up unable to move. I wasn't entirely sure where I was, but it didn't take me long to realize that I was tied to something. I pulled at my arms, but there was no give in the straps. I glanced down and saw Deimos sitting at my feet.

"We're going to play a game," he said. "It's called 'Let's Make Nate Relive His Worst Fears and Memories.' It's not a catchy title, I'll admit, but it's pretty accurate."

Somewhere inside me I knew what had happened. Deimos had used his empathic ability on me from the moment I'd stepped toward him in the hallway, and he'd started to raise my level of terror. The moment he'd touched me, he was able to invade my memories, finding the ones to use against me. But knowing what he was up to and being able to do something about it were two different things. Deimos was easily powerful enough to force me to relive whatever he chose, and there was nothing I could do but continue to try to fight it in the hope that he screwed up.

I glanced over at the door and saw Jenny walk toward me, as if she'd just appeared out of nowhere. Jenny had worked for Mordred, but at some point she'd decided she didn't want to work for a monster anymore and had tried to save the lives of two young girls who were essential to Mordred's future plans. She'd been key to me recovering the memories that Mordred had stolen from me. I knew what was coming, but there was nothing I could do to stop it.

She was exactly how I remembered her—bruises on her exposed shoulders, running up her neck. There was a cut just above one eye. Stitches had been applied to close the wound. All of this was so familiar. The anger and pain at seeing her that way, the fear at what was going to happen to her, to me. I'd lost all of my memories, I didn't even know who I was. I had no power, no nothing. I'd played the fool, jumping from beautiful woman to beautiful woman, playing thief while I tried in vain to block out the fact that I was just scared. Scared of who I was, of what I might become if my memories ever returned, but more scared about never getting them back.

"They said you could go free," I found myself telling her. I wanted to scream at her to run, to leave and never come back, but that wasn't how it really happened. That wasn't how Deimos was going to play the game.

Jenny nodded. "Death is their version of setting me free. They only let me talk to you because they want to watch you suffer."

Time shifted, moving in fast forward. It was only a few seconds, but it was enough.

Jenny touched my cheek, a tender moment between two people who had been lovers. Who could have been more. "I want you to know something," she told me. "I really liked our time together. It made me feel normal."

Another fast forward as I screamed in rage at what Deimos was making me relive. Jenny kissed me gently on the mouth. A grating sound started, coming from the side of the table, but it didn't last for long as the kiss intensified and she grasped the sides of my head in her hands. I returned the passion, and suddenly, without warning, memories exploded in my head.

I tried to yell out. I knew what was happening, what *had* happened to me. I knew what Jenny had done, as more and more memories came into the forefront of my mind. But the kiss intensified once more, unlocking chunks of my past with every heartbeat. Deimos was making me relive all of those unlocked memories for a second time, all of the pain and rage and heartbreak that they brought with them.

I moved my head slightly, noticing dark marks on Jenny's wrist and forearm. Another memory exploded, giving me instant knowledge of what it meant. She was killing herself so that I might live. She was giving me back my memories, my abilities; she was remaking the man I used to be before Mordred tore my mind asunder, before I spent a decade playing games and pretending that nothing bothered me.

Outwardly, I followed through the memory, feeling the wetness of Jenny's tears as they fell onto my cheeks, mixing with my own.

Deimos touched my hand and everything faded, only to be replaced with me in the house I shared with Selene. We'd lived in New York for four years. I'd quit Avalon decades earlier, and for the first time in a long time I was happy. And then I walked through that door and found our house empty, found the note on the dining room table. Smelled Selene's scent as I read it, and felt the pit of despair as the realization of its contents hit me. She'd left me. I wasn't to contact her, I wasn't to try to find her; she was going to marry Deimos and her mind was made up.

"There's not enough terror or horror here," Deimos said from beside me. "I just always wanted to see the moment, you know?

I expected more crying. Maybe we should just change your memory so that you cry. I think I'd like that."

I dropped the yellow paper onto the table and my heart felt as if it were ready to burst.

"Oh, I've got a better idea—how about this?" Deimos taunted.

I was walking toward a house, a two-story building made from wood and brick. There was a porch on the front, and the door was banging open in the wind. The ground beneath my leather-booted feet was wet and soggy. It had been raining heavily for some time and had turned the grass into something resembling a swamp.

I took a step and fear lanced my heart. "Please don't," I said.

"Oh, you're gaining some control," Deimos said from beside me. "That's actually quite impressive. It's not going to stop me. Nice clothes, by the way."

I wore a set of black leather armor, similar to that worn by the Faceless. I had one of their cloaks, which billowed out behind me in the wind despite the strip of metal placed in the bottom of it. I took another step, the mud making horrific noises that even the wind couldn't mask.

"That's it—keep going."

I walked on as if nothing were bothering me, stopping at the banging door. "Jane, I'm home," I bellowed into the house.

There was no response.

I stepped inside and shook my cloak, removing it and draping it over the back of a chair, leaving it to drip water onto the floor.

"Jane," I called again. I doubted she'd be out in the weather we were having, but maybe she'd gone to town and decided that she'd rather stay with people during a storm.

I took the first step on the staircase and froze. The smell of death careened into me like a runaway carriage. I ran up the stairs, taking them two at a time, and crashed into our bedroom door, removing it from one hinge.

The horror before me was almost too much for my eyes to bear witness to. I didn't understand what I was seeing. Jane was on the bed. She was naked, except for a sheet that covered part of her torso and one leg. The sheet had, at one time, been a cream color, a present for our wedding day. It was now dark red. A huge pool of my wife's blood formed under the bed, cascading out around its legs and seeping into the crevices in the floor.

I walked toward her, my hand to my mouth, stifling screams of terror and pain that would not come. There was no sound that could temper what I was feeling, no noise that would do justice to the sight of what used to be my wife.

Jane's throat had been slit, her torso stabbed repeatedly. Her hands were tied to the top of the bed with thick rope. I reached out slowly to her face, and tears fell freely from my eyes as I climbed onto the bed. I rubbed her stained cheeks with my fingers, as if anything I did could make it better.

I howled in pain. Lightning struck a tree outside, and it burst into flames, but even the elements couldn't make me so much as glance up from Jane's face for long. Her beautiful face. Her natural red hair was now crusted and stained, her eyes still open. Looking at me, as if pleading for my help.

I used fire magic to cut through her bonds, and she sagged against me. "I'm here," I cried out. "I'm so sorry. Please, please don't go. I'm here." Words fell as tears, tumbling out of my mouth. I pleaded and begged with anyone and anything that might have been listening. All the while I cradled her dead body against me.

I offered my own life countless times, but no one was listening or no one cared—I didn't know which.

"Now this is more like it," Deimos said with a slight clap. "You know, I've wanted to do this for so long. You had everything. People who feared you, people who loved you. Selene. Do you know how long I used to just watch her? To wish she'd take notice of me.

"And now she's my wife and she won't even touch me. She hates me and loves you. But by the time I'm done, there'll be nothing left of you but a gibbering wreck. Let's see how much she can love you then."

"I'm so sorry, Jane," I said, ignoring him. "I'm so sorry."

In an instant, I was crouched beside Deimos, watching myself weep for the woman I'd loved. Watching my own heart break with grief. The rage would come, and there would be a reckoning the likes of which few had ever seen, but for the hours I stayed, holding my wife in my arms while the storm continued outside, it felt as if nature itself was grieving with me.

"Take two," Deimos said, and he made me relive it over and over again. Each time, it was either first person or I was forced to stand beside Deimos while I watched with horror while my younger self went through one of the worst experiences of my life.

"What are we at now, six?" Deimos asked as I watched myself hold Jane yet again.

"Let's change things around a bit." He paced up and down through the pool of blood that had crossed my bedroom floor. "Oh! How about we show you what you imagined happened when they came for your wife. Shall I show you that?"

I would have pleaded for him to stop right there. I would have begged a million times, if it could have made him stop forcing me to see Jane. I'd relived it in my memories a thousand times, but nothing could compare to that first time. And Deimos had constructed a way to make every time feel like that first time. He was breaking me. I knew it, and so did he. And soon there would be no point of return.

The picture faded, replaced with my wife running toward a man, dagger in hand. The man—I'd later come to know him as Henry—punched her in the face, and the dagger clattered to the floor. I had no idea if that was how it had happened, but there had been a dagger there, and again and again I'd gone over in my mind what must have happened to Jane. Reliving the horror that I couldn't be there to stop.

Jane tried to crawl toward the dagger, and Henry laughed, removing his belt and throwing it on the floor.

"Now, I bet this gets good," Deimos said to me.

Everything froze.

"Well, that's odd," Deimos said. "I don't remember hitting pause."

"I did," said my voice, and Erebus appeared beside him. "You, Deimos, are a selfish, cruel little man who should have left well enough alone."

The vision disappeared, replaced with everything exactly as it was when I found Jane.

"Who the fuck are you?"

"My name is Erebus," he said. "And you tried to make Nathan see an altered memory. If you'd made him relive the actual thing over and over again, you'd have broken him. But you decided that wasn't enough. You wanted him to suffer more. You tried to change the moment from what actually happened to what he imagined happened. And now I'm here, because although I can't interfere with his memories as they are, I sure as hell can interfere with those that are made up."

Deimos grabbed Erebus's arm, but nothing happened.

"Good try. My turn." Erebus placed a hand on Deimos's chest, and the entire wall behind him exploded outward, taking him with it. I turned to watch as Deimos and most of my house hit the mud outside. He bounced along until a large tree stopped him.

"Make him suffer for this. Make him know real fear." Erebus's words were said to me with a cold detachment, but his eyes revealed the fury within. He touched me on my head, and the fear and pain that had been coursing through me vanished, replaced with something else. Something much more terrifying. The need to hurt the one who had wronged me.

I stood up and shook Erebus's hand. "Thank you."

"This meeting between you and me—this one you'll remember. I'll make sure of it. Just because this is your memory, that doesn't mean you can't change it to suit the moment. The imaginary and the real aren't so different. One doesn't erase the other. You're in charge now. When you want to leave this place, kill him. He's the anchor holding you both here."

I didn't understand what he meant. Had we spoken before and I couldn't remember? But I pushed it aside and stepped through the remains of the door and into the howling winds outside.

As I made my way toward a motionless Deimos, the house itself moved to create steps for me, those parts of the ruined structure vanishing once they had finished with their usefulness. There was no magic here—just Erebus allowing me control over my own mind once more.

Planks of wood covered the mud until I was standing above Deimos, who was bleeding slightly from his nose.

"How'd you do that?" he demanded. "This is my domain."

He grabbed my hand. And fear awoke in him as he realized there was nothing he could do.

"This is my mind," I told him as Deimos released me and scrambled away. "You wanted to fuck around in here so badly— let me show you the sights."

I moved quickly and grabbed his hand, crushing it by wrapping it in air and squeezing while I ignored his screams. I released it and the limb was whole once more. I gripped his collar and dragged him to his feet, head-butting him and then slamming the back of his skull against the tree.

"You should not have done this," I said as he slumped to the ground. "You should not have shown me these things. No one should be forced to relive the worst moments of their life. No one." I looked back at my house. "But maybe you should be forced to live someone else's." I clicked my fingers, and the world changed. We were no longer outside; there was no longer a storm or mud, or anything I'd loved.

We were underground in the cellar of a house that belonged to a rich merchant who had worked for Avalon over the years. There was a wooden table beside where I sat, and on it were a collection of bladed instruments of various shapes and sizes. On the opposite side, on an identical table, were two bowls. One held clean water, with a towel beside it, but the other's liquid was now dark red. I doubted it could truly even be described as water any more.

I picked up the bowl filled with bloody water and poured it over Deimos, who was strapped to a chair before me. The blood and water mix saturated him, doing little to clean the grime from his naked body. I refilled the bowl with fresh water from a large jug on the floor and then sat back as Deimos gasped while the bloody water ran into the grooves in the floor and out under the wall behind him.

"Why can't I see?" Deimos demanded. "What have you done to me?"

"Calm down," I said. "I wrapped a cloth over your eyes. I'll take it off in a minute."

"Where am I?"

I explained about the castle and merchant. "The man who murdered my wife was called Henry. He was in the King's army. You're currently occupying his place in my memory. You sort of look like an amalgamation of Henry with your body shape. It's a weird thing. Anyway, I kept Henry down here for some time. Basically, you're going to go through the exact same things that Henry did."

"*Fuck you!*" he screamed, bucking against the chair, but it was no use.

"Henry couldn't break free. He was human, and so in here you are too. You never should have forced me to do this. But you're about to live out the worst few weeks of anyone's life. I won't make you do it over and over; once should be enough.

"When we're done here, you're going to remember the kind of man I am, the kind of man you threatened and tried to break. I want you to remember what happens to those who cross me. I want you to tell people. Tell everyone what happens when Hellequin is pushed too far."

"You're Hellequin?" he asked, his voice full of fear.

"You didn't know?" I was a little surprised. "Well, now you do." I walked over and removed the damp cloth from his head.

"It's so dark in here," Deimos said after a few seconds.

"Oh, I should have mentioned. By this point, Henry had already been here a few days." I removed items from the small jar on the table and placed them in Deimos's hand, and then I whispered into his ear, "I'd already taken his eyes."

Deimos screamed himself hoarse while I picked up a short, sharp blade from the table. I turned to him. "Shall we begin?"

CHAPTER 40

It took me a few blinks of my eyes to realize I was back in Earls Court. Deimos was in the fetal position on the floor beside me, half-hiding under a table. His bowels and bladder had both forsaken him.

"Remember what happened here," I demanded.

He started to gaze up at me and stopped, refusing to look any further than my knees, before nodding furiously.

He'd lived a week of the worst things I'd ever done to a person. He'd felt all of Henry's pain and suffering as if it were his own, but with the added bonus of being unable to actually die. When I finally put Henry out of his misery, we'd come back to reality. The emotions I'd felt during the episode had been real, and it took me awhile to realize it was just a memory.

I walked past Deimos as the humans around him began to remember I was prey once again. They hadn't moved from the time Deimos had forced me to relive my memories, and I doubted more than a few seconds of time had passed in the real world.

I changed from walking to sprinting within a few steps, and used air magic to tear to pieces the door that Pandora had gone through, flinging them aside as I ran through the doorway and up the stairs.

The corridors above were mazelike, and I had no idea exactly where Aphrodite was having her meeting.

I took a moment and calmed myself, trying to listen for any sign of where Pandora had escaped. I heard nothing for a few seconds, and then a gunshot rang out. I ran toward the sound, and although I couldn't pick out the exact place, due to the confines of the corridors, I at least had a rough direction.

A second gunshot rang out after a few steps, and I followed the noise down one hallway, toward a blue door. It was easy to spot Pandora through the glass panel on the front of the door, but as I got closer, I noticed it wasn't Pandora holding the gun, but Selene, who had transformed into her dragon-kin appearance.

"Selene, *no!*" I shouted as I barged through the door. She glanced at me, a glazed expression on her face. Pandora was in control of her.

The gun looked awkward and silly in her hand, her talons barely able to hold the weapon and manage the trigger.

I turned to look at Pandora who was standing in front of a window looking down on the floor of Earls Court. "Stop her," I demanded.

"Fuck, you Nate," Pandora snapped. "Look at them—look at Hera and her cohorts."

I glanced over at the far end of the room, where Hera, Ares, Demeter, and Aphrodite all stood, all of them with the same glazed expression on their faces. There were three other middle-aged men, all in suits, who were cowering in the corner. None of them appeared to be under Pandora's power.

"Why control them?" I asked.

"Can't risk them fighting back," Pandora said. "Selene here is going to kill all but Hera. Then I'll release her and let her see what she's wrought. And then I'm going to kill her myself."

"Why Selene? You don't need to use her."

"She can die knowing what she did."

"Don't," I said. "Don't do this."

"Why shouldn't I?" Pandora snapped. "She's just as bad as them. She joined them, and she hurt you. You should want her dead."

"I can't let you kill anyone here," I informed her. "And I'm certainly not going to let you use Selene to do it."

Pandora stared at me. "You still love her."

"Yes," I admitted. "Despite everything that's happened, despite all the anger and hurt, I still love her. Now let her go."

Pandora appeared to consider it for a second. "No. Say 'bye to Ares."

I blasted Pandora with a gust of air that threw her out of the window with a crash. Then something unexpected happened: all the people regained their minds.

Selene blinked twice as I took the gun from her, emptying the magazine and the bullet in the chamber and dropping them in a bin. "You okay?" I asked.

She nodded, and her body returned to her human appearance.

"I'm going to fucking kill her," Hera roared.

"You're all too groggy. Just stay here." I jumped out of the window, my air magic letting me glide the thirty feet to the ground.

A lot of the humans were back to their normal selves but appeared confused and shaken as an apparently uninjured Pandora got back to her feet.

"You knew," Pandora accused.

"I guessed," I said. "Enthralling all of these people must have taken a lot of concentration on your part. Falling thirty feet onto hard ground probably knocked your power out for a second or two, just long enough for everyone to recover."

"I can just as easily take them again."

"Not without going through them all one at a time. How did you manage to enthrall Hera and the others upstairs, anyway?"

"Selene was in the corridor and Ares, standing guard outside. After that it was just a case of overwhelming force. Hera almost got me, but she wasn't quick enough to realize what I was doing."

"You're coming with me now," I said.

"No, I don't think so." She turned and sprinted off into the crowd, and I followed without getting too close. She touched a few people as she went by, but when we reached the center of the convention room, Tommy appeared out of nowhere, subduing the newly enthralled humans. She could enthrall Tommy, but by the time she could have gotten past the throng of people and done it, I'd have caught up to her. She changed course.

Another aisle had Sky at the end and a third held Hades. Pandora took a fourth, and I slowed to a walk after she discovered Persephone waiting for her. I let her take a fifth, but she came back to the center after spotting Olivia. There was nowhere to go, no path she could take that would lead to her escape before I caught up to her.

"We're done here," I said.

"*No!*" she screamed. But most of the humans had been evacuated from the building, and none of those that were left were close enough for her to grab and enthrall.

I glanced over at my friends and nodded. Each of them turned and walked away. Once everyone had gone—leaving just Pandora and me staring at one another—I offered her my hand. "Give it up," I said.

"No," she repeated and swatted my hand aside. "If I go, I'm going to grab someone and use them. There's no one you can trust near me. And this time, I'm not letting you bring me in."

"I don't want to hurt you."

"Spare me your pity. If you want to take me out of here, you're going to have to kill me to do it." She snapped her fist toward my face, which I pushed aside before giving her a shove and allowing her momentum to carry her beyond me.

She snapped one leg up toward me, catching me on the chest, which made me stagger, and she followed up by planting that foot, spinning around and hitting me in the face with her opposite foot.

The blow split my lip, but I recovered enough to avoid the rest of her kicks and punches. It wasn't that I didn't want to strike back because she was a woman; I'm of the opinion that if someone is trying to kick your ass, you defend yourself no matter the sex of the attacker. I just didn't want to hurt someone I liked. I'd hoped once the initial flurry of rage she had inside her had been burned out, she'd surrender, but it soon became apparent that wasn't going to be the case.

She weaved toward me and caused me to block or dodge more blows. The more they continued, the more force I had to use to slow her down. I pushed her away, tripped her, and tried to lock her arm in place in an effort to subdue her with minimal damage, but she was always moving and never stayed down for long.

It made fighting her incredibly difficult, but I refused to be drawn into a full fight with her. Pandora was thousands of years old, but she wasn't a hand-to-hand fighter. And any training she'd had wasn't something she'd been able to continue practicing on any sort of regular basis while in a jail cell.

Pandora launched herself up to catch me in the side of my head with a vicious kick, and I decided I'd had enough. I grabbed her thigh and twisted my body, dragging her up and over me before dumping her on the floor with a crack. She kicked out at me with her free leg, but I connected with a blow of my own on her knee, which caused her to roll aside in pain.

I released her leg and stepped back, hoping she'd had enough, but she had other ideas and swept out at my legs. I jumped back, giving her enough time to get to her feet.

"Enough," I said. "Seriously, you can't beat me in a fight. Just surrender and we can leave. No one needs to be hurt here today."

"Never! Now fight me."

She put up her hands in a fighter's stance and walked toward me before throwing a punch that I caught in one hand, at the same time driving my other fist into her solar plexus with immense force.

"Breathe," I said as she collapsed to her knees. "Breathe steadily. You're okay."

Tears fell down Pandora's cheeks, and I wasn't convinced they were from the pain of the blow. "They deserve to be punished," she gasped weakly. "Why won't you let me punish them? Look what they did to me."

Realization of a previous thought's accuracy dawned on me. "It's not Pandora who took charge of the body is it? How long have you been in charge?" I asked. "Hope, how long have you been in charge?" I repeated when she didn't answer.

Hope glanced up at me through misted eyes. "Since Berlin. Pandora is gone. There's only Hope now. Once she'd left, all of the knowledge she'd been learning about controlling a person's soul, not their mind, became mine to use as I wished. It was as if our merging unlocked all of these possibilities. When did you realize?"

"Just now. I thought Pandora was in control, but only you ever described yourself as an individual. Pandora never could. So, I should have known it was your personality taking over, not hers, when I heard you say 'me.'"

"I was trying so hard not to screw it up ever since I saw you again."

"Also, Pandora would have actually had people plant bombs in London. She didn't care about the people if it meant getting her way."

"I wondered if that was going to reveal the truth," she said sorrowfully.

"Are you done weeping?" Hera asked from behind me. "Because I'd like to kill the fucking bitch."

I stood and turned to Hera and her group. "You're not having her," I declared.

Hera glanced around. "Everyone appears to have left you. There's no Hades here to stop me from just taking her and killing you if you get in the way."

Ares cracked his massive knuckles, and I wondered if he'd discovered what I'd done to his boy.

"You're not having her," I said again.

Selene appeared and walked past Hera to stand beside me. "How much noise do you think it would take before Hades came in?" she asked.

Rage erupted onto Hera's face. "How dare you! Clearly you've forgotten why you owe me your allegiance. Maybe I should remind you."

I was about to say something when Hope launched herself past me, toward Hera, her hands outstretched to grab her creator. I reacted instinctively, creating a blade of lightning and driving it through Hope's back, stopping her in her tracks. Hera's mouth dropped open in shock or horror at either the lightning blade or the expression of agony on Pandora's face, I didn't know. I removed the blade and caught Hope before she collapsed toward the floor.

"I'll remember this," she said weakly as I laid her down. Suddenly, the sounds of doors opening and people running toward us echoed around the room.

"I'm sorry. I had to," I explained.

"You'll wish you'd finished the job," she said before I was ushered away by LOA agents.

CHAPTER 41

The few hours after I'd put Hope down were hectic to say the least. Hera and her people scarpered once it became apparent that both Hades and Avalon had Brutus's okay in terms of working within London, something Hera wouldn't have gotten even if she'd paid for it.

The last I saw of them was Ares helping a dejected Deimos out of Earls Court. Selene stayed behind, talking to various Avalon members about what had happened and what she'd seen. Occasionally, I found myself staring at her, but I looked away when she glanced toward me. It was childish and silly, but I felt angry with myself for what had happened between us, and angry with her for never revealing the truth.

"So, Pandora is no more?" Tommy asked as he sat beside me, carrying a sandwich.

"Where'd you get food?"

"Went to the shop," he said and took a bite. "So, you going to answer my question?"

"Hope's in charge now. I assume she's much less happy with me than she was."

"Last I saw, she was cursing your name while being loaded into an Avalon transport. I get the feeling things won't be done between the two of you."

"I couldn't let her get to Hera. We'd be at war if she died."

"Tough choice to make. Save Hera or allow a war to happen. Neither of those outcomes is all that great." He finished his sandwich. "So, you and Selene. You spoken to her yet?"

I shook my head. "What do I say? For a century I was led to believe she'd discarded me through some act of callous self-advancement. 'Sorry' doesn't seem to really sum it up."

"You'll figure it out. Oh, Brutus says thanks by the way. I think he was pretty happy how this ended without a bloodbath in his city."

"Probably for the best. I forgot to ask: Where's Kasey?"

"Olivia had her agents take her to Winchester. She had a little temper tantrum, but I'm led to believe none of the agents were going to allow a fourteen-year-old girl to tell them what to do. I suggested they tranquilize her. They told me that it was always an option. I think they were joking."

Selene was suddenly walking our way, and Tommy made his excuses and left, patting me on the back for good luck as he went.

"We need to talk," Selene said to me after nodding a thanks in Tommy's direction.

"Probably."

"My sister told you why I had to leave."

"Yes. She explained about the threats and blackmail. About how you did it to keep me safe. You should have told me."

"I couldn't. I had to keep it to myself. No one could mention it."

"So, why did Eos? And what about Petra? Did she know more?"

"Petra figured out that something wasn't right just after we separated. She didn't know it all, but she knew enough. Eos told you because she's got a big mouth and no longer cares what Hera thinks. She figured if you knew, you could do something to stop Hera from telling everyone. Can you?"

"Are you leaving Deimos?"

"I think that's pretty obvious. I was never really with him except in title. I don't know what he thought was going to happen, but having a wife who didn't care about him probably wasn't on his bucket list." She reached out and took my hand in hers. "Can we work again?"

I shrugged. "A century of feelings won't just vanish. I think we both need to find out what we feel."

"I need to find out who I am," she admitted. "A century in that regime has changed me. Maybe we could be friends."

"I'd like that. If it happens, it happens, but maybe you need to take some time for yourself. I don't want to rush back into something and then fuck it up because I'm still angry and hurt by everything that happened."

"Deal," she said with a smile. "I don't expect you to wait for me, Nate, if you find someone . . ."

I stood and kissed her on the cheek. "Go see your family. Don't worry about me."

"Can you stop Hera from releasing all of that information about you?"

I shrugged. "We'll see. I have an idea or two."

"I never loved you any less," she whispered. "When I found out. If anything, I loved you more for beating the darkness inside you. I'm not sure I could have done it. I want you to know that."

I took her hands and pulled her toward me slightly, kissing her on the lips as I moved one hand up to the side of her head. I pulled away and she licked her lips.

"I missed that," she said.

"I missed you," I whispered.

"I will come find you. When I know who I am and what place I have in this world. I promise, I'll come find you. I love you."

Hades called me over. I turned and waved that I'd be a moment before turning back to Selene who was walking out of the rear double doors at the back of Earls Court.

"I know," I whispered with a smile.

CHAPTER 42

Pretty much everything was dealt with so that what had happened in Earls Court was put down to some drunken idiots' gate crashing. Most of the people there would have put the whole incident out of their mind as a weird moment they'd rather forget, and to the best of anyone's knowledge, no one was going to write a book about what had happened. Or if someone did, it would be fiction, and no one was going to believe it.

Hades called me at home after a few days and told me he needed me at the complex above Tartarus in Mittenwald. I made my way there and was surprised to find both Lucie and Sky at the entrance when the car that had picked me up from the airport stopped.

"Hi," I said to them both. "What's going on?"

"Hades has arranged a meeting between yourself and Hera," Lucie said. "She's in one of the meeting rooms in the complex. She's not very happy at being called here. She arrived with her entire entourage in tow."

"Well, he left that little bit of info out when he invited me here," I said. It would have been nice to at least be asked if I wanted to see Hera, but I was here now and quickly resigned myself to the idea of the whole process. Hera still had a lot on me, and I doubted very much she was going to give it up without getting something in return. I hadn't managed to figure out what I was going to do to stop her from going public with the information she had on Hellequin. Hopefully, Hades knew.

"How's Pandora?" I asked Sky and then paused. "Sorry, how's Hope?"

"Pissed off," she said as we walked through the compound. "Mostly at you. She was secured in Nevada this morning. Unless she can enthrall rock and metal to do what she wants, she's not getting out of there in a hurry."

"She'll escape one day," Lucie said. "She always does."

"Probably," Sky conceded, "but not for a while."

Cerberus met us at the entrance to the underground lift. He was walking without a stick for assistance.

"I assume your leg is okay?" I asked.

"It's getting there. Thanks for your help here. You saved lives."

"What happened to that piece of shit, Wayne, who's now missing his hands?"

"We have him," Lucie said. "He's undergoing *questioning*. He'll crack. Sooner or later."

We took the lift down to the floor where Hades had given his talk to the class of children, and we walked to a meeting room in which Hera, Ares, and Demeter were all sitting in chairs around a small table. None of them appeared all that pleased to see me.

The sadness I felt that they had decided not to like me was, obviously, overwhelming, and for a second I did consider throwing myself upon their mercy, but then I remembered they were all nasty little fuckers and decided I couldn't be bothered.

I sat opposite them, with Sky and Lucie on either side of me.

"So, Mr. Garrett," Hera began with an air of smug satisfaction, "please tell me why I shouldn't reveal your horrific deeds to the world. You have, after all, ensured that the marriage between Selene and my grandson is no longer viable. She knew what would happen if she were to betray me. Apparently, her love for you is less than you imagined."

"Hera," I started, "I think I can speak for everyone when I say—"

Before I could finish my incredibly witty reply, Sky interrupted. "Although it was Pandora's plan, you didn't know that. You followed it through and had people arrange for Cronus to escape."

"I believe I explained to Avalon that Hyperion and Sarah Hamilton were the ones responsible for that. Sarah was suckered into Pandora's plan, and Hyperion fell for her lies in an attempt to remove me from power. In fact, I believe your father is arranging for his transfer back to Tartarus."

"Yes, that was well timed," Sky said. "Selene leaves your employ, and Hyperion is found to be the one responsible."

"You think you know someone," Hera said with a sly chuckle.

"Except we know it was you who hired Sarah, after Deimos brought her to your attention. It was her information—fed to her by Pandora—that you used to break Cronus free."

"Where is the evidence?" Demeter demanded. "You can't accuse people without evidence. And Ares's son, Deimos, is a deeply disturbed individual. We had no idea he was working with Pandora to try to kill his own grandmother." She turned to Ares and patted him sympathetically on the arm. "We're heartbroken by the betrayal."

That part at least was true. Not the heartbroken bit— that was bollocks. She probably hadn't known her grandson Deimos was working against her. I'd have liked to think she wouldn't have let it go as far as it had.

"Well, this has been fun," Hera said, standing. "But it'll be even more fun when this information is made public."

"Oh, you're leaving so soon?" Hades asked as he entered the room. He pushed a file across the table. "These are the e-mails between Demeter, yourself, and Sarah, planning Cronus's little excursion."

Hera's face contorted with anger.

"I'm not an idiot, Hera," Hyperion said as he walked through the open door. "I kept files of everything you were doing. If we go to Avalon with this information, what would happen?" he turned to Lucie. "For those who don't know, Lucie here is the assistant director of the SOA."

Hera sat down.

"Well, you'd be expelled from Avalon," Lucie explained. "Merlin and your enemies would certainly want you to be branded traitors, and any control you have in Avalon projects would be removed. Your assets would probably be frozen too. You'd likely get them all back, but it would take *years* to sort out."

"What do you want?" Hera asked.

"The information you have on Nate," Hades said. "All of it. You will also relinquish all claim on Tartarus. You have one week to do both. If it's not done, Lucie here will go to Merlin with the information we have on your role in Cronus's escape. And one last thing: you will never take action against Eos, Selene, or their friends and family."

I was dumbfounded. I had no idea that Hades had any kind of plan in place to deal with Hera, but the fact that he was doing it, even partly, to protect me made me very grateful for his friendship.

"And if we say no and decide to go it alone anyway?" Hera asked. "I'll have destroyed Nate's life; that's quite an attractive prospect."

One second there was no one behind Hera, and the next, Eos was standing there with a blade against Hera's throat. "If you do, then I'll kill you," she said, her voice utterly calm. "Also, now that my family and I are free from your influence, if you ever cross us again, there's not enough light in the world to stop me from getting to you."

Hera had no option but to agree to the terms. Everyone left happy. Well, not Hera, but I didn't give a shit how happy she was.

Ares stopped at the door and turned toward me. "You hurt my boy," his voice was deep and menacing. "There will be recompense for that."

Images of Mordred and what he'd done in Ares's name flashed into my mind. "One day, you'll try," I said without breaking eye contact, "but not today."

He looked around the room as if really considering it. "No, not today." And then he left.

Everyone else filed out, leaving Hyperion and me alone. "You hated me for a long time," he said.

"I was wrong," I admitted. "I'm sorry about that."

"Nothing to be sorry for. You got Cronus back without having to kill him, stopped Pandora, and helped my children break free of Hera. I'm sorry you needed to be lied to for so long. I assure you Selene didn't want to do that."

"I know, and thanks."

"So, you two . . ." he trailed off.

"I don't know. We'll see, I guess."

He walked over to me and offered me his hand, which I took. "You're a good man, Nathan. If it does work out between the two of you, you have my blessing. She's been unhappy for too long. Change it."

"I'll do my best."

"One last thing," he said before he left the room. "Don't come back to Tartarus anytime soon. Cronus will kill you. Or at least try. I'm only going back to ensure he doesn't do anything stupid."

"I'll make sure it's not on my list of holiday destinations."

Once the meeting had finished and Hera had stomped her way off the grounds, I found Lucie and Sky as Lucie was getting into her helicopter and thanked them for their help. Sky punched me on the shoulder and walked off.

"What you did back then, after your wife was murdered," Lucie said, "it was wrong. But right now, having you on our side is better than not. We're going to need your help one day, Nathan, and you will say yes to that."

"Who's 'we'?" I asked as the helicopter's engine started.

"You'll find out. Good-bye."

I watched her fly off and was suddenly joined by Eos. "You should stop that," I said.

"I like making people jump," she said with a smile. "Have you spoken to my sister?"

"Not since we caught Pandora. I get the feeling that's a question I'm going to be answering a lot. Your dad got there first. We both need time to deal with things."

"So no wedding bells in the immediate future." She gave me a piece of paper with two phone numbers on it. "Top one's mine, bottom one's Selene's. She doesn't know you have it. Don't call unless it's an emergency. But I think she'd like you to have it. I'm sure she'll contact you soon enough; after all, she'd lost you for a century. I saw her yesterday, and she was like a teenage girl. She fucking giggled, Nate. I don't know what you did, but it's very discombobulating to hear my dragon-kin sister giggling."

I laughed. "Sorry."

"Yeah, well, I just wanted you to know. I think my father likes you. He feels bad about everything."

"We spoke. He gave me his blessing to date his daughter."

Eos laughed again. "Bloody hell, did he try to crush your hand or tell you not to stay out after curfew too? I think maybe he's been watching too much TV."

I joined in the laughter. It felt good.

"I'm sure I'll be seeing you again." She walked off, and I went to find Hades, who was sitting on a bench overlooking a small pond at the rear of the complex.

"Thanks for what you did," I said.

"I look after my own. Even those who aren't technically my own. You did a lot to help me, Nate. I owe you more than I can possibly say."

"You don't owe me anything," I said and sat beside him. "Did Persephone tell you how much of Cronus's ass she kicked at Stonehenge?"

Hades nodded. "She's a rare woman. You pissed off some powerful people, Nate. Ares isn't about to give you a pass for what you did to his son, and Hera will definitely be keeping a close eye on you. And then there's Pandora."

"I'm used to it," I said and got up.

"You staying in town?" he asked. "Persephone is in Tartarus, but we've got some of our other children over in a few days. It's been awhile since the whole family was together, and it would be nice to have you there."

"I'll be around. I'm off to go see Kurt and Petra."

"Give them my regards."

I took a few steps and then paused. "We still don't know who the Vanguard's *liege* is. Pretty much everyone who worked for him is dead, but someone is out there pulling the strings. Could it be Hera or one of her people?"

"Possibly, but they're unlikely to tell us, and I think I've used up my ability to get answers from them for the foreseeable future. They'll all be watched more closely now. Whoever it was made a move and lost this time. They'll make another. No one puts this much effort into a plan that fails without having a plan B in store. Someone screwed around with those Vanguards' heads and someone sent them here to die. We'll find out who did it and stop them."

"And if we don't?"

"Then we'll be dead. So it won't matter."

"Maybe I should go back to Avalon. Someone there is definitely involved. I could talk to a few people."

"You really think you'd be welcomed back? You think you could stand to see Merlin again?"

I thought about it, about why I left, about what had happened between Merlin and me. "No. There's almost nothing in this world I'd rather not do."

EPILOGUE

It was a few weeks after I'd left Hades's compound in Germany when I finally got the information I needed on Mara and her witches. Almost everything else had been dealt with, but I wasn't about to let someone who used her own daughter as bait and helped Cronus escape the compound get away scot-free.

I found myself sitting in the dark, in a small meeting hall in the New Forest. I'd been waiting for about an hour when the front door opened, and the lights switched on. Emily Rowe and Mara Range walked in, Emily closing the door behind them.

Emily wore casual jeans, a white T-shirt, and trainers, and Mara wore a bright yellow dress that on anyone else might have been called pleasant. On Mara, the happiness and joy the yellow signified were diminished by her presence.

"I wondered how long it would take you," Emily said, removing a revolver from the back of her jeans waistband and holding it by her thigh.

"Well, I had a few problems tracking you down," I explained.

I looked around the room. It was also used as a hut for Scout meetings and other occasions that would need the dozens of chairs stacked up against the walls under the barred windows. There was a small stage behind me, and although it was only a foot off the floor, it still had curtains on either side.

"I wondered if you guys put on plays?" I asked. "*Macbeth*, for example."

"Is that meant to be a joke?" Mara asked.

I shrugged. "Take it how you wish."

"Why are you here?" Emily asked.

"Put the gun away. I'm not going to attack anyone. I came to talk."

"Sorcerer's lies," Mara said.

"If I wanted you dead, you'd both be dead. I know where you live. I know where you drive every other day at 1:00 p.m., Mara, when you go to meet that lovely man who's married, while he's on lunch break. I know a lot about you. About you and all thirty-eight members of this coven."

Emily put the gun away.

"What are you *doing*?" Mara screamed at her.

"He's right, if he wanted us dead, he could have attacked at any time."

"Thank you," I said. "I'm most disappointed in you, Emily. You lied to me. Mara's not just a member; she runs this whole coven. And you're their enforcer."

Emily shrugged. "People lie. I'm not going to feel bad about it. You're right, though, I am the enforcer. I didn't lie about everything. Too many witches do follow Demeter and Hera without thought. And Mara is an idiot. But she's also the coven leader and I'm honor-bound to protect this coven."

Mara glared at Emily, who pointedly ignored her.

"That's why you killed those Vanguard in Germany, yes?" I asked. "Because they screwed up and let Cronus escape? But they also knew too much, didn't they? Did Sarah know you were going to do it?"

"It was her idea," Emily admitted.

"You used the same chameleon potion you brewed in your hotel room to cover yourself. The one you gave to Cronus. It was obviously a good potion."

"How'd you know it was me?" she asked.

"Because you just told me."

Emily's smile faded. "So you're here to take us to Avalon?"

I shook my head. "There's no evidence. Anything between Mara and Sarah is never going to be found, and while I'm loath to allow Chloe to stay with the psychopath who used her as bait, I can't really do much about that. Mara behaved in such a way as to ensure all attention was on her at all times. The annoying, shrill pain-in-the-ass who berates people and says unpleasant or unnecessary things. I imagine it didn't take much acting on your part."

Mara's face darkened.

"But," I continued before she could interrupt, "there's no evidence you did anything other than act strangely and brew a potion in your hotel bath. At best, you may have to pay a hotel fine."

"Then you can leave," Mara told me. "This place will have to be cleaned as is, just to get your stench out."

"But you'll wash away all of your lovely runes."

Mara's eyes grew wide and she readied a spell, but nothing happened.

"I had a friend of mine, a lovely lady by the name of Lucie . . . well, 'friend' is the wrong word. I get the feeling she doesn't like me, but she does trust me. An odd combination. Anyway, she's an enchanter. She can't remove the runes placed by another enchanter, but she can remove the ones put there by a bunch of witches. All of them are gone, replaced with brand new ones that stop anyone from using magic."

I glanced down at the rune on the back of my hand, and I clicked my fingers, drawing a small flame onto them. "Except for me, of course. I can still do magic."

"What do you want?" Emily asked.

"Well, I considered burning this place down as a warning, but that was counterproductive as it's in the middle of a forest. So I was going to threaten you to leave, but I don't have the time to go around checking that you've actually done anything."

I stood and folded the chair, placing it over by the rest. "No, I figured I'd come here to tell you that, while no one has any proof of your wrongdoings, we all *know* what you did. This coven has been marked because of your actions, and Avalon will be keeping a very close eye on you. Not because we believe you're doing anything wrong, of course, but because you were involved in a traumatic event in Germany, and they want to make certain you're all okay.

"There will be site visits, probably at random, maybe in the middle of the night. There might even be interviews with all the members, just to verify that everyone is happy and healthy."

"You can't do that," Mara said with barely contained rage.

"I'm not. Avalon is—well, technically, Lucie is, but she helps run the place, so she's probably qualified to tell whether people here are happy and healthy. Did I mention the random visits?"

"You think this is funny?" Emily asked.

I shook my head. "I think it's deadly serious. A group of witches used by Demeter and Hera broke Cronus out of Tartarus, witches who used the coven leader's own daughter to get the job done." My stare could have bored holes in Mara.

"Emily, I'm not going to underestimate you again. I promise you that. And Mara, dear sweet Mara. Your daughter is a delight. If you remove her from school, if you hurt her, if anything happens to her in any way that results in my friend's daughter telling me of her unhappiness at your parenting, I will come find you. And I promise, once I'm done, no one will ever find out what happened to you."

I made my way toward the door, my piece said.

"You think that you can threaten me, Mister Garrett?" Mara said, her body shaking with anger.

I continued walking and opened the door before pausing for a second.

"You can't come into my coven and demand things," Mara continued. "You're a thug, a man with no vision who does what his masters tell him. I'm not afraid of you. You don't scare me."

I didn't turn back toward the two women as I spoke, "Then clearly you haven't been paying attention."

ACKNOWLEDGMENTS

My wife, Vanessa, is always going to be the first person I thank, and not just because I don't want to sleep on the couch for the next month. She's supportive, helpful, and allows me the time to write. I can never really thank her enough.

My three beautiful daughters, who inspire me to write every day. Except when they're misbehaving; then they inspire me to buy a shed and live in it.

My parents, who constantly sound interested when I talk about the next tiny plot detail. Thank you for your enthusiasm.

My family and friends: without their support I wouldn't be where I am today.

The incredible D. B. Reynolds, Michelle Muto, and Melissa Olson, all three of whom helped make the book what it finally became. I'm very lucky to know you all and to be able to call you friends.

My agent, Paul Lucas, whom I've enjoyed working with very much. I look forward to where the future leads.

Denise Grover Swank, Richard Ellis Preston Jr., Mark Barnes, Amber Natusch, Jack Horn, Stant Litore, and all the other 47North authors who help create a group of people I'm proud to call my friends. Never have I met a greater hive of scum and villainy, and I couldn't be happier to be a part of it.

Sana Chebaro, Emilie Marneur, Neil Hart, and everyone else with the Amazon publishing UK team: Thank you for time, friendship, and help; it's been great working with you all. It means a lot. Also, to Britt Rogers, the force behind the 47North US team: you were a joy to work with.

My editor, Fleetwood Robbins. An awesome name for an awesome editor. I look forward to working with you in the future.

Ken McDaniel, who's always available to answer questions about the military or weaponry—thanks, man. Any errors that ever exist to do with those things are mine and mine alone.

There are probably dozens more people who should be mentioned by name, but to everyone out there who has supported me over the years, thanks. It means a lot.

Last, but not least, thanks to Scott Hollander, Zoe Mountain, and Kyle Felis Key, the three people who won the chance to name a character in book 4. They picked Sarah Hamilton, Magali Martin, and Robert Ellis, respectively. I hope the three of you enjoyed reading about the fates of the characters whose names you picked.

ABOUT THE AUTHOR

Steve McHugh is the author of the popular Hellequin Chronicles. He lives in Southampton on the south coast of England with his wife and three young daughters. When not writing or spending time with his kids, he enjoys watching movies, reading books and comics, and playing video games.

16293665R00303

Printed in Poland
by Amazon Fulfillment
Poland Sp. z o.o., Wrocław